CUCKOO

ALSO BY
GRETCHEN FELKER-MARTIN

Manhunt

CUCKOO

GRETCHEN FELKER-MARTIN

NIGHTFIRE

TOR PUBLISHING GROUP • NEW YORK

CUCKOO

A Nightfire Book
Published by Tom Doherty Associates / Tor Publishing Group
120 Broadway
New York, NY 10271

www.torpublishinggroup.com

Nightfire™ is a trademark of Macmillan Publishing Group, LLC.

The Library of Congress Cataloging-in-Publication Data is available upon request.

ISBN 978-1-250-79466-6 (paperback)
ISBN 978-1-250-79467-3 (ebook)

Our books may be purchased in bulk for promotional, educational, or business use. Please contact your local bookseller or the Macmillan Corporate and Premium Sales Department at 1-800-221-7945, extension 5442, or by email at MacmillanSpecialMarkets@macmillan.com.

First Edition: 2024

Printed in the United States of America

0 9 8 7 6 5 4 3 2 1

For all unwanted children

CUCKOO

THE GOOD NEWS

Angel's Climb, Montana
1991

Monica Howard couldn't stop cleaning. It was two days until her daughter, Casey—seventeen in three weeks—came home from camp, a thought that nagged at the back of her mind every moment she wasn't scrubbing, sweeping, tidying, mopping, or folding something. *If the house is clean enough*, her subconscious whispered to her as she lay awake most nights beside her husband Wayne's snoring bulk, *then maybe it will be all right. Maybe Casey's problems will be cleaned up, too.* She didn't know what Wayne had paid that place in the desert, he didn't like to worry her with things like that, but she knew it was a lot because she'd heard him talking it over with Cal Olson in the den one night just after the camp's people came for Casey.

It's an arm and a leg, Cal, but I'll be goddamned if any girl of mine turns bull dyke. I'll drown her first.

Mm, Cal replied, as though mildly interested.

Monica, a tray of ham and cheese sandwiches and glasses of cold Coke balanced on one hip and her ear pressed to the door, had whispered, "You misheard," out loud to herself without meaning to, then gone in to bring the men their lunch.

"Too much ice," said Wayne. "You know I only like a little. Where's your head this week?" The air was thick with cigar smoke. On the television, one boxer pounded on another. Monica had thought of the dull thud of her mother's meat tenderizer against a piece of veal. Sunday dinner.

"I'm sorry, dear," she said, forcing a smile.

It had to work. Two years now of screaming, cursing, sullen looks, the stink of marijuana clinging to the jeans and sweatshirts Monica found balled up in one of Casey's backpacks. And then the magazine. You expected it with boys. They couldn't help themselves, dirty little animals rooting around in the filth, always touching themselves, chasing girls on the playground like a pack of baboons, grimy hands tearing her blouse open, serrated teeth on her nipples, her sons, but her daughter? Her little girl? Tan limbs twined together in those glossy pages hidden under the mattress. Teased manes of hair, pink lipstick glistening, and the dark forks of their legs, those obscene curls and shadowed clefts. Roadside ditches, overgrown and choked with muck.

A phase, said Pastor Daniel. Just a phase some girls go through. A dirty, nasty little phase brought on by MTV and communism and free love and grass and the tribadists haunting locker rooms all over the country. A brochure pushed across his desk. Smiling children in ranch clothes. A huge man in a suit of cream-colored linen, a smile on his face, his hands on their shoulders. Camp Resolution. That night as she'd sat beside her husband in the den, watching college football reflected in his glasses, her empty stomach tied in knots, she'd asked Wayne if maybe there was another way, if maybe they should try counseling or medication first, or sending Casey to stay with her parents in Flint for the summer.

"She's going," said Wayne, still watching the game, and the flat, dull dismissal in his tone nearly drove Monica to allow herself to know what she had spent nearly sixteen years *un*knowing every day, to tell him that he could blame her for coddling their girl, for raising her wrong, but that she knew the real reason Casey had turned into such a mess. Then, as it had perhaps a half a dozen times before, that small urge to poke holes in her family shriveled up and died. She was making up stories. She had simply *misheard*.

The next morning Monica had started to clean. First the windows, scouring each pane inside and out, squinting to make out streaks and water spots in the late summer glare. Then surfaces until her hands were red and itchy from all the cleaning product. The girl on the plastic bottle of Fairy smiling mindlessly out at her. On her knees wiping stray hairs from the bolts on the toilet in the den bathroom. Cleaning urine from under the toilet seat. Wayne and the boys never checked. Their pubic hairs stuck in nameless residue.

The baseboards, furred with dust. The red wine stains on the den carpet, usually hidden by Wayne's navy La-Z-Boy recliner. Hydrogen peroxide fumes stung her nostrils as she watched her cleaning mixture fizz between the carpet fibers. It was the same one her mother had used. Peroxide, club soda, and dish soap. Monica still tasted it in dreams sometimes. She scrubbed until her shoulder burned and her knees ached from kneeling. She was so tired that night she nearly forgot to make dinner. As she cleaned the dishes afterward her hands began to shake. She chipped a plate. The rough edge cut through her glove and opened her palm as easily as a letter opener slides through paper. No one asked at breakfast why her hand was bandaged.

The days passed. The house rebelled against her. Her sons, Brian, eleven, and Stevie, thirteen, tracked dirt through the kitchen and the dining room. Wayne and his friends left constellations of crumbs and broken chips ground into the carpet. In the attic she found oceans of little black mouse turds, and for weeks afterward the high-pitched squeaks of mice caught in the glue traps she'd set out tormented her through sleepless nights. She lost weight. The women at church and at the Moms Against Satan group said she looked wonderful, then asked if she was all right, then stopped mentioning it. Her sister, Jane, asked delicately over coffee if she'd seen a doctor lately.

Still, the house fought her. It fought her with water spots in the tiles of the basement's drop ceiling, with mold in the vegetable crisper, with dry rot under the sink and grime in the basin of the bathtub, and a clotted string of hair and nameless gunk she fished out of the drain with the aid of a bent hanger. The smell of it, dank and flatly mineral, like lake water, made her think of the box at the back of Wayne's closet, a worn and sagging cardboard box that had once, perhaps two decades ago, held little miniature Snickers bars like the kind her parents had given out on Halloween. She had never touched that box, not once in eighteen years of marriage, and she never would, because it wasn't there. It had no smell. It was just another thing that she'd *misheard*.

At night she dreamed of Casey torn apart by lions on the African veldt, of hyenas with matted red faces cracking her daughter's blood-slimed femurs in their jaws, of black flies swarming over exposed viscera and vultures roosting on the rotten arch of a scraped knee, plucking Casey's eyes out of their sinking sockets. Casey baptized dead at Righteous Savior in Lincoln, where they'd lived before Wayne's job with the ministry, her big brown eyes filmed and staring under the clear water, her curls floating on the surface of the font. Casey kicked by other girls behind the school until her mouth and anus bled. Night after night she woke soaked in sweat, hours before dawn, and polished silverware or dusted shelves until it was time to pack lunches for Wayne and the boys, and then to make breakfast.

Five weeks after the men in their van came for Casey, Monica broke down crying in the middle of a meeting of the Angel's Climb Christian Decency League. Veronica Peterson handed her a pecan sandy and she burst into tears. She told them everything, weeping on Carol Anne Forester's shoulder, clutching at her blouse with its ugly paisley print. The magazine. The fights. The call from the principal's office. And then finally, shamefully, the camp. "They'll kill her," she screamed, not caring that Carol Anne's elderly mother was upstairs, that there were children playing in the yard who looked up from their games as though they'd heard a wolf howl. "They're going to kill my baby. I did it. I did it."

"Hush, now," Carol Anne said awkwardly, patting Monica on the back. "You did the right thing, hon. She needs help. You remember everything we went through with Terry? They put him right. It was a miracle, Monnie."

Monica only cried harder. She felt as though something in her chest was tearing open, as though behind the frail cage of her ribs was a terrible box with no smell and no feel to it, a box that had been *misheard* and *unseen,* that had never existed at all, and she had opened it up without looking and shoved her daughter inside. She had never liked her daughter. She felt it now, a thought she'd kept wriggling under her thumbnail like an earwig for seventeen years. She had never liked Casey.

"I'm a terrible mother," she wailed.

Patty McMahon, the League's chair, took a different approach from Carol Anne's. In three quick steps she was across the room, frightfully quick in spite of her sixty-four years and considerable bulk, and without expression she slapped Monica across the face hard enough to make her ears ring. When Monica stared up at her in openmouthed shock, Patty hit her again.

"Smarten up," Patty snapped, adjusting her bifocals on their chain. She rubbed her hand, working stiffness from the joints. "The good Lord wants you up shit creek, you shut your mouth and *paddle.*"

Later, drifting on a gentle tide of Valium in the back seat of Carol Anne's Volvo, Monica wondered what had come over her. Wayne wouldn't send their daughter anywhere dangerous (*drown her first*), would he? He loved the kids. He was a wonderful father. She just needed to trust him. *It has to work,* she told herself as Carol Anne and Cynthia Ludgate whispered about her in the front seat, the huge open sky beyond them. *It has to be the right thing.*

The dreams grew worse. One stifling August night she didn't sleep at all, just sat awake in the empty living room, staring at the photos on the wall. Wayne and Cal and other men on Wayne's bass boat, *Glory,* a huge striper in her grinning husband's arms. Casey's fifth-grade ballet recital, not the screaming, kicking two-hour tantrum it had taken to get her into her tutu, but her and the other girls in her class turning clumsy circles up onstage. When Monica could no longer stand the sight of all her memories, she returned to her work. She went over the ministry's books, in which Wayne, their congregation's treasurer, sometimes made careless mistakes. She went over grass stains on the knees of Brian's baseball pants with Didi until her head swam with the fumes.

The next night she slept an hour and a half. She had almost forgotten why she was cleaning when, on the fifth day of the eleventh week of her crusade, as she was knocking dead insects from the dining room fixture's frosted dome into the trash, there was a knock at the door.

Monica found Casey standing on the front stoop, bags at her feet. The pale, untoned girl the camp's staff had dragged out to their van three months ago was gone. In her place was a lean, wiry young woman, hair a little bleached from too much sun, a smudge of freckles across her snub nose. For a long moment they stared at each other across the threshold, and Monica felt with a clarity that slid into her breast like a knife that she had made a terrible mistake, that something in her life, in her home, was very wrong, and that she had pushed her little girl straight into its waiting teeth. She was seized with a sudden memory of holding her newborn daughter to her breast, of that little pink body squirming and fussing, refusing to latch. A feeling, which had come with her out of twilight sleep, that this child was not hers. Was no part of her.

Casey stepped across the threshold and wrapped Monica in a tight embrace. She smelled of dust and sweat and something else, something unpleasantly sugary and wet. "I know why you sent me," Casey said, her voice muffled against Monica's shoulder.

Monica felt as though Patty McMahon had slapped her again. "What?"

Casey broke away. She wiped her nose on the back of her arm, sniffing. Her eyes were rimmed in red, her cheeks wet with tears. "I know why you sent me," she said thickly. "I was out of control. I was disrespecting you and Daddy. Pastor Eddie and Mrs. Glover helped me see that I was never really . . . gay." She spat the word out like it was a maggot on her tongue. "I was just trying to hurt you, because I was confused. I had the wrong friends. I was trying to fit in with people who weren't good for me, who didn't want what was best for me, like you do."

Monica took a step back.

That night at dinner Casey said grace for the first time in years. Brian and Stevie ignored her. They shoveled chicken Kiev and mashed potatoes into their mouths. Monica thought of their sweetness as toddlers, of their soft little hands and the clean, milky smell of the tops of their heads. Wayne ate without taking his eyes off their daughter, fork and knife moving mechanically between his plate and his mouth.

"I learned so much," said Casey, smiling shyly. "How to build a fence, how to hull peas, how to milk a cow—"

Brian snickered. Without a word, Wayne reached across the table and slapped him.

"Wayne," said Monica, but that was all.

"There are ladies present," said Wayne, ignoring her. "If you can't behave like a man, you can go to bed right now."

"Yes, sir," said Brian, staring at his plate.

Wayne leaned forward. "Are you going to cry now? Is that how I raised you?"

Brian blinked fiercely, his shoulders trembling with what Monica thought was rage. She wondered suddenly if he ever fantasized about killing Wayne, and how he would do it. If he did.

"No, sir."

"Apologize to your sister."

Brian turned his simmering gaze on Casey, who stared back at him placidly. "I'm sorry, Casey."

"Thank you, Brian." She smiled. "Thank you, Daddy."

Wayne looked almost surprised. Monica couldn't remember the last time one of the children had called him that. It made her cringe, that word. Daddy. A performance of weakness. Calculated. Cynical. A cringing ploy for table scraps.

Daddy.

"Your sister's been through something very hard," said Wayne in the broad, expansive voice he always used when he thought he was being magnanimous. He had a smear of breading at the corner of his mouth. It made him look like a mental patient, nodding in his chair as an orderly spooned slop into him. "And she's had to be brave for all of us, so I want us all to give her a little extra respect."

"Yes, sir," Brian and Stevie choroused.

After dinner Casey gathered plates without being asked and joined Monica at the sink. For a while she dried and Casey washed, the only sounds Wayne and the boys watching television in the den and the gentle clink of dishes. It felt wrong to have her daughter back so suddenly, to have this helpful girl beside her, uncomplaining and composed. She glanced at Casey. She'd grown her hair out; it looked better, more feminine. Monica still had a scar on the heel of her right hand from a struggle they'd had years ago when she caught Casey trying to shear off her curls in the bathroom. Her daughter had kicked her in the elbow as they wrestled with the scissors. It had taken months to heal.

"Let me finish up, Mom," said Casey, smiling.

"What?"

Her daughter's brown eyes glittered under the overhead light. "The house looks so beautiful; you must be working hard. Can I finish the dishes?"

Ungrateful, thought Monica. She didn't know why she thought it, which made her angrier than the thought itself. "Was dinner that bad?" she said through gritted teeth. "I can't be trusted to wash a dish?"

"Oh, I'm so sorry, Mom," said Casey, and somehow being treated as reasonable made Monica even more furious. "No, dinner was so great. Can I do anything to make it up to you?"

"Go watch television," Monica snapped.

Casey left, looking puzzled. A few moments later, a burst of Wayne's laughter came from the den. *She's telling them all I'm crazy,* thought Monica, scrubbing fiercely at a smear of oily butter.

They're laughing at me. She felt sick to her stomach. Something was wrong. Something was wrong with Casey, and she couldn't put her finger on it. They'd taken the daughter she'd hated all her life, whose mouth at her breast had felt like a leech's boneless orifice, who she'd left one day at six months old in the back seat of their old sedan when it was ninety-five degrees. She could still remember the red flush of Casey's skin, the slick of sweat on her small body. She'd stood beside the car and stared at her child sitting slumped half-conscious in her car seat, and wondered what would happen if she just waited half an hour. That feeling that had always lain between them, unspoken, uncomprehended. Now it was gone.

Now there was . . . nothing.

Laughter echoed in her ears.

Monica woke just after three from troubled dreams. She had been in the woods, caught in the thorns of a dark and tangled thicket, and something had been creeping closer. The more she'd struggled the deeper the thorns dug. The house was dark and silent, except for the thin whistle of Wayne's deviated septum. There was no moon, only faint starlight between the blinds. The Kirks' yard was empty and still outside. Gradually she became aware of the distant thrumming of crickets.

She sat up and slipped out of bed. As her eyes adjusted to the gloom she saw that Wayne's closet door was ajar, and the thought that he had taken out the box and opened it while she was sleeping crossed her mind in a horrible rush, a thought like a centipede skittering across a bathroom floor.

There isn't any box, she told herself. *It isn't real. It was only something I* misheard.

The hall was quiet. No light under the boys' door. No light under Casey's. In the bathroom Monica splashed cold water on her face, hoping it would take the edge off her prickling nerves. She felt as though she'd rolled through nettles. The least caress of her rayon dressing gown shifting as she moved was enough to make her want to crawl out of her skin. Then she saw it, and her irritation vanished.

There was a light under the basement door. *Casey's down there smoking reefer,* she thought with something very like relief. *She's looking at smut. Little hussy.* And then, with a twinge of frustrated concern: *She's cutting herself again.*

Quietly, carefully, Monica opened the basement door. She took each step with care, stretching to skip the third stair from the top, which creaked. The light, which flickered and buzzed every few seconds, was the bare hanging bulb over Wayne's workbench. The surface had been dusty with disuse until she'd cleaned it the week before. Wayne had no real interest in woodworking, no real knack for home repair. The sagging love seat and armchair were empty. The old TV, the one Wayne's father had given them for a housewarming gift, was dark and silent.

Monica sniffed, but the only odor hanging in the air was the last faint trace of mildew she'd been unable to scour and spritz away. The light flickered again. Maybe one of the boys had been messing around with Wayne's things and had left it on. She crossed the carpet and put a bare foot over the line where it gave way to cold concrete. The boiler loomed dark and silent in its corner. The lightbulb whined. It was nothing. Monica felt curiously deflated. Disappointed, almost.

"Mom?"

Monica screamed, clapping her hand over her own mouth to stifle it as she spun around. Casey was crouched in the shadows under the stairs. In the darkness Monica couldn't see her daughter's face, only the soft crescent of her mouth and the faint suggestion of a nose. "I'm so sorry, Mom. I couldn't sleep." Casey's lips curved into a smile. "I came down here to pray."

"Are you out of your mind?" hissed Monica. "You scared me half to death. And praying? Missy, I have dragged your behind out of bed enough Sunday mornings—"

Casey's face fell. "You have every right not to trust me."

Monica slapped her. "Stop it," she snapped, not caring that she might wake Wayne, not looking at the memory that surfaced like a bubble through thick mud of a little girl with an overbite and big jug ears cowering in front of a shrieking woman in a tatty housedress. That girl's shoulders had been red with welts. Her ribs had been painted with bruises. She wasn't real. She was shut up in a box somewhere in the back of a closet, on the highest shelf.

She seized Casey's shoulders and shook her. "What did they do to you? Did they touch you?"

"Mom, no! Mom!" Terror in those big brown eyes. Real fear. "You're hurting me!"

Monica let go of her daughter and stepped back, stumbling a little. "Honey, I'm so—I'm—"

Casey burst into tears, hugging herself and doubling up. She cried silently, fat tears falling to vanish into the carpet. Finally she sank onto the floor. "I kn-know why you're mad." She gulped. "I know why you don't trust me, Mom, but I want to show you that you can now. I j-just want to stop hurting you."

She doesn't really look anything like me, thought Monica, staring down at Casey's loose blond curls, her little ears and button nose. *She's all Wayne.*

"It's okay if you c-can't believe me," Casey sputtered. Her eyes were red and swollen, her upper lip glazed with snot. "But I'm better, Mom. I r-really am."

"I didn't mean to hit you," said Monica. Her own voice sounded flat and dead to her. She took Casey by the elbow and got her on her feet and over to the old green corduroy couch. They sat side by side, Casey still sniffling, Monica awkwardly holding her arm. "I didn't—I don't think we should discuss it outside the family. Do you understand why?"

"I do," said Casey, eyes downcast.

Monica patted Casey's arm weakly. She tried to picture her daughter kneeling in the dark under the stairs, eyes closed, lips moving in fervent prayer. "What were you praying for, honey?"

"For you and Daddy and Brian and Stevie," Casey said. "And

for Pastor Eddie, and Mrs. Glover. Everyone at camp. So many of them are still fighting for themselves. For their souls."

"What was it like?" asked Monica.

"It was hard," said Casey. "Meredith—Mrs. Glover—told us it's like suicide to change who you are. That most people are too afraid ever to admit they might be wrong." Her eyes glistened in the faint, flickering light of the overhead as she stepped out from under the stairs. "I didn't want to believe her. I was so angry at you and Daddy—"

Daddy.

"—it was like that was all I could feel, even in sessions with Pastor Eddie, when we were talking about, you know, the things I did, and why I did them, I was so angry, I could hardly sleep I was so angry, and then one day a few weeks ago I was scrubbing the floor in the farmhouse—"

Cleaning.

"—and it just . . . fell away. I felt this light in my chest, this white fire, and all my anger was gone."

I opened a box, and I put my daughter inside it.

"That's very good," said Monica, not knowing what else to say, not knowing why suspicion still gnawed at the pit of her stomach. "I'm . . . that's good, Casey."

Casey leaned her head against Monica's shoulder. "I love you, Mom," she whispered.

Monica's skin crawled.

Days passed, became weeks, then months. Fall blew in over the Rockies.

Casey's grades improved. She joined the baking club. Sundays she volunteered at the church daycare. Monica had looked in on her once or twice, disturbed somehow by the thought of Casey around little children, but they adored her, crawling over her, demanding stories, cuddling in her lap for naptime. Mrs. Hansen, the harried, bone-thin woman who ran the daycare, said that

Casey was so sweet, so responsible, she felt she hardly had any-thing left to do herself.

By Thanksgiving Monica had almost grown used to this dutiful, even-tempered new daughter. Casey helped her roll out pie crust, bake biscuits, stuff the turkey—a twenty-eight-pound monstrosity from one of Wayne's fishing buddies who had a farm in Gelton, two towns over—and lay the table. She led the grace at dinner, and that night, once the bones were picked, the talk among her family and Wayne's was what a fine young woman Monnie's girl had turned out to be, how gracious, how lovely, how obedient, and what a fine, fine wife she'd make one day soon.

Two days later, Pastor Brian told the congregation that Carol Anne Forester and her son, Terry, had gone home to Jesus in a terrible accident. There were prayers. Tears were shed. The whole church entered mourning. It wasn't until Monica read it in the paper that she learned the truth: Carol Anne had made her fam-ily turkey sandwiches the day after Thanksgiving, then gone into the kitchen and returned with a loaded shotgun. With the first barrel she blew her son's brains onto the walls. With the second she'd added her own.

"She was always crazy," said Wayne when she told him.

"No, she wasn't," argued Monica. "She was as normal as you or me. I knew her for fifteen years."

"What do you want me to do about it, Monica?" he snapped, looking at her with faint disgust and irritation. On the television, Pat Robertson was explaining the ways in which teaching chil-dren about evolution made them homosexual. "I didn't ask her to put a sunroof in her head. You lost your friend, well, that's sad and I'm sorry, but don't make it my problem."

She stared at him for a long time as Robertson continued his tirade. She wondered what it would feel like to ask Wayne for a divorce, if he would laugh at her, or hit her, or simply nod and say he'd been meaning to get around to it himself. She would have to find a new congregation. Righteous Heart was full of Wayne's people, though without her they might soon realize he wasn't the accounting wizard they believed he was. *Marriage is a sacrament,* she heard her mother say. She could almost see the ugly purple bruises on Mary Lampell's throat, the cuts and scrapes on the side of her pretty face. It says in the Bible, "Wives, be subject to your husbands." Her mother had put up with much worse than she got from Wayne, and she had been a beauty in her day, too. Monica, with her overbite and stuck-out ears, had never turned heads.

At Terry's funeral—Carol Anne had been quietly cremated and her ashes left in a repository—Monica thought it was strange how Casey wept. The two children had never been close, not even in a playful, teasing way. Could it really be nothing more than that Terry had gone to Camp Resolution a summer earlier? The strength of that place, the strength she and Wayne had prayed for, disturbed her now.

Across the open grave, Stan Forester stood looking dazed and broken, his bent little mother beside him holding his toddler, Maggie. When Monica squeezed Stan's hand after the service it was like touching a dead man. He looked straight through her. Maggie screamed and kicked in her grandmother's arms. And then, just as she was set to pull away, to chivvy the boys into the caravan and head home to begin Casserole Patrol for the grieving family, Stan's grip tightened. His eyes focused.

"I didn't know," he said, his voice hoarse. "Did you?"

"I didn't," said Monica, deeply uncomfortable with how much Stan reminded her in that moment of Stevie at the age of six, his big blue eyes wide with shock as he clutched his cheek where Wayne had slapped him. "You can't blame yourself, honey."

"Do you have her diary?"

Monica blinked up at him. "What?"

"They're all there, back to eighty-two, but this year's . . ." His face crumpled. "I can't find it. I thought if I could find it . . . if I could . . . do you know where it is?"

"I'm so sorry," said Monica, backing away. She pulled her hand from his. The hairs on the back of her neck stood on end. "I don't know. I don't know anything about that."

She left the church—not Righteous Heart, but a much smaller Episcopalian ministry nearly an hour's drive from Angel's Climb— at a walk quick enough to flirt with running, ignoring the stares and murmurs that followed her. Her heart was pounding as she hurried down the whitewashed wooden steps. "Brian!" she called, her voice wavering. There were children at the graveyard's edge, girls standing together at the wrought-iron fence, boys whipping rocks and clods of earth at one another, scaling the side of the groundskeeper's shed. Animals. "Stevie! If I find you making fools of yourselves on holy ground, you will be very sorry!"

They met her at the van, both of them red-faced and sweating, Brian still surreptitiously wiping his hands on the seat of his pants where later, Monica knew, she would find grass and dirt stains. "Car," she said. "Now."

"But Mom, we didn't do anything," whined Stevie.

"Can I sleep over at Trevor's?" Brian interjected. "It's not a school night and his mom said—"

The boys fell abruptly silent, like rabbits when a dog is near. Monica stared at them in confusion for a moment until she felt Wayne's familiar crushing grip on her wrist. "What the hell is the matter with you?" he snarled in a tone a stranger might have mistaken for solicitous. He was standing close. She could smell the spearmint on his breath, and the earthy stink of chew beneath it. "You ran out of there like you were on fire."

"I . . . I think I left the oven on," she lied, grasping for the first excuse that came to mind as she turned to face him. "I'm so sorry, honey."

He was silent, his dark eyes narrowed. "You'd better hope you didn't," he said finally, his voice low and dangerous. "Go and get Casey. She went back to the grave to say goodbye. Some people have a sense of decency."

Monica scampered away, rubbing her wrist where he'd gripped it. Wayne had always been strong. He'd pulled Brian's left arm out of its socket once when he'd found the boy poking around his office. In the emergency room, four-year-old Brian sobbing in her lap, Stevie hungry and bawling in her arms, all Monica had been able to think about was Wendy Torrance stammering to Danny's doctor in *The Shining* that Jack hadn't meant to hurt him, and that he'd felt just awful. She'd seen the movie on television late at night as a teenage girl, sitting enthralled and disgusted by its dark spell, moved to wonder at a world beyond church and school and the kitchen. A world of secret thoughts and hungry ghosts, beyond the grace of God.

Wendy, she thought, still feeling a little hysterical. *I'll never touch another drop.*

She hurried through the graveyard, cutting between headstones and monoliths, ignoring the leaf-strewn walking paths. The sun was setting and a light sprinkle of autumn rain had just begun to fall when she reached the final resting place of Terry Forester. Casey knelt at the edge of the open grave. Monica walked briskly toward her, wondering again what had gone on between Carol Anne's son and her daughter. Then she heard the whispering. It wasn't words, or at least not words she understood, but her daughter was speaking into that hole in the ground, and above the gentle autumn wind, Monica heard something whisper back.

"Casey?" she husked, but the words died in her throat. She couldn't draw a breath.

Nevertheless, her daughter stiffened and fell silent. Slowly, very slowly, she turned to look back over her shoulder at Monica, and there was a cold, alien shrewdness in her stare that Monica didn't like at all, that made her think for a single terrifying, exhilarating moment of rushing at Casey and pushing her into the open grave. And then it was only her daughter, looking at her with mild concern. Casey rose. "Are you okay, Mom? You're so pale."

"I'm all right," said Monica. Her mouth was dry. It took every inch of willpower she had not to take another step and look into that yawning hole, look down at the thing that could not have whispered to her daughter. She wet her lips. "We're leaving, honey. Your brothers are in the car."

"Oh," said Casey. "Okay. I was just saying goodbye."

They walked back in silence. A light mist was rising in the fading daylight as rain swept the graveyard. The last leaves clinging to the oaks and maples danced dark and wet on the gusting wind. It was on that walk to the car that Monica finally allowed herself to think what her shocked mind had volunteered when Casey first returned from camp.

This girl was not her daughter.

"Monica," Pastor Daniel sighed, massaging his lined forehead with clear frustration. Monica had always thought he looked more like a personal trainer than a pastor, with his broad shoulders and clearly defined muscles, his short blond hair and icy eyes. He was softening a little as he came to the end of his forties, but not much. "It's so easy not to trust success when we've grown used to failure. Your daughter is home. She's happy. She's healthy. Her issues are behind her, and she's going to have a warm and blessed final year of school. You should be thankful."

They had been talking for close to two hours in the gray of early morning. She'd come straight to the church after bringing Brian, who'd missed his bus, to school. Righteous Heart was an enormous complex off of I-90 just over the Greer town line, one of the new breed of vast white churches with neon crosses and gigantic billboards that had been steadily creeping north and east since the Reagan administration. A lot of money moved through Righteous Heart. Millions of dollars a year. Her proximity to Wayne, the steward of that fortune, meant Daniel had to take her early morning walk-in, but his patience was obviously beginning to fray as they went in circles around the issue of Casey's transformation and her strange behavior at Terry Forester's funeral. Monica had omitted the voice from the grave.

"I am," said Monica, though she wasn't. She wasn't grateful at all. She hadn't slept in close to thirty-two hours. When she'd gone to the bathroom and seen a light under Casey's door at half past two, she'd been too frightened so much as to knock. She gripped her skirt, twisting the fabric in her knotted hands. "I just can't shake the feeling that something is wrong, Pastor. I can't stop thinking about it."

"You had a hard time with Casey these past few years," said Daniel. "Wayne shared with me some of what you and your daughter went through. That kind of strife can be very rough on a family, and sometimes even after it's gone, we keep trying to recreate it because that's what we know. Our hearts want what's familiar, even when it leads us into sin."

Monica frowned. Wayne? Shared? It didn't sound right. She forced herself to take a breath. "I'm not worried she's gone back to . . . to what she was doing before. I'm worried there's something else. Something worse. Schizophrenia, or . . ." She could hardly make herself say it. "A demon."

Pastor Daniel's eyebrows shot up. "She's a straight-A student, Monica. She volunteers three days a week right here, where she's a beloved member of the congregation."

"I know how it sounds, it's just—"

"I'm going to be frank with you," said Pastor Daniel. "I think you should consider a rest, Monica. Stay with your sister. Or a bed-and-breakfast, maybe. Somewhere you can get away from all this stress and give yourself a chance to catch up."

Monica stared at him. He wouldn't help her. She'd known that, but she'd come anyway, because where else was there to go? She had seen evil in that graveyard yesterday. She had heard its quiet voice at work beneath the ground, but nobody was going to believe her for the simple reason that she wasn't very likable. "No," she said, brushing back a stray lock of her lusterless, graying hair. "No, of course, you're right." She allowed herself the luxury of tearing up. "I've just been worried for so long. My nerves are . . . and losing Carol Anne, and Terry . . ." She let out a sob. "I just don't know my left from my right, Daniel."

He rose and came around the desk to rest his hand on her shoulder. "God knows," he said, smiling kindly. "Let Him do the worrying for you, at least for a while. We forget it's Christian mothers who've always had the weight of our future on their shoulders—you deserve a rest."

"I'm sorry for being so silly," she hiccup-laughed, still crying. "I know how busy you are. I'll get out of your hair."

"It's no trouble at all," said Daniel, his smile taking on a pained quality. "I'll see you at the silent auction this Wednesday. Wayne tells me it should be quite a crowd!"

"Th-that's good," said Monica, rising from her chair. "Thank you, Reverend."

He resumed his seat, reaching for his cup of coffee and the book he'd been reading before she arrived. *The Turner Diaries.* She'd seen her father reading that once. Years ago.

"Thank you, Monica."

When Monica pulled into the driveway half an hour later, Wayne's car was still in the garage. She had a strange feeling as she got out of the van and locked it. Wayne never overslept. He never called in sick. She went inside. The house was silent. In the kitchen she found PB&J detritus. Casey must have made lunch for Stevie before walking him to school. Monica sniffed. That wet, sugary smell hung in the air. The smell of Wayne's box. The smell that had wafted out of Terry Forester's open grave as Casey knelt beside it, whispering to something.

Stan's voice echoed in her memory. *Do you have her diary?*

She heard a sound. A faint groan of bedsprings coming through the ceiling. The thought that Wayne was having an affair flickered briefly through her mind, but it inspired no real anger. He wasn't interested. He had his box. Sometimes she imagined him fucking it, creasing its corners as he pushed himself against its velvety, ragged cardboard. She imagined it was full of his dried secretions, a milky lake concealed in total darkness, hiding its true purpose. Slowly, she moved toward the stairs.

The noise grew as she reached the second floor. Someone had drawn all the curtains, and the hall was gray and dark. She could hear the bed's headboard thumping against the wall of her and Wayne's bedroom. *The box is open,* she thought. She opened the bedroom door. The noise grew louder. Clearer.

It was dark in the bedroom. As Monica's eyes adjusted to the gloom, she saw something moving on the bed. Her first thought was that Wanye was having a seizure. Limbs thrashed under tangled sheets. There was a sound as of someone trying to inhale in the midst of an allergic reaction, an awful sucking, thin and desperate. The silhouette was wrong. Monica stepped closer. Her heart pounded like a drumbeat in her chest.

"Wayne?" she whispered. "Wayne, honey?"

The shape convulsed. There was a tinny rattle as something caught hold of the blackout curtains beside the bed and yanked them out of position. A blazing swath of sunlight lit the room, and Monica saw Casey. She was on top of Wayne. *Straddling,* thought Monica, grasping for the filthiest words she knew. *She's straddling him. He's inside her. She made him do this.*

Casey turned to face her, shoulders heaving, breasts and stomach slick with sweat. There was a division in her lower jaw, a gap between its left and right halves, and a thick secretion dripped from it. Monica could see her daughter's teeth right back to her molars. Her inner forearms were open, too, and glistening tendrils of opaque white tissue spilled from the parted lips to coil around Wayne's neck and penetrate his mouth, his ears, his tear ducts. He moaned, one eye twitching in Monica's direction. Casey's jaw sealed itself shut. Her tendrils began to withdraw as the flaps of skin along her arms fluttered and closed.

"Mom," she breathed, her voice crackling.

Monica turned and ran. She screamed as she sprinted out into the hall, banging her shoulder hard against the far wall, clawing along the wallpaper toward the stairs. She screamed as she tore down the steps, slipping on the second to last and banging her chin on the hardwood floor. Rapid footsteps on the stairs behind her. A weight on her back, crushing her as she tried to scramble to her feet. "No," she wailed. She could feel her mind beginning to break. "No, no, no."

"Don't be afraid," said the thing that looked like Casey from where it knelt astride her spine. "It's okay. Hey. Hey." It touched her cheek. "I've got you." It pressed her flat against the floor, its palm on the back of her head. Monica whimpered. Her bladder released, soaking through her panties and nylons and the front of her skirt. The Casey-thing kissed her just behind the ear. She could feel the slippery parts of its mouth shifting against her skin. "Are you going to be good?" it whispered.

"Please," sobbed Monica, not knowing what she was begging for, not knowing if she was alive or dead and in Hell, if Christ had abandoned her, abandoned all the world, because how else could something like this happen? He was gone. He had left them all to rot. "Please, please."

As easily as a man lifting a child, the thing flipped her over onto her back and punched her twice, breaking her nose and cracking something in her eye socket. As she struggled to draw breath, it sat down backward on her stomach, took her right leg in its hands, and hauled back on it, unbearable pressure mounting in her calf, her muscles knotting, cramping, and then the sickly snap of her tibia breaking. Her ears rang. The pain was like frozen lightning in her flesh. She stared at the thing as it rose and took hold of her arms. It dragged her down the hall and through the dining room into the den, where Stevie sat crouched in the far corner facing the wall and *I Love Lucy* played silently on TV Land, washing the room in black and white. "What did you do to him?" groaned Monica. "Stevie. Stevie! It's Mommy. Can you hear me, sweetheart?"

"Yes," he whispered, not turning.

The Casey-thing pulled her to the couch and dragged her up and onto it. Pain lanced up and down Monica's broken leg. She could hardly think. Lucy and Ethel were stuffing bonbons in their brassieres and into one another's mouths in an effort to manage a conveyor belt in a chocolate shop. She'd always hated that gag. So obscene. The Casey-thing stepped between her and the television. Its eyes were very dark. Almost black, with only a faint hint of sclera. It smiled. "Have you heard the good news?"

Her daughter's face opened up like a flower, splitting into fleshy petals lined with jumbled baby teeth and dripping thick, opaque secretions. A wet red mouth gnashed mindlessly. Monica began to laugh as it tore her blouse and bent to seal itself against her breast, its tentacles cutting into her chest and collarbones, something within the raw, squirming mass of its split face fastening tight around her nipple, squeezing so hard that her laugh became a scream, a strangled hiss, fingers in her mouth and that sweet, damp taste on her tongue, and then nothing opened up beneath her, vast and wet and dark, and she fell into it.

And she was gone.

Part I

TOUGH LOVE

This is what we hear when you mourn over our existence. This is what we hear when you pray for a cure. This is what we know, when you tell us of your fondest hopes and dreams for us: that your greatest wish is that one day we will cease to be, and strangers you can love will move in behind our faces.

"Don't Mourn For Us,"
Jim Sinclair
Our Voice, volume 1, number 3, 1993

I

TWO FOR FLINCHING

Manhattan, New York
1995

Shelby walked past Penn Station in the broiling August heat, hurrying so that no one would ask why she was crying. So that no one would look too close. She was sure her mothers had at least one PI sniffing around by now; they'd never go to the police, never do anything to risk their socialite friends finding out that their precious little baby boy, secured from the very best and most expensive orphanage in all of Korea, had run off to be some kind of transvestite. Shelby's eyes darted between faces before she realized anyone tailing her wasn't going to do her the favor of looking like a character in *Dick Tracy*. It would be just another sweaty nobody in the tide moving along Thirty-Fourth to the crosswalk where it bisected Eighth.

In the weeks since she'd left she had often dreamed about Stel and Ruth sliding after her through crowds. In elevators. On busy sidewalks. Once at some kind of nebulous function where everyone else wore masks and her face kept slipping off her skull so that she had to plaster it back on, only she got it wrong and when she caught sight of her reflection in the moment before their claws found her, it was a Picasso tangle of fat, twitching features. Nose snuffling upside down at her right temple. An eye staring from the circle of her puffy lips and swags of jiggling flesh hanging slack from her chin.

At the corner she gave an old bum sitting against the station's stone wall a dollar and he smiled toothlessly at her and said,

"God bless you," and she wondered if that was how she'd look in twenty years, or thirty, or however much older he was. Wrinkled and sunken and smelling of stale cigarettes and unwashed skin. She'd tried, really tried, to convince Charlie to give her a room, but the older girl had said her age would be a problem, that it could attract too much attention from the neighbors. *It's a cathouse, honey; the pedos catch wind of you and we'll never get rid of them.* It had been Shelby's last idea, her last desperate hope to find somewhere to live. She was sure Tyler wouldn't want her for much longer. He was getting sick of her; she could feel it in his awkward silences, his cruel little comments.

You don't have much of an ass, for a fat girl, he'd said while she sucked him off a few nights earlier. When she'd gone quiet he'd scoffed, told her not to be so sensitive, that it was just a joke. *A lot of guys would think you're ugly,* he told her. *No, not me, Jesus; I'm just saying. You think I'm that shallow?*

He wouldn't hold her hand in public. Didn't like to go out with her at all, if he could avoid it. When his college friends came over to smoke weed and watch shitty movies he'd make sure to clear her out an hour beforehand, not to come back until an appointed time. When she did, sunburned and drained, the counters would be sticky, the linoleum dribbled with coke, the toilet seat furred with loose pubes stuck in slicks of urine. He never *asked* her to clean, but if she didn't he would sulk and stomp and slam the doors and tell her nothing was wrong, to stop asking, to stop being such a bitch, and so she cleaned until the shithole sparkled. Sometimes it was two or three in the morning when she finished.

But where else could she go? She was a tick. A parasite who couldn't survive without a body to cling to. Stel's family had always treated her with a kind of benevolent disgust she had no reason to suspect concealed any secret fondness, and Ruth's were all Bible psychos living on a rotting compound somewhere deep in Alabama. They probably didn't even know she existed, not that they'd take her in if they did.

Sure, sure, just send the little faggot on down and Peepaw and the boys'll make a man out of it, praise God.

The LIRR was mostly empty, the upholstered seats with their geometric patterns in pale blue and yellow smelling of years of soaked-in sweat. Shelby, cheek resting against the scratched plexiglass of her window, wondered as she always did if this was the car Colin Ferguson had stepped aboard in 1993, an automatic pistol tucked into the waistband of his suit pants. Did the ghosts of the six men and women who'd died that day drift moaning down the central aisle late at night when the train was out of service? Did they smear the windows with their sticky ectoplasmic fingerprints, washed away each morning before the commuters came?

She got off at Jamaica, the sultry breeze smelling of rain and fragrant garbage, and watched the train roar back into motion. Its wheels threw sparks. The platform shook. Down the iron steps, stepping around gum and pigeon shit, into the cool gloom of the underpass and then cutting through the alley behind the Citibank. Two blocks to Tyler's building. Air conditioners dripped onto the sidewalk, puddles forming in the narrow troughs between the cracked and crumbling concrete slabs. In front of the barbershop next to the apartment, an old man sat dozing in a white plastic patio chair, his sunken chest rising and falling slowly. Silvery hairs glinted on the vee of skin left bare by his half-unbuttoned bowling shirt.

Garbage bags sat piled and stinking on the curb at the foot of the steps. She went up past them and into the cool front hall, shoving the humidity-swollen front door until the bolt clicked into place. The inner door was easier, the cut-crystal knob hot to the touch from the sun filtering in through the outer's transom, and beyond it the stairs to the second story with their worn Oriental carpeting and the dark first-floor hall to the landlord's apartment. Each step felt heavier than the last as she climbed toward Tyler's landing. Her thighs were chafed, her dress dark under the arms with sweat, and her cock and balls tucked back between her legs and taped in place, a fetid swamp.

You're fat. You're ugly. You reek. One look and anyone could tell you're not a real woman. He's going to throw you out. That's why Charlie didn't want you, because you're a freak. An ugly freak. Who'd pay to be with you?

Through the door and into the tiled front hall, kicking off her flats into the jumble of Tyler's neglected shoes on the dusty rubber mat beside the doorway. He only ever wore the same ratty pair of sneakers, black Skechers with duct tape wrapped around the right one's toe. He'd seemed so grown-up to her the first time she'd come to visit him. The way he smoked, sucking the gray cloud back in and breathing it out through his nose in lazy jets. The way he made her a whiskey sour with a shaker and crushed ice, just like Stel made cocktails at parties. He'd even cleaned before she got there, and his long arms had felt so good around her. His stubble rasping against her freshly shaven throat.

"I'm home," she called as she hung her purse on one of the wall's pegs. Most were empty. Tyler's down jacket, green with pale yellow stripes along the arms. A battered Yankees cap. She lifted her right foot and twisted to look back with a hiss of disgust at the yellowish blisters on her pinky toe and heel. She'd have to pop and bandage them before Tyler saw. He hated things like that. Pimples. Zits. Boils. It practically made him turn green.

He's going to throw you out anyway.

"Tyler?" She passed the bathroom, glancing at the creased and water-spotted Iron Maiden poster opposite its door. A withered, mummified-looking judge raising a gavel to hand down a ten-year sentence as a crowd roared in the foreground. She'd never liked the thing. It made her think of witch burnings and public hangings. The ecstasy of the crowd as the trapdoor banged open and the condemned dropped. Then there was the linen closet—her innovation—and a sharp left turn into the kitchen where Tyler was waiting.

He sat at the table, not looking at her. There were men with him. One, the younger of the two, sat on the counter with an empty glass in his hand and a milk mustache on his upper lip. The other was older, maybe forty, with wind-burned cheeks and a thick gray mustache, and wore a brown leather bomber jacket. He stood beside Tyler, resting a hand on his shoulder. For a moment Shelby thought that she'd fucked up, forgotten Tyler's friends were over, except these weren't cruel, grinning twentysomethings in hoodies and basketball shorts, all big ears and scrawny necks and stupid grade school secret handshakes. She'd seen them once in the line outside the AMC in Harlem. She wasn't supposed to follow them, but she'd been so curious, and Tyler hadn't seen her, so what was the harm?

You're a dirty little sneak.

"Hello, Andrew," said the older man. He had a nice smile. It made his dark eyes crinkle at the corners. "I'm Dave, and this is Enoch." He waved a hand in the direction of the blond man perched on the counter. "Why don't you sit down?"

Shelby took a half step back. Her chest felt tight, her mouth dry. There was a high-pitched ringing in her ears. "Tyler?" He still wouldn't look at her. "Tyler, what's going on? Who are these people?"

Dave's hand left Tyler's shoulder. He came toward her, moving around the table. He had a slight limp in his left leg. "Your parents are worried about you, Andrew."

She broke for the hall in a desperate sprint. Four yards. Three. Her heart pounding in her chest, her chafed thighs burning. Her hand closed on the doorknob. Enoch caught her from behind just as she yanked the door open. He kicked it shut and hauled her away, pushing her back against the wall. She could smell the milk on his breath. Milk and something else, meaty and pungent. "Take it easy," he grunted, dragging her wrists to the small of her back as she tried to push off from the mold-spotted drywall. Cold metal against her skin. The click of a mechanism locking. "We're here to help you."

"Rape!" she screamed, her voice cracking. "Rape, rape!"

Enoch put a palm against her head and thumped it hard against the wall, cratering the sheetrock. She blinked. Stars swam in her field of vision and then he was shoving her and she was stumbling toward the door as behind them in the kitchen Dave spoke to Tyler in hushed tones. ". . . won't press charges," he was saying, "but man to man I'd give serious thought to finding help. You don't want this life."

"Yeah," Tyler mumbled. "Thanks."

"Tyler!" Shelby shrieked as Enoch reached around her to open the door. The stairwell yawned below, and at the bottom another man stood holding the inner door open and looking up at them. He wore sunglasses and a light, faded denim jacket. A car was idling outside. Shelby could hear the low, insistent rumble of its engine. She tasted vomit at the back of her throat as Enoch forced her out onto the steps, her bare feet sliding on the worn carpeting. "Tyler, help me!"

But he didn't. Not as Enoch shoved her down the stairs, vertigo stretching the front hall into a dark canyon, and not as he and the other man bundled her into the back of a white van while the old man sleeping in the chair snored fitfully and a thin, nervous-looking woman out walking her dog cried, "What are you doing to her?" and Dave slipped between them, soothing and explaining, saying things like "parental consent" and "accreditation" until the woman shrank into herself and the van's doors slammed shut, plunging Shelby into blackness with only her screams for company.

For the first hour she could still hear the sounds of the city through the van's padded walls. She tried scooting up against it and tearing at the foam padding, but it was thick and spongy and impossible to get a grip on between the constant jouncing and the angle. If anyone could hear her screaming through the insulation, they didn't do anything about it. When the van stopped at what she assumed were traffic lights she threw herself against the wall until her shoulder was raw and nearly numb. She screamed until her voice cracked and gave out.

When they hit highway, their stop-and-start progress smoothing out into the roar of the open road, she began to cry. It started in her throat, a lump she could hardly swallow past, and then she was sobbing so hard that she nearly retched, her whole body bent over by the force of her misery. No matter how many times Ruth had threatened her with reform school or the cops or wilderness retreats way out in the linty navel of Nebraska, she'd never really believed the hammer would come down. She'd heard them arguing at night, Stel sniffling and saying "It's just a phase, it's just a phase" while Ruth ranted about gender roles and autogynephilia, and somehow she'd thought it would just blow over, that ten years later it would be an ugly memory.

Even the night she'd left for Tyler's, her great escape, when Ruth cornered her in the kitchen shrieking *You want to be a woman? You want to be a woman? See how you like it, see if you can take it* and hit her again and again, vicious little slaps across her face, her throat, her chest and shoulders, she hadn't really believed it. It would just end, sooner or later, and they would pretend it had never happened at all, like they had when Stel caught her trying on Ruth's pantyhose or the time on the Cape with Julian Donner. Now here it was. She'd guessed wrong, so unbelievably wrong, and she was going to pay for it.

She cried herself out after a while, lapsing into a dull, sticky half consciousness to avoid the infuriating itching of her snot-coated upper lip, the pins and needles creeping up her arms. With her ear against the van's metal bed she could hear the rolling hiss of the tires, feel the vibration of the engine. She thought of the *How Things Work* picture book Ruth's sister, Jean, had bought for her when she was little. Pistons and turbines and the little deaths of controlled explosions flashing in the heart of the hidden machine. A cutaway of everything unspoken and ignored that drove the world onward, onward, faster, with everything exactly where it was supposed to be and moving at terrible speed.

Sleep came somewhere in the long, monotonous hum. Shelby dreamed of babies crawling over an abandoned kitchen, cutting

their little fingers on broken glass and cookware, and of their unformed heads collapsing when she tried to take them in her arms.
When she woke her mouth was parched, her nose stuffed and
running. She could feel the little puddle of snot under her cheek.
The car wasn't moving. The engine was off and she could hear the
muffled sounds of gas pumping, the hiss of the pneumatic grip,
the thrum of the pump building suction. Voices, too. Men talking.
Laughing.

"Help," she croaked, rolling onto her stomach. Her face itched
where her stubble was coming in, thin and wispy as pubes. She
squirmed forward a few inches, dragging herself like a worm toward the rear doors. "Help me."

The doors are going to open, she thought as she heaved herself
up onto her knees and leaned against the cold metal. *Tyler's going
to be there. He's going to say baby, I'm so sorry, and he'll pull me out,
or my moms, we couldn't go through with it, we made a mistake.*

It had to open. Something had to happen to make sense of
the day's long, dark blur. She was dead. She'd had a stroke. She'd
fallen asleep on the LIRR and this was all a dream, just an angry
ghost whispering in her ear that Whitey was coming for her, that
Whitey had gotten her before she could talk, before she could
crawl, and now she couldn't get out of the stainless white sheet
they'd sewn her into, couldn't be anything but a fat, smudged
carbon copy of the women—the *real* women—who'd reached
halfway across the world and plucked her from her crib.

"Help me," she cried, her voice cracking. "They kidnapped me.
Please, please, help me."

The voices outside fell silent. There was a loud *chunk* as the
pump shut off, and then footsteps circling the van. A man's voice
came, flatter and harsher than Enoch's or Dave's. "You got someone in the back there, Davey?"

"Let me out," wailed Shelby. She banged her head against
the door, hard enough that a squirming gray thread of nausea
crawled from the pit of her stomach up into her throat. "Please,

mister, please, help me! They dragged me in here, I'm from New York, from Long Island, I don't know where I am."

The man snarled. "You didn't say nothing about a girl."

He knows them. She started to cry even before Dave could clear his throat and answer: "It's a transvestite, Jimmy. Didn't think you'd be interested."

There was a short silence.

"Show it to me," Jimmy said.

Shelby squirmed back from the door as Enoch threw the left-hand panel open, then the right. Cold artificial light flooded the van's interior. Three men stood silhouetted against it, and behind them a semitruck idled at the edge of a huge expanse of cracked and broken pavement. A weigh station, maybe, not a regular gas station. No one would hear her screaming here. No one would find her if they dragged her out and raped her under the light of the moon and put a bullet in her head.

"Fat," said Jimmy, once a moment had passed. "Little titties and everything. Coulda fooled me, tell you the truth."

As Enoch tossed a package of crackers and a bottle of warm Poland Spring into the van and slammed the doors again, Shelby felt a flush of perverse pride, pride she clung to as she unscrewed the bottle with her teeth and choked on lukewarm water, as she tore open the package of smashed peanut butter crackers and ate them like a pig, face-first, snorting and snuffling. The cab's doors slammed and the van pulled away from the pump, creaking and thumping back onto the open road. Those eyes, nested deep in leathery skin, going wide.

Coulda fooled me.

Blossom, Kansas

Nadine slammed the back of her head into the woman's face again, relishing the crack of breaking bone and cartilage. Her mother was screaming. Her sisters, too, all held back by the bulwark of her father's bulk. There were tears in Mark Donovan's eyes and somehow that was the worst part, his indulgence in his own weakness as he did this to her, as he let it happen, wet and weepy as though he hadn't paid to have her socked away in whatever funny farm or backwater revivalist rapist reserve the people who'd been waiting for them in the rest stop parking lot were running. As though he had no more choice in how her life went than the wind howling through the desolate visitor center and the derelict cars at the edge of the dusty, gritty lot.

"We're trying to help you," the woman holding her snarled, snaking an arm around Nadine's throat. She had a tattoo on her thick forearm. Names and dates. Nadine hoped her kids had died. "Stop *fighting me*."

Nadine twisted, bared her teeth, and bit her. The woman howled, wrapping a fist in Nadine's hair and trying to drag her off her other arm. Her skin tasted like sweat. It stretched between Nadine's teeth. Her mother was screaming "*Do* something, Mark!" as though the whole mess weren't his fault, and her little sister Alice, four years old, kept wailing "*Naddy!*" in her lisping voice as Nina, eight since her birthday three days earlier—white sheet cake with pink icing, *Happy Birthday Princess* in big bubble letters— and wide-eyed with terror, held her back.

The other muscle, the bearded man in the Orioles cap who'd been waiting with Names-and-Dates by the unmarked van when they pulled up, ducked down to grab Nadine's legs, wrapping his thick arms around her calves. "You're doing the right thing," he growled to her family as he lifted her bodily into the air. Names-and-Dates took a half step back, her grip loosening, and Nadine dug a shoulder into her side and wrenched her head back with all her strength, the flesh between her teeth stretching, stretching. With a sickening squelch it tore away from the woman's arm in a long, ragged strip, snapping taut again as the screaming started and the woman lost her hold. Blood flooded Nadine's mouth. She thought of Tess's pussy, of the deep iron stink of the other girl's period as she pressed her nose into the slit, and spat, laughing. A closed fist slammed into her cheek and rocked her head back like a speed bag. She saw stars.

"Oh Jesus, Mark," her mother screamed. *"Do something."*

Names-and-Dates, retching and gasping, a string of bloody skin swinging loose from her forearm, shoved Nadine at the Beard, who wrapped her in a crushing bear hug from behind. He twisted her arms behind her back and snapped a cuff on her right wrist. He did it easily, by rote, like tying off a garbage bag or hefting firewood. Names-and-Dates, gray-faced and swaying a little, followed them toward the van. She'd wrapped a handkerchief around her wounded arm. Nadine kicked, spat, went limp, and finally forced herself to piss, a urine stain darkening the crotch of her overalls, but the Beard was unfazed.

"Why don't you just fucking kill me?" Nadine screeched as they manhandled her into the back of their van and onto a bench seat bolted to the side panel. Names-and-Dates snapped the other end of the cuff around the bench's left support as the Beard let Nadine go and climbed down over the tailgate. Nadine kicked out at the older woman, clipping her shin. "Don't let them take me!" she screamed, ashamed of the way her voice cracked, of the hot piss running down her legs, of how afraid she was. "Don't do this! It was just a joke, we didn't mean it, please, please, Mom, please!"

Nadine couldn't see her family, but she could hear her mother and her sisters crying, and she could see her father's white-faced horror as he walked into the garage at three a.m. to find her tangled up with Tess behind his tarped Harley panhead. He'd dragged her across the cold concrete by her hair, bruising her tailbone on the edge of the step up to the kitchen, where he dialed Tess's mother while she cried, begged, groveled.

The Beard slammed the van's rear doors. The sounds of Nadine's family being sad about what they were doing to her, what they'd paid other people to do to her, faded to a wet and distant blubbering as the overheads flickered weakly to life. A moment later the van rocked, another door slammed, and the engine growled awake.

"You fucked my arm up pretty good there," said Names-and-Dates, crouching down just outside Nadine's reach. "You're scared. I get that. And you're all fucked up in there, too." She jabbed Nadine's forehead with two stiffened fingers. "Dykes, man. They'll drive you crazy. Get you chasing your tail." They rumbled into motion, jouncing over broken pavement and potholes toward the highway cutting flat and straight across the featureless void of the desert. Light and dark jumped over the woman's sweaty face as they went over a speed bump. She was pretty, in an average sort of way, and had a little pit in her nose where she might have had a piercing once.

Names-and-Dates straightened up, shifting her balance easily with the sway and rattle of the van beneath her feet. "Anyway," she said, tugging the bandana wrapped around her oozing arm a little tighter, "I'm gonna show you what that kind of shit'll get you at the camp, but that doesn't mean we can't be friends once we're evened up." She made a fist, knuckles cracking.

Nadine wished for her lacrosse stick in that moment, a need so powerful she almost moaned at the thought of that reassuring length of titanium with its taped-over butt and the neat lattice-work of its head. Split that hateful smile in two. Bash this bitch's head in until it broke down the middle, red and wet.

I'm going to murder you, you fucking cunt. I'm going to beat your brains out.

Names-and-Dates feinted toward her, fist raised, and Nadine banged her head on the van's side jerking away on pure reflex. She blushed furiously as the older woman cocked her bloody fist back, smiling.

"Two for flinching."

II

CAMP RESOLUTION

"Do you know why you're here, Gabe?" asked the woman at the desk in the air-conditioned trailer. Hard, bright desert sunlight fell across her face in narrow bands filtered through dusty Venetian blinds. Her wheat-colored hair hung pin-straight to her shoulders, framing a pinched mouth, pale eyes, a chinless slope of neck. She wore a ruched white blouse with puffy sleeves and a tan skirt that clung awkwardly to her narrow hips.

Maybe to teach you how to dress yourself so you don't look like a nun going to prom?

Gabe shook his head. His skin felt grimy after who knew how long in the back of a van. Two men from Camp Resolution, which so far consisted of a couple of trailers and some rows of wind-scoured cabins with chicken wire on the windows in the middle of an endless, anonymous desert, had ridden with him the whole way. *This is an opportunity for you, man,* the blond one had kept saying. *I wish I'd had a chance like this when I was your age.*

Yeah, the other man had agreed, not looking at Gabe. *Yeah.*

"Your"—her gaze flicked down to the open manila folder on her desk, then back up to Gabe—"parents are worried about you. They want you to have a full life, to get into a good school, make a name for yourself, fall in love, raise children of your own. They want you to contribute to society, Gabe, and they know none of that can happen until you get help."

He imagined spitting in her face. "Help with what?" he asked, folding his arms across his chest.

She smiled at him, the same smile of feigned warmth he'd seen his aunt and mother use on one another when they were getting into it good and didn't want to admit it. "With your homosexuality," she cooed, pronouncing it carefully, as though she was afraid to let the word touch her tongue. "Another boy can't give you a family, Gabe. He can't give you love. All he can give you is the sickness they spread to each other."

Gabe's cheeks prickled with what he thought was probably an ugly flush, brick red and blotchy like his dad got when someone beat him in Scrabble, or the day Gabe had refused to come out of the locker room at his first swim meet. *You made a commitment to Coach Hauser and the rest of your team.* Staring down at his pelvis where the black Speedo clung to his skin and his flat, bony hips and the soft little bulge of his twelve-year-old crotch, feeling as though he might vomit. And then closer, like the older man was right up flush against the door to the pool. *Do not make me come in there, Gabriel.*

He clenched his teeth and forced a smile. "I'm not gay."

"What a surprise that would be for the boy your father found you with." She said it so tartly and with such tight, quivering relish that Gabe was sure she'd had it locked and loaded from the moment he walked in out of the baking desert heat. "What was his name?" She thumbed through his file, her French tips scratching at the printed pages, before stopping on a handwritten page near the end. "Francis."

That big, strong body dwarfing his. A swaying mop of hair, strawberry blond, and gray eyes looking down at him with something between love and nausea. A thumb pressed to his bottom lip and his chin cupped like china by long fingers. *Do you mind being the girl?*

Never.

"Wrestling," he bit out. "We were wrestling."

"Your father tells us there was another boy. Michael Olsen." Her eyes sparkled with delight even as a look of simpering concern plowed across her face. "When the counselors at Camp Sapawan found you together, were you wrestling then, too?"

He said nothing. The air in the trailer seemed suddenly thick, pressing in on his chest, wrapping tight around his throat. *You don't know what you're talking about,* he wanted to scream, but no words would come. He imagined the relief of dragging a bent safety pin's dull point along his inner arm.

"What about the clothes you stole from the camp's laundry facilities? I wasn't aware skirts and stockings were typical wrestling attire."

Michael's mouth in the hollow of his armpit. Michael's breath on the back of his neck. Michael's tongue, Michael's fingers, Michael's soft, husky voice and quick little hands, Michael's penis, Michael's whispered promises and the sour taste of panic as the lights came on in the storeroom. Michael's screams the next night, muffled by a dirty sock, when the older boys came to his bed after lights-out.

"We're going to do our best to help you, Gabe," she said, and somehow the tears in the corners of her eyes made Gabe so angry he could hardly see, so angry that he wanted to lunge across her desk and sink his teeth into her throat right above the silver cross necklace she'd probably bought at a kiosk in some mega-mall, or from a Kmart jewelry counter. "But if it's going to work, you have to be honest with us. You have to want to get better."

He never heard the man come up behind him, had no idea he was there until a thick, hairy arm coiled around his throat. His attacker tipped his chair back as Gabe kicked at empty air and clawed at the steel cable of muscle cutting off his oxygen supply. Then, over the strained hiss of his own breathing, he heard a high, whining buzz.

"No!" he screamed, but the clippers were already in his hair, sawing through the long auburn waves he'd fought his parents over month after month, year after year, the woman looking down at him with an expression of such smug, complacent contentment that he sobbed in frustrated rage and terror. He stubbed his toe kicking the edge of her desk, his vision darkening at the edges as the mosquito whine of the clippers slid over his skull, high and stupid and monotonous, going on and on and on until finally there was nothing left and he was hustled to the door by the man, whose face he never saw, and shoved down the creaky steps onto packed earth, gasping and blinking in the white-hot blaze of afternoon.

His scalp was covered in a fine dusting of peach fuzz. Loose hairs pricked and poked him as he plucked at the neck of his sweat-dampened T-shirt, staring as he did at the dusty dirt parking lot where another van was pulling up. There were already a dozen parked—more, maybe—and boys and girls around Gabe's age lined up in the smothering sunlight under the watchful gaze of a man dressed head to toe in filthy denim who leaned against a solitary fence post, smoking. The long barrels of the shotgun resting on his shoulder glinted in the sunlight. Gabe had never held a gun in his life. Had seldom so much as seen one, except for at his uncle's in the fall when the men and the other boys would suit up in camo and reflective neon orange and go stomping out into the woods to kill things.

Maybe it's loaded with rubber pellets, he thought, hypnotized by the gun's oiled gleam. *Or rock salt. That's a thing. Unless the plan is just to kill us if we run.*

He pictured it for an exquisite moment, the arc of his body caught in the small of the back with a blast of lead, flesh shredding, the red heat of his spine coming apart as he bent like a bow in midair and the scabby desert soil rushed up to kiss him. It must have been fifty miles from the nearest gas station out here, and it was so *flat.* Nothing cast a shadow but the mountains. His mouth was already drying out, his eyes stinging from the glare.

I'm going to die out here.

At the edge of the compound, near the chain-link fence enclosing it, was a dusty, worn pavilion the color of oatmeal into which the staff herded the kids. Shelby shuffled with the others through the sagging entrance, its flaps drawn back and tied in place like the petals of some ugly carnivorous plant.

Her shaved scalp itched and burned after an hour spent standing in the sun as one by one the others were led up to the trailer with its pretty secretary and the bearded man and his clippers. The *real* girls got to keep their hair, of course. They were clustered together, nine or ten of them, around a tall, lean white girl with a mane of tawny hair, a butterfly Band-Aid across the bridge of her crooked nose, and two spectacular black eyes, the left swollen to a small, wet slit. She gave Shelby an appraising look as the crowd in the pavilion swelled, forcing them all toward the raw pine platform at the back of the space. The work lamps hanging from the poles swung to and fro as the crowd jostled for position.

"Whaddya think?" asked a skinny Black boy, arching an eyebrow at her. "Bet you they're gonna teach us close-up magic. Maybe juggling."

Shelby stared at him, unable to comprehend the joke, and then the crowd sucked him away and she was jostled back as, with a groan of bending wood, a man climbed onto the platform's sanded boards. He was huge, closer to seven feet than six, with a deep chest and massive shoulders. A thick salt-and-pepper mustache covered his upper lip and he wore a light linen blazer over a white button-up. In a wicker chair behind him, far to the back, sat a tiny white woman with wispy blond hair and huge, pale eyes. She wore a long-sleeved white blouse and a dark skirt that brushed the boards.

"Welcome to Camp Resolution," said the man. He had a deep, velvety voice with a slight crackle in it, as though his lungs were made of dried-out paper. "I'm Pastor Eddie. I bet some of you are pretty angry right now."

He paused as though expecting laughter.

"Fuck you," someone shouted. Shelby couldn't see who.

"That's good," the pastor rumbled. He sounded contented, like a big cat stretching out before a nap. "You get that out your system, because starting right now, I hear one word of nasty talk from you, you get the belt. Out in the world you may be teenagers, might think you're big tough rebels because MTV tells you so, but at

Camp Resolution you're a child until we say otherwise, and you will learn to live as children are meant to: in silence, with respect for your elders and betters. So I don't want to hear no nasty talk"—the thick fingers of his right hand tapped the length of brown leather holding up his slacks—"and if I do, well, you've been warned."

Another pause, this one tense and ugly.

"You're here," said Pastor Eddie, and all of a sudden there were tears in his dark little eyes, "because your parents love you. Because they don't want to see you sell yourselves on street corners for pills and marijuana. They don't want to see you lying in hospital beds with sores on your faces, lesions like the ones God laid on the Egyptians holding the children of Israel hostage the way you—*you*"—he jabbed his forefinger at them, sweeping it like a scythe—"are hostage to the pornographers in Washington and Hollywood and New York City, to the ideas they've planted in your heads, the lies they've told you."

He calmed. The color faded from his sun-roughened cheeks. Behind him the little doll-woman in her chair had a hungry look on her gaunt, pinched face. Not far from Shelby a big fat white boy started crying, sniffling like a baby, and a lanky brown girl—*boy?*—with a butch haircut and a little mustache observed his tears with a look of flat disgust. Shelby hugged herself and dug her nails into her forearms.

"You're here to learn how to be men. How to be women. First thing tomorrow you'll have help from young people of quality, people who know your struggles and have overcome them, and from me and my staff. For tonight I'm only asking you to sit, work through that anger you're feeling, and think about the kind of life you want." The big hands made fists, knuckles standing out. "I think you'll be surprised what you can figure out just sitting quietly." He smiled. "Now get some supper in you, then it's lights-out."

Gabe poked at the mound of steamed spinach heaped in the corner pocket of his plastic dinner tray. Grayish creamed corn. A sticky lozenge of something like cornbread. The chili was the worst of it, thick and glutinous and an awful shade of neon red. All around him the mess tent was full of the sound of kids eating, shoveling food into their mouths, chewing noisily, talking to each other in low voices.

You should eat, he thought, but the voice in his head was his mother's, colorless and coolly mocking under its veneer of commonsense advice. *Cover up those collarbones.*

Skinny girls made him angry. He didn't understand it, but just the sight of one was enough to make him want to scream. *I'm better than you,* their ribs and the knobs of their spines seemed to hiss at him. *My every step is effortless. Weightless. While you plod on the dirty earth I soar above you, drenched in sunlight.* His mind kept straying back to the woman sitting in the wicker chair on the platform in the pavilion, to the fleshless lines of her skull, the elegance of her long, thin fingers, and the blue traceries of veins visible on her scalp through her hair.

He thought of her, and he ate nothing. His stomach snarled and begged until he drained three plastic cups of tepid water from the beading red cooler on the serving table. A fake wood top and folding metal legs. Two big women in aprons dishing chili out to kids, the youngest of whom looked about thirteen, the oldest maybe a few years older than him. Seventeen. Eighteen, maybe, if that was legal. Or probably even if it wasn't. He went back to his table at the edge of the mess cabin. There were about sixty kids under its sagging roof, most of whom he recognized from the tent. The others, sunburned and weathered, he guessed had been here longer. Eight counselors strode the aisles between plastic folding chairs, one or two tapping nightsticks against their legs, others stopping to talk and joke.

"You should eat," said the girl sitting across from him, who was fat and thus, according to the hidden calculus of how Gabe saw the world, safe. "They work the boys really hard."

He flashed a smile, the most charming he could drag out of his sweaty, itchy, crop-haired walking skin suit. Fat girls usually liked him. In eighth grade he'd had a friend named Bea who'd followed him everywhere like a sad-eyed little puppy, doing his homework and laughing at his jokes with nervous, almost frantic intensity until finally he'd let her jerk him off in the woods past the playground. After that the sight of her had made him sick, made him think of the pearlescent slick of his cum on her soft forearm, the jiggle of her breasts as her wrist moved and the skin of his penis slid up and down with the motion of her palm, exposing its swollen purple head. After they'd parted he'd thrown up over the roots of an old pine tree not far from the river where the other kids were jumping off Black Moth Rock and hunting for crayfish in the shallows.

Before that, though, she'd been nice, and kind of comforting to have around. He caught himself staring, the girl looking back at him with wary incredulity. *You're going to need friends if you want to survive here.* "Sorry," he said, clawing another smile up from somewhere deep in the pit of his stomach. "This place is freaking me out. I'm Gabe."

She blushed a gratifying shade of pink. "Candace. I got here last week. It's not . . . not that bad, if you do what they say."

A week. How long are they going to keep us here?

"What do they make you do?"

"Mostly we just work. The girls cook and clean and stuff in the big house and the barn; the boys are outside. There are cattle. Fences. Getting rid of prairie dogs and coyotes." She said it *kai-oats*, like Foghorn Leghorn. "They have etiquette classes, too. Like how to be a lady, how to be a man. And they make us exercise." Her blush deepened, real shame reddening her cheeks as she looked down at her tray. "That'll probably be easy for you."

"That's really unfair," he said, trying his best to sound sympathetic. The thought of her round, heavy body jiggling as she labored through a set of jumping jacks made him feel both contemptuous and keenly interested. "I bet you're better at it than you think."

She smiled shyly, eyes flicking up, then down again. The servers were clearing off the tables, assisted by a handful of kids, as the counselors started going table to table and rousting everyone to their feet. Gabe took a hasty bite of spinach, chewing fast. "Is he serious about the belt? The pastor guy?"

Candace met his stare again, and this time she held it. "He's really, really serious," she said. "Don't make him mad. Just do what he tells you to do. If you piss him off it's not even the belt you have to worry about."

"What, is he a pedo or something?"

She shook her head. "After the belt, he gives you to the other kids."

After dinner, counselors broke the new arrivals into ten groups of four and led them through the dark to their cabins, which had bars on all the windows and locked from the outside. The other kids, fifteen or twenty of them, remained behind with Dave and a few other ranch hands.

They put Shelby in with a tall, skinny boy named Gabe, a younger kid with an overbite and a rat tail who couldn't stop crying long enough to tell her his name, and John, the fattest boy she'd ever seen, who stared at them all like they were aliens abducting him. Their names—the names on their birth certificates—were on little steel plaques nailed to the frames of their bunks.

Their counselor couldn't have been older than twenty, a sunburned ginger in Wranglers with a flat-top buzz and acne scars dotting his cheeks and throat. He'd introduced himself as Corey Fudder—Gabe had mouthed "motherfudder" at her behind his back on the walk from the mess to their cabin—and now stood blocking the doorway, the white glare of sodium spotlights blinding behind him.

"You'll do orientation tomorrow," he said as they settled into their bunks, Shelby scurrying up into the one over Gabe's. It made her feel a little safer, looking down at the rest of them. "For tonight, all you need to know is that you might be able to break out of the cabin. Put your back into it, use your head, and maybe. But if you do, there's about a hundred miles of open desert in every direction, and when we bring you back you're gonna sleep cuffed to your bed. You're boys, and you don't want to be here, and Pastor Eddie says it's healthy you fight back a little, but think about the desert before you waste all our time and maybe get yourselves snakebit."

He left, shutting the door behind him and locking it. First the thunk of the deadbolt, then the click of a key in its hole and the smooth, heavy turning of tumblers. The bunks' plastic mattresses crinkled as bodies shifted in the sudden gloom. White light leaked in through the doorframe.

"Motherfudder," came Gabe's scratchy voice, unmistakably faggy.

Shelby giggled nervously into her hands. The boy with the rat tail—the nameplate on his bunk read BRADY—just kept crying, and John didn't say anything at all. He turned toward the wall and lay down on his side on top of the sheets and the single thin blanket, ribbed and pea green. Shelby thought about saying something, about putting out some feelers to the others, but as her eyes adjusted to the dark the boy-ness of them seemed to close in tight around her, pressing her back against the wall and driving her under the covers. She could feel the name nailed to the side of her bunk as though it were a burning coal, and the last two days of unshowered misery—squatting to piss in a bucket bolted to the truck's bed, eating what Enoch or Dave threw in to her—crashed down and flattened her against the crinkling mattress, a leaden weight like a barbell sitting on her chest.

I can't do this, she thought, wanting Stel, wanting her on a good day when Ruth was traveling or at the gallery and the two of them would make pizza bagels and ice cream sundaes and snuggle on the couch watching scary movies. The kind of thing Ruth hated.

Classless, she'd say when she caught them at it. Cold, thin line of her lips. Shelby sucked in a ragged breath and pushed her fist into her mouth to stifle her sobs. *I can't do this.*

It was a long time before sleep came.

III

FUN RUN

The desert was endless and Nadine was digging in it, her undershirt sticking to her sweaty back, her hands blistered where they gripped the shovel's shaft. Sometimes it rained and the rain was thick and viscous and smelled like the hairy trench of skin between pussy and butthole, rank and sour and gamey. Her little sister Nina called her "butthole" sometimes, when she was angry. She shouted it like a real swear. *Butthole, butthole.* As though it meant something on its own.

The hole Nadine was digging in grew deeper. She could hear Tess's voice somewhere under the hard, dry dirt. That voice. Valley girl with a hint of a lisp, and those baby blues looking up at her, that soft little mouth moaning *another finger* like a question. *I want your whole fist. I want it. Nate . . .*

She dug faster, the shovel biting into the rain-soaked earth with wet, flatulent squelches. *I'm digging up Roy,* she thought suddenly, remembering the way the old hound dog had whimpered after her father backed his truck over him. Wet and shaking, parts all twisted the wrong ways. They had buried him in the backyard, shoveling in silence in the sweltering Kentucky heat, and she was digging him up here, who knew how many thousand miles away, and people were watching from the edges of the grave above. Her parents. The Kleins and the Heisses from First Lutheran, and Reverend Joseph. Tess and her mother. Her lacrosse team. Jody and Alison and Danielle. They all expected something of her.

The shovel's blade found something hard, the shock of impact traveling up through her blistered palms and aching arms. She panted as she yanked it free and drove it into the dirt a short

way off, then knelt to continue with her hands. The people looking down at her were talking, but she couldn't understand what
they were saying, only hear the mush-mouthed susurrus of it, like
they were grown-ups in a Charlie Brown movie. *Wa-wa, wa-wa-
wa-wa*. It hurt to dig. Her nails chipped and tore. Her blisters
burst. She clawed at dark, wet soil that gave way to blue clay and
then to fine white sand that spilled through her fingers as she
scooped it from the hole. There. Something pale. That taint smell
again, thick and sweaty, and she dug deep and had it in her hands,
pulling it up as white sand ran down its cheeks like tears.

Her own face, expressionless and serene, eyes shut, hair still
mostly buried. The voices on the lip of the grave went quiet all
at once. Nadine could hear herself breathing. She could hear her
heartbeat and the churn of her guts. Her mouth was so dry. When
had she last had water?

The face—*her* face—opened its eyes and she recoiled from it,
scuttling backward on all fours until she slammed into the stri-
ated wall of the grave and it gave way against her, spilling her out
of the dream and into the predawn silence of the cabin.

She lay very still. *I'm in bed,* she thought, looking across the room
to where Jo and Felix slept in their bunks, the former curled up like
a roly-poly whose rock had just been lifted, the latter sprawled and
snoring. Light fell gray through the doorframe and chinks in the
walls and the flat roof. A line of ants marched in and out of shadow
from a knothole in a floorboard to the wall. Already the dream was
sliding away from her. Something about buttholes.

Smith stirred in the bunk above Nadine's, mumbling in her
sleep. The cabin's steps creaked. The lock rattled. *Hide beside the
door,* Nadine thought, sliding her legs over the bed's edge. Adren-
aline sang through her, bringing the cabin into brutal clarity. Her
toes met the floorboards silently as she gathered the sheet around
her. *Twist this up, loop it around her neck when she comes in. Get
her on the floor and put your knee on her spine. Pull. Pull hard.*

Except it wouldn't matter. Maybe she'd turn out to be a real
badass and kill the counselor, John McClane–style. Maybe the

counselor would put her on her ass. Either way there'd be a dozen more people waiting outside for her, and even if she somehow got past them then there was the desert stretching away flat and endless except for the mountains, which she'd die trying to cross without supplies or warm clothes. She didn't even know which state she was in. So she sat on the edge of her bed, pulse thundering, and forced herself to stay still as the door swung outward and their counselor, Cheryl, stepped inside.

Cheryl was tiny, maybe five-two or five-three, the only one of Pastor Eddie's staff Nadine had seen so far who was shorter than most of the kids. Still, there was something serious about her, something that frightened Nadine in a way even Names-and-Dates's fist crashing into her face hadn't done. Her cold black stare slid over the cabin's interior as she came to a halt in the middle of the room, crushing a section of the ant column under the sole of her left boot. The survivors filed onward, uncomprehending.

"Out of bed," said Cheryl. Her voice, high and a little breathy, filled the cabin effortlessly. "Now."

Nadine got up, letting the sheet drop to the mattress. Felix, blinking sleep out of his eyes, rolled out of his bunk and dropped to the floor in his T-shirt and briefs as Smith climbed down to stand next to Nadine, hugging herself. Jo didn't move. Whether she was asleep or faking Nadine never found out, because in three quick steps Cheryl had crossed the cabin, pushed Felix out of her way, and dragged Jo out of bed by the ear and a fistful of fabric. The stocky girl crashed to the floor with a cry, thrashing in a tangle of sheets and limbs. Cheryl flipped her over neatly with the toe of her boot.

"I said out of bed," the counselor repeated. "Tomorrow you will be dressed and standing at attention when I come in. Beds will be made, clothes folded or in the hamper." She put her foot on Jo's chest. "You are not butches. You aren't studs, bull dykes, or any other macho perversion. You are ladies, and you're going to learn to act like it." She turned toward Nadine and Smith. "Let me hear a 'Yes, Cheryl.'"

As she said it with the others, Nadine pictured the butt of her lacrosse stick breaking Cheryl's pretty nose.

"Yes, Cheryl."

A smug, tight smile. "Good. Now we're going for a run."

Felix jogged through the desert in the middle of a ragged line of a dozen other kids, wondering which of them was going to drop first. It wouldn't be him. He ran every day at home, and he'd gone to sleep the night before as soon as his head hit the pillow, ignoring the sniffles and whimpering that filled the dark interior of Cabin Four. The counselors and the rest of the freakshow Mormons or whatever they were could call him Inez and make him wear whatever they wanted; he'd put his head down, do what they told him, and when he got back to Philly he'd apologize to his father for the quinceañera—shredded taffeta and broken glass and his brother, Leo, screaming, blood on his face—and do his time until he could move out. He'd lost the round. Spun out. He could live with that.

Easy.

Ahead of the joggers a rust-spotted white pickup bumped and rattled over the uneven desert earth, its tires throwing up thin clouds of dust. A blocky blond man named Enoch sat in the bed with one leg hanging over the tailgate. He watched them through scratched sunglasses, his face expressionless. Felix wondered if Enoch had been through this, if he'd put on his mother's nylons or given his boy cousins handies at Christmas and gotten his white ass shipped off to wherever the fuck they were—Utah or Arizona or whatever—so Pastor Eddie and the rest of his boy band could help him pray away the gay.

It didn't matter. Just another thing to think about while the rutted earth flew past beneath his sneakers. A little to the left of their line Cheryl paced them easily, occasionally turning to run backward at a mocking reverse lope. Even sweaty and flushed she looked untouchable. Felix picked up his pace. On his left Nadine matched him stride for stride. She had a couple inches on him and her fucked-up face didn't seem to be slowing her down, but he thought she was probably running to beat him, not to last. Most of the group's girls had been at the camp for weeks at least. He and the rest of Cabin Four were the new meat, and he'd felt the eyes of the other eight on him since they'd met in the yard among other blocks and columns of counselors and kids.

"Pick it up, Blanchard!" Cheryl yelled.

Felix looked. Smith was flagging, her fine corn-silk hair plastered to her face and neck, her pale skin blotchy. He turned back to the truck. What was he supposed to do? Not like he could run *for* her. He could tell by the way the others darted looks in Smith's direction they were all thinking the same thing. Ahead, the truck hit a patch of sand with a reverberating hiss, tires churning up a cloud of grit that swallowed them at once. Felix squeezed his eyes shut, stumbling over the loose, shifting terrain as flecks of stone and sand stung his face, his forearms, his ankles. A few desperate heartbeats and they were through it. Felix blinked rapidly, grit caught in his eyelashes, as Cheryl shouted, "Line up, line up!" at the straggling runners.

That was when Smith dropped. Whether she tripped or collapsed Felix couldn't tell, but one moment she was wobbling along, face pale and blotchy, shining with sweat, and the next she was sprawled in the dirt, her whole body convulsing with dry heaves. The line came to an uneven stop. The truck drove on a few seconds longer before halting with a groan of metal and worn-out suspension. Felix stared at Smith, his own pulse loud in his ears.

"On your feet, Blanchard," barked Cheryl. She jogged back through the midst of them to stand over the fallen girl. "Up."

Smith struggled to her hands and knees, then retched. A string of yellow bile hung from her chin. "Can't," she husked. She retched again. "H-help. Can't. Can't."

"All right," said Cheryl after a short pause. She turned her back on the shivering girl. "Cleaver, get her moving."

A big sunburned redhead, one of the "upperclassmen," as Felix had heard others call the kids who'd been there longer, with her hair tied back in a tight, sleek bun, started toward Smith, a look of pure glee on her freckled and peeling face. She wore tight red shorts and a ratty T-shirt with an Indian brave's head in profile on it and the legend GO TOMAHAWKS! A few of the other upperclassmen exchanged knowing looks. Giggles ran up and down the line. "Help her up, Betty!" someone shrieked, plainly delighted. If Cheryl heard them, she chose not to say anything. Betty Cleaver sank down on one knee beside Smith, laying a hand on the back of the girl's neck as Smith retched again, her spine arching, more bile splattering against the loose red soil.

"Got it all out?" Cleaver asked, her voice dripping with sympathy.

Smith nodded shakily.

Something bad is going to happen, Felix thought. Blood and taffeta. Broken glass and screaming.

Cleaver patted Smith on the back, and then in one smooth motion she seized a fistful of Smith's white-blond hair and shoved her face into her own puke. The smaller girl clawed desperately at Cleaver's hand, but Betty held her there, grinding her face into the bile-soaked dirt. "You're gonna make us miss breakfast, you fuckin' gash," Cleaver snarled. "That happens, I'm gonna tie you to the truck's tailgate on the way back. You want that? You wanna be my little doggy?"

She rose, dragging Smith with her. The skinny girl's face was covered in mud and yellowish-tan slime. She sobbed convulsively, hugging herself. "N-no," she blubbered. "I'm s-s-sorry."

Betty leaned in close. Felix hardly caught what she hissed in Smith's ear.

"Then *run.*"

Smith ran.

Corey and the Beard, both on horseback, led the eight of them toward the mountains as the sun rose on the eastern horizon from a sea of heat shimmer. Shelby's feet hurt. The sneakers they'd given her didn't fit right and she could feel new blisters forming where they rubbed against bare skin. Her Wranglers pinched at the waist and the work shirt, which Ruth had bought for her years ago, made her feel like a misshapen sausage. She had stubble, her thighs were chafing, and she smelled like piss and sweat. The brim of the worn baseball cap—HINDLE HARDWARE: GET HAMMERED HERE!—Corey had tossed her itched against her freshly shaved scalp.

I wish I was dead, she thought. *I wish the pills had worked. I wish I'd used a razor, or Stel's gun.*

The dry, crumbling earth dipped down into a canyon, walls of red and yellow rock rising to either side of their little party as they followed the incline. The sound of running water echoed from the stone and gorse, and stunted thorn trees grew wild in the shade. Lizards scurried under rocks and into holes and crevices as their party passed by. Bugs rose whining from the witchgrass, midges and horse flies and grasshoppers with their vivid brown and yellow wings.

Some of the others were doing even worse. Weedy little Brady looked like he hadn't slept at all, and John was red in the face and wheezing like a pug with sunstroke, a far cry from his pompous handshakes—*John Calvin Bates, so good to meet you*—that morning when they'd gathered in the yard beside the flagpole. *At least I don't look like that,* she thought with a guilty species of relief, watching him lumber along, thighs jiggling in his loose silver basketball shorts. It made things easier when she wasn't the fattest, when she could protect herself from mockery simply by keeping her head down and trusting it to take the path of least resistance. She hated how secure it made her feel.

They crossed a fast-moving stream spilling down from the canyon's wall and plunging into a crevice in its far side. Smooth stones shifted under Shelby's feet. Her sneakers squelched as she climbed the far bank behind Gabe and Brady. "What do you think they're gonna make us do?" Brady whispered. He had a high voice, thin and nervous.

"How the fuck should I know?" Gabe snapped.

"We're gonna cornhole your mom, Brady," said Malcolm, the skinny Black kid Shelby had met in the pavilion. He pushed his glasses up his sweat-slicked nose. "We're all the way out here so civilians don't have to watch."

"Fuck you," Brady shot back, blushing furiously.

"Quiet," Corey shouted back over his shoulder. He frowned at Shelby, though she hadn't spoken.

They went on in silence for a while. The canyon opened up around them, dotted with shocks of saw grass and bur sage and piles of fallen rocks sloughed from the stone walls. Little brown songbirds speckled with white hopped through the undergrowth, hunting for bugs in the dirt. John Calvin Bates, esquire, was practically gasping by the time they reached a broad flat stretch where someone had left a cluster of shovels driven into the earth beside a huge roll of cut wooden posts and wire fencing. Shelby felt like sitting down and crying. Her wet feet itched and stung.

"Postholes are marked," said the Beard as he brought his horse around in a tight circle. It was huge, much bigger than the dainty little mares Shelby had ridden her summer at equestrian camp, its brown coat rough and dirty. "Need 'em three feet deep, then you take that bale and roll it out, get the ends of the wire around the bolts we sank here"—he gestured toward the nearer of the two stone walls where a pair of thumb-sized lengths of steel stood out from the rock at hip height—"and plant 'em."

"What's it for?" asked Gabe.

"Cattle," Corey answered. His horse came around more slowly than the Beard's, shaking its head as it picked its way over the uneven ground. "They graze down here. The fence should keep them out of the water. On a hot day they'll drink too much and sweat themselves out. Die, even, if we don't stop them."

He reached into his saddlebag and pulled out a tall bottle of Poland Spring, the sight of which transfixed Shelby instantly. "Look alive," he said, and tossed it underhand at John, who almost fumbled it, before throwing another to Malcolm. The Beard flipped a third to Shelby. She grabbed for it, missed, and had to crawl after the rolling plastic cylinder to snatch it before it went down the embankment and into the stream. A few of the boys chuckled. She straightened up in time to see the counselors riding back toward her.

"Do you have any moleskin?" Shelby asked, face burning, as the Beard's horse drew even with her. "I have a blister."

He rode past without answering, Corey beside him. The horses started down the bank. Their tails swished from side to side, whisking flies off their haunches.

"We need sunscreen!" she shouted after them, but neither man turned, and after a few minutes they had crossed the stream and started back along the canyon, dwindling into the long shadows. Shelby's chest felt tight. Adults might forget to pick you up from school, they might hit you or scream at you or rip up your diary and throw it in the fireplace, but what they *didn't* do was abandon you in the desert with a couple bottles of water. This was something that happened in horror movies, car wrecks where the parents died and their plucky teens had to cross the Mojave on foot, wetted T-shirts wrapped around their heads.

"What do we do?" Brady asked. His voice shook.

"We should kill them when they come back," said a muscular boy named Vick. His expression was hard, his olive skin flushed dark with anger and the heat. "Beat their heads in. Two of us could take the horses and bring back help."

Shelby couldn't think of anything to say. She knew she'd fuck it up if she tried to fight. She'd hurt herself, or someone else. She'd run. Cry. *You just don't want to be responsible for anything,* she told herself in a voice that sounded much like Ruth's. *You don't want to try so you won't be able to fail.*

"Ride where?" Gabe asked, his tone edged with hysteria. "Some hick town where everyone has Pastor Eddie on speed dial?"

"At least it's an idea."

Shelby wet her lips. "They have guns. Some of the staff had

them when we got in yesterday. There must be twelve or thirteen counselors, half as many ranch guys. Pastor Eddie."

Vick glared at her. "Well, what do *you* think we should do, General Tso?"

She stared back at him, openmouthed.

"There's no need for that," John said in a small voice, which made her feel bad for everything she'd thought about him earlier. "They want us to fight each other."

Malcolm, who had plopped down on a flat-topped rock as soon as they'd stopped walking, got to his feet with a groan and held his arms out like a referee as Vick advanced and John retreated, cowering. "Gentlemen," he said. "I think we better shut up and build the fuckin' fence."

IV

HOUSEWORK

The camp's showers were outdoors, a single wooden stall big enough for ten of them to wash at once attached to the back of the mess hall. Jo hated them as soon as she stepped through the creaky plank gate. She hated the smell of mildew, the crunching gravel underfoot, the bare pipes of the showerheads and the graying particle board walls of the stall where they hung their clothes on metal hooks. It made her think of locker rooms, of the smell of chlorine in the air and her parents' faces when she'd told them, still floating from her win in the day's last freestyle relay, a towel draped over her shoulders like a cape. It made her think of the ride home.

The water pressure was slack. It drooled over her, tepid and smelling of chemicals, as she palmed a chunk of rock-hard soap from a metal tray nailed to the mess hall's plank siding and started working up a lather. The other girls and the transsexual, Felix, who bunked in her cabin, stepped under the misting, fitful spray. *He's kind of hot,* she thought, wondering if that made her less or more of a lesbian. *Tall, strong, little Gomez Addams mustache . . .*

She soaped between her legs, hating the way her thighs felt, jiggly and formless. After her parents had made her quit swim team, she'd spent months lying in bed while her muscle tone dribbled away like the sudsy water soaking into the dirt beneath the packed-in gravel. The morning run still throbbed in her legs and hips. *Maybe I can get back into shape out here,* she thought, trying not to stare at wet skin, at bare breasts, at water trickling into asscracks and dripping from bushes. It was so close to some of the porn she'd watched hunched in the den in the middle of the night and then studiously deleted from the family computer's browser history. Shoddy reproductions of prison showers and locker rooms. Cheap fabric tearing. Lip gloss. The artificial glow of bronzer and the gleam of clear undercoat on pointed nails.

Mom, Dad, there's something I want to tell you.

Faces falling. Smiles growing brittle. They'd driven in silence to pick up Oji-chan from his shogi night, a dozen old Japanese people pushing tiles around wooden boards and smoking awful imported cigarettes, and Jo's mother had turned to her and said "Not one word" as Oji approached across the parking lot. He'd known something was wrong, though. The whole ride home he'd held Jo's hand while she cried and her parents refused to discuss the reason why.

"What is it? What's wrong? Did something happen to Joanna? Asuka! Explain yourself."

Her mother speaking terse and rapid Japanese, too fast and low for Jo to follow as they pulled out of the parking lot and into traffic. Downtown West Caldwell all lit up at night and a thin scum of dirty snow and slush still on the sidewalks.

A long, dead silence, and then he spoke, his voice heavy. *"She would be ashamed of you if she were still alive."*

By the end of the week her parents had put him in a retirement home in Essex Fells, though half their Japanese friends stopped talking to them over it, and the house on Lincoln Street, never lively, became a tomb. Sometimes at night Oji would call, and if Jo reached the phone before her mother he would say, voice trembling with grief and fury: *"I love you. There is nothing wrong with you, my brave girl,"* and she would mumble something back, feeling dead, feeling like meat rotting on a scaffolding of bone.

I want to fuck all of you, she thought at the girls around her, a black void opening in the pit of her stomach. In the corner of the stall the big redhead, Betty, who'd hurt Smith during the run, was touching herself under the farthest showerhead, the muscles in her broad shoulders flexing, tensing. Another girl, slim and olive-skinned with thick black eyebrows and rows of scars on the insides of her skinny thighs stood on tiptoe next to her, whispering in her ear. Jo's throat felt tight. Her clit was stiff and aching. *Please, don't look at me.*

The water cut out. Jo drew a shuddering, sucking breath that was almost a sob. As the last drops spattered on the gravel underfoot she heard what the girl with the eyebrows was whispering to Betty.

"... *beautiful baby, my little thing, helpless and weak*..."

The voice trailed off. Naked bodies jostled for rough towels at the hooks. Jo fought the urge to cry as she watched a fat girl help a shaking Smith towel off and dress herself. *I don't want to be here,* she thought. They spilled out of the shower; Cheryl was waiting to escort them to breakfast.

I don't want to have to be brave.

You're such an idiot, thought John, planting his foot on the back of his shovel's head and throwing his weight against it. The blade bit into the hard, dry earth. At least being fat was good for something. *Telling them your full name? Shaking hands? What are you, running for office? Are you workshopping campaign slogans? John Calvin Bates, a dork you can kick in the nads.*

"You're making me feel bad for that shovel," said Malcolm, who was digging at the marker to John's left. A few of the other boys laughed and the Black kid's grin widened as John blushed. "When you hear 'all you can eat' at the buffet, do you think it's an ad or a dare?"

Two markers over, Vick busted out laughing like Malcolm's joke was the funniest thing he'd ever heard. The stocky boy doubled over, leaning hard on the handle of his shovel as he wheezed. "I have a slow metabolism," John said stiffly, raising his voice to be heard over the laughter. He levered a load of dirt and pebbles out of the hole and jammed the blade back into it, kicking down on it harder than he needed to. He jiggled with the force of it and felt his blush deepen. There was a roaring sound in his ears.

"Well, when it finally gets here it sure has its work cut out for it," Malcolm drawled. He was pretty, which made John even angrier. Sharp cheekbones, soft mouth, and long, dark eyelashes. "You ever hear of Richard Simmons?"

"He probably ate him," Vick wheezed. He was laughing so hard there were tears in the corners of his eyes.

Of course it's the same here, John thought, driving the shovel in again. He set his jaw and heaved, levering a stone the size of his fist out of the posthole and tipping it onto the growing pile of reddish earth beside it. *Of course it's just like Saint Peter's, just like Concord High, just like fucking Bible camp. Just like home.*

All night he'd lain awake with a dull ache in his throat, a lump of homesickness so bad he'd hardly been able to breathe, but what was at home? His father's disgusted expression at the dinner table. Grant and Lisa, so thin, so perfect, looking at him like he was something mildly interesting they'd found under a rock while his stepmother ranted about how no one at her WeightWatchers group could really be honest with themselves, how they were always lying and backsliding, sneak-eating candy bars from their purses, sabotaging and enabling each other and everyone knew but the facilitator was so soft on them, so forgiving even though it hurt them in the end, even though it really wasn't professional, and they all resented *her*, poor innocent Sheila—who had married John's dad after cancer picked his soft, round mother's bones clean and flicked the shriveled stick of her away—for her self-control and because she'd joined to work on body fat percentage and not weight, wasn't that sad, wasn't it sad, didn't they all agree it was sad, sad, sad the way those cows just couldn't control themselves and made it everyone else's problem?

"Seriously, man, did you watch *The Blob* and think *There's a look I could pull off*?"

Crunch. Heave. Thud. Another shovelful onto the pile. John's shoulders were burning, but it felt good to hurt. It made Malcolm's voice and Vick's hysterical hyena cackle and the chuckling of the other boys feel far away and small. He was strong. Stronger than them. He could bench two hundred pounds, even though it made him sick and woozy. His dad had looked excited when John sat up red-faced from the padded bench, like he was seeing John for the first time, or like he was seeing another son, useful and handsome and not at all embarrassing to him.

When that son had failed to materialize, had stayed buried under the rolls and folds of disappointment now sweating and itching in the brutal sunlight, his father had gotten a different look, pinched and furious and wide-eyed.

"If you're not going to take this seriously," he'd said at dinner one night, and John had known with an instant flush of shame that "this" was his body, his entire existence, "then for your own good, I'm going to do it for you."

Malcolm's voice punched through his fugue.

"Mr. Michelin, what sets your tires apart from your competitors'?"

John started toward the other boy before he knew what he was doing. His grip tightened on the shovel's haft. He saw the moment Malcolm went from trying to think of another joke to knee-jerk fear and it made him feel strong and rotten at the same time. Vaguely, he sensed that the other kids were drawing back, dropping their shovels and saying things like, "Ah, fuck!" and "Kick his ass, Shamu!"

A hand fell on John's arm. He turned, tensing up, but it was just the Asian kid, Andrew, short and kind of pear-shaped, hair shaved down to black stubble. The one he'd spoken up for earlier. *Oh,* thought John, somehow completely certain, as he met Andrew's stare and all the anger drained out of his body. The shovel's blade thunked to the dirt. *She's a girl.*

"Come on," said Andrew. She had a soft, high voice that crackled just a little. "Let it go."

"I was just fuckin' around," said Malcolm, smiling nervously as he edged back toward his half-dug hole. "My grandma says I don't know when to shut up, and I guess she's right, but you're okay, aren't you, killer?"

"Fuck you," said John, but he smiled a little as he said it. It was hard to stay angry with someone so beautiful. Behind the skinny boy Vick stood looking embarrassed, cheeks flushed and shoulders hunched. The tall, good-looking kid, Gabe, watched John with what looked like respect.

"Yeah," said Malcolm, his smile widening. He punched John's shoulder lightly. "If you can find your dick under all that—kidding! Kidding!" he squealed as he danced back a few steps from John's raised fist. "Fuck me. I get it. Fuck me."

They went back to their holes, John tired and aching, thighs rubbed raw from walking in the heat, but with a feeling of relief in his chest, a feeling that something quick and cruel had made its play for him and missed the killing bite.

"Thanks," he said softly to Andrew. She smiled back at him, sad and pretty with her big, dark eyes, and then picked up her shovel and turned to her hole.

After breakfast, Enoch and Cheryl herded Nadine's group and a few upperclassmen, one of them the Cleaver bitch, into the back of the pickup, Cheryl heaving the tailgate up and shoving until it locked into place with a metallic *clunk*. From her seat on top of the wheel well Nadine watched Names-and-Dates pass with another group of girls out by the cabins and smirked at the sight of her swollen nose and bandaged arm. *I hope that bite gets infected,* she thought, relishing the mental image of skin swelling red and tight, of pus leaking from fissured skin. *I hope your fucking arm rots off, you cunt.*

The counselors got into the cab and the truck roared to life and jolted into motion, throwing girls against one another. Felix had a blank, fixed look on his face. Betty, perched on the opposite well, and the unibrow who seemed to spend her waking hours glued to the red-haired girl's side like one of those flat-headed fish that sealed themselves onto sharks' bellies, stared at the incoming campers with open contempt.

Nadine brought two fingers to her mouth, spread them into a vee, and licked the gap between them until Unibrow turned red and looked away. The new girls on her side of the truck bed giggled. They were past the last of the cabins now, a staff member in denim and sunglasses dragging a chain-link gate open for them as they headed out on a rough dirt road. In the distance a rock ridge rose up from the bare, dead earth.

"You don't wanna fuck with Athena," said Betty.

"Why not?"

A sharklike grin. "Because that would mean you were fucking with me," she said. "And I'd drag you out of bed some night and drown you in a toilet."

"All right," said Nadine, wondering if Betty had ever actually killed anyone. She'd known a girl at school when they lived in Texas who people said had killed her brother and done time in juvie. It happened. *She probably just talks tough,* thought Nadine, though she didn't quite believe it. *She's just some ugly dyke who wants to be teacher's pet.* "Try it. See what happens."

The truck cut north toward the mountains, hitting a pothole that nearly unseated Nadine. She gripped the wheel well's hot metal sides and pushed the heels of her sneakers against the plastic ridges of the truck's bed.

"Get off the thing," hissed Jo, leaning across the swaying and still ashen-faced Smith. "You're gonna fly out of the truck."

"Shut up," said Nadine. The thought of sliding down onto her butt, of abandoning Betty's eye level, made her want to bare her teeth and snarl. It had been like this with Sam DiScalia on the lacrosse team, this sense that the first to show weakness would get her throat torn open. The early part was crucial.

They came around the rock ridge, the roar of the truck's engine shifting and deepening as it braked on the downhill slope, and suddenly the world was green, the air cool and moist with clouds of water vapor left by whisking sprinklers. On either side of the road grass rioted ankle-high, not the saw-edged scrub Nadine had seen on their drive, but lawn grass, lush and overgrown.

There were stands of sumac, too, and wild strawberries growing free among the nodding paintbrushes and white clover. As the truck slowed, tires crunching on the rutted gravel drive, Nadine made out the fat black-and-gold motes of bumblebees drifting between blossoms, and the iridescent shimmer of the humming-birds that darted among them and hovered around plastic feeders with yellow imitation flowers into which they plunged their needle-thin beaks to drink.

This is impossible, thought Nadine, staring in openmouthed shock at a decorative fish pond beside which two counselors were talking on a wrought-iron bench. *It must take so much water. The grass alone . . .*

It was a crater, its slopes gently tiered, its overgrowth an assault on Nadine's eyes after the barren rock and hardpan of the desert. It made no sense. Nothing grew out here but creosote and rocks. This was past irrigation, past anything Nadine knew about groundwater. She'd worked a few summers with the landscaping company partnered with her dad's design firm, and no one in all of Arizona had been able to make anything like this, no matter how much they spent. As they got deeper in, she saw what looked like a salamander the size of a man's shoe scurry out of the grass and into a little stream winding back and forth along the slope. Below, a crooked crabapple tree bloomed delicate pink beside a slant-roofed farmhouse, weeping petals from its branches where the gauzy webs of gypsy moths tented leaves and stems.

The truck ground to a halt, brakes squealing, in a little dirt lot at the depression's base. From here it seemed they were much farther down than Nadine would have guessed, and without the sun in her eyes she could see other spikes and broken curtains of stone rising from the earth amid the overgrowth. Betty kicked the tailgate open and the other girls began to get out, stretching and muttering. In the tree's shadow, wearing a dress of white linen buttoned all the way up to her chin, a woman stood waiting for them. She clasped her hands as they filed into the shade, a few of them looking up nervously at the gossamer webs sagging in the boughs above. Dark, hairy shapes squirmed within. "Good morning, girls," she said.

It was the wispy little blond woman Nadine had seen onstage with Pastor Eddie. She looked older up close, the skin on the backs of her hands a little papery, lines radiating from the corners of her pallid eyes and rosebud mouth. She was also the skinniest person Nadine had ever seen. Her cheekbones were as sharp as razors, her cheeks gaunt hollows in their shadows. Even her hair was thin, her pink scalp visible through its combed waves. It made Nadine think of a baby mouse, new and bald and feeble.

"Good morning, Mrs. Glover," Betty and the rest of her clique chorused, and for a moment they sounded so needy, so pitifully desperate for this shriveled cunt's approval, that Nadine forgot to hate them. They were just stupid little babies.

"Mama," said Enoch, taking off his baseball cap.

"Meredith," said Cheryl.

The woman smiled. What little she showed of her teeth was a nightmare, gums receding from eroded brown and yellow stumps. "I hope you ladies aren't afraid of a little hard work," she said, turning to Nadine and the rest of the new campers in the group. She had a beautiful voice, high and soft and pure. She turned, leaning hard on her cane, and looked back at them over her shoulder, pale eyes narrowed, the house looming huge and still and silent beyond her. "Follow me."

Felix followed the pinched little skeleton in through the front door. A long, narrow coatroom, hats and jackets on pegs, wood paneling giving way to stenciled wallpaper. The screen door banged shut behind them as Meredith led the group into the living room, which was full of the same spindly legged furniture Felix's grandparents had in their trailer. A pea-green sofa bracketed by spidery end tables draped in lace, a faded azure love seat and its swaybacked ottoman. An old-fashioned television, antennae cocked at odd angles, stood before the curtained windows.

A carpeted staircase set along the far side of the room led up the second floor, an oil painting of Pilate showing Christ to the mob hung halfway up it.

They split there, Cheryl dragging Felix and some of the others toward the clatter and boiling heat of the kitchen while Enoch and the rest—except for kiss-ass Betty, who went upstairs with all ninety pounds of her surrogate mommy—vanished deeper into the house's sprawl. Sweat beaded on Felix's forehead and upper lip as he followed Smith, Jo, and Nadine through an empty doorway and into the sweltering, breathless space.

Something hissed and crackled in the gigantic gas oven, the blandly meaty stink of it filling Felix's nostrils. Peeling linoleum underfoot, a twin sink piled with filthy plates and crockery, dirty plastic compost buckets overflowing with eggshells and coffee grounds, potato skins and browning apple cores. A fat blond girl with her hair tied back under a red paisley kerchief was plucking a chicken at the little square table in the center of the room while another, dainty and curly-haired with a blue armband worn over her long-sleeve shirt, shelled peas over a paper bag.

There were muttered introductions—the two girls were Candace, the plucker, and Laurie, who seemed to Felix like one of Pastor Eddie and Mrs. Glover's brownnosers—and then Cheryl put them to work. Methodically, as the girls chatted and Nadine half-assed her way through the dishes with much clattering and clanking, Felix scrubbed the floor. He filled a lacquered steel basin with hot water from the tap, Nadine elbowing him as she cleaned, and dug a filthy sponge from the cabinet under the sink. That was fine. Let her take her shit out on his ribs. She'd probably be bent over Pastor Eddie's knee getting her ass belted raw by tomorrow.

He heaved the basin from the counter down to the floor and squeezed lemon-scented soap into the steaming water from a half-empty plastic bottle. His knees still ached from the morning run, but it was better to be down below the smells and the heat and the sounds of the girls' voices, so hatefully like his own no matter how hard he fought to pitch it down, no matter how much smoke he breathed. *Is this the scam?* he wondered, squeezing excess water from the sponge and starting on the corner where the kitchen cabinets and the ones under the breakfast bar met. *They drag us out here and make us do their housework? There had to be more convenient Mexicans around.*

He missed the smell of his mother's kitchen with a sudden chest-tightening fierceness. Paprika and vinegar, chilis and poblanos, bitter chocolate and onions simmering in butter. His father complained sometimes that her cooking was too Mexican, that it embarrassed him to bring his business partners home to her spicy oxtail stew, her pickled beef tongue and peppery machaca and eggs. Felix had heard her tell him once that *he* could always cook, if he was that ashamed of her. He'd bounced her head off the wall for that.

My father didn't come to this country to eat like a fucking ranch hand. You hear me? You hear me?

It was always some version of that when the hitting started. Your grandfather didn't come to this country so you could run around in khakis like a manflor. Your grandfather didn't come to this country so you could bitch to me about Nintendos. Border crossing. Clothes on his back and shoes on his feet. Six to a room. Secret police. Cartels. When Felix had cut his hair, though, when he'd come out of the bathroom after their screaming fight with that hideous purple dress trailing in slashed and shredded strips from his hands, there had been no anecdote, no colorful commentary on the crimes of the Ordaz administration. Just Manny Vargas hurtling across the room and then those thick, soft hands tight around Felix's neck and Leo shouting "Papa, Papa, get off her!" and the guests who'd come early screaming. And then the reeling stumble and the crash, the vase, Leo rolling on the carpet with his hands clamped over his eye and blood everywhere, blood staining everything, and their father bellowing like a bull with a spear in its side, bearing Felix down to the floor as a dozen pairs of hands tried to haul him back.

Stop thinking about this shit, he told himself, tensing his stomach muscles as he drew the sponge back toward himself. A clean streak gleamed wetly on the sticky floor. *In three years you'll be eighteen. You'll leave for college. Someplace cheap in case he cuts you off. You can be a pussy once it's over.*

At the kitchen table Smith was snuffling miserably as she peeled potatoes, the skins spilling over the rim of the metal mixing bowl she held in her lap. Her flyaway hair was lank and colorless in the smothering heat that radiated from the oven. Her eyes were red and puffy from crying and Felix, still scrubbing, thought as he looked up at her that someday he would have a daughter, and the sight of her tears would not disgust him as the sight of Smith's did, and she would be happy and free and she'd never daydream about beating his head into tomato sauce with an aluminum bat.

Someday.

Nadine heard footsteps from the living room. The sound was clear even over the rattle and crash of the dishes and the thin, whining wheeze of Smith's crying. Heavy footfalls like a storybook giant's. Fee fi fo fum, don't do drugs, have sex, or cum. Pastor Eddie's reflection appeared in the window over the sink, his huge frame filling the doorway. The bass rumble of his voice seemed to force all the air out of the kitchen.

"Everything under control here?"

"Yes, sir," simpered curly-haired Dana, wiping her hands on her apron. "Cheryl just went out to talk to Mrs. Glover and Enoch. We're finishing up the prep work now."

"Good." The giant stepped into the kitchen, the plywood under the linoleum creaking beneath his weight. A hand like a dinner plate came to rest on Nadine's shoulder. She froze, fighting the urge to drive an elbow back into the pastor's stomach and then turn and go for his eyes. He was huge, almost a foot taller than her and probably a hundred and fifty pounds heavier. He could pull her apart without trying.

"Why don't you get that roast out, sweetheart?" he purred. She could *feel* his voice in her bones. "Smells just about done."

Nadine slid out from under his palm, fumbling through the kitchen drawers until she found a set of mismatched potholders scarred black with carbonized fabric where they'd been used to grip hot metal. The oven belched a cloud of thick, greasy steam into her face when opened. She wrestled the black pan and its sizzling cargo up onto the range. Yellow bone glistened where it jutted from rings of half-molten fat. Slices of pineapple clung to the grayish-brown meat that bulged between the roast's twine trusses. An inch of oily, clouded drippings sloshed in the pan's bottom. She reached over it to shut off the oven, and as she did a flash of motion through the window caught her eye. A grinning face in the undergrowth. Limbs pushing through the vegetation. Then it was gone. Nadine couldn't breathe.

It took all her restraint not to scream, but something must have crossed her face, some look of horror, because suddenly Pastor Eddie was beside her, one huge hand tipping her face up toward his, the other like a vise on her upper arm. "What's wrong, honey?" he asked, and his breath stank the same as the meat, but with an edge of mint and something else. A feeble, sugary sweetness. "You burn yourself?"

The other girls were watching. Only Felix kept at his cleaning, scrubbing on his knees in the corner of the kitchen. Doing his time. "It was the steam," Nadine lied, casting her eyes down in the way she knew men like him wanted her to. Shy. Embarrassed. Her heart was racing. "It . . . it was hotter than I thought it would be. That's all."

He chuckled. "You girls," he said. He released his grip on her arm and swiped a finger over the roast's flank, then brought it to his mouth. The juices stained his mustache as he sucked them off. "Always jumping at something."

He left, heavy footsteps receding into the house, and gradually the kitchen's quiet chatter resumed. The *click-click-click* of knives on cutting boards. The soft, fleshy ripping sound of Candace plucking her fat chicken. Nadine drifted back to the sink, turning the hot water on and reaching for a gunk-crusted serving bowl afloat in the soapy basin. The ceramic burned her palms and there were no rubber gloves that she could see. It didn't matter. Outside, the hummingbirds darted like little jewels through the sunlight, bobbing and weaving around one of their plastic feeders, but Nadine couldn't shake what she'd seen through the smeared and spotted kitchen window.

Cheryl, face twisted into a lined rictus, crawling roachlike through the garden on all fours.

V

PELLETS

Once the fence was up they walked back to camp for lunch. The return trip was worse; not only was Gabe exhausted, starving, and sunburned, but the other boys—even that whale who'd gone around shaking their hands that morning—had done what boys always did, clicking together in some unspoken ritual of insults and raised fists until they were *us* and Gabe was *them*, left to stand outside their little warrior circle. His hair was bothering him, too. The short, fuzzy feel of it, like a small animal's pelt. Francis had loved his hair, had liked to play with it when they lay together, after. Chestnut locks spilling loose between pale, callused fingers.

Even Francis didn't talk to you at school, whispered a nasty little voice in the back of Gabe's mind. *He knew you didn't fit. He knew everyone would* smell *you on him, the loser stink of you. He's probably doing damage control right now, telling the other baseball team douches you tried to suck his cock, that you're in love with him, a pathetic little fag he feels bad for. Disgusting.*

The other boys laughed at something Malcolm had said. Gabe hadn't heard it. On their hike out he'd felt them all watching him, peeling sweaty clothes from his body with their eyes, drawn in by his beauty and his silence. Now they'd sniffed out its real name— awkwardness—and there was nothing left to draw their eyes. He dropped back behind the others, making space for his self-pity. A ways ahead Corey and Enoch rode atop their horses with the sun at their backs, and past them the compound danced in a shimmering heat haze. The world's most depressing oasis.

He didn't see what tripped him. A rock. A patch of sand. A prairie dog hole. Through the thousand ways his feet were crying out in agony it was impossible to log one more. All he felt was a flat, gray sense of bottomless despair as he plummeted face-first toward the ground. *Of course.* It slapped him breathless before he could get his hands out to break his fall, leaving his head ringing and his lungs straining fruitlessly for air. He rolled a little way down a shallow incline, ledges of brittle earth collapsing under him, and managed to suck in his first breath just as he flopped into a pile of something soft, wet, and reeking of vomit and moldy cheese. Sour dust and clinging debris coated the inside of his mouth. He scrambled back with an undignified squeal of horror, spitting and wiping his face on the sleeve of his flannel. On the ground where he'd landed, his face and right shoulder imprinted in its mashed length, was a heap of wet, hairy, knobby little bundles no bigger than two fingers held up side by side.

"Back on your feet, Horn," Corey yelled from the front of the line. A few boys were coming toward Gabe, sliding and hopping down the shallow incline so that waves of dust and loose dirt washed over Gabe where he sat sprawled on his ass, coughing up flecks of who knew what.

"Pretty boy fell in some cow shit!" Malcolm hollered back. "We'll get him!"

"That's not shit," said John, puffing and red in the face, as he skidded to a halt, one hand going to Gabe's shoulder before he drew it hastily back. He looked befuddled, and Gabe felt a moment of white-hot attraction to the huge and reassuring bulk of him. The soft, broad strength of his presence. "Are you all right?"

"Yeah," Gabe wheezed, not knowing what else to say.

"It's pellets," said Brady, crouching beside the pile. He had an absurd voice, high and squeaky, and up close Gabe could see traces of dried, cracking eyeliner at the corners of his eyes. "Owls throw them up after they eat something." He blushed, looking from John to Gabe to Andrew and back in a nervous series of twitches. "A-all the parts they can't digest, like hair and bones."

"Gee, thanks, Ranger Rick," said Malcolm, but he squatted down to look just the same as John helped Gabe to his feet. A little way up the incline Andrew stood looking queasily down at the heap of owl pellets, or whatever they were. Malcolm leaned forward a bit, drawing a collective hiss from the rest of them, and snatched something thumb-sized out of the pile. Gabe saw part of a little skull. A mouse, maybe, or a songbird. "Well, then what the hell threw *this* up?"

An uneasy silence fell. Andrew had gone pale and Brady looked nauseous. Gabe cleared his throat and spat on the ground. "A big fuckin' owl, genius."

The other boys laughed, and just like that, for the first time in his life, Gabe felt the curtain part, felt himself led through into the warmth of brotherly love, and for a few minutes he forgot about his blistered, throbbing feet and sunburned shoulders, his parched mouth and the flecks of owl pellet still stuck to his face. For a few minutes, walking up the hill with the other boys to rejoin the disgruntled marchers and their counselors, he felt like he belonged.

In his heart, though, he knew no owl that ever lived could have vomited up that awful thing.

Lunch was cold black beans with little shreds of pork rolled up in stale tortillas. The other boys came in late as Felix was wolfing down his second. They were sunburned and filthy, their shirts soaked with sweat, and for a moment he felt an awful, wrenching pain in the pit of his stomach that he didn't stink like they did. He crushed it down. *You aren't going to cry,* he told himself, and under the table he dug his short, square nails into his palm until he calmed. *Eat.*

A few of them came to sit at his table. Gabe and Malcolm and the fat boy, John. Candace, seated to Felix's left, gave Gabe a shy smile. "How many Michelin stars you guys think this place has?" asked Malcolm, picking at his dry triangle of cornbread. "Two? I'd say three, but the sommelier is really phoning it in."

Candace laughed. Felix took another flavorless bite. None of the food at Camp Resolution smelled or tasted like anything.

Just different textures and configurations of oily, salty nothing that sat like a brick in his stomach. He chewed, glancing over at Nadine at the next table. She still looked shaken after whatever she'd glimpsed through the kitchen window. He'd seen her go pale. Maybe a counselor raping a kid in the garden? This seemed like the kind of place kids got raped.

It's not your problem, he told himself, forcing down another mouthful of cold, chewy burrito. *Let her worry about it, if she's so fucking tough.*

". . . and there were all these, like, lumps of hair and bones and stuff in a big pile," Malcolm was saying, gesturing rapidly as he spoke. He slung an arm around Gabe's shoulders and pulled the taller boy into a one-sided hug. "He wiped out right in the middle of it and came up looking like he blew a Fraggle."

Gabe had a fussy, irritated look on his face that made Felix think of his little sister, Clara, when she stayed up too late and started turning everything into a fight. *Don't think about Clara,* thought Felix, chewing faster. He swallowed, almost choked, and then ripped off a huge mouthful of greasy nothing. *Get ready for the next thing they do to you. Eat. Hydrate. Sooner or later someone's going to hurt you. Beat you. Someone's going to wait until you're down and then start kicking. Push your face into your own puke.*

He felt a sudden surge of nausea at the thought of Betty with Smith's hair wrapped tight around her fist. That grin. That freckled, peeling skin, like something underneath was trying to get out. *What leaves a pile of hair and bones in the middle of the desert?* A scene from an old *National Geographic* nature documentary surfaced in his mind's eye. A pale, ghostly looking owl hacking and retching until it brought up a turd-shaped clot of indigestible material. *Maybe they do it together, in a flock.*

"Hey, Speedy Gonzalez." He looked up. Malcolm, elbows on the table and chin cupped in his hands, was grinning at him from a bare few inches away. "Save some for the war orphans."

Felix stared at him, cheeks bulging with half-chewed burrito.

What the fuck was wrong with everyone else? Why were they acting like this was all some big adventure at sleepaway camp? He swallowed and dropped the heel of the burrito to his tray. "Why don't you fuck off?"

"Jeez," said Malcolm, his smile fading. "Tough crowd."

"Do you ever shut up?" Felix snapped.

Malcolm's smile returned at once, like a light switching on. "Put your cock in my mouth and find out!"

Felix stared, mouth hanging open, as Gabe and John started laughing. Even Candace let out a shrill little giggle. Felix shook his head, smiling in spite of himself. "You couldn't handle it," he said. His voice sounded pleasingly gruff to his own ears. He missed his brothers with crushing, all-encompassing despair, a need deep in the pit of his stomach to have Leo ruffle his hair and the twins, Marco and Julian, whining at him to help them beat a level in *Super Mario Brothers*. Tears threatened, and perhaps a little more than threatened, but the other boys turned graciously to talk to one another as he dried his eyes on the sleeve of his shirt, and he felt himself begin to love them for it.

Don't think about that.

He cleared his throat. "So," he said to Gabe. "You fell in a bunch of owl shit?"

"We're gonna get caught," hissed Jo, scrambling to keep up with Nadine as the taller girl slunk out from behind the trash cans in back of the mess hall. "We should have gone to lunch with everyone else!"

"Then stop following me," Nadine shot back. "Maybe if you suck Enoch's dick he'll let you off the hook."

Jo flushed, but she didn't turn back. Wherever Nadine was sneaking off to, it was probably more interesting than cold burritos. "You don't have to be such a bitch about it."

Nadine ignored her. They crossed the open stretch of dirt between the mess and Cabin Ten at a brisk clip. Jo's legs still burned from their morning run, but after an afternoon in the cool, musty darkness of the farmhouse's laundry room it felt good to warm her muscles up again. They circled around the back of the cabin, passing under its barred windows. "At least tell me what we're doing," Jo panted as Nadine, hugging the splintered clapboards, peered around the corner of the cabin.

"*I'm* following Cheryl," Nadine hissed. "*You* need to shut the fuck up before you get us caught."

Just go back to lunch, Jo told herself even as she scurried after Nadine, crossing the gap between Cabins Ten and Eight in a few breathless steps. *Slip in and pretend you were there the whole time. Nobody's going to notice.* Still, she hunched down when Nadine did, advancing at a snail's pace until they were practically on top of each other at the end of the cabin's rear wall. There, walking down the empty lane between the rows of housing, was Cheryl. A cold thrill ran up Jo's spine. The petite counselor, so effortlessly doll-like and perfect with her dirty blond bob and her fitted khakis, had flipped her out of bed that morning without so much as a grunt of effort.

"She fucking scares me," she whispered to Nadine.

"There's something wrong with her," Nadine whispered back grudgingly, apparently resigned to having an accomplice. "I saw her crawling around in the garden at the house, like an animal. I wanna see what she does when no one's around."

It should have seemed funny, but Jo couldn't find it in her to smile. Instead her mouth went dry, and when she spoke her voice quavered like an old woman's: "Maybe she dropped a contact or something."

Jo had dreamed the night before of a woman crawling on all fours, more like a spider than a baby, long white hair a curtain hiding her face and trailing over the ground. *It's just some weird coincidence,* she thought, watching Cheryl vanish beyond the next cabin. They waited a breath. Two. Three, then dashed across the gap. Jo felt like she was back at practice with the rest of the swim team, helpless to stop herself drifting after Angie Ceriello wherever she went, sneaking glances at the girl's long, muscular legs as she mounted the dive stand or leaning forward to smell the chlorine and the lilac shampoo in her hair while sitting behind her in the bleachers between heats.

Oji had always told her she was like a cat, wanting only what she couldn't have, and here she was again, sniffing after another mean white girl who didn't give a shit about her or anyone else. When Smith had gone down on the morning run, Nadine had just looked annoyed at the delay. It had been Jo who'd dragged the skinny, gasping girl back to her feet. *So why aren't you sitting with Smith right now?*

"What the fuck is she doing?" Nadine murmured. Jo sidled over beside her and peered around the corner of the cabin, standing on tiptoe to look over the other girl's tawny head.

Across the stretch of bare dirt, Cheryl knelt by Cabin Five, fiddling with something near the ground. It was the plywood lattice closing off the crawl space underneath. She worked a yard-long section of it loose, set it aside, then dropped to her belly and slithered through the gap and out of sight. Jo watched the counselor's boots disappear into the dark beneath the cabin. Waiting in silence, a creeping awareness of the lattice rising halfway up Jo's own calves put the hairs on the back of her neck on end. What if another counselor was under there now, watching them from the dark, just waiting to slip out and creep silently after them until they were close enough to touch . . .

"Maybe she went out the back," Jo whispered, fighting the urge to crouch down and peer through the flaking pressboard slats into the gloom under Cabin Six. *Do the counselors slide under there to sleep at night? Do they listen to us through the floorboards?*

The seconds dragged, piling up like a wave about to break until finally Cabin Five's front door banged open and Cheryl stepped out, bolted the door behind her, and set off back toward the mess, brushing dirt from her windbreaker as she went. Jo followed Nadine around the corner toward the cabin's front to watch the counselor go, a petite silhouette with her shadow thrown out long and spidery behind her by the sinking afternoon sun.

"How did she do that?" asked Jo. "Some kind of trapdoor?"

Nadine smiled, showing teeth. "I don't know," she said with relish, "but I'm going to find out."

Shelby looked up from the picked-apart remnants of her burrito, ripped up in search of offending slivers of meat, as the muted babble of the mess hall quieted. Corey stood at the head of the room in front of the serving counter, the people bustling behind it just dark shapes veiled in the steam from a big industrial dishwasher. He clasped his hands behind his back. "Campers," he began. "Chef Jason and the kitchen staff worked hard to make your lunch; you're going to show them some respect by cleaning up after yourselves. Bates, Glass, you're in the kitchen. Parisi, Horn, start bussing tables. Trays stacked on the counter, leftovers in the orts bucket here." He kicked a white liquid sheetrock bucket around which a few flies circled lazily. "The rest of you, get these tables into rows facing the far end of the hall. Class starts in ten minutes."

She barely had time to wonder what the hell "class" meant at Camp Resolution before Dave appeared at her shoulder. "Up and at 'em, Glass," he said, his tone as warm and even as it had been in the kitchen of Tyler's apartment; as it had been the whole way from New York. "Come on, you could use the exercise."

It made it so much worse, somehow, the way he joked around and smiled. He looked like he probably had kids at home. She wondered, as he gripped her arm and towed her from her seat and toward the kitchen door, if he dragged them around the same way. The kitchen was like a sauna, the air thick enough to chew and stinking of grease and oil. Dave led her past a pair of young Latino men in stained whites chatting in rapid-fire Spanish as they wiped down stainless steel counters and a crooked, pockmarked old white man smoking a drooping cigarette and chopping a wilted head of lettuce. The dishwasher, a huge steel cube fitted into a stand bolted to the floor and fed by a fat tangle of pipes, released a boiling wave of steam at the back of the crowded, noisy space as John, already sweating freely, lifted it by the handle. Dave let go of her arm.

"Good skill, working in a kitchen," he said, scratching his stubbled chin. "World always needs dishwashers."

He left, brushing past her and trading a few hushed words with the smoking man on his way back to the door. Already the dry, stale air of the mess felt like a distant memory. Her shirt, only half-dry after the ordeal in the canyon, was clinging to her skin again, her boxers riding up into the swamp between her thighs. She stepped toward John, who edged aside to make room for her between the dishwasher and the drying rack. "Hey," he said, his voice small. "They won't give us gloves, so it's best to just go as fast as you can."

His soft little hands were already red and swelling. He plucked a cookpot from the billowing steam and swung it over to the rack and Shelby dove in beside him and seized a Pyrex pan by its upper edge. It burned, so hot she almost screamed, almost dropped it, slotting it into the drying rack crooked and then stuffing her smarting fingers into her mouth. A memory threatened. Ruth. A burner glowing orange, then cherry red. John stopped for a moment, his expression softening. "I know," said the fat boy. "Take a second. I'll keep going."

Reluctantly, she took her fingers from her tongue. "No, that's okay. I can do it."

They shuttled cookware to the rack, the pain of each contact between flesh and metal, glass, or crockery layering atop itself until it seemed like from the wrist down she was just one giant throb. She wondered if this was what Paul Atreides had felt like with his hand in the Reverend Mother's box of pain, forced to prove he could endure any agony in service to a greater goal. One of the young prep cooks wheeled over a plastic bus bucket full of dirty trays just as they were finishing. John brought the hood down and pressed a red button on the stand. More steam squirted from its rattling bulk. Shelby ran a stinging palm over her scalp, wiping sweat from her cropped hair. She and John exchanged a look. The hood came up. They dove back into it.

The smoking chef watched them for a while, his expression flatly reptilian. Shelby found it hard to care. She could hardly breathe in the smothering heat, and a cloudy blister the color of spoiled milk had formed on the heel of her hand; she had to concentrate to avoid popping it. And then they were done, the trays all scoured and racked, the clatter of dishes replaced by the low murmur of conversation from the mess and the slow, deliberate *thunk* of the smoking man's chef's knife against the butcher block as he diced tomatoes.

"Done?" he growled, a fine dusting of ash drifting from the cigarette's end as he spoke.

"Yes, sir," said John.

He turned back to his tomatoes. "Then get out of my kitchen."

They left, scalded and trembling, hands blistered and clothes damp. Shelby felt somehow worse emerging into the clear air of the mess than she had in the kitchen's dank swamp, as though she were an amphibian lost in the desert. Nausea seized her stomach and she nearly pressed her palms to her belly before remembering how raw they were, and how little she wanted the rest of the camp looking at her middle where her jeans squeezed her tummy into two doughy rolls. She closed her fists instead, fighting the urge to retch as her nails touched gummy pink burns.

The other kids had rearranged the mess. The tables stood in four rows with a few school desks and folding chairs pulled in from elsewhere in the building sprinkled throughout and a whiteboard on a rolling wooden stand set at the head of the room. A tall, handsome middle-aged woman stood in front of it, her steely gaze locked on John and Shelby. Her lips twisted with distaste. "Take your seats, boys."

They separated, John trudging toward a seat at one of the tables at the back of the room, Shelby making her way stiffly toward the middle where a single desk chair stood empty. For a moment she was paralyzed with the fear she might not fit, that the folding desk would squeeze her, make her look like too much sausage in not enough casing. Relief washed over her as she settled in and found two or three inches between the desk and her stomach.

The woman at the front of the room was writing on the whiteboard, her dry-erase marker squeaking with each stroke and loop. "My name," she said in tandem with the marker, "is Ms. Armitage." She turned back toward them. She had a strong jaw and wore heavy plastic-framed glasses with fine chains hanging from their arms. In her long, billowing gray dress and dark cardigan she looked like one of Ruth's gallery friends. "The pastor retains my services to see that you stay current with your schoolwork. I have yet to let him down and do not intend to start now." She pursed her lips. "To that end, your performance in this classroom is directly connected to your privileges at Camp Resolution. Desserts, free periods, phone calls home—all of these things can be yours so long as you apply yourselves, and all of them can be taken away should you fail to do so."

The mess was silent. By the door, Dave sat in a folding chair with one leg stretched across the threshold, a line of golden sunlight cutting across the toe of his work boot. On the desk in front of Shelby was a scratched and battered textbook with a bland illustration of a lighthouse on the cover above the text THE LAKE METHOD printed in faded type and then in smaller font, beneath it, CORE CURRICULUM GRADES 8–12. Ms. Armitage was still going over the finer points of crime and punishment, so Shelby opened the book, flipped to the middle, and picked out a word problem at random.

If the cardinal of Utrecht and the cardinal of Bamberg build a summer house in Naples, will it help the leper's stammer?

She scanned down to the next one, perplexed.

If the moon is waxing gibbous and the limpid limpets shimmer, who is watching from its zenith as the bursar carves his dinner?

She flipped forward a few pages. There were dozens of them. More than that. Hundreds. Tongue twisters, maybe? Some kind of elocution exercise like they'd had at her friend Cara's private school? Shelby paged through the textbook until she found the start of a new chapter, announced with the title EIDETICS in a stacked block font. Someone had doodled a little cartoon Ms. Armitage getting railed by Ronald McDonald just under the header and above the lesson.

The following exercises are intended to strengthen and expand your memory. From the fragments provided for each problem, reconstruct the original sentence to the best of your ability.

1. H v   n ea c l i be en nfo di g f sh.
2. i g h mu c f he sp er .

"Am I boring you, Mr. Glass?"

Shelby looked up and sank down into her seat at the same time, her cheeks burning. Ms. Armitage was staring at her, dark eyes flat and merciless behind her glasses, which burned like the corona of a double eclipse in the sunlight falling through the high, small windows near the ceiling.

"I'm sorry," she stammered. "I was—"

"Distracted," Ms. Armitage finished for her, a cruel sneer twisting her mouth. "Focused elsewhere. Not. Paying. Attention."

She seemed to want to make some kind of point, so Shelby kept her mouth shut and her eyes downcast. When an adult wanted to take a piss on your head, it was best to close your eyes and let it happen.

"Tomorrow morning," said Ms. Armitage, and the smug, breathy pleasure in the woman's voice made Shelby feel uncomfortable, like she was hearing something she shouldn't, "you and the other boys will join Enoch for an hour of calisthenics before bed check."

A collective groan rose up around the mess, then faded just as quickly when Ms. Armitage raised a single slender finger. More than one boy shot a dirty look at Shelby. *Don't cry,* she told herself as her eyes burned and a lump formed at the back of her throat, the unfairness of it pressing the breath from her lungs. *It'll only make it worse. Just take it. Take it.*

"Open your textbooks to chapter one," said Ms. Armitage, turning back to her board. "We'll begin with basic psychobiology."

Gabe's brain felt like pudding as he filed with the others out of the mess and into the fading light of early evening. Someone had strung low-wattage bulbs between the cabins' eaves and the rows of housing sat immersed in overlapping pools of soft yellow light. Moths and midges circled the burning filaments, battering themselves against the glass. The pavilion was dark, its entry flaps billowing slightly in the hot, dry breeze, but beyond it in the direction of the parking lot a bonfire had been lit and the dark silhouettes of people sat on logs and folding chairs around it. The counselors were waiting in the gathering dusk to shepherd them from the mess hall toward the blaze.

"Think they'd let us out of here if we jumped in the fire?" Malcolm muttered from the corner of his mouth. "We probably wouldn't die."

Gabe stifled a giggle. He felt a little lightheaded; he'd only picked at breakfast and lunch, and class had left him turned around and listless, his thoughts popping like pimples before they were fully formed. First a lecture he hadn't understood about cellular memory and something called recombinant evolution he hadn't gotten to yet at Saint Michael's. Evolutionary lines coming apart and reuniting, coming apart and reuniting until they were more like a braid than a tree. It kind of made sense. The word problems Armitage had given them were slipperier, some kind of algebra that had given him an intense but short-lived headache right between his eyes. He didn't even know what the Lake configuration was, much less how to solve for its obscure and oddly named variables.

Corey and the Beard, who Gabe had overheard Enoch call Garth earlier, shepherded them toward the firelight's edge. Gabe sank down onto the dirt and pebbles, grateful to be off his feet and out of the stale, stifling air of the mess. The day seemed to fall on him all at once. The sunburn on the back of his neck and his shaved scalp were starting to sting and itch in earnest, his skin tight and hot where it had cooked while he dug postholes for the cattle fence. His back, shoulders, and arms ached fiercely. All around the fire the other kids settled cross-legged or onto logs mummified by the desert air and polished smooth by use, faces bathed in dancing firelight. Red and orange painting skin.

Pastor Eddie pushed his stick into the fire, sparks and cinders flying as a burnt-through log collapsed. Five kids Gabe didn't recognize sat around the pastor, apparently exempt from class. There was something about them that made him uncomfortable, something quiet and still and unnervingly watchful. It was hard to get a clear look at their faces in the firelight, which threw deep shadows on them all. Dave and a few of the other ranch hand–looking men who seemed to always hover at the edge of things stood smoking off in the dark near the chain-link fence, the glow of their cigarettes' cherries waxing and waning with each drag.

"First day's tough," said Pastor Eddie after a few moments had passed with only the pop and crackle of the fire to break the silence. "Bet your blood's pumpin', though. Bet you haven't worked that hard a day in your lives. Am I right?"

No one said anything.

"I was down the mines when I was a boy. Eight years old, pickin' up spill, humpin' water sixty, seventy feet underground."

His small, dark eyes glittered in the firelight as he looked around at them, and Gabe felt a sympathetic spasm of claustrophobia clutch his throat. "I bet most of you haven't been *worked* yet. Not really. Rich parents, soft hands, think the world owes you something just for waking up."

Gabe thought it was pretty fuckin' bold of a guy forcing teenagers to work his ranch land for free to carp about their lack of calluses, a sentiment he saw reflected in more than one hard, angry face around the fire.

"And why wouldn't you expect it?" Pastor Eddie asked. He sounded genuine. "Look where you are now, tossed to someone else by parents who don't have the guts to teach you themselves how to be in the world. The minute things got hard, they pushed you out of the nest and paid someone else to fix the problem. Throw money at it, right?"

Gabe wondered what it had been like, the conversation when his parents decided to get rid of him. He could picture his father swearing, pacing, jabbing a finger toward the floor as he said things like "unbelievable" and "learn some respect" and "sissy." Had his mother cried? Somehow he didn't think so. Maybe she would have for his little sister, Mackenzie, or even for Celia, his father's daughter from his last marriage who kept cutting herself and getting detention for smoking on school grounds, but not for Gabe. There was something cold between them. Something ugly. There always had been, since the lake.

"You're confused right now," said Pastor Eddie. "Your age, that's natural. What isn't is what you've all gotten yourselves into without real men to show you limits, set some boundaries. With your mothers out playing boardroom power games instead of giving you a household. They're weak, and they abandoned you."

A few of the kids around the fire were crying. Gabe swallowed, fighting the urge himself. A few places down the circle, the fat boy, John, was sniffling and wiping his nose on the sleeve of his shirt. Crying like a girl. He *looked* like a girl, with his fat tits resting on top of the shelf of his belly and his soft, round face, his double chin and the stretch marks on his big heavy thighs. He looked like a fat girl, and Gabe found himself hating him for it, contempt bubbling at the back of his throat so hot it almost burned to keep it inside. *If our parents are weak, what are we?* He wrenched his gaze from John and stared at Pastor Eddie, at that huge, long slab of a face with its thick mustache and little glasses. *We're supposed to, what, thank you? Love you?*

He thought of Francis straddling his hips, of that lean, muscular ass rubbing against his hard cock, pressing it against his belly until he could hardly breathe, until he wanted to scream. *I'm not fucking confused,* thought Gabe. *Just say it. Just call us faggots. Stop fucking lying and* say it.

"I know this place seems harsh right now, but you can trust us," said Pastor Eddie. "We only want what's best for you."

Oh, there it is, thought Gabe, realizing with nauseous disgust that in some frightened corner of his heart, some little piece of himself still cowering behind the locker room door against which his father stood pressed and breathing angrily, he'd been hoping against hope that there was something gentle hidden inside Pastor Eddie. *The thing they say when they want to hurt you.*

There were hot dogs, blistered and split by the heat of the fire, and more lies. Lies about hard work, about movies and TV, about heavy metal and makeup and women's clothing. Gabe kept thinking about Ms. Armitage and her psychobiology lecture, the way everything familiar in what she said seemed to morph midsentence into something alien. Evolution wasn't a braid. That was bullshit. Fake science. Evolution was a road continually diverging, an unimaginably vast tree stretching back to a single squirming cell, each generation a billion coin tosses fed through the meat grinder of eat or be eaten. How the fuck would it be a braid? Snakes didn't turn back into lizards. Birds didn't grow fangs and swell to huge and terrible sizes, dinosaurs reborn out of chicken coops and pet shops. He picked at his hot dog bun, putting a shred of mushed white bread on his tongue for every two he dropped to the dirt or flicked into the fire.

Why was she telling us all that shit?

Malcolm grabbed his sleeve, jolting him from his thoughts. "The fuck was that?" the other boy hissed in his ear.

Gabe followed Malcolm's stare, squinting out into the dark beyond the fence to where the black outlines of the camp's small fleet of vans and trucks loomed against the stars. Nothing. He jerked his arm from Malcolm's grip, annoyed. "What?"

"Eyes, like when you see a skunk in the headlights, you know? The way their eyes glow?"

Gabe looked out at the cars again. He had a dim memory of seeing eyes like that on a camping trip in Maine. The flat, silvery gleam of something watching him from the woods beside one of the campground's wide dirt trails. The hoarse chuff of an animal's breath. He'd almost peed himself. Had nightmares for weeks. He swallowed, the night suddenly colder than it had been. "What about it?"

"I saw that, the eyes, over by the fence. A lot of them. I think it was dogs or something. Coyotes? Are there coyotes here?"

"What would they eat?" asked Gabe, and now the hair on the back of his neck was on end, and was that a smear of deeper darkness in among the cars? A shadow moving in the shadows. He swallowed. *Calm down,* he told himself. *You're freaking over nothing.* "There's nothing out here."

"What else could it be?"

He looked back to the fire. Pastor Eddie was deep in conversation with Enoch, and some of the other counselors were getting their campers back into their groups, getting ready to head for the cabins. The five strange campers, the ones he hadn't seen before tonight, stared at the rest of them, oddly expressionless. "Fuck should I know?" he hissed, tossing the rest of his hot dog into the fire and standing up abruptly. The blood rushed to his head and for a second he thought he might keel over, the firepit yawning huge and distorted, flames licking at the soles of his sneakers. Then it passed. Corey was coming toward them, clapping his hands together.

"All right, Cabin Six!" he called. "Form up on me!"

VI

LIGHTS OUT

ONE WEEK LATER

Malcolm didn't remember the day his brother had died. He'd been four years old when Ian, just barely sixteen, drew his last breath in a shitty apartment on the outskirts of Riverside. He'd been staying with friends—Malcolm later pieced together from gossip and eavesdropping that Ian had run away from their parents' home a few weeks earlier—and one night he'd gone into the bathroom in their little apartment, locked the door, and opened up his wrists with a razor. There hadn't been a note. Malcolm had a vague memory of wandering among headstones while his mother screamed and screamed and screamed, her voice getting hoarser with each awful shriek until the only sound left was a raw, guttural sucking, like a pig rooting through mud.

Ghuh-ghuh-ghuh.

Sometimes he wondered what they'd been like, his parents, before Ian died. His aunt Charlotte always said his mother, Gloria, had been *wild* as a girl, though she hadn't deigned to expand on what exactly that meant. As for his father, everyone liked Don LeFay. He was handsome and charming and knew how to make people comfortable, and how to make himself scarce when things got ugly. *Why do you always leave when she gets going?* Malcolm had asked the older man once, not long after his ninth birthday. *It's just me and Mary with her when you're gone, and she gets so mad. She made Mary put her hand in the door and—*

Little man, Don had said, cuffing him playfully on the shoulder. *Sometimes you just need to get away.* He slipped off the side of the bed and brought his fists up, jabbing and feinting. *Float like a butterfly, sting like a bee.*

What's that mean?

Means you can't get into trouble if trouble can't find you.

Except Don never stung, and whenever Malcolm tried to do what he did, to put a smile on people's faces, to disarm them and endear himself, create an easy little bond in the space of a few words, a handful of expressions, it just got everyone pissed. That, he figured, was why Betty and her little gang were beating on him now. He'd never worked out how to do the floating part.

"Fuckin' immigrant piece of shit," she spat, pistoning her foot into his stomach. "Go back to fucking Africa."

"I'm from Connecticut," he groaned. He tried to curl around the blow, tried to get his arms around her leg, but she was already drawing back for another kick. Stomach again. He coughed and spat a glob of bloody phlegm onto the dirt. "I haven't even taken Africa out to dinner yet."

For Christ's sake, shut up.

The toe of her shoe caught him in the chin and his head snapped back against the wicker lattice that screened the crawl space under the cabin. He saw phlox, the spiky leaves and delicate tissue pa-per flowers, pale pink and purple, and his mother's long, elegant hands turning the earth. *I need you to be a man for me, Malcolm,* she said, wrist-deep in that dark earth. *God knows your father won't. He doesn't love me. Doesn't love any of us. He's leaving me.*

Something warm and wet slapped his cheek. Spit, oozing down to drip from the tip of his nose. "I'll tell Pastor Eddie if I catch you by the girls' cabins again, you fuckin' porch monkey."

"I'm gay," he croaked.

"Then what"—a kick to the chest—"the fuck"—and another, scraping his knuckles and shoulder as he curled into a ball—"are you doing"—and one final cannonball to the belly that left him gasping and heaving—"*here.*"

"Good question," he wheezed, once he had the breath.

Shut up. Shut up. For once in your life, shut up.

The truth was he'd been on his way to the showers with the other boys when he saw something, or thought he had. A skinny dog, white and tan with a long pink tongue lolling from its muzzle, loping between the cabins. It seemed stupid now. Gabe had said as much at the bonfire back on their second night. There was nothing to eat out here, so how could a dog survive? The sole of Betty's shoe on his ear squeezed the thought from his head.

"You've got a big mouth," she said. Celine and Dana giggled. They were all clustered around him, the two of them and Athena. He could see their shoes. Their ankles.

"What's going on here?"

A grown man's voice. Garth's. Malcolm squinted down the alley between cabins, looking between the girls' legs at where the bearded man stood on the line between sun and shade, hands on his hips, leathery face impassive. In his mirrored sunglasses he looked like a shitkicker Secret Service agent.

"He was sneaking around," Betty said sweetly. "I caught him looking in our window when we came back to change for house chores."

"Get him up," said Garth. "He's had enough."

The girls dragged Malcolm to his feet. Someone brushed dust from his T-shirt as Garth approached. "All right?" asked the older man as the girls parted before him. He was so big up close, only a few inches taller than Malcolm but probably forty or fifty pounds heavier, not sculpted but *hard* in the way men who worked all day were hard. Wide and thick and solid. He put a callused hand on Malcolm's shoulder.

"Oh sure," Malcolm wheezed. "I'm ready for my close-up and everything."

Garth pushed him back against the cabin wall and seized his crotch in one hand, his throat in the other. Malcolm froze. He couldn't breathe. He couldn't find his voice. The girls were staring at him, Dana and Celine in shock, Athena with the same cold indifference she stared at everything, and Betty with a disgusting tangle of blind rage, fear, and breathless arousal pushing and pulling at her blunt features, her lips parting and sealing with each panting breath, sliding over red gums and big white teeth. Still it was safer to look at her, to lose himself in that horrible landscape of sunburned skin and twitching muscle, than it was to look at Garth, or to feel the man's hands on him.

"You want to try that again?" the ranch hand said softly.

"Yes," Malcolm heard himself say. He didn't recognize his voice. He sounded like a little boy. "I'm fine, sorry."

"Get to the showers," said Garth. He let Malcolm go. "Girls, Cheryl's looking for you by the flagpole. Now."

The girls and the counselor left together, Betty throwing one last hateful look over her shoulder at Malcolm. She mouthed a word he'd been hearing all his life and he couldn't find it in him to smile back at her or flip her off. What would it matter? He thought of his father joking and smiling as his mother worked herself into one of her moods, of the way he'd burned up and blown away out of their lives like paper touched to a lit match. A smile couldn't save you. It was for you, for your own dignity. A way to say "You didn't hurt me" to someone busy sticking a knife in your guts. It had never occurred to him, really. The idea of how much pain his father had endured.

Malcolm sank down into a nauseous crouch, trying to catch his breath. His stomach hurt. His head was pounding. He thought probably he had at least one broken rib. He stayed like that for a handful of heartbeats as his breathing evened out, his eyes adjusting to the gloom under Cabin Six, the darkness waiting there.

The dog stared back at him through the peeling lattice, panting in the heat.

Ms. Armitage's lessons gave Jo a headache. It started between her eyes, a dull white heat burning at the center of her forehead, and crept out in both directions until it was throbbing behind her eyeballs, as though she could feel the optic nerves diagrammed in the Lake Curriculum chapter on the physical process of perception slowly and silently catching fire. At night after prayers or evening calisthenics or midnight hike or whatever their counselors decided they were going to do, she lay in her bunk and touched herself, trying to wash the pain away with the numbing wave of an orgasm. She would think of Cara Sobhian from swim team with her thick, strong thighs, or of Michelle Pfeiffer's catlike face and mysterious smile in *Ladyhawke,* and brought herself over the lip of climax and into floating emptiness, but the white-hot point remained.

By the time the next day's morning run was over, the last vestiges of the headache had usually faded. Her head stayed clear through kitchen or laundry or garden duty at the Glover house, though one morning she'd tried pulling up a patch of ugly brown weeds with tough, woody shoots and translucent seed pods and her hands had broken out into disgusting blisters, hives rising from her wrists and forearms until she looked as though she'd battered her arms and dipped them in boiling oil. That had brought the headache roaring back. It had gotten so bad as she sat in the cool darkness of the laundry room, bandages soaked in honey wrapped around her swollen forearms, that after a while spent staring at the wall while the others loaded, switched, and folded, she began to hallucinate a little white dot in the water-stained concrete. It felt like boiling bleach piped one droplet at a time onto the center of her forehead.

The white point on the wall crackled, and from it descended a thin white line until the whole of it resembled a kind of keyhole. The next day her headaches were gone, though the worst of the blisters lingered for several days afterward. At night the other girls oohed and ahhed over the crusty, oozing mess when she unwrapped her bandages to change them. No one had bothered giving her gauze, so she'd started tearing up some of the random assortment of T-shirts they'd taken from her dresser when they came to drive her south. Courtney Love and Eric Erlandson wrapped tight around her oozing wrists, their peeling faces all coiled together in mismatched strips.

The garden out back of the house was so lush, bursting with life and color. Even the air was heavy with moisture, the sun sparkling in drops of dew and hanging water vapor. Jo had heard one of the counselors call it the crater, and looking up from its basin, where on her hands and knees she weeded among the strawberry plants, it felt like the right word for it. *There must be water underground,* she thought, watching jewel-colored hummingbirds flit around one of the hanging feeders. Cheryl and one of the ranch hands were smoking on the porch, half-hidden by the crabapple tree. *How else could this place exist?*

A short way off Candace knelt among rows of sweet peas with her back to Jo. The other girl had been quiet for a few days now. Her cheeks looked hollow, like she'd lost weight, and at lunch she seldom spoke and only picked at her food listlessly. It wasn't like the way Gabe avoided eating, spreading food around his tray, shredding little bites—Jo recognized her own bony mother's fetish for starvation there. Candace's sudden loss of appetite seemed more like the way animals stopped eating at the end, or how her Oba had refused food during chemo, even when her best and oldest friend, Mariko, had begged her, had sat by her bedside for hours, first pleading, then shouting, then crying in the stick-thin woman's arms while Oji sat whey-faced in the corner and Jo and her parents waited outside with her mother's cold, unsmiling sisters.

"Hey," Jo called to the other girl. "You okay?"

Candace was silent a long time before answering. She wasn't even weeding, just crouching with her hands in the dirt. When she did speak, her voice was oddly flat. "I can't sleep. Can you sleep?"

Jo yanked a particularly stubborn weed out of the bed and tossed it over her shoulder onto her rapidly growing pile. "I sleep okay." Long yellow grubs squirmed through the loose soil in the hole left by the weed's roots. "Feels like they're trying to wear us out so we don't plot our great escape at night."

In fact it felt like Mrs. Glover and the counselors had a special grudge against Candace. They assigned her all the worst jobs—scrubbing toilets, mucking the horse's stalls in the barn and the chicken coops behind the house, raking up the rotten grass left behind by the mower—and seemed to delight in watching her sweat. They ignored her in the water line, refused to let her break to piss, and made her carry every bag of fertilizer and pile of gardening tools the yard crew needed.

"I'm tired," said Candace. She was weeding now, though slowly. "I just can't sleep. I have this headache . . ."

One of the grubs, which had squirmed to the surface of the soil, began to squirm out of its skin, which flaked and cracked as the wet flesh beneath oozed out, diaphanous wings unfolding limply from its sides. Jo watched it with disgusted fascination, the ghost of her own headache fluttering inside her skull, until the sound of footsteps drew her attention toward the distant house. Cheryl was coming toward them across the gardens, passing Nadine and Smith where they knelt digging potatoes out of mounds of dark soil, pushing through the tepee-shaped tomato frames. She stopped not far from Candace.

"Gruber. Mrs. Glover wants you at the house."

Candace got up, wiping her dirty palms mechanically on her shorts. Her clothes looked loose. Her face was ashen. Cheryl led her away toward the house without another word as the newly hatched insect's wings whirred into motion. It flitted away over the tilled rows and sumac stands, past the glazed panels of the greenhouse and up over the yew tree overtaking the glass oblong's southern end where it vanished among pale green needles. Jo stared after it, her head throbbing.

Shelby had always sat to pee. When she was younger Ruth had liked this, had considered it the first sign of budding homosexuality and encouraged it the same way she encouraged Shelby's love for *Sailor Moon* and baking and dancing to ABBA. She wanted the kind of polite and waifish gay boy her friends sometimes produced, something witty and dry and tastefully aristocratic to go with the little cream-colored Dior clutch she carried at openings.

Peeing while sitting down, though, proved to lead to an entirely different set of qualities. Stealing Ruth's pantyhose. Trying on her lipstick, applied in messy smears and painstakingly shaped with a wetted cotton pad. It led to slumped shoulders and long hair—she missed her hair so badly then, sitting in the graffitied stall attached to the camp's mess, that she began to cry a little—and to falsies lifted from Pussycat, the sex shop over on Fourth she'd slipped into one day after school where she'd seen two girls kissing in a back room, one sliding her fingers past the waistband of the other's skirt to stroke the clear arch of a cock. That night Shelby had lain awake in her bed, the little rubber breastlets hidden beneath her mattress, her face burning at the memory of that hand and the coarse dark hairs at the root of the penis its thumb had stroked.

She wiped, not looking down, and stood to shimmy back into her ill-fitting jeans as a whirlpool formed in the stained porcelain bowl with a sound like a gurgling inhalation. It made her think of a movie Stel had shown her once, something scary and sticky with a man who grew a wet vaginal slit in his stomach for some reason. It had made that same glottal sucking sound when he put his fist inside himself. Ruth had come home halfway through and made them turn it off. *Brain-dead garbage. Do you think this is the kind of thing he should be watching?*

Baby, let's talk about this lat—

We're going to talk about it now. Andrew, you stay right there, and I don't want any tears. You have no right to be upset right now.

Shelby was washing her hands when movement in the dirty mirror over the sinks caught her eye. She turned, heart thumping, but it was only Nadine. The girl stood in the recessed doorway, her face in shadow. The worst of her swelling had gone down, her bruises faded to greens and yellows. Her dirty flannel, its sleeves rolled up to her elbows, and torn black jeans, her tawny hair up in a huge, unruly ponytail, she looked like something out of a fantasy, some log-splitting butch all sweaty from stacking cordwood against the wall of a mountainside cabin.

"This is the boys' room," said Shelby. She regretted it immediately, heat rising in her face as her stomach did a queasy kind of flip.

Nadine stepped closer. She was thinner than Shelby, but three or four inches taller, and in the dusty sunlight slanting through the little windows the bruises on her cheekbone looked like wax, tight and shiny. "What, are you gonna narc?"

"No. I—I wouldn't."

The other girl cracked her knuckles, first her right hand's, then her left's. "Good," she said, flashing a chipped incisor with a sudden smile. "I'm Nadine. Pretty sure one of the counselors hid something here. Wanna help me find it?"

If she'd asked Shelby to get on her knees and lick the floor tiles, Shelby might have hesitated. She nodded, not trusting her voice, and followed the other girl into the stall farthest from the door.

"I heard that bitch with the names and dates on her arm banging around in here earlier," said Nadine as she lifted the cover off the toilet's tank, revealing rust-red water and the rubber and steel guts of the pump. She bent down close, then straightened and replaced the cover, roughened ceramic grinding against porcelain. "I bit the shit out of her arm when they put me in the van. That's how I got these." She tapped a forefinger under each of her black eyes in turn.

I wish you'd bite my arm. I wish you'd punch me in the face.

"Her name's Marianne," said Shelby, turning her attention to the toilet paper dispenser. The plastic housing came off with a squeak, revealing the runty last few sheets of a roll of cheap brown tissue. "I heard her and Corey, our counselor, talking. She said she has a yeast infection."

Nadine wrinkled her nose. "Gross."

Shelby tried not to stare at the back of the other girl's neck as Nadine squatted to run a hand over the tile wall behind the toilet. Lean muscles shifted under freckled skin. A faint smell of sweat hung in the air over the bathroom's mélange of mildew, piss, and lemon. All Shelby needed to do was reach down and brush her fingertips over that smooth skin, that constellation of cinnamon spilled over cream. *What would it feel like to touch you there?* she wondered, and then with an effort of will she forced herself to look at the graffiti cut into the wooden walls of the stall instead. Nadine wouldn't want some fat loser half-girl. She could have anyone. Shelby ran her fingertips over the words *I love you Terry F.* cut crudely just under the door latch. Below them was a little carving of what looked like Pastor Eddie, his face scratched out by a penknife or a nail.

They moved on to the next stall. Shelby was working another dispenser case loose, struggling with the plastic catches, when Nadine's tapping produced a hollow sort of *clink.* They exchanged an excited look. The first tile came free with a little wriggling. The second slipped out with a tap. The third clattered to the bathroom floor on its own as Nadine thrust her arm into the gap and pulled out a short-necked glass bottle as long as her forearm, its front covered in cursive under the word ABSOLUT. The tall girl grinned, hefting the fifth. "Bingo."

"Glass!" came a shout from just outside the bathroom.

Shelby nearly jumped out of her skin, but Nadine only turned and eased the stall door shut. She shot the bolt, then looked back at Shelby, smiled wickedly, and took her by the shoulder to guide her up onto the toilet seat. Shelby crouched down, her brain whirring frantically as she stared into Nadine's twinkling blue eyes. The other girl's feet were planted in a wide stance and she was undoing the buttons and zipper of her jeans, exposing sandy curls. She thrust her hips out, hands braced on the stall's sides, and with an expression of extreme concentration she started to piss, the untidy stream speckling Shelby's shoes and splashing into the bowl.

"Hey!" Corey called again, and now she could hear his footsteps echoing from the tile walls, could see the shadow of his legs stride past the next stall over and come to a halt before their own. The door shook as he tried the handle. "What's the holdup, Glass? You expect us to wait on you?"

Shelby swallowed. Nadine, still peeing, though now in spurts, gave her a little nod. *Tell him something,* the other girl mouthed. Shelby tried not to stare at her mound and the pink lips of her vulva as she tugged her panties up and rebuttoned her jeans. "Just . . . I'll just be a minute," Shelby squeaked. She felt hot. Her balance was precarious, her belly squished against her legs.

A pause. The worst pause in the world, and for a moment Shelby was sure Corey would rip the stall door from its hinges and she'd wake up in her bed at home, and it would all have been a daydream stuffed inside a nightmare. Nadine's face would be sucked up into nothingness, would fade within an hour into a vague blur of overlapping crushes.

Corey cleared his throat. "We're hiking out in five minutes," he said. "You're late, Garth comes in here and gets you. You think he'll be as polite about it as I am?"

"No, sir."

Another pause, and then the satisfied reply: "Then I'll see you at the flagpole."

"Yes, sir."

Footsteps. They held their breath together, she and Nadine, the stall smelling of piss and disinfectant, until they were sure he was gone. Shelby let out a nervous titter and immediately felt herself turn purple. *What are you laughing at? Why is she staring at you? She probably thinks you're insane, sitting here giggling while—*

"What's your name?" Nadine whispered. Her face was so close Shelby could see the tooth marks in her lower lip and where the Band-Aid across her broken nose had started peeling away from her skin. A thin residue of adhesive made a ghostly outline where the strip had clung to her.

"Shelby."

The other girl smiled. Her lips parted as she leaned in. Their mouths came together and she tasted like morning breath and cinnamon, like sweat and orange juice and pussy, gross and hot and perfect. Sucking and nipping. Spit between them when they parted to breathe. Too much tongue, teeth scraping Shelby's chin. Hungry.

Perfect, perfect.
Perfect.

Malcolm started wide awake, the dream he'd been having already swirling into rags of wet, disjointed images. Pale phlox blooming. His cousin Leon's dog, Bones, barking madly at a man without a face. Five little fingers clutching a doorjamb.

The other boys of Cabin Nine were sound asleep. Franklin's snoring filled the cramped space—two bunks, a linen closet, and a bathroom little bigger than a phone booth, its only partition a heavy canvas sheet hanging from a curtain rod. In the bunk above Vick was talking in his sleep, a ceaseless nonsense mutter, and across the room Carlton Sweet, the camp's only other Black kid, lay curled into a ball under his blanket.

Something was scratching at the cabin door. Malcolm rose up slowly onto one elbow, fumbling for his glasses in the dark. Every inch of his body hurt like hell, the bruises where Betty had kicked him throbbing in sync. There was something moving in the slit of moonlight coming in under the door. His fingers found plastic and he slid the lenses up his nose, squinting as the gloom came into focus, a wash of grays and browns and blacks, and beneath the door a wriggling shape. Fingers? His heart was pounding in his ears. Vick's muttering grew louder. Malcolm listened for a moment as the other boy hissed "*Mommy, Mommy*" in a flat, cold voice.

He slipped out of his bunk, the floorboards rough and cool under his feet, and took a step toward the door. *You're having a nightmare,* he thought calmly as he lowered himself to the floor. *This isn't real. You're home in Riverside in your bed and Mom is crying in the next room over, crying and crying like she always is, but never any tears.*

The things—fingers?—under the door withdrew without a sound. Malcolm knelt, holding still, and pressed his bruised cheek to the floorboards. He could see the scratches where whatever it was had dug into the door's soft and graying pine. Nothing else remained.

The moonlight vanished. A pair of gleaming silver eyes replaced it. Malcolm lay very still. In some deep recess of his brain a little voice was screaming that now was the time to run, that he should roll under his bunk and hope against hope whatever it was looking in hadn't seen him yet. A low, meaty waft of breath washed over his face as whatever it was let out a rattling exhale, and then in an instant it was gone, the moonlight shining once more on the splintered boards.

His heart pounding, his mouth dry, Malcolm got up from the floor and went to bed.

VII

THE HOLE

The first thump yanked Shelby up and out of sleep. By the second, Gabe and John were out of bed. Brady sat hunched in his bunk, his eyes wide and the blankets pulled up to his chin. Shelby set foot to the cold planks just as the third thump rattled the door to the linen closet.

Gabe darted forward and opened it. He'd gotten a match from somewhere and its flame cast a wan yellow light over the interior. Threadbare sheets and pillowcases sealed in plastic waited silently within, some fallen from the highest shelf, others neatly stacked, and for a moment they all looked shamefacedly at one another.

Then the tallest stack began to tip.

Part of the closet floor swung upward with a groan of rusty hinges, a bar of moonlight from the main room illuminating a vicious smile in the inky black below. A hand slid through the gap, nails clutching at the boards, and whoever it was hissed *"Heeeere's Johnny!"* in a deep, gravelly voice. It made Brady scream and recoil so ferociously he fell backward off his bunk, so that by the time Gabe and Shelby pulled first Nadine and then Felix and Jo up into the cabin he was nursing a lump the size of an egg while John waved a finger back and forth in front of his face to see if the dazed boy could focus on it.

For a terrible moment Shelby felt sure that Nadine would ignore her, would pretend nothing had happened between them in that rank bathroom stall just like Tyler had pretended every day that she was just part of the furniture, an embarrassing stain he was too lazy to scrub out of the upholstery. Then the other girl smiled at her, warm and wide and kind of smug, and a few minutes later

Shelby found herself on the floor with her head in Nadine's lap as they passed the bottle of Absolut around their little circle. A flashlight stood on its head and draped with a washcloth in the center of their group gave off the only light.

It was real, she thought, looking up at the hollow of the other girl's throat, at her long collarbones and the spill of her dirty blond hair falling over her shoulders. Nadine was stroking Shelby's scalp as she took a shot from the clay mug Gabe had dumped their toothbrushes out of and rinsed in the bathroom, and the other girl's touch seemed almost to burn. A fingernail catching the edge of Shelby's ear. The pad of a thumb at the nape of her neck. *It really happened.*

Gabe took the mug and poured more vodka. "So she was crawling in the garden. So what? My mom used to crawl for primal therapy or something."

"No," said Nadine. "Something's really wrong, and you all know it. I'm not crazy."

"They're just Mormons or something," Gabe slurred, spilling a little on his shirt. He snorted, then giggled, snuggling into John's side as the fat boy poured himself a fastidious shot. "They fuck their kids. Maybe she's inbred."

Jo looked thoughtful. "That Black kid, Malcolm, said he saw a dog under one of the cabins the other day while Betty and her little shit-eaters were beating him up."

Across the circle, Felix snorted. "He's a loudmouth."

"He mentioned dogs to me at the first bonfire night here," said Gabe, his brow furrowing. He was so pretty, long and slender and elfin like one of the characters on *Sailor Moon* or the bootleg *Escaflowne* tape Stel had brought back for Shelby from her business trip to Singapore. All the folds and bumps and bulges ironed out. "He said he saw eyes outside the firelight."

I wish I looked like you.

The mug and bottle rounded their little circle again. Shelby had never had a drink before, except a little wine at Thanksgiving, and her head was already swimming when Nadine bent down to kiss her with a mouth full of vodka. Shelby's face burned. She struggled not to cough as Nadine's tongue slid over her teeth. *If you throw up on this girl she will turn around and disappear back down that hole,* she thought. *And the next time she looks at you, it'll be like she's noticing she stepped in something.*

"He *is* a loudmouth," said John, "but I don't think he's a liar. He's just nervous. Imagine being Black out here, especially if Pastor Eddie really is a Mormon. My dad told me they didn't even let Black people inside their churches until a few years ago."

"No," Nadine repeated. Even flushed and tipsy she had that quality that made everyone in the circle sit up straighter when she spoke. "It's not Mormons—not just Mormons, anyway. It's these fucked-up classes, it's those weird fucking plants in Mrs. Glover's garden, it's . . ." She paused to catch her breath, and when she spoke again it was like someone had jabbed them all with a hot needle. "Has anyone else been having nightmares?"

The cabin fell silent. Vague unease stirred in the pit of Shelby's stomach, splashing in the bitter pool of vodka that had gathered there. The sound of Felix pouring another shot seemed suddenly as loud as a waterfall. *I can't remember my dreams,* Shelby thought. *I wake up, and my hands hurt. I can't remember where I am. Tyler was there, and Ruth . . .*

"I keep having the same one," said Brady suddenly, his voice cracking. "I'm digging a hole, like when they make us put up fences, but it's really deep. I'm in it up to my neck."

Nadine's grip on Shelby's shoulder tightened.

"There are people watching me dig. Sometimes it's camp people, Pastor Eddie and the staff, and sometimes it's my family. People from school. My friends. I keep digging until I'm all the way underground, and they're all talking but I can't really hear what they're saying."

There were tears on Nadine's cheeks. Shelby sat up, the room swimming slightly as she took Nadine's hand and looked around the circle. John was white as milk. Felix looked as though he was about to vomit and Gabe's bottom lip was trembling.

"Eventually I find something, but when I go to pull it out of the dirt, it's . . . me. It's my face."

I've had this dream.

Felix ran for the bathroom, wrenching the curtain aside. Knees hit wood with a hollow *thump*. The seat clattered against the tank, bright and clear, and then he was puking, his dry heaves echoing through the cabin. A bubbling splash of vomit. Jo scrambled to her feet and went in after him.

"I've had that dream twice," said Nadine.

"I had it last night," John squeaked. "The face in the dirt."

More heaving and splashing from the bathroom. Jo's voice, soft and low and comforting.

"The lessons don't make any sense," John piped up suddenly. "I thought it was just religious stuff, but it's not. The whole book is insane, and is anyone else getting—"

"Headaches," Jo finished from the threshold of the bathroom. She was rubbing Felix's back.

"Maybe it's the bariatric pressure or something," Shelby ventured, knowing it wasn't. She could hear the fear in her own voice, could understand on a level just above the churning surface of her subconscious that she'd had a blinding headache during class the day before, black spots swimming in her field of vision, white auras flickering around the other students in the mess. "Like when migrating birds get confused because of, like, magnetic fields, or storms . . ."

"Barometric," said John.

Jo came back out of the bathroom, Felix leaning heavily on her. Shelby realized with a delayed jolt of something like homesickness that she'd never actually met another transsexual her own age. The only ones she'd known in New York were the big blocky woman who did Charlie's accounts at the cathouse and one of the girls there, pretty Saffron with her sharp cheekbones and heavy eyeshadow, who she'd been too frightened to talk to. She felt an overwhelming urge to take Felix in her arms.

"It's like there's this . . . light," said Brady. "It starts burning right between my eyes, inside my head."

"Like a point of white light," Jo said grimly. "Like a cigarette burn? Does that make sense?"

Shelby's stomach clenched around the sour churn of the Absolut. Her hand in Nadine's felt suddenly lifeless, the whole arm like a dead hunk of meat someone had sutured to her living body. Ruth only smoked when she was drunk, and it had only happened once. The lit butt pressed to Shelby's arm. The smell of burning flesh. *You cannot do this to yourself, Andrew. You cannot do this to me.* They'd gone to therapy about it. Tears. Apologies.

"I saw it, too," Felix croaked into the silence. He sat with his eyes closed and his head resting against John's bunk. "Like you said. The hole, in my dreams."

"So, what?" Gabe was sweating. He poured another shot, the neck of the bottle clattering against the lip of the mug. "We've been *digging holes,* for like, a week. Someone's beaming shit into our heads like Professor X? I mean, come on." He let out a nervous bleat of laughter.

"Yeah, maybe," said Nadine.

No one laughed.

"Whatever's happening here, I want to get out." Nadine let go of Shelby's hand and leaned forward. To Shelby it felt like the sun going behind a cloud. Nadine's lean, hungry face with its fading bruises looked so grown-up in that moment, a shadow cast through time of the woman she'd grow into. "Mouth off however much you want, but you know this place is fucked. You know it is. You see the kids who've been here longer than us. The way they stare, like they're fucking brain damaged. You want that to happen to you?"

"We don't know where we are," said Felix, his voice hoarse. "We don't know where the nearest town is. We don't know how many ranch hands there are hanging around. These people aren't playing. What do you think they'll do if they find us drinking? What do you think they'll do if we try to *run away*?"

"You guys are so serious," Gabe giggled, pouring himself another shot. His face was flushed. She thought maybe from the way his eyes were glistening that he was holding back tears. "Can we just have a good time before tomorrow gets here?"

Nadine's expression softened. She leaned back against the bunk. "Yeah," she said. Shelby thought her heart would explode when Nadine casually took her hand again. "Just, you know . . . keep an eye out. I don't have so many friends I can afford to let you guys get brainwashed."

Friends, thought Shelby, leaning her head on Nadine's shoulder as Gabe passed the bottle to Jo, who took it with a nervous smile. The dreams didn't seem so frightening, all of a sudden. The headaches. Ms. Armitage's silly classes. She closed her eyes, the heat of the vodka a pleasant burn in her stomach.

I have friends.

In Malcolm's dream he was digging a hole. The ground was hard and rocky, fighting him for every shovelful of earth, and the sun beat down mercilessly on the back of his neck. He heard someone who sounded like his father say, "The shirt on his *back*!" but he didn't know who they were, or where they might be. His father was gone. Sometimes Don would come home to sweep Malcolm and Mary off to dinner, to grin and joke and tell them stories about his work in Texas for one of the big oilfields, stories about men with names like Gatwood and Cotton, but he never stayed, and after dinner there was their mother crouched in the doorway like a starving vampire, watching them walk across the lawn, already rehearsing in her mind a litany of the sins committed against her.

Malcolm looked up. The hole had gotten deeper. He was in over his head now. On the lip above a crowd stood watching him, their faces lost in shadow, backlit by the sun, and from time to time warm droplets of their spit would strike his face or fall to the dirt beneath his feet, absorbed at once by the hungry earth. He kept digging. Deeper and deeper, the soil growing darker, turning muddy as moisture welled up from it. At length the shovel's blade struck something solid, the shock of impact reverberating up its handle and his arms to rattle his teeth in their sockets. He set the implement aside and knelt to dig by hand.

Slowly, the shape of the buried thing took form. A long nose, slightly crooked where a neighbor kid, Mark Sussman, had broken it with a baseball bat. Cropped hair, tight and coarse. A wide, smiling mouth. High cheekbones and a little scar, barely noticeable, at the corner of the left eye where the emerald set in his mother's ring—

The face's eyes opened. Malcolm froze. The people above were talking now, voices low and excited. The face's mouth moved. Mud dripped from its chin as it spoke in a voice he recognized at once as his fifth-grade teacher Ms. Landsman's, soft and precise and respectably white.

"Kiss me, Malcolm."

The voices above grew louder. He heard frantic wingbeats, though he couldn't see a bird. "I don't like girls," he said as their lips met. His mouth tasted of earth and rain and something oily and bitter that he didn't recognize. A tongue thrust its way into him, gliding over his teeth and then slipping back into the sour trenches between gums and lips. It was a kiss like nothing he'd ever experienced. The dry, chaste pecks he'd teased and wheedled from his fellow Boy Scouts. The sloppy lip-locking with Bruce Ramapoe, who'd thrown up on him right after and given him a black eye the next day at recess. This was a real kiss, a grown-up kiss, hungry and intimate.

Muddy fingers brushed his throat and the line of his jaw. His mouth felt oddly full, as though the questing tongue were swelling, and as a hand took hold of the back of his head he felt that slick, fat muscle split and split again, tendrils forcing themselves deeper, caressing the back of his throat, the tender clapper of his uvula. He gagged, recoiling, and the face came with him, the mud erupting as the buried thing emerged, kicking its way free of its slimy, shit-colored womb and forcing its tongues deeper into

Malcolm's throat. His back was against the wall of the shaft. He could see, at an oblique angle, that its face was hollowing out, becoming gaunt. He retched, bile burning in his nostrils, but the thing only reached deeper as the muscles of his esophagus convulsed.

Something came unstuck, and for a moment he surfaced flailing from the dream, confused by the sheets entangling him, by the warm, sticky wetness soaking into the front of his boxers, by the alien shapes of the bedframe and metal springs of the bunk above his, and somewhere beyond wood and air and the harsh light of the overheads strung up between the cabins, seven wild pink lanterns burned in a circle, and beyond them something huge and raw and hungry snuffled at the edge of their campfire, and then he was back in the hole and the thing that was him and not him stood over where he sagged slack and powerless within the negative impression it had left climbing out of the dirt. A womb in the earth that fit him like a second skin down to the last pube.

"Wait," he tried to say, but only a strained breath escaped his lungs, and then mud rained down on him, hard enough to bruise and stun, and did not stop until the world was black and cold and silent.

Nadine pulled herself through the trapdoor in the floor of Cabin Two and knelt to help Jo and Felix up after her. Her head was swimming pleasantly as they restacked the linens. She felt warm. Her stomach fluttered with the memory of her kiss goodbye. She'd never really thought about being with a transvestite, but Shelby felt like a girl in her arms, soft and shy and so achingly sweet. She found herself grinning as she shut the door, though in the pit of her stomach a little worm of guilt squirmed restlessly at the thought of Tess's dimpled smile.

In silence they replaced the closet's false bottom. Smith stirred in her bunk when Felix closed the closet door. She blinked owlishly at them from within her blankets, her big eyes catching the light that fell through the gaps in the cabin's walls. "Was it fun?" Smith whispered.

"You should come next time," Nadine whispered back, fighting the urge to giggle. Beneath her drunken euphoria she could feel her niggling doubts about the dreams trying to resurface, but maybe they'd gotten overexcited, started convincing themselves they'd seen things they hadn't. She knew it happened sometimes. Her mother was like that; whenever someone got sick, an hour later she'd be retching in the bathroom and moaning about her fever. "I'll tell you all about it in the morning."

But when she woke in the gray gloom just before dawn, her head pounding and her mouth sour, Smith's bed was empty, her sheets and blankets folded neatly at its foot.

VIII

THE BARN

Gabe felt sick. The heat, even with the sun still creeping up over the horizon, was boiling, and his head felt as though someone had put it in a vise while he was sleeping. His stomach churned sourly, cramping with each shaky heave of the shovel's blade. They were digging postholes again. Corey and Garth had led their cabin and two of the boys from Eight out while it was still dark, the last faint blush of starlight making the counselors' horses appear limned in silver as they rode. One of the other boys, a stringy little fifteen-year-old named Ben who Gabe didn't know well, had cried for most of the walk out.

He couldn't shake the dream, the one they'd all had. He'd told himself a dozen times that it was mass hysteria, that they were all feeling scared and alone and looking for things to pin those feelings on, trying to comfort himself with his therapist mother's cold platitudes, but nothing worked. *People don't have the same dreams,* he thought as he dug. Not far off the ranch's cows were ambling down a broken slope, mothers nosing their calves over the rocks and desert driftwood, lowing in the heat as the first ghostly shimmers danced atop the nearby ridge. *It's impossible.*

By silent agreement the other boys stopped digging and joined him to watch the herd pass. Gabe leaned on his shovel, breathing hard. There must have been fifty cows. Maybe more. He wondered how you were supposed to keep track of all of them. The desert seemed endless, and the more he saw of it the more he realized that beneath its flat expanse and empty sky was a second infinity, one of canyons and shale and hidden riverbeds run dry and snarled with gorse and creosote.

"Max and James were gone when we woke up," said Ben, his voice hoarse. Fat, pimply Stuart Carmichael, the other boy from Eight, nodded, looking like he wanted to cry, too.

"Their beds were empty," Ben croaked. "Stripped. Dave said they left for a hike with Pastor Eddie, that it's a retreat for kids who've shown they're ready to really commit."

"Do you believe him?" asked John. The fat boy's face was pale beneath his sunburn.

Ben shook his head, eyes wide and frightened. "I heard something outside the cabin last night," he said. His voice was small. "It was scratching at our door and . . . it was *sniffing*."

The hairs on the back of Gabe's neck stood up. He felt suddenly exposed out on the open ground in the shadow of the ridge. There was an ache in his chest for the idea of a home that wanted him, that would care if he was safe or not, if he was warm, if he was fed. *You're not going to have this life,* his mother had said to him a little while before the men from Resolution came and dragged him from the house. Her narrow face was pinched with fury, her hands curled together white-knuckled on the kitchen table. *You have no excuse for behaving this way. You're trying to hurt me. To hurt your father.*

The smell of her perfume came without warning to the forefront of his memory. A thin and clinging cloud of citrus over the buttery scent of vanilla. He nearly retched. He could smell her sour sweat beneath it, and the musty stink of the lake house his grandparents had left to her. They'd been alone. His dad and his little sister, Mackenzie, had gone out for ice cream. Gabe hadn't wanted any. Already at eight years of age he had begun to feel out the unspoken virtue of starvation, the sickly shadow pleasure of denying himself something in which others would indulge.

I'm going to give you an examination, and it's best we keep it between just the two of us. That's called doctor-patient confidentiality. Do you understand, honey?

She'd never called him honey before, and although he knew something was wrong, although his skin prickled with goose bumps and his thoughts began to stretch into a single timeless, disembodied smear as she bent in front of him where he sat at the kitchen table, he wanted her to say it again. He wanted her to love him, to act the way the other moms at Hebrew school acted when they came to pick their kids up. Hugs. Ruffled hair. He could feel the wrongness sweeping through the camp. He could feel the lake reaching for him from out of the past, a wave driving the other kids before it, sweeping them all toward something at the edge of understanding.

We have to get out of here, he realized, staring out into the vast and empty desert. *I don't know how, but we have to get out. Before it's too late.*

"Where's Smith?" Nadine asked Cheryl as the counselor entered the cabin. Cheryl looked at her with cool disinterest. Nadine had to fight to keep from blushing. She knew she was breaking out. Her hair was tangled, and she had a slight hangover, a kind of fuzzy, dirty feeling in the pit of her stomach. She could feel her period coming, twisting the soft tissues cradled in her pelvis into a tangle of writhing eels.

"Good morning, girls," said Cheryl. She paused, expectant.

"Good morning, Cheryl," Jo and Felix chorused back unevenly. Nadine did flush, then, with anger at her friends for caving in so easily.

The counselor gave a little nod and stalked past Felix to inspect the bunks. Jo shot Nadine a panicked look. They'd been up talking half the night while Felix snored—he'd fallen asleep as soon as his head hit his pillow. They'd rinsed out their mouths as best they could, but the tap in the bathroom was on some kind of meter and only ran for twenty seconds a night, its flow sluggish and lukewarm even after the temperature dropped. The bottle of Absolut was buried in the loose soil under the cabin, but Nadine knew the look on Jo's face, the unreasoning terror of someone certain she'd been *bad* and could not escape the consequences of it. She narrowed her eyes at the other girl and mouthed *Be cool* the moment Cheryl's back was turned.

"Can you tell us where Smith went?" Felix asked as Cheryl straightened up from his bunk, apparently satisfied by its tight corners. "She wasn't here when we woke up."

The counselor smiled, just a little, an expression of such maddening smugness that Nadine immediately pictured herself bashing her teeth in with a brick. "That's really none of your business, Vargas."

"We're not going anywhere until you tell us where Smith is." Nadine regretted it as soon as it was out of her mouth. It was a stupid thing to say, a stupid hill to die on, but trying to walk it back now would just make her look stupid *and* weak. "What did you do to her?"

Cheryl looked Nadine up and down. The counselor's expression was unreadable. She was so composed, even this early in the day, her short black pixie cut freshly gelled, her stare dark and cool and catlike. "Not a thing," she said at last. "Enoch and the pastor came and collected her early this morning for private counseling, which she requested herself." She took a step toward Nadine. "Anything else I can clear up for you, Donovan?"

Nadine held the older woman's stare. "No."

For a moment she thought Cheryl might hit her, but the counselor just nodded and turned to lead them out. "What the fuck are you doing?" Felix hissed in her ear as they went down the cabin's steps. The other campers were flooding into the thoroughfare. "You're going to get us all in trouble."

"She's lying," Nadine muttered back. The other girls were joining them now. Betty and Athena. Sarah Becker, who everyone called Pecker, and Fawn DeAngelis with her scar where she'd had her cleft palate repaired. "Whatever they did with Smith—"

"Donovan!"

Cheryl stood a few yards off, pointing toward the worn-out tires piled against the south wall of Cabin Four. The other squads of campers were starting to stare. "Get me one of those. Now."

Nadine's heart sank into her stomach, but there was nothing to gain by stalling. She trudged over and hefted one of the frayed and ragged tires, sliding her arm through its center so its weight rested on her right shoulder. It was already starting to rub her skin raw by the time she lugged it back to where the other girls were waiting for her.

"The truck's been riding off-center," Cheryl said with bored disdain. "I want a spare with us on the morning run, just in case. You don't mind carrying it, do you, Donovan?"

Betty, standing with her clique behind the counselor, gave a shrill, dirty little giggle.

"No, ma'am," said Nadine, her cheeks burning. *I'm going to fucking kill you, you bitch. You fucking asshole. I'm going to cut your face up.* "Not at all."

That smug smile again, this time without a hint of pretense that it was anything else. "Good."

Felix jogged a little way ahead of the others, trying not to listen to the sound of Nadine's labored breathing. Even with the tire she was keeping up, more or less, but the last time he'd looked back her face had been a waxy, ghoulish gray. Sometimes he thought he had the hots for her, with her long, slender legs and that wild mane of tawny hair, her broken nose and crazy grin. Other times she made him sick and angry, made him want to cover himself up and hide.

Keep your head down, he thought, trying not to think about how hungover he was. His head pounded with every loping step. His stomach churned. He tasted bile. *Do your time.*

The ground melted away beneath his feet. He thought of Linford Christie winning gold in Barcelona, those legs scything over the track's pebbled red-brown surface, that smile breaking like dawn at the finish line. That was going to be him at the end of the summer. He'd blow through the ribbon and never look back, never think about this place or his weird dreams again. Who cared if they'd all dreamed about some hole? It's not like it meant anything. He'd had lots of nightmares before. At six years old he'd woken up screaming every night for a week from dreams of a bear getting into the house, its huge claws ripping the wallpaper, its hot breath snorting in rancid puffs under his bedroom door.

"Pick it up, Igarashi!" Cheryl shouted back at Jo. The truck went through a patch of loose earth, tires filling the world with a smoky haze of grit. "Let's see some hustle!"

That was when Nadine fell. Felix felt it in his bones at the hollow *pwup* of the tire bouncing off hard-packed soil. The rest of the group stumbled to a ragged halt. Felix nearly tripped. His head was swimming. His mouth was dry and still tasted faintly of puke. A short way back Nadine was struggling to get to her feet, the camp a hazy blur in the distance beyond her. Her shoulder was raw and bleeding where the tire had rubbed against it while she ran. Part of her dirty tank top was soaked with it.

"On your feet, Donovan!" Cheryl barked, striding back toward the rest of them. Betty and her clique fell in around her like jackals slinking after a lioness. Nadine got her knee under her and shrugged the tire from her shoulder. It fell with another hollow *thwack* of rubber against dirt, raising a little ring of dust. Nadine's hair was dark and matted with sweat. Not so tough now.

Keep your head down. Do your time.

Cheryl came to a halt an arm's length from Nadine, hands on her hips. In her dark, form-fitting tracksuit she looked like she'd just stepped out of *Enter the Dragon*. Her bare arms glistened with sweat. "Did I tell you to put that down?"

Nadine looked up at her with such pure hatred that for a moment Felix thought the other girl might try to throw herself at Cheryl, but instead she bent and looped her arms around the tire, flipping it up on its edge before trying again to stand. Points of color burned in her pale cheeks. Her legs trembled.

Keep your head down. Do your time.

"Benson, Schwarz," said Cheryl, her lip curling in disdain. "Help her up."

Celine and Dana started toward the struggling girl. Celine's big, bulging eyes were wet with excitement. Dana looked nervous, almost tearful, hanging back a little as Celine grabbed hold of Nadine's hair and bounced the girl's face off the tire, blackening her mouth with dirt and soft rubber. Nadine groaned, collapsing on her belly, and Dana shuffled forward and kicked her half-heartedly between the legs.

The shout tore out of Felix before he could stop himself, not the shrill complaint he always feared when he raised his voice but, for all that it cracked a little, a *man's* voice, hard and stern. "Leave her the fuck alone!"

Betty grabbed him from behind just as he started toward Nadine. Cleaver was bigger than him, two or three inches taller and at least thirty pounds heavier. He struggled, trying to stomp on her foot and only succeeding in bruising his heel on a rock. She got an arm across his windpipe. "Let her go!" he wheezed, thrashing in the redhead's grip. "You're gonna kill her!"

Cheryl looked at him. "They're just trying to help her, Vargas." Her dark eyes gleamed with a kind of flat, satisfied complacency more terrifying than the most naked malice. The other girls watched, frozen. Jo was crying, her arms pinned to her sides by Athena. Celine kept dragging Nadine forward by her arm, then bending down to simper with fake concern as Nadine got to her hands and knees and crawled a few pitiful feet. There was blood on the inner thighs of her Wranglers.

"You're next, faggot," Betty whispered in Felix's ear.

Nadine hated the sounds Mrs. Glover made during sex. Even in the kitchen, even through the ringing in her right ear where Celine had kicked her, she could hear the pastor's wife keening like an animal upstairs. Bedsprings creaked and groaned. Flakes of plaster drifted from the kitchen ceiling to float in the sink. It made her think of her own mother, who she'd heard gasping and moaning more than once when her parents thought no one was listening. It was so fake. So staged. The breathy, girlish exclamations of "*Oh, Eddie*" like he was taking her on a magic carpet ride beneath a sea of stars instead of ramming his dick up into her mildewy box. Nadine scrubbed at a copper-bottom stock pot, scratched hands raw and stinging. She wanted to march into their bedroom and dump the pot of filthy, boiling water on both of them, even if she'd have to gouge her eyes out later.

Godddd, came Mrs. Glover's deep, guttural groan, muffled by the intervening floor. *Oh Godddd, Eddie, Eddie.*

Felix and the girls pretended not to hear it, though Jo's face was beet red as she hulled peas at the kitchen table. The thump and creak of the bed frame and box spring grew louder. Faster. Nadine scrubbed harder at the Pyrex baking dish she was cleaning. *They get to do this to us, and I had to put my hand over Tess's mouth when I got her off.* She scrubbed faster, fighting the stubborn crust of whatever the dish had held. *I have to kiss Shelby in a bathroom stall, breathing in the smell of piss and bleach.*

Oh, Eddie. Yes. Harder. Harder.

A phone rang, an earsplitting clatter of handset against cradle. Nadine dropped the Pyrex, which broke cleanly into three pieces. "Shit," she hissed, trying to fish the shards out of the soapy water. The phone rang again, and suddenly the pounding from upstairs stopped cold.

"I've got it, I've got it!" someone shouted from the living room. Enoch, she thought. The screen door banged, then the sound of a key fumbled into a lock. The phone's third ring cut off abruptly. Ignoring Jo's warning look, Nadine crept toward the door to the living room, wiping her soapy hands on her jeans. Heavy footsteps overhead. She peered around the doorframe just in time to see Pastor Eddie come bounding down the stairs in nothing but a pair of wrinkled tan slacks. He met Enoch coming through the little office, always kept locked, to the right of the front door, and without pausing grabbed his son by the front of his shirt and shoved him back against the wall.

"You called Harlon last night," Pastor Eddie rumbled, his face brick red. "About the truck? Isn't that right?"

Nadine couldn't see Enoch's face from where she stood, but she could hear his terror. "Yes, sir."

"Did you turn the ringer on?"

Enoch mumbled something.

"Speak up," said Eddie. Nadine knew that tone. Her father had used it with her more than once before the belt came off.

Enoch swallowed. "He had to step away and I didn't want to miss his call back in case—"

The pastor slapped his son across the face with a crack that echoed from the walls and silenced the whole farmhouse. Nadine didn't care. She wasn't listening. *They have a phone.* She smiled, the effort tugging at the fresh scabs on her cheek and over her right eyebrow. *They have a fucking phone.*

Too late she realized Felix and the girls had gone silent for another reason. Blinding pain lanced from her ear as a hand seized hold of it and twisted cruelly, dragging her back from the doorframe. It was Cheryl. The counselor pulled her farther back into the kitchen, jaw set and nostrils flared. "Don't stick your nose where it doesn't belong," she snapped. "You're a guest in this house. Don't forget it."

Nadine almost laughed, but the pain in her ear and jaw was overwhelming. When she grabbed at Cheryl's arm, the counselor seized Nadine's wrist and twisted it behind her back, forcing her to turn while keeping her neck taut and burning. At the table, Felix stared fixedly at the potato he was peeling. Jo was crying. Nadine's face felt hot, caustic shame burning her cheeks. "Let me go," she said, and felt pitiful as soon as she'd said it.

"March," said Cheryl, pushing her toward the back door. Nadine hobbled forward, helpless, so angry she could hardly see. "I'm not done with you."

Cheryl marched Nadine across the yard and toward the ramshackle hulk of the barn. Chickens scattered from their path, squawking and flapping. Nadine thought for some reason of

Gonzo's pet chicken, Camilla, on *The Muppet Show,* every episode of which her uncle Rick had fastidiously taped during what her grandmother called, with quivering disapproval, his Mary Jane years. Cheryl smelled a little like her grandmother, a slightly chemical reek of mothballs and herbal liniment. *I'm going to kill you,* Nadine thought matter-of-factly, looking at the counselor's smug profile. *Whatever kind of fucking freak you are, scuttling around on your belly, I'm going to cut your throat and shit in the slit.*

Even thinking it felt flat and pitiful. She wasn't going to kill anyone. She wasn't going to change anything. Cheryl had her by the ear, the same way her father had dragged her around as a little girl when she did something to set him off, or when he decided she had. Cheryl set her shoulder against the sliding barn door, splintered wood rattling in its rusty track, and the warm, grassy stink of cow manure flooded Nadine's mouth and nostrils. Horned heads turned toward her. Big, dark eyes blinked slowly. Cheryl released her ear and kicked her, hard, in the back of the knee. Nadine dropped with a grunt to the straw-covered concrete floor, the impact rattling her teeth.

"You're a slow learner, aren't you?" said Cheryl. She sounded pleased, like the prospect of Nadine's stupidity was a little personal gift for her. "Shovel's by the door. Wheelbarrow's in the empty stall. Compost is around the back at the edge of the garden. Muck the rest of these stalls out. And watch out for Doris; she bites."

"Which one's Doris?" Nadine coughed, but Cheryl was already gone. A brown cow stuck her head over her stall door and snorted in the silence, flicking her ears to dislodge flies. Nadine stayed kneeling for a while, indulging in sullen fantasies of sinking her teeth into Cheryl's face. Truthfully, though, mucking stalls sounded better than washing dishes. She'd done it a few summers at Gorse Brook Farm, where she'd taken riding lessons. She liked the stink of it, the burn in her arms after hours of shoveling shit. It made her think of her father coming home from rec league basketball, or a job site on a hot day, his T-shirt dark under the arms and around the neck.

The shoveling was hard with her bruised ribs and aching arms, but it felt good to be alone for once. The cows were mostly content to chew their cud as she worked, heaping the dented and rusty wheelbarrow with manure and pushing it around behind the barn to where flowers, weeds, and what she thought might be bamboo grew from a huge hill of refuse. Broken eggshells, apple cores, corn cobs, and other detritus lay heaped among piles of cow shit, some of them already growing grass. By the time she'd finished half the barn's twenty stalls she'd built up a pleasant sweat. She liked to build up a sweat. It made her feel the same way she did when Tess called her Nate in bed. Once she thought she heard something moving in the hayloft, but when she made her way up the groaning ladder there was nothing to see but a couple of rats skittering among the moldy bales.

It took her the better part of the afternoon to notice the smell. She caught her first whiff of it as she was cleaning out Doris's stall, eighth on the left—she'd identified the cow when Doris tried to take a bite out of her ear. It cut through the sweet, grassy stench of the manure and the warm musk of the cows themselves, a note a little like the stuffy, slightly tallowy perfume her great aunt Christine always wore. *They put little bits of shit and weasel oil and rotting things in perfume,* she remembered. *To make it smell like sex, and like death.* There was a sweetness to it, though, a sticky, syrupy scent. She leaned the shovel against a post and followed the stink toward the rear of the barn. As she did, the buzzing of flies emerged from the stamping and chewing of the cows.

The smell was coming from the last stall on the right. Flies swarmed over the half gate and the cracked and weathered lintel. The drone of their wings filled the air. It set Nadine's teeth on edge. Her skin crawled as she lifted the heavy wooden latch and the insects, taking flight, bumped against her and crawled over her arm and the sleeve of her flannel. She hauled the gate open, its rusted hinges creaking. The smell intensified. She raised her arm to cover her mouth and nostrils, her eyes watering at the putrid stench.

Inside the stall, beneath a living carpet of flies, a dead cow lay on its side, tongue protruding from its mouth, one empty eye socket staring at her in mute judgment. Maggots writhed in that dark pit. Beetles burrowed through the matted, shit-caked hide, which had begun to slough from the bones and rotten meat beneath.

The seething whine of the flies became a roar, a staticky sound like a TV blasting on a dead channel. The glistening black carpet of their bodies undulated over the carcass, circling the yellowed pillars of its ribs, the fat ropes of its guts, which had spilled from its burst belly. Nadine took a step back without meaning to, her hand flying to her forehead as a headache burned itself in through her temple, a white-hot needle from her eye to the nape of her neck. The world swam before her, shadows stretching and melting in the corners of the barn's dark alcoves. She swayed, grasping for something to hold on to, and as her hand found the splintered wood of what felt like an antique plow, a voice spoke from the stall.

Nadine.

Her childhood dentist, Dr. Campbell, who had died in a car accident when she was eleven, was crouched beside the carcass, flies crawling through the pitiful landscape of his graying combover and on the lenses of his thick Coke-bottle glasses. **Open wide, Nadine,** he said, but his voice wasn't his, it was the dead static howl of the swarm. He smiled hugely, flashing crowded rows of rotten teeth, and crept toward her on all fours. His nails were mottled blue and green, as though his hand had been slammed in a car door. He reached for her and she saw that there was shit trapped under them, a toxic brown crust of sludge. She felt something in her belly *stretching,* a feeling somewhere between gagging and the hot, convulsive pressure of a hand inside her.

It's only going to hurt for a second.

His index finger touched her lip. Behind him, the dead cow's foreleg twitched. Something squirmed within the gawping, vacant mouth. Nadine screamed as her headache burned brighter. She squeezed her eyes shut and in a flash of acrid purple and white light she saw a foot-long clot of matted hair and crushed slivers of bone lying half buried in the loose, crumbling desert earth. There was something inside it. A wet thing, rubbery and slick. A mouth full of baby teeth. A finger where its tongue should be.

Nadine vomited. Her knees gave out, and she fell hard on her rear, legs splayed to either side of the puddle of her own puke, around which flies already gathered. Dr. Campbell was gone, and with him the sickly, feverish sensation of being stretched, replaced by a sense of griminess, as though her skin had been sprayed with rotten honey.

Sitting in the hay, the hot pain of the headache ebbing now, Nadine could make out ragged bite marks in the cow's flank and belly. They were too big to have been made by rats or weasels, the wrong shape for a coyote or a dog.

Oh, God, she realized with mounting horror, bile welling up again at the back of her throat. *They're human.*

Shelby looked up from her hole just in time to see Gabe puke. He stretched back like a bow, staring into the sky at an angle, and then bent double and vomited all over his own shoes. John hurried toward Gabe. He caught the smaller boy as Gabe's legs buckled, and for a moment Shelby thought he'd fainted.

"Get it out of me!" Gabe screamed, jerking upright. He kicked and struggled in John's arms. His eyes rolled back into his head until only the whites showed. Shelby's mouth felt dry. She was nauseous and couldn't seem to find her breath. Her shovel fell to the dirt with a clank. The others were running toward Gabe and John. "Get it out! Get it out!" Gabe vomited again. This time there was blood in it. He began to thrash, the sinews in his throat standing out like cables.

"Help me!" shouted John. His mouth was bleeding where Gabe's skull had split his lip. He dragged the spasming boy toward the shade of a nearby boulder. "He's gonna hurt himself."

Shelby scrambled out of her half-dug hole. It took her, Ben, and Stuart together to hold Gabe down once John had wrestled him to the ground. Brady stripped off his shirt and folded it to stuff under Gabe's head, then stood by with a fearful look. Slowly, Gabe's convulsions slackened, becoming tics, and then faded to nothing. He blinked. He had such pretty eyes, deep and gray with long, thick lashes. Shelby let go of his ankles as the others stepped back.

Brady knelt and held a water bottle for him. Gabe took slow sips, then turned his head and spat into the dirt. "What happened?" He croaked. "My head hurts."

"I don't know," said John. The fat boy's face was the color of milk. Stuart was crying while Ben held him, looking helpless and lost. "You were begging us to get something out of you."

Shelby's headache pulsed at her temples. She saw the point of white fire again, the mote of light dancing on the boulder's side just above Gabe's head. On her right, Stuart squeezed his eyes shut and put the heel of his hand to his forehead, as though he had an ice cream headache. Gooseflesh crawled up Shelby's arms, heat or no heat. "I want to go home," she whispered to nobody, though what she really wanted was to have a home she could go back to.

"It's getting closer," Gabe murmured, his eyelids fluttering. "It's kissing Nadine now."

"Keep him in the shade," Shelby forced herself to say, stepping back from Gabe and the others. Her heart was pounding. She wanted to bolt, to run back to camp and make someone bring her to Nadine, get a knife and threaten to kill herself unless they let Nadine go. She sounded like a stranger to herself as she kept talking in that calm, measured tone. "Give him water. A little bit at a time. I'll finish digging his hole."

"Closer," whispered Gabe. "Getting closer."

At lunch the mess was dotted here and there with empty seats. Jo thought of Smith's bare mattress as she worked her way mechanically through her beans and meat loaf. Wonder Bread and margarine on the side; a white-person-food triple threat. Her friend

Sammy's mother cooked the same way. Skinless chicken breasts, unseasoned. Undercooked boiled potatoes cut into glistening chunks. Plain broccoli steamed until it was barely solid anymore. It made her want to cry, all the bad food she'd eaten. She pushed her meat loaf around its lonely partition of her scratched and heat-warped plastic tray. Her mother had never really cooked. Her grandparents had done most of that, and then Oji by himself after Oba-chan died of cancer. In the last few years, since her father's promotion to junior partner at his firm, they had mostly stopped having dinner together at all. The thought of eating bowls of charcoal-cooked chicken and sticky rice in the kitchen with Oji after finishing her homework, of his lumpy homemade mochi and the smell of spicy stock simmering on the stove, brought tears to her eyes. She wiped them on her sleeve as Felix joined her. Nadine hadn't come back with them. Cheryl had dragged her away during the drama over the phone.

The phone. Jo kept turning it over and over in her mind. If they could just figure out where they were, what state, the name of a town, they could call someone. It was just conceivable they might even be able to get out of this place before whatever insane shit was in the air finally chose its moment. It would be soon. She could feel it coming.

"Nadine here yet?" she asked Felix. He shook his head and started wolfing down his meat loaf the way he always did, like it was an enemy fortification he had to demolish.

Jo spotted her a moment later coming from the serving counter. Nadine limped toward them through the milling campers. She looked terrible and smelled worse. Her hair was lank and damp with sweat. There were fresh bruises layered over her fading ones, and blood on her flannel work shirt. Her boots and the cuffs of her jeans were crusted with nameless muck. Slowly, as though it hurt her to do it, she lowered herself onto the bench across the table and leaned forward, resting her head in her hands. Kids at neighboring tables stared at her.

"Are you okay?" Jo asked.

Nadine only shook her head. For a while the three of them ate in silence as more counselors led their groups in. Jo sank down a little in her seat as Names-and-Dates arrived with Betty and her little minions in tow. The big redheaded girl was laughing shrilly about something while Celine and Dana tittered. Athena, trailing a little behind the others, scanned the mess with her cold, dark stare. Jo didn't like the way Athena looked at people. It was the way you were supposed to look at the things you found when you flipped over a rock: interested, but a little repulsed, too.

"Was it Betty?" Felix asked. "Did she fuck with you again?"

"No," said Nadine. Her voice sounded raw and strained. She looked up from her plate. "We have to get out of here," she said. Her knuckles were white on her spoon. "There's something bad happening. Something wrong." She took a deep breath, like she was about to climb that last rung and step up onto the high dive. "I think they're going to kill us.

"We have to get out."

IX

GRADUATION

The boys' cabin was dark except for the moonlight spilling through the windows when Felix led the girls in through the trapdoor. The boys were awake in their beds. Felix felt a twinge of jealousy when he noticed the sparse stubble on Gabe's cheek. He had the same little mustache his mother had painstakingly plucked from her own upper lip for as long as he could remember, but it was soft and feathery. He wanted Leo's, thick and bristly, or his tío Lalo's, covering his mouth like the sweep of a push broom. He sat down on the edge of John's bed, hands folded between his knees. If anyone but Nadine had told him the story of the dead cow and the thing in the barn, he'd have looked around to see what kind of glue they'd been sniffing, but there was a seriousness to the tall, rangy girl. He trusted her, an uncomfortable feeling.

Shelby and Nadine were kissing and whispering with each other to everyone else's intense boredom and embarrassment by the time Malcolm popped his head up through the trapdoor, cobwebs stuck to his glasses and a scowl on his face. "Can't believe you bonded without me." He climbed up into the closet and brushed dust and dirt from his clothes. "You know how boring my cabin is? The liveliest it gets is when Vick farts in his sleep."

"Sounds riveting," said John.

Malcolm chucked him lightly under the chin. "He's not bad once he gets warmed up," he said, grinning, and dropped onto the bed beside John, who had turned beet red. For a while they settled into the easy back-and-forth that Malcolm always seemed to bring out in them, even though small talk usually made Felix feel like his head was being slowly crushed in a drill press. It was nice to forget for a minute that they'd all been sent here by their own parents, that they couldn't call home and say they were in trouble because none of them had ever really had one.

"There's a phone in the farmhouse," said Nadine once everyone was settled. She sat on the floor, holding hands with Shelby, shadows darkening the bruises on her face and arms. "If we're going, we'll need to hike out there and use it. We'll need food. Jackets. Water. I was in Scouts for like eight years; if we can get a map and compass, I can take us through the desert."

"Who are we gonna call?" asked John. Felix thought it was a mark of how afraid they were that no one ventured even a feeble "Ghost-*busters*." The thing in the barn. Cheryl crawling in the garden. Malcolm's story about something scratching at his cabin's door. Those weird, huge owl pellets, the ones Gabe had fallen on their first day building fences. And now they'd lost Smith. It made him feel cold and angry that he'd needed someone else to connect the dots for him, to show him that he couldn't just keep his head down and do his time.

"Don't look at me," said Malcolm, holding up his hands. "You think I know anyone who wants to drive out to wherever we are just to pick my ass up?"

"Can you be serious for five minutes?" Nadine snapped.

Malcolm's smile vanished like the sun going behind the clouds. A look of pure venom twisted his features, then disappeared just as quickly. He looked down at his feet. "Yeah."

Felix wondered if there was anyone who'd come to get him. His mother had cried when the Camp Resolution people came for him, but she'd always cried when his father hit him, too. It had never stopped Manny's fist. He didn't know Tío Lalo's number, he couldn't call Leo without risking getting one of his parents—and even if he got through, Leo would have to believe him, and get a car, and figure something out for afterward. He realized he was clenching his fists hard enough to make his hands ache. He forced himself to relax.

"We could call Oji—my grandpa," Jo said shyly. "He's in a

retirement home in New Jersey, but he'd . . . I think he'd come. I think he'd believe me. I don't know for sure."

"No one's for sure," said Gabe. He sounded bitter.

Nadine turned on him. "Do you actually want to help, or do you want to sit there finding new reasons it's okay to be a useless fucking pussy?"

Gabe stared in astonishment. Silence fell again. Felix still felt hollow, his skin prickling with dread, but after a few heartbeats he forced out, "I'll help."

"Me too," Brady whispered.

One by one the others muttered their agreement. It didn't feel much like the Three Musketeers crossing their swords, but Felix knew that was a little kid's way of looking at it anyway. They were talking about pitting themselves against adults, against people whose authority over them was as total as it was unquestioned, who had the right to drive and carry guns and drink themselves stupid without worrying they'd get caught. They were talking, he realized with a cold thrill, about fighting their parents.

"All right," said Nadine once the last of them had given half-hearted assent. "Cheryl told us it's more than twenty miles to the nearest town. A long way. It would take, like, two or three days to walk that far. At least. Next person to get kitchen duty, see if you can take some of those shitty granola bars they give us. They're light and they have a lot of calories."

Felix looked around at the others. Soft, shy Shelby. Gabe, just skin and bones, and Malcolm not much more than that. John, who he'd seen struggle to walk three miles. Out there in that heat, no cover, nothing to eat or drink but what they could carry . . . could they make it? He shoved the thought out of his head. They had to. For the first time in his life he had *friends*, real friends; he wasn't going to let them get murdered by Jesus freaks or die of dehydration.

Malcolm shook his head like he was trying to dislodge something. His lips peeled back from his teeth. "So we have to get past the fence, hike to the farmhouse, get inside, call Jo's grandpa and hope he feels like a road trip, then make it who knows how many miles to a town we know nothing about where, if all of these things go the way we want, he'll be waiting for us so we can . . . what? Go on the run? What do we know about surviving on our own? We're supposed to just trust this geezer to figure it out?" He was crying now. "You have no idea what you're doing. You're going to get us killed. I don't know what was at my door. Maybe I was dreaming. We won't even make it past the fence."

"Shut UP," Nadine snarled, loud enough that the rest of them fell silent, listening for the sound of footsteps or the rattle of a key. Just when Felix thought Malcolm would start ranting or Nadine would lose it and deck him, Jo cleared her throat. The whole room looked to her.

"Um," said Jo, working her hands back into the sleeves of her too-large turtleneck. "Malcolm, you said you saw a dog last week, right?"

Malcolm blinked slowly, tears still streaming down his cheeks. "Yeah, so?"

"If it could get in through the fence," said Jo, "there must be a way out."

Felix stared at her, wondering what it was like to be able to un-pick a situation like that, to know what to say to calm everyone down and show them a new way forward. He didn't have it. He'd felt the lack of it all his life, the same way he so often felt others pairing off by means of some hidden language, disappearing into private worlds he couldn't see or hear or touch. He'd watched it happen between Nadine and Shelby with a dull ache of envy in the pit of his stomach, a certainty that no one would ever show him the way to that beautiful place of being wanted, and of wanting.

The crisis was over. They were committed. In the dark of the cabin, they made their plans.

The next few days passed quickly for Gabe, though at first he felt a horrified certainty that every counselor who glanced his way was about to uncover their secret. It was even worse when they started stealing from the mess during kitchen duty. The pantry and the tiny restroom for the kitchen staff were off the same corridor, and if you were quick you could slip from the bathroom and load your pockets with protein bars and trail mix, but it made his heart pound and his palms sweat. He was grateful he was off duty today; he didn't think he could face it two days in a row, especially not after the miserable class Ms. Armitage was inflicting on them.

"The arm is made up of four independent muscle groups," Armitage continued, jabbing the point of her dry-erase marker at the diagram she'd drawn on the whiteboard. Gabe blinked, trying to bring his notebook into focus. His head was swimming, his stomach sour with anxiety. He could hardly read his own handwriting. Something from yesterday's lesson on metempsychosic transmission, the movement of thoughts as discrete chemical entities through physical matter.

"Each subgroup receives impulses from the *cogitare carnis,* which roughly translated means 'gray matter,' which in turn pass through the *evictii carnii,* or ganglion clusters, secondary processing centers for the commands our brains send to our limbs. The end result is that the hundreds of different muscular structures in our bodies act as a unified whole, even though the human animal is in fact a colony of independent organisms. Now, can anyone tell me what keeps our muscles functioning in unity?"

A hand shot up. Betty's girlfriend, the unibrow with the smug smile. Ms. Armitage nodded in acknowledgment. "Allostatic pressure," the girl said crisply.

"Very good, Athena. Can you define that for us?"

"The intersection between social and environmental stressors and the body's natural impulse to change in order to maintain homeostasis."

"That's right. The body wants to change, but it wants to stay in balance, too."

Gabe had no idea what any of it meant. Horseshit, probably.

Except there was *so much of it,* and it all made a kind of horrible internal sense. Just like John had said. Gabe felt cold. His body kept trying to force those thoughts out like pus from a wound, but he couldn't stop thinking about Jo's tear-stained face when she'd told the rest of them at lunch the other day that Nadine had been badly beaten during their morning run, and how they'd woken to find Smith's bed empty. His collapse that same day, which he didn't remember, though he still felt tired and vaguely sick. It had scared John, though, and the fat boy wasn't the chicken other people pegged him for.

They scratched through incomprehensible word problems and short two-paragraph essays for the next forty minutes—*What is the smallest number of phonemes needed to command thought? Define the haptic requirements involved in crossing the stochastic threshold*—and then suddenly the sun had sunk behind the mountains and the others were returning the tables to their original positions. The cook and his helpers had pulled the segmented steel partition down over the serving window to the kitchen at some point and now the chafing dishes stood empty, the cans of Sterno under them squirreled away somewhere.

If we're going to get out, Nadine had said during their planning session, which they'd started referring to half-jokingly as "the summit," *we're gonna need food.*

They're panicking, he told himself as he helped another boy maneuver their table back into position. *It's just a fucked-up Bible camp teaching us fucked-up shit. Where exactly are we supposed to go after we get out, anyway? Even if Jo's grandpa does come for us, what can he do? Our parents will call the cops. They'll call the FBI.*

No. There was no way they'd make it to a town, much less out of whatever state they were in. Safer to stay and let Pastor Eddie feel them up and speak in tongues, or whatever he wanted to do. Afterward they could go home and maybe, if they were lucky and played their cards right, they wouldn't have to go to military school. Hoping for anything better was just daydreaming, though a little part of him knew he was just turning away from his terror. He knew something was wrong.

Ms. Armitage cleared her throat, silencing the last hushed murmurs and the scrape of metal table legs dragged over concrete. "Tonight the outgoing campers return from their wilderness expedition with David and Marianne for a fireside graduation dinner." Her dark eyes swept the room. The single antique air conditioner mounted in one of the high windows chugged pitifully, leaking down the concrete wall to where a puddle spread over the floor and seeped into the cracks in it.

"Some of you have made a real effort in your work; I imagine the young people returning from the culmination of theirs will have a great deal to offer you. Those of you who have elected to treat your lessons with the same flippant disregard with which you approach the question of your development into adults of quality, perhaps you'll learn something. To that end, the following campers have performed with the least distinction in this week's lessons and are solely responsible for tomorrow's cleanup and kitchen shifts. Cross, Babbage, Glass—"

Gabe glanced at Shelby, trying to catch her eye—it still felt weird to think of her as a girl, a roiling knot of discomfort in his chest that put an edge on everything he said to her—but she was holding her head in her hands and didn't see him. Probably freaking out about Nadine, who'd showed up for lunch yesterday looking worse than Gabe did. Or maybe about the trek through the desert Nadine was telling them they had to risk. Like they'd last ten minutes out there. Kids were getting up now, leaving their desks. John, a few seats over from Gabe, smiled shyly at him before joining the crowd pushing toward the door.

He'd never make it, Gabe thought. It felt like a cruel thing to think, but wasn't he just being honest? *He's too soft. He'd never last the whole way, and he eats so much . . .*

A sudden sharp, stabbing pain lanced through Gabe's thoughts.

It felt as though someone were forcing a nail out through his forehead from the inside of his skull. *Is anyone else getting headaches?* He staggered after John and Shelby. Ahead of him John was deep in conversation with Malcolm, still bruised and limping—they were all beat to shit, really—and beyond them the doorway yawned out onto the barren thoroughfare, washed in sunset colors and sparkling with little points of blackness that burst and faded in his vision. The air conditioner rattled in its rubber and plastic window mount.

"Where are Felix and Nadine?" asked Shelby.

"They were gone when the lesson ended," said John. The blood drained from his face.

It's just a headache, Gabe told himself, gripping the door frame for purchase as he stepped outside. He kept thinking about phlox. A flower. Purple. Spiky needles.

It's just a headache.

"When I first got here," said the boy who had come down from the mountains, "I was confused. I was angry."

The other graduates stood in the shadows behind him, firelight flickering across their faces. They didn't look like they'd been hiking. They didn't even look like the rest of the campers around the fire. They looked like catalog models, almost, even in their scuffed and soiled flannel shirts and ripped-up jeans. The girls were slim, the boys broad-shouldered. They had been silent since they took their places.

Light and shadow from the bonfire danced over the speaker's handsome face, slightly sunburned and with a spray of freckles across the bridge of his nose and spreading out onto his cheeks. Beside him, Pastor Eddie sat in a canvas camp chair with his long legs crossed and his huge dinner-plate hands folded on his knee. The firelight flashed in his glasses. Jo couldn't stop thinking about the sounds she'd heard from upstairs in the Glover house a few days earlier, the grunt and creak of an old mattress getting a hard workout. The thin, feminine cries of "*Oh, EDDIE.*"

"Back home in Montana I was getting into trouble. I had the wrong friends, made the wrong choices, let myself get fooled into thinking I knew what was good for me." The boy chewed his lower lip. "I thought I was in love with a boy. An older boy. A man, I guess. He'd give me things. Take me out. I felt special. Wanted. And when he kissed me, when he'd do things to me . . . I'd tell myself that it was what I wanted."

Dave, sitting on a log on his other side, put a fatherly hand on the kid's shoulder. The other counselor who'd gone out with the graduating class sat across the fire from where Jo sat with John and Shelby, who was still sniffling as she had been since lunch. Marianne, the woman Nadine had called Names-and-Dates. Her arm was still wrapped in bandages where Nadine had bit her. *Remind me not to fight Nadine,* thought Jo, staring at the other woman as the boy kept talking tearfully about getting his butthole stretched out by some college freshman.

"Pastor Eddie . . . you helped me understand how to move forward with my life. How to want a future. That you had the patience to reach out to me, that you even wanted to, after what you went through with your daughter . . . I'm so grateful. I don't have any words."

Daughter?

Pastor Eddie nodded his huge head in acknowledgment. Jo thought again of the grunting from upstairs, the steady thud of headboard against wall. She'd walked in on her parents once, when they'd still shared a bedroom, and she could remember the trail of silvery slime her father had left along her mother's thigh when he'd pulled out in a fumbling hurry and crossed the room in three long strides to slam the door. Did the pastor leave a trail like that along the sunken plane of his wife's belly? Did his huge hands press bruises into her thin and birdlike arms?

The handsome boy put his hands on his knees and rose to his feet. "Our bodies have a memory of what we're supposed to be," he said. "Dave taught me that, and when I get home I'm going to live by it. I'm going to tell my father . . ." He stopped, and for a moment Jo felt a deep and total certainty that this was all rehearsed, right down to his emotional pause and swallow, and then he continued, eyes glittering with tears: "I'm going to thank him for making me do this, and I'm going to become a man he can be proud of."

I wish I'd tried harder to get Smith to come with us the other night, Jo thought suddenly, digging her nails into her palms. *I wish Nadine was here. I wish my parents weren't such fucking Nazis.*

Dave started applauding. Pastor Eddie and the graduates picked it up and a lukewarm wave went around the circle. The kids on kitchen duty were passing out paper plates of hot dogs and beans. Just outside the ring of firelight stood Garth and a few of the camp's other ranch hands. The tips of cigarettes glowed red, like dying stars. Jo saw the gleam of metal. A shotgun's barrels. For a while there wasn't much sound except for the scrape of plastic forks and the mushy, muted chorus of chewing mouths.

"We should look for them tonight," John whispered in Jo's ear. "Shelby's freaking out."

Before she could respond, Pastor Eddie stood and the whole circle fell silent. Slowly, the pastor began to unbuckle his belt as one of the graduates brought out a backless canvas camp stool and set it up not far from the fire. A moment later, four others emerged from the shadows, each pair supporting a third figure between them. First came Nadine, and when the firelight touched her face Jo's breath caught in her throat. The other girl's old bruises were mottled with dark, shiny new ones, her nose swollen, and her cheek scraped and lacerated, little shreds of skin dangling from tiny cuts. Her escorts forced her to her knees and pushed her across the camp stool.

The pastor's huge fingers moved deftly, and the fine leather slithered through the belt loops of his slacks with a rasping hiss. Once he had it wrapped around his fist, he stepped behind Nadine and jerked down her jeans and underpants. A few people gasped. Even Enoch looked queasy. Pastor Eddie spoke, his voice a velvety, crackling rumble. "I told you all back on your first day what I'd do if you took advantage," he said. "A camper caught this little hussy stealing from the mess."

Jo looked for Betty and found her grinning like a jackal a few yards from where the pastor stood. The belt cracked like a whip against Nadine's bare ass. A little way down the circle Shelby tried to get to her feet. Malcolm pulled her back. Jo's ears were ringing. Her thoughts kept slipping through her fingers, little dribs and drabs of the last summer her family had spent on Lake Winnipesaukee before Oba-chan got sick. The way her giggles had echoed from the pontoons under the Ketterings' raft, where she'd had her first kiss with Jamie Kettering, the younger kids' feet thumping against the boards just overhead. A glass shattering two rooms over and her father's voice rising in a cruel, needling whine as her mother began to sob.

The belt rose and fell. Nadine jerked against the seat, arms pinned by the two graduates escorting her. Their faces showed a mix of sympathy and grave seriousness, as though they were bailiffs and the campfire a court. Jo thought of the winter her aunt Mariko's house burned down, of the day they'd driven out so that Jo's mother could help her file her insurance claim and Jo had sat in the car and watched the cold wind strip ash from the house's blackened skeleton.

Nadine screamed at the belt's sixth stroke. Her voice broke at the next, and before the twelfth she was sobbing like a child. She *was* a child. They all were. Jo couldn't look away. It felt like watching Linda Hamilton cry, or Batman. Nadine was still crying when the graduates dragged her upright and turned her to face Pastor Eddie. The big man was breathing hard, his face flushed. "You got anything you'd like to say to me, young lady? To your fellow campers?"

She spat in his face. Bloody mucus glistened in his mustache and on the right lens of his glasses. He brought his hand up and the buckle of his belt split her lips and rocked her head back. That was when it registered for Jo that the girl holding Nadine's left arm was Candace, Gabe's friend, who she'd eaten lunch with a few times. A split second later, as the graduates led Nadine away and two more of them hauled a gray-faced Felix toward the stool, she realized she hadn't seen the other girl since she'd been called in at the house four days earlier. *She's thinner, too,* she thought, watching Candace retreat into the darkness. *She's too thin. That's impossible.*

She caught a glimpse of Nadine's backside, a horror of bloody welts and open wounds, and then the night swallowed all three retreating figures. Something in the fire popped with a noise like a firecracker going off, logs collapsing inward, sparks and cinders rising in a scintillating cloud that lit the faces of the campers up like daybreak. Terror. Nausea. Something that looked for a fleeting moment like arousal.

"You've got a choice to make here," Pastor Eddie rumbled. Felix knelt in front of him, head bent, a graduate to his either side holding him down by the shoulders. "Grace or punishment. Responsibility or rebellion. As hard as I'm hittin' your little friends, the world's gonna hit you one hell of a lot harder if you don't wise up.

"You think if you make it through the summer and go home the way you left it, things are going to get easier? No. Next comes reform school. Juvie. Some of you maybe get tried as adults, wind up doing real time. Plenty of queers in the big house, but those people don't look like you want them to look. They won't touch you how you want to be touched." He licked his lips and bared his teeth in a humorless snarl of a smile. "You remember, no matter what happens next, you can't say nobody ever gave you a chance."

His arm went up. The buckle caught the firelight with a dazzling flash and then it came down and the sharp, hard slap of leather against flesh echoed through the dark.

Gabe caught up with Candace under the hanging lights while the other campers were still lining up to brush their teeth in the mess hall bathrooms. "Hey!" he called, reaching for the sleeve of her shirt. "Wait up! Are you okay?"

She turned just before his fingers brushed the fabric of her shirt. Gabe took an instinctive step back; her face was lost in the deep gloom between two pools of light, which faded in stages up the length of her body. "I'm fine," she said. He could just make out the shape of her face, thinner and more angular but still recognizable. He thought she was smiling at him. "I'm going home tomorrow."

He'd wanted to ask her why she'd helped them beat Nadine, what had happened to her in the wilderness, why she looked so different, but the words seemed to dry up and stick in his throat. Even more than the sight of Pastor Eddie with blood sprayed across his face he found that Candace frightened him, that there was something here he wasn't seeing but could feel, like the film of oily pond scum that clung to you when you got out of the water at Elm Brook Park. He fumbled for something to say.

"I'll . . . I'll give you my address," he said lamely. "We can keep in touch."

She didn't move. He couldn't see her eyes, but he could feel them boring into him, peeling back his face to expose the falseness of his smile, the hesitation in his words, and something deeper, something he wanted to hide from her the way he hid the sissy porn he watched on the family computer, something frilly and weak and maggoty soft that squirmed away from her deeper into the recesses of his thoughts. He couldn't bear to look at it himself. He cleared his throat. "Or . . . or not. We don't have to."

"No," she said at last. "I'd love that. Give Corey the details and he'll get them to me."

He nodded, not trusting his voice, and before he could think whether to hug her or shake her hand or what, she turned and left, her golden hair catching the lamplight. On the back of her neck was a strange little constellation of moles, raised and dark. And then she was gone.

I'm digging up Roy, Gabe thought suddenly. He didn't know where the phrase had come from, or what it meant, but he could feel it in his gut. The others were coming now. He could hear them. He stepped into the alley between Cabins One and Three, waiting for the throng to reach him so he could slip into it.

"What the hell is wrong with her?" asked Malcolm as they followed Corey and Garth through the dark and back toward the cabins. "What *happened* to her? She was only gone a week."

All Shelby could think of was *Invasion of the Body Snatchers*, which Stel had shown her once on a rainy October night. People running in the streets. Emotionless faces in a crowd swiveling to follow any trace of feeling. She'd seen Candace too, fifty impossible pounds lighter, sleek and glistening like a backup dancer in a music video, but she couldn't make herself speak. It was too insane to say out loud.

She's been replaced.

And besides, Shelby couldn't stop thinking about Nadine, about that beautiful face deformed by bruises and swelling, about the horror of her striped and bloodied ass when the graduates had dragged her off with her jeans still down around her ankles. Felix, too. The toughest kids in camp beaten until they screamed, until snot dangled from their nostrils and their mouths hung open in silent agony. *Being tough doesn't mean shit. It won't save you. They don't want us to have leaders.*

She was still trapped in her own thoughts long after the cabin lights went out and the boys of Cabin Two had drifted into their own troubled dreams. Barbs of moonlight slid over the warped floorboards. She thought of the time Stel had left, of the two months last winter when it had been just her and Ruth in the big, empty apartment. There was a feeling in the air, then, a kind of aching, sticky tension like the humid low-pressure fronts that ran ahead of storms. Until the morning after Christmas.

You have no idea, the pain of being a woman. What we go through every month. Do you see this? Judy Chicago painted it in her menstrual blood in 1971, before anyone had ever thought about you. Her body ripped itself apart, tore itself open, and she made art out of it, and you think you can just sweep in and make it yours?

I don't—

Stop. Just stop. If I hear one more lie out of you—

You're hurting me.

The kitchen. The burner. Squeal of metal against metal as she pushed the cast-iron skillet back. *You want to know what it feels like? You want to know what you're trying to take from us?*

Shelby threw off her blanket and slid out of bed, dressed only in her T-shirt and a pair of ugly briefs. She rubbed the pad of waxy scar tissue on the heel of her left hand. The temperature had dropped and she felt uncomfortably aware of her balls, which were stuck to her thigh by sweat, and of the flush in her chest. She adjusted herself, wiped her face on her shirt, and let out a long, quiet breath. Gabe was sucking his thumb in his sleep, all his grown-up vanity melted away. John and Brady were both snoring.

It wasn't hard to move the linens and slip down into the cobwebbed crawl space under the cabin. Loose, pebbly earth shifted under her hands and knees as she crawled through the darkness toward the alley between their cabin and the girls'. She felt for and found the movable section of plywood latticework, backing out awkwardly through the gap and into the bitter desert cold. A minute later she was wriggling through the trapdoor into Cabin Four. She lowered the hatch gently behind her, flushed and sweaty and already second-guessing herself as she squinted in the gloom, looking for Nadine's bunk. Jo, face caught in a beam of moonlight. Felix sleeping on his stomach in the bunk under hers, legs and backside bare, blanket tight around the rest of him.

On the far side of the room Nadine lay propped up on one elbow, looking back at Shelby. Her expression was lost in the shadows of the empty bunk above her, but Shelby could feel the heat of her stare. She crossed the room in a crouch and slid into the bed at Nadine's feet, just able to make out the other girl's outline. Her heart hammered in her chest. She wet her lips, painfully conscious of her belly spilling over the waistband of her underwear, of her little nipples, hard like tight pink rosebuds, and the sparse, itchy stubble on her throat and jaw.

"Are you okay?"

Nadine shook her head. When Shelby, hardly daring to reach out, touched her cheek, she felt the hot, wet trails of tears. The other girl's voice trembled. "I should have killed him," she whispered. "Pastor Eddie, Dave, Enoch—all of them. I'm going to kill them. Gouge their eyes out. Bite off their f-fingers." She sobbed, shoulders shaking. "I should have . . . I should have . . ."

Shelby kissed her. For a moment Nadine stiffened and Shelby felt a horrible certainty that she'd done the wrong thing; then the other girl's mouth opened against hers. Her split lip had scabbed over but she still tasted like blood, hot iron and copper mixing with their spit, which caught the moonlight as they pulled apart and Nadine took hold of Shelby's head and guided her down toward her naked crotch. The taller girl lay back, wincing as she wriggled into position, and Shelby smelled the deep, dark heat of her period in the moment before her lips met Nadine's bruised and swollen pussy. She could hardly think. In her fantasies of slipping into Nadine's bed she'd pictured stroking the other girl's hair, cradling her as she wept; things you'd see on the cover of one of Stel's weepy lesbian romance novels. She licked the soft, wet flesh in front of her, trying not to hyperventilate.

What if I eat pussy like a man?

"Like this," Nadine whispered, pushing Shelby harder against her. "Use your whole tongue. Use your nose."

The taste of blood was overwhelming at first, but Nadine's hands on the back of her head made it easy to sink into the experience, to run the flat of her tongue over fragrant skin and nose at the other girl's clitoris, which was bigger and firmer than she'd expected. The bunk was cramped, her feet against the footboard, Nadine reaching up to grip one of the slats above for balance, and as Shelby wormed her way deeper into the other girl she found herself unable to breathe, mouth and nostrils lost in musky, perfumed folds which slicked her face and gummed her eyelashes.

This is happening, she thought, a thrill pricking its way up her spine to where short nails clung to her scalp. *It's real.*

Nadine wrapped her thighs around Shelby's head, pulling her closer. "God," she whispered. She ran her thumb along the edge of Shelby's ear. Melting. Taste of life and blood. Her smell was everywhere. Her skin. The scabbed edges of the wounds on her backside rough against Shelby's fingers. "My good girl.

"My good girl."

Smith woke in the dark to a terrible smell. It reminded her a little of the stink that had led her to the body of her guinea pig, Peter Pan, who had escaped his cage one night and gotten into the walls of the house in Tucson. He'd died in there, and the smell of his tiny body decomposing, ripe and sickly sweet, had flooded the whole downstairs. In the end her father's friend Jim had to cut out a piece of drywall to get to him. Not long after, Smith had seen them together behind the pool house, Jim's big hand between her father's legs, his mustache brushing her father's throat. Even the memory made her feel hot and sick and flustered, distant from herself, like she was on her period.

She sat up, sleep falling away. It was warm, cloyingly so, and she was soaked in sweat, the T-shirt she'd slept in stuck to her skin like melted taffy. The ground beneath her was wet rock, slippery and furred with some kind of slimy algae or moss. The sound of water dripping echoed and re-echoed. It felt like she was in a basement, or a cave. Her stomach clenched with claustrophobic terror at the thought.

Gradually, Smith realized it wasn't quite dark anymore. She *was* in a cave, and on the cavern ceiling pinpricks of bluish light were kindling slowly from the gloom, some still, others moving in slow waves. She thought they must be glowworms, or some kind of firefly. Alan loved watching nature documentaries. Smith thought they were boring, could find nothing moving about footage of howler monkeys scratching themselves and eating fruit, but it meant a chance to press her leg against Alan's, and to see the blush rise in his round face, to hold his sweaty hand in hers. Everyone else called him Tabitha, or sometimes Tabby, but they were speaking to a ghost. Only Smith and a few friends at school knew the truth, had been entrusted to hold it between them. She missed him so badly. She wished they could have seen each other one last time before his family moved, but after her mother found them together it had been nonstop hellfire. Her new church was scary. Smith had heard other women tell her mother she'd been raped her whole marriage, that a faggot had profaned the sacrament to humiliate her.

More glowworms lit the dark. Smith screamed, the sound echoing monstrously as she scrambled back over slick rock and what felt like some kind of lichen. No more than five or six feet away, Dave and another counselor, a pockmarked woman of twenty or so whose name Smith didn't know, were crouched among lumpen stalagmites, watching her in silence. Their eyes shone like coins, like the eyes of animals at night. More eyes gleamed beyond them, their owners' faces too deep in shadow to make out. There were dozens of them. Smith's back hit stone. The cavern wall. She froze, breathing hard.

Where are you going, insect?

The voice burned. It itched. It felt as though something had crawled up her ear canal and out into her brain, something soft and raw and many-legged skittering over the lobes and folds hidden away inside her skull, feelers swishing over her gray matter. The smell in the air grew stronger. She curled against the cavern wall, digging her nails into the sides of her head. *It isn't real. This isn't happening.*

Are you ready for me, Smith? Are you loose and wet and dripping? Did you touch yourself when you spied on Daddy and his special friend? Did you know he diddles little boys, Smith? They all do. I can show you, if you want to see.

Smith peeked out through her fingers just in time to see the people in the shadows scatter. The patter of their footsteps faded as they vanished in among the jagged spires of rock. Her heart pounded. She fought for breath in the close, humid air. *Please,* she thought, her nails beginning to draw blood from her forehead and cheeks. *Please, make it stop.*

Soon, Smith. Very soon it will all be over. You'll never have to feel afraid again.

Something soft brushed Smith's arm. She screamed, flailing in an ecstasy of terror and disgust, and ran headlong into the dark. Every step felt like tripping. Every moment she was certain she would smash her skull open on a stalactite, or slip and break her leg. Silhouettes darted around the edges of her vision. Her glasses were all fogged and grimy. Something ran across her path. The pockmarked counselor, a hideous grin splitting her features, sprinting bent nearly double with her arms folded tight against her chest. Smith broke right. Her foot slid on the slimy stones, but she caught herself on all fours and scrabbled forward, skinning palms and knuckles on rough rock, so terrified she could hardly think. One of her nails split with a sharp, sickening shock as she dragged herself up over a fallen stone.

Please Daddy please Daddy please please please help me, help me, I'm so scared.

She found a tunnel and squirmed into it without thought. More worms lit her way. Strands of silk beaded with luminous moisture dangling from their distant bodies caught in her hair and stuck to her face, stinging her skin. The tunnel narrowed. Whoops and screams behind her. The glimmer of water ahead. Her shirt tore on a protruding rock. A line of pain across her belly.

Poor girl. Come to me. Let me taste you. Wear you.

She forced herself through the choke point and into the gallery beyond, leaving skin and blood smeared over the rock. She was crying. She wished the other girls were with her, or handsome Felix, so tall and strong. She was useless. Stupid. Weak. She tripped over a ridge in the cavern floor, biting her tongue as her jaw hit stone. She tasted blood. By the time she got to her feet, the worms above had brightened enough that she could see the clots of matted hair and oddments of bone and keratin lying around the filthy water of the pool. She'd fallen close to one, and to her horror she could make out the faint outline of a body through its filmy skin. It squirmed. There were close to a dozen she could see. The cries from behind her were getting louder.

You'll never be alone again. Poor girl. Darling girl. The flesh is warm. We're waiting for you.

She forced herself to climb over the horrible cocoon. It shifted under her. Something tore with a wet pop and suddenly her arm was wet up to the elbow. She touched soft flesh. An arm. A breast. Pruny fingers caressed her wrist. She sobbed and pulled herself onward, putting her foot straight through another caul. A skinny leg flopped out onto the cavern floor in a rush of stinking fluid. She stumbled onward. *Am I dead? Is this Hell? Jesus I'm sorry I'm sorry please don't.* She slipped. A blow to the side of her head. The water. Things in it. Squirming. Eager. Her glasses gone.

Never alone touch you feel you mine wear your skin stretch out your little holes baby worm before me bow, crawl in the dark blind fetus, little clot.

She fumbled after the glasses with shaking, bloody hands. Her fingertips found the frames. She put them on, blinking blood and condensation from her eyes, and as she did something reared up from the pool, something huge and pale and awful, all flaking skin and filthy hair and dirty, shedding feathers. Thought fled. Smith tore her glasses from her face and twisted them, broken glass and metal digging into her scratched palms. She heard herself screaming, or laughing, but it seemed a very long way away. The only mercy left to her as the thing seized hold of her and pressed her to the stone beneath its crushing, fetid bulk, fronds and tentacles unfolding from the lump of suet that was its head and feeling for her nostrils, her tear ducts, the canals of her ears, was that she had already lost her mind.

X

MRE

The cows were the one thing at Camp Resolution Malcolm liked. Their big, dark eyes were soft and gentle, and they smelled like it did out by his aunt Charlotte and uncle Ruben's place in Redding. Dry grass and dung and the spicy musk of their sun-warmed flanks. Today they were grazing in the foothills of the mountains a two-hour drive outside the camp, which at least meant there was some distance between him and Betty. She'd had a hard-on for him the last few days, ever since Nadine and Felix got the belt. The next day the graduates had all been gone, packed onto buses and driven off in the predawn glow, the air in the camp charged with a sense of sudden change.

Betty was getting worse. Just that morning she'd tripped Brady as he came out of the mess; the kid hit the ground so hard he'd lost a tooth, and no one had done anything. Digging ditches in the middle of the desert sucked, but at least the cows and the backbreaking work were a distraction after two days of looking over his shoulder for any sign of ginger. He'd tried striking up a chorus of "Sixteen Tons," but Shelby and the Tighty-Whiteys had just looked at him like he was insane. So. Digging.

Corey and Garth had stuck around to watch them for the first few hours before taking off in the truck. He'd watched the plume of dust and grit it left in its wake snake away across the flat hard-pan below until it vanished into the afternoon glare. The ditch's parameters were marked out with surveyors' stakes with ribbons of orange plastic fluttering from their tops.

"What the fuck is this even for?" snarled Vick. He threw down his shovel. "Fucking ditch in the middle of nowhere."

"They're gonna bring your sister out here for her next period," said Malcolm. "This is like, you know, a spillway, like they have for dams."

"Malcolm," Gabe warned, shooting him a look.

Vick stared at him, face red and blotchy. "Say that again."

Malcolm dug his spade into the ground and leaned on the handle, grinning, and launched into his best Foghorn Leghorn. "Ah say, ah say, boy, when ya sistah's puss-ay gets ta gushin', this heah trench goan absorb that theah ova-flow."

John and Gabe caught Vick before he got to Malcolm, but only just. The olive-skinned boy struggled and stamped. "Let go of me! I'm gonna bust his fuckin' head. He has it coming. You know he does!"

"God damn it, Malcolm," shouted Gabe, hanging onto the back of Vick's shirt. "Take a walk!"

Malcolm put his hands up, backing away. *Why'd you do that?* he asked himself. *He's a shit, but he didn't do anything to you.* "All right, all right." It was hard to tear his eyes away from the sight of John, muscles bulging in his big, thick arms and sweat standing out on his broad forehead, wrestling Vick back in a bear hug.

Vick's eyes narrowed to dark slits. "You're dead, bitch," he snarled. "Just wait until your girlfriends aren't around."

Gabe let go of the other boy as though he'd been burned, his face a mask of rage, and suddenly John was on his ass in the dirt and Vick was storming toward where Malcolm stood fantasizing about a fist crashing into his jaw, about a man's hand holding his head in place, about the night he'd kissed Artie Merman at Logan Corder's sleepover birthday party. Another boy had seen them, it turned out, and when Malcolm got home his mother was waiting in the kitchen with soap and a soaked washcloth tied with knots.

"Malcolm," John shouted. "*Go.*"

Malcolm ran. He was fast. He'd always been fast, and Vick wasn't much of a runner. After a few minutes of sliding down slopes of loose, sandy soil and hoofing it over broad stretches of sun-heated rock, the sound of the other boy's labored breathing started fading. By the time Malcolm made it to the thin belt of dead pines he'd glimpsed from the truck bed when they'd driven out, there was no sign of Vick at all. Malcolm stumbled to a halt, looking back over his shoulder at the slopes and plateaus and crooked slabs of rock calved from the mountainside rising back up toward the dig. Scrub brush grew sparsely from the red and tan soil. He sucked in deep, shuddering breaths until his heart stopped pounding.

Why'd you do that? he wondered, wiping sweat from his throat with the sleeve of his work shirt. It was like a heat rose up in him sometimes, an urge to slide the right jab like a needle into any opening, an ache in his mouth that only running it could satisfy. It was so easy with other boys. Most of them lost it the second you mentioned their mothers, which he thought was kind of a pussy move. He wouldn't care if someone went after *his* mother. They could fuck her for all he cared. He wiped his face on his sleeve, sniffing.

Something wet touched his palm. He yelped, spinning around as his mind conjured visions of Pastor Eddie erupting from the tree line to cut him in half with a sword or some kind of wet, dripping monster like the thing in *Alien* rearing up over him. He staggered back a step. It was the dog. She sat on her haunches, feather-duster tail sweeping back and forth in the dirt as she panted, grinning at him. Behind her the dead pines leaned drunkenly over a carpet of dry needles, most of them bare-branched and stripped of their bark.

"Jesus," he breathed, crouching down to give her his hand to sniff. "You scared the shit out of me, girl."

She licked his knuckles and stared up at him with soulful eyes. He wondered what kind of dog she was, with her long muzzle and silky, tangled cream-and-brown coat.

"I don't have anything for you," he told her, scratching her behind the ears. "How'd you wind up out here?"

The dog yawned, stood, shook herself, and trotted back into the woods. *I should go back to the site,* he thought. *Apologize. See if John's okay.* Instead he found himself heading in among the dead gray teeth of the pines, the spicy scent of layered needles filling his nostrils as he followed the dog's wagging tail across dry creek beds and over fallen trees scrawled all over where beetles had eaten pathways into the pith of their trunks. They passed the stripped and fleshless carcass of what he thought must be a deer, the dog pausing to sniff at its ribs and the scraps of leathery hide still clinging to them, and twice Malcolm heard rustling as though something small were fleeing through the sparse and dying undergrowth. Mice, maybe, if there were mice out here. He didn't know what lived in the desert.

I don't even know what state I'm in.

The dog turned uphill, the shadows deepening as the trees thickened. Malcolm ducked under an arch where two fallen trunks supported each other over a dry gulch. It looked as though water had cut the ground here, but it must have been a long, long time ago. His lips were dry and cracked, and as he scrambled up the stony incline after his guide, he realized just how hot he was, his shirt sticking to his back, sweat stinging his eyes. *What if Corey and Garth come back for us while I'm out here?* he thought, watching the dog's hindquarters as she flitted nimbly up the slope ahead of him. *What if I can't find the way back?*

The trees thinned out as they got higher, the stone faces of the little cut in the hillside closing in until Malcolm had to turn sideways to follow his guide. "Whaddya got up here, girl?" he puffed, sidling through the narrow gap. The edges of the cut met overhead, forming a small tunnel. Dead roots and nubs of rock caught at his clothes. Loose soil sifted down onto his face. Probably she was leading him to a dead gopher or something, just in case he was hungry. He forced his way onward, dirt pouring down on him now as he scraped against the stone, hardly able to see, and then he was stumbling over open ground and ahead of him was total blackness.

A rectangular doorway gaped in a concrete facade set back at the end of the short tunnel, which he now saw was shored up by sun-bleached beams. The dog, with one last quizzical look back at him, trotted through it and disappeared into the gloom. For a moment he quailed. He was still, to his shame, afraid of the dark. He hated so much as to open the basement door at home. Hated to creep down the hall to use the bathroom in the night. He always felt as though something in that dark was going to grab him, was going to croon his name as it wrapped itself around his legs and dragged him screaming out of the reality he knew.

But the dog had brought him here, and he was curious. Burning with it. He couldn't pass it up. He swallowed, set his jaw, and followed her in.

Nadine hated crying. She'd hated it ever since she could remember, ever since she'd seen her older half sister, Tiffany, sobbing through the keyhole of the bathroom door and felt a hot, compulsive stab of loathing, a certainty that she would never look that weak. But she had. In front of everyone in camp she'd cried and screamed and begged like Tiffy with one of her boyfriends. *Don't say that, don't do that, you're hurting me.*

The clatter of dishes shifting in the sink as Celine scrubbed nearly made her jump out of her skin, which made her tear up again out of frustration, which made her furious. *Fucking pussy,* she thought, pushing her little pile of chopped peppers to the left of her cutting board with her knife. *Pussy. Pussy.* She set the knife down and pinched the skin on the inside of her wrist, twisting it between thumb and forefinger until her eyes dried and the kitchen swam back into focus. *Get it together.*

Her head hurt. All of her hurt, from her bruised legs to her scabbed and lacerated ass, but her head hurt the worst. When she closed her eyes she saw a point of white light burning in the dark, a pinhole flare so bright it felt as though she were staring into the sun, and stray thoughts kept interrupting her inner monologue like pedestrians bolting into traffic. For an hour in the morning she'd kept thinking *What are you, running for office?* until she wanted to claw through her ears to get at whatever part of her brain was repeating the stupid phrase.

". . . died when she was, like, a toddler or something," Celine was saying to Jo, who dried and racked dishes with mechanical efficiency as the other girl babbled. "And they started this whole place to give kids in trouble a home and I just think it's totally inspirational to turn something so sad into this amazing opportunity, because honestly we're so lucky to be here. Marianne says sometimes they take on graduates as counselors, and I'm going to apply as soon as I'm old enough."

"Yeah," said Jo.

From upstairs came the creak of bedsprings and a woman's high, thin scream of pain. The ceiling shook, flakes of plaster spinning through the air like a giant's dandruff. They'd been doing it on and off all morning, ever since Pastor Eddie sauntered through the kitchen with his dry, papery voice and his big, soft hands, saying *Somethin' smells good, girls* as he squeezed their shoulders, and then on into the living room and up the stairs to fuck his matchstick wife. Nadine imagined Mrs. Glover clinging to the headboard with her skeletal hands, inner thighs raw like chicken skin, teeth clenched as her husband thrust himself into her, fucking and fucking until finally she started to tear open.

What are you, running for office?

She hit herself in the head with the heel of her hand hard enough that the others on kitchen duty stopped what they were doing. Celine and Jo looked at her strangely. Nadine flashed them a tight, split-lipped grin. Celine was the kind of cunt who was only tough when you were curled in a ball and pissing yourself from sheer exhaustion at her feet. She and Dana hadn't dared come near her since the beating.

Try it, thought Nadine, a real urge to hurt someone bubbling up in the pit of her stomach. To break her knuckles on the soggy hamburger mess of a ruined face. *Give me a reason and I'll choke you with your French braid you sniveling cuntbreath American Girl doll bitch.*

The ceiling kept shaking. A flake of plaster fell into the soapy water standing in the sink. It floated tranquilly over the submerged cups and dishes, the shimmering drifts of flatware. Nadine turned back to her pile of unchopped peppers. Suddenly she didn't want to beat on Celine, or anyone for that matter. She wanted to cry again. She wanted her mother. Her vision swam as she set her palm against the knife's back and cut into the next pepper, splitting it neatly in half. Halve the halves, gut the seeds, walk and rock the knife along each section until she had six neat slices for each quarter. The rhythm of the kitchen blending with the creak and thump above.

Does Shelby like having her dick sucked? she wondered, shifting cut sections aside to make room for the next vegetable. Penises unsettled her, wrinkled and soft and so horribly vulnerable, but the thought of Shelby's in her mouth only made her feel curious. *I'll ask her. I'll go over there tonight the way she came to me*—for a moment, before she tamped the feelings down and set a lid over them, she felt an overwhelming surge of emotion at the memory of the other girl crawling into her bed, of that tender little hand on hers.

"Are you okay?"

She didn't notice she'd cut the tip off her left index finger until she was on the floor, her head in Felix's lap as he gripped her injured hand, wrapped in a dishcloth, to keep pressure on the throbbing digit. Celine sat white-faced on the floor in front of the sink, staring at the red bloom in the center of the cloth and the dark droplets staining Felix's jeans. And then Cheryl was there, crouching low, her face close to Nadine's, and the smell of hydrogen peroxide bloomed sharp and harsh and chemical. The cloth peeled back. Stinging. *I'm crying,* Nadine realized, tears of pain leaking down her cheeks. There was snot on her upper lip. *They can see me. They can see me.*

She could smell her mother's perfume, always covering the stink of flop sweat, always hugging her *after,* holding her so smotheringly close, saying *He didn't mean it, you just need to give him a little time,* and the oil and sawdust smell of her father as he sank huge and heavy onto the edge of her bed, hands clasped between his knees, and heaved out another tired apology while his big, sad, hungry eyes gnawed at her until she said *It's okay, Dad,* and sometimes he'd put a hand on her shoulder and sometimes he'd say *No, it's not* and then the tears would start and she'd sit there, her hand numb in his, and think *I'll never cry. I'll never be like that.*

"Watch what you're fucking doing," said Cheryl, and for a moment all Nadine's self-pitying thoughts withdrew like a crowd from the sight of a drawn gun. Something was wrong with Cheryl's face. For an instant, just the briefest of split seconds, she had seen something *flex* under the counselor's flawless skin. She thought of thin, smiling Candace dragging her toward the pastor's camp chair.

It wasn't her. She's been replaced.

Cheryl's eyes narrowed. Her fingers tightened on Nadine's calf. Nadine forced herself not to scream, not to start kicking and fighting. She did her best to look merely frightened. It wasn't hard. A moment passed, then Cheryl rose and left. Felix helped Nadine to a sitting position, asking if she was okay, if she needed anything, but she couldn't answer.

What the hell is she?

The first thing Malcolm noticed as his eyes adjusted to the dark of the bunker's entryway, lit only by the tunnel mouth behind him, was the sedimentary layer of dark, shredded plastic packaging strewn over the cool concrete. He crouched down to get a closer look, the dog panting somewhere ahead so that her breaths echoed from the walls, as though a dozen dogs were all around him. He found one scrap still largely intact and picked it up between his thumb and forefinger, wrinkling his nose at the earthy chemical smell emanating from its greasy interior. It was about the size of a softcover and in plain, faded typeface it read:

MEAL, READY-TO-EAT, INDIVIDUAL
MENU NO. 12
SCALLOPED POTATOES WITH HAM

He let the bag slip through his fingers and flutter back to the floor. "Holy Red Scare, Batman," he muttered to himself, standing. He'd heard about places like this. His dad had told him that a bunch of wackos built themselves bomb shelters back before the Wall came down. Sometimes, Don said, their families didn't even know about the bunkers right under their feet. That had kept Malcolm up at night for weeks, until his mother caught him digging in the garden at three a.m. and he'd broken down in tears, unable to explain what he was doing.

He stepped over the threshold of the iron pressure door, rusted open so fully that it didn't budge an inch even when he leaned his full weight on it, and into a little antechamber, more packaging rustling underfoot. In the next room a dim yellow panel of overhead lights flickered on as the dog loped by, a plastic packet in her jaws. *It must be a motion sensor,* Malcolm thought. He ducked through the inner airlock and stepped down to the sunken space beyond.

Another panel of lights buzzed to life, half of them flickering, most of the rest long since dead, throwing the recessed bookshelves stuffed with disintegrating paperbacks and the moth-eaten couches set along the walls into sharp relief. A big wood-frame television hunched on the far side of the room, right where a fireplace would have been in a real house. He could hear something rustling around under the couches. Rodents, maybe. Pale little moths no bigger than quarters fluttered through the flickering light. He hugged himself against the cold.

I should get back, he thought again, but the lure of the rooms opening off the main area was too strong. The first was a pantry, row after row of those packaged meals spilling off of wire racks, some torn at, some gnawed through by little teeth. The dog was shaking her head to tear one open even as he stepped inside. Malcolm scanned the shelves. Franks in red sauce. Bacon and greens. More ham and scalloped potatoes. Who had lived here? Someone sick? Insane? It felt like a sad place.

The bathroom was small and cell-like, tile over concrete, the shower recessed in the wall behind a glazed plastic sliding door. The door fought him when he tried to get it open. It was jammed, maybe the metal rim had rusted shut, or it was stuck on something. *This is how people die in horror movies,* he thought, and at that moment the door flew open and slammed into its slot in the wall, and Malcolm screamed in terror as the flickering lights reflected off something smooth and white and—

Bones. It was just bones. A skeleton lying curled on its back at the bottom of the shower. Some of it had been disarticulated and strewn over the dirty tiles, showing marks where something had chewed on them. A splintered rib. A length of shinbone cracked and gnawed at one end. *Coyotes,* he told himself, but his imagination bubbled over with stick-thin cave dwellers, hair matted and filthy, eyes sunken in deep sockets, lipping leathery flesh from their father's remains. *They'd be blind after so long in here. Afraid of the sun. Afraid to leave this place.*

He knelt for a closer look and wondered with a sudden surge of nauseating fascination if the body in the shower had slipped and broken something, perhaps aggravated some miniscule spinal deformity, and then starved to death folded up in that tiled cell, the water beating down on them until there was no water left, only the rattling and groaning of empty pipes. Was it really that different from a coffin, though? Either way you were dead and gone. *Cold cuts,* his dad always called corpses. Just meat. He forced the rusted shower door shut anyway, if only because he didn't like the way the skull's dark sockets seemed to follow him.

The last room held only a small dresser set into the wall, a twin bed covered in rumpled, rotted linens in which it looked like something had made a nest for itself, and a tall, narrow wall safe, slightly ajar. The dog appeared at his side as he stood in the doorway. She licked his palm and for a moment he thought about going right then, about ditching this sad little hole in the ground where some poor weirdo's whole fucked-up worldview had slipped and fallen in the shower and then lain there staring at its own limp junk and jumbled limbs, waiting to die. He felt like someone was watching him.

Somehow instead he found himself gripping the wall safe's corroded handle. He pulled. Nothing. Harder, and a growl of rusted hinges. He set a foot against the wall and heaved. The locker swung open, first an inch, then all at once so that he fell and bruised his ass and the dog jumped back with a frightened yelp. It took him a moment to stop shaking, to step close again so he could make sure what he'd seen was right.

It was. The cabinet was full of dynamite.

"A bunker in the hills," said Felix, crushing down the dull ache in his chest. The stiff, chewy corn tacos the mess was serving today made him think of his mother's tortillas, thick and fluffy. He kept thinking about things like that. He could feel himself softening. Opening up. He didn't like it. "What were you even doing out there?"

"We were digging holes for a fence," said John. "Malcolm picked a fight with Vick, because he's an idiot. Vick chased him off, and there was a whole, like, fallout shelter in the woods. There were guns, food, a skeleton, so—"

"Who's telling this story?" Malcolm asked, exasperated.

"Keep your voices down," said Nadine. Felix followed her stare to where Cheryl prowled the edge of the mess, circling the tables like a shark. "A bunker's good news. If the MREs are still in plastic, they should be edible. My uncle Jason's in the army and he says those things last fifty years if you store them right. That means we can stop worrying about granola bars. After we make our call, we'll stop off there to stock up."

"It was . . . kind of sad there," said Malcolm. He shrugged at their looks of incredulity. "Just a feeling. But yeah, it's better than stealing two granola bars at a time and getting whipped for it."

"I've been thinking, we should do something to make sure they don't follow us after we make the call," said Felix. "Some kind of distraction, maybe." The idea of hurting the Glovers excited him in a way he didn't fully understand, except that it felt like his fantasies of strangling his father did sometimes. "The knobs are always coming off the stove; the metal's all stripped. You could leave the gas on—"

"No," said Nadine, shaking her head. "This shit is too fucked up, we don't know who we might hurt. What if they're keeping Smith in the house? The rest of the kids who've disappeared?"

"Should we, um," John interjected, visibly flustered. "Should we maybe try to get other people out of here with us? Should we try to find Smith?"

There was a moment of silence. Felix knew they couldn't do it, that to add another step to a plan already hanging by a thread would all but doom it. Still, he hoped someone would say they should. It felt like the kind of thing good people were supposed to do. The silence stretched on. Finally, Nadine spoke.

"We can't," she said. She looked exhausted. Drained. Even beyond all her bruises, scrapes, cuts, and other injuries, she looked tired in a way Felix had only ever seen adults look tired. Like she wanted to lie down and close her eyes and not get up. "We'd fuck it up trying to add more people. We'd need more cars, more places to escape to, more food. We'd keep making it more likely that someone would grass on us to Pastor Eddie. It has to be just us, and it has to be now. We're leaving tonight."

"Tonight?" Brady squeaked through a mouthful of taco.

"We've got no way of knowing when it'll be our turn for their little wilderness walk," said Nadine, her voice low. "I don't know about you, but I don't want to find out what they do to kids out there. Remember all the graduates around the fire? Just . . . staring. Empty. I won't wind up like that. Boys, Shel, you come to us after lights out. We'll figure it out from there."

Gabe was frowning down at his tray, where a lone taco, some wilted romaine lettuce, and a square of grayish cornbread sat almost untouched. "Does this taste weird to you?"

Shelby, silent through most of lunch, seemed to come back to herself at that. "Yeah. Kind of, like, dry and crunchy?"

"Yeah."

Malcolm elbowed Gabe, breaking the taller boy's concentration. "Will you fuckin' eat something, Horn? Kate Moss called; she wants her rib cage back."

Gabe sighed as the others laughed, though Felix could tell he was pleased with the comparison. He'd seen that giddy, feverish look before in the eyes of the girls at school who threw up in the bathroom between periods, and who had razor burn on their arms from shaving the dark fur that grew there.

Felix took a bite of his own dinner, stale corn tortilla splintering between his teeth. It *did* taste funny, under the spices. Probably mold or something, but he'd need his strength if they were going to hike out and break into the house tonight.

So much for keeping my head down.

XI

FREE YOUR MIND

It was dark when Jo woke from a dream of white cloth billowing over hidden flesh. Moonlight spilled over the floorboards, which seemed almost to ripple like a lake's surface in a high wind. Nadine's bed was empty, she realized, and the cabin door was open. When she swung her legs over the edge of her mattress she could feel the air caressing them, stroking her bare skin with love. Felix's bed was empty, too. *I want him to make love to me,* she realized. *I want him to put his hand inside me.*

The cabin door was unlocked. Jo stepped out into the night, taking a deep breath of the cool, dry air. She felt as though she could have inhaled the world, as though each breath coated her insides with a reflection of the night sky and the blazing beacons of the bulbs strung up between the cabins. Something in her ached to float away among those lights. *Everything Oji-chan ever said to me, he meant. He meant it with all his heart. He said I'm brave, so I must be brave. He said there's nothing wrong with me.*

She closed her eyes, swaying where she stood, and the thought that she was probably high on something flitted through her mind. She'd smoked weed a few times with Carly Prince, who she'd known since kindergarten and whose breasts she regularly imagined burying her face in when she masturbated, but this didn't feel like that. It felt like falling into herself, like missing the last step on a set of stairs and then hanging forever in that moment, your senses all blown out of your body as you tried to recalibrate, to summon some response to the collision between certainty and chaos.

They put something in our food.

She opened her eyes. For the first time she noticed that there were others in the thoroughfare between the cabins, close to a dozen of them. A few lay on their backs, staring up into the void. Two girls down at the far end by Cabins Eight and Seven looked like they were having sex. Just the idea of the sound of a wet mouth on the flushed and tender skin of her throat made Jo shudder with euphoria. The air grew tight around her. The lights burned brighter and she saw that they were caged in soapy matrixes of some translucent substance, shifting fractals that collapsed and formed and fell apart again in scintillating bursts of color. "Wow," she whispered, and the word flashed purple, gold, and silver as it tumbled from her tongue and spilled into the world. She laughed, snorting a little.

I am very, very high.

She made it down the cabin's steps and the shock as the soles of her feet met cold earth shivered up through her body in blue-white waves of static. She giggled again. Someone grabbed at the hem of her shirt as she passed by them and she danced aside, her body tunneling through the air so that as she looked over her shoulder at their shadow she saw a dozen of herself smeared back along her path in a rainbow of wild colors. "I get it," she said, raising a hand to feel her own lips. They were so soft. A red sensation, tinged with deep, warm pink. "I get it."

"What?" asked a boy sitting sprawled against the side of one of the cabins. Vick, who'd called Shelby those awful names. He was looking at his hands.

My parents would shit if they knew I was friends with a Korean transsexual.

"I said I get it," she breathed, but he wasn't paying attention and the gong-like ripples of her voice passed over him without his notice, leaving him pale and haggard. She left him there, drifting past the lights of the mess hall, where dark figures stood in doorways and at windows, watching her with eyes that burned like starlight, and on to the embers of the bonfire and the empty logs and camp chairs set around it. The ghost of the fire still danced in the air, sparks and cinders drifting on the cold night wind. When she'd seen Nadine and Felix beaten, part of her had wished that it was her, not them, on display like that, her ass clenching in anticipation of each crack of the belt, her snot and tears mingling and dripping from her chin as she squirmed and wailed. For a moment she was in the locker room of the Concord YMCA, a travel meet three years before, and a dozen girls were pinching and groping her, hissing "*Dyke, dyke, dyke*" and calling her "jap" and "gook" and her friend Helen Strand was staring at her through the press of bodies, eyes wide, not going for help, not moving, not trying to stop it.

I want to be nailed to a cross and burned, and I want everyone to think how beautiful I look and how sorry they are.

At the edge of the camp she found Brady, waifish in boxers and a too-big T-shirt, staring up at the top of the chain-link fence. He turned as she approached. His eyes were huge. "Are we still doing the plan?"

"The plan?"

"Calling your grandpa."

She looked out at the open desert. Through the lattice of the fence it seemed as though the world were carved apart into dark little diamonds, none of it quite fitting with the rest. To pick up a phone and light a golden line of fire between this wasteland and New Jersey seemed like magic, and Brady had come here to do it with her. She reached for his hand. He gave it to her. There was no need to find whatever entrance Malcolm's dog had used, because they were made of air. They could step over the fence. They could rise up forever into infinity.

"Let's do it. Give me a boost."

"What do you think pretty boy's doing over there?" asked Malcolm. They were outside, though John couldn't remember how they'd gotten there. Gabe stood a little ways off, just past the end of the row of cabins. It looked like he was staring at the moon.

John had never noticed just how big the moon looked out here in the flat country. It seemed to take up half the sky, as huge and round and pale as he was.

Are those bad things to be? Do I dislike them?

It had never occurred to him to think about it, but here in the watery light with Malcolm beside him and the camp's other kids all around them, thoughts felt looser, prone to crumble at a single touch. In the back of his mind John knew something was wrong, that maybe they'd been drugged, but whenever he tried to imagine why the pastor and his staff had done it he was swamped by waves of pure euphoria, the world around him blazing with wild color, the cabins transformed into soaring spires of oak and shingles like something out of a fairytale. Maybe it was like Ms. Armitage's lessons. Some kind of brainwashing.

"Why do you call him that?" asked John. He knew he'd waited too long before answering, but he could see the lines connecting words, sagging wires of gold along which glowing beads slid silently, conveying thoughts from mind to mind, so it was harder to know when to speak, and what to say. Anyway, Malcolm would understand. He was so close, taller than John. They were holding hands, somehow.

Malcolm's brow furrowed for a moment. "What, 'pretty boy'? Just look at him."

John brought a hand to Malcolm's cheek before he could stop himself, before he could bury the urge to touch the other boy beneath a thousand different excuses. *Fat. Useless. Stupid. Chickenshit. Why would he want you?* Malcolm's eyes went wide. He was speechless, for once. "But you're prettier," said John, and as a fierce blush washed over his chest and face he rose up on the balls of his feet and kissed the other boy. Malcolm let out a little squeal of delight and wrapped his long, thin arms tight around John. That cutting mouth was alive against John's, that acid tongue jammed overenthusiastically past his lips and teeth to lap at nothing in particular.

Oh my God, he's so bad at kissing, thought John. It delighted him, somehow, that someone so beautiful could be such absolute shit at making out. Their mouths made a seal, Malcolm trying to eat his nose and upper lip. They broke apart and John saw tears on Malcolm's cheeks, diamond-bright and trailing silver fire behind them.

"It's okay," said John. He smiled. "I'll show you how I like it."

"That's where you go," whispered Nadine, running her fingers through the fuzz on Shelby's scalp. The soft hairs parted the skin of her palms, but there was no pain. Her body had begun to open. Every sensation seemed to echo through it and rebound out into the night, magnified to a thundering pitch, a shout of joy that resonated at reality's precise frequency and so became it. Every breath tore her open wider, a joyous wound gaping in the moonlight, Shelby's fingers inside her and her mouth on Nadine's throat.

"I want to touch you perfectly," said Nadine. "I want you to feel nothing but joy. I love you so much. Are you here with me?"

Is this real?

"It is," said Shelby. "It is. I'm real. I'm yours. They cut me out of my mother and shipped me to America, they stole me for themselves, but it was really so I could be here with you. I'm going to be with you forever." Shelby's mouth found Nadine's ear and waves of bright white pleasure washed over her, cupping her skull in their foamy swells, racing up her sinuses and bursting from her pores in a clean mist. She opened her mouth to taste the air. The earth was cold and stuck to her bare ass as she shifted, the rough wood of the cabin's side scratching her back.

Shelby's lips moved like a moth's wings, soft against the inner ridges of her ear. "Sometimes I pretend my mother, my real mother, knew I was a girl."

Nadine thought maybe she came then, a gentle roar passing through her, her legs going weak and the muscles banding her pelvis unclenching, and she wrapped the other girl in her arms and kissed her on the lips, the chin, the eyelids. "You're a girl," she whispered back. Someone was screaming somewhere, but the shapes in the thoroughfare were just shapes, twisting and shifting in the light. Shelby's face was the surface of the world. "You're a girl. You're a girl."

She guided Shelby's hand down the neck of her shirt to cup her breast. "Are you here with me?" she asked again. The word was red and white and yellow, flashing as it sank into itself like Wile E. Coyote leaving a hole in the shape of his silhouette through wall after wall until the outline of it shrank down to nothing, reduced to a pinprick by perspective. She fell into it and it closed soft and warm around her and grew arms that held her tight and a round, earnest face with a button nose and a little double chin, which she loved.

"I'm here with you," said Shelby, leaning her forehead against Nadine's. "I'm here. I'm here."

For a while Gabe lay in the dirt and watched Malcolm's glistening finger, slick with spit, push slowly up and into John. *He looks like ice cream,* thought Gabe. *He looks like a dish of ice cream, so sweet and big and soft. I want to hold him on my tongue. I want to sleep against him and be a baby again and start over with different parents. I want to put his breast in my mouth. He has breasts, and it's not fair that he does, it's disgusting, or it's beautiful, or I hate him, or something is very wrong.*

He closed his eyes. When he opened them he was alone, the cabins a ways off and the voices of the others rendered soft and insubstantial by the distance. He kept picturing himself tumbling over the ground, driven by a great, wild wind that roared until his skin began to peel from his bones, until ice seeped into the cracks in his skeleton and broke him apart over the long, slow centuries until he sank into the sand of a long, dark sweep of shore and then was gone.

When he was nine, his aunt and uncle, his mother's sister, Lorraine, and her husband, Glen—with his pink polos and moussed blond hair—had taken him to the Massachusetts Museum of Fine Arts to see *The Birth of Venus*. There had been a fight afterward, his mother and her sister cutting at each other with the cold politeness that was their family's favorite knife, exchanging words like *concerned about the impact of pornography on his development* and *things are changing; it's not like it was in the seventies,* but Gabe hadn't cared about that. All he'd been able to think about was Venus in that shell, the sweet candy curves and folds of her, the faraway look in her eyes and the wind pulling at her pale golden hair as she stepped out into the world. He had looked at himself in the mirror that night and then spent half an hour dragging a safety pin along his inner arm until the huge and awful feeling in his stomach went away. He hadn't seen his aunt since, except at Christmas and Thanksgiving up at Nana's house in Madbury.

I want to come out of the sea, he thought, and all that desperation climbed up out of him as though he were throwing up a snake, a centipede as long as he was tall. He was on his knees coughing and bile was clinging to his lips, and where it puddled in the dirt he saw those foaming breakers smashing themselves on the sand, and the clear wash as they kissed the earth and drew back to the sea, and her pale feet, fat and soft like little dinner rolls, sinking into the silt, crabs no bigger than fingernails scuttling over her toes, and he felt her hand on the back of his neck and the salty kiss of her wet lips, the weight of her soaking mane of hair like the one the unknown man had cut away from him the day he'd come to camp.

"Oh my God," said Gabe, and his voice broke. The air was shimmering and something was calving from him like ice from a glacier, falling away and taking with it a terrible, crushing weight he hadn't known was resting squarely on his chest. A cascade of other nameless things went with it and then he was rocketing up into the stars and sinking down into the warm embrace of earth and waves were breaking over him with awesome force, as they had on the molten rock at the dawn of creation when the first bacteria wriggled to life in pools of sulfurous water. A flower opening, and opening, and opening. "Oh my God."

I'm a girl.

It was easy to sneak into the crater past the few ranch hands smoking around its perimeter, as though the rest of the world were blind and it was only Jo and Brady who could see. The moonlight led them down the paths of the garden tiers, past the little pools and rivulets where pondweed waved in obscure currents and strange segmented creatures Jo had never seen before undulated through the crystal flow, armored bodies shimmering. The word that came to mind was "trilobite," but they didn't look like that. They looked older. Stranger. She bent to touch one and it squirted away from her hand in a rush of bubbles, eyes blinking along the edges of its plates.

In a clearing in a bamboo grove they found a nest of hummingbirds, a bulb of dry grass spun into a little house hanging from the stalks, and inside the jewel-bright birds were sleeping in a pile of glinting feathers and sharp beaks. *That's what I want,* thought Jo. *To be beautiful and loved and always touched, always against the people who are mine, who I belong to.* She thought about touching one of them, feeling the sleek shine of its feathers, but as she drew closer the pile of iridescent plumage resolved in the moonlight into a nightmarish spectacle. She drew her hand back from the entrance to the nest, staring in fascinated horror at the thing that looked like a hummingbird but wasn't, which had buried its needle-thin beak in the back of another bird's neck and now drank from it as though its body were a flower. Eyes opened in the false bird's flank, watching her.

Cuckoo, she thought suddenly, not quite knowing why. Huge body swelling from a hidden egg. Beak gaping, never sated, dumb cry, silly like its name. A nature program? One of her old Discovery Channel tapes? Gray feathers. *Cuckoo. Cuckoo.*

"What is it?" Brady whispered.

"Nothing," she answered. They went.

By the time they reached the house Jo felt as though she were surfacing. Colors were less vibrant, sounds less clear and cutting. She felt gray and drained and frightened, worn out after their long walk from the camp and grateful they'd had the presence of mind to go back to their cabins for their shoes before climbing the fence and striking out into the boundless dark. What had happened to them? It was like a pit was opening up inside her, a dark void of exhaustion. Her headache was coming back and for a moment she thought Malcolm was beside her, a tall shape moving in the shadows, dark eyes afraid behind their mocking glint, but just as she opened her mouth to call his name she realized that it was only one of Mrs. Glover's tomato frames. She blinked, white spots dancing in her vision.

"There's someone on the porch," said Brady, crouching down and pulling her with him. "I think it's Garth."

Float like a butterfly, sting like a bee, thought Jo. It kept happening, thoughts slipping away into strings of nonsense. It didn't matter. Garth stood at the rail maybe fifteen yards from where they crouched, the cherry of his cigarette glowing in the dark. With the porch lights behind him he was little more than a silhouette, but Jo could see the shotgun resting on his shoulder. The front door stood at his back. Jo thought frantically.

How can we get him to move?

All around them, a chorus of metallic clicks rose from the grass and undergrowth. A chorus of hisses like a nest of rattlers waking from deep sleep, and then the lukewarm arcs of sprinklers flashing silver in the light. Garth stepped back to avoid the spray. He hesitated, then turned and set off around the corner of the porch toward the other door on the barn-facing side of the house. The sprinklers *chik-chik-chik*-ed, catching Jo and Brady across their backs. Even the tepid drizzle felt frigid in the cold.

"Come on," Jo whispered, taking Brady's hand.

They went.

Gabe could hear the others, but he couldn't see them. He'd wandered off from the avenue between the cabins and he wanted to find Shelby, wanted to tell her that he understood, that he *got it*. He wanted to cry with her and ask her what to do, to apologize for avoiding her and every unkind thought he'd had about her. Things were starting to come back into focus. There was no light yet but he could sense the sunrise coming like a premonition. A white seed burning high above the horizon. He swayed through the cold, fluid gloom by the showers and ran his still-tingling palms over his chest and the concave plane of his stomach, trying to drag the image of his womanhood he'd touched at the height of whatever it was they'd all been through over his real flesh. Pelvic bones too prominent, emphasizing narrow hips, flat ass, his legs with their hatefully stubborn thighs, always jiggling no matter how strictly he stuck to his diets or how long he went without water. Euphoria, picked at like a blister, voided itself.

The backwash of his vision flooded his stomach and after a few more tottering steps he doubled over and threw up, acrid bile splattering at his feet. He lurched past the puddle, still retching, and puked again before he reached the back of Cabin Five and sagged against the wall.

I'm never going to look right, he despaired. *I'm never going to be a real girl. Never. I should fucking kill myself. I should slit my wrists. Drink bleach. Lie down on the train tracks.*

Something whined. Gabe straightened, wiping his sour-tasting mouth on his sleeve. Whose flannel was he wearing? He hadn't had one on him when he'd woken. He limped to the corner of the cabin. A whimper, fainter this time. A dark shape lay sprawled in the dirt.

It was Malcolm's dog, only something was wrong. It lay on its side in the shadow of Cabin Five, and as Gabe drew closer, he saw that its legs were splayed limp in the dirt and a dark puddle soaked the soil around its belly. He thought at once of his collie, Eli, who had slept on his bed every night since he could remember, and for the first time in his life he felt real love for Idaho's dark woods and windswept fields, and with that love a deep and aching homesickness. He knelt beside the mangled thing and saw the trail of blood droplets leading to the dark under Cabin Seven. The flat, silvery glow of coin-like eyes stared back at him from the blackness.

A hand emerged from the shadow. An arm. An elbow. The bottom half of Corey's grinning face, mouth and chin still slicked with blood and something *moving* under sunburned, freckled skin, bone and muscle shifting and converging. Gabe fell back, paralyzed by terror, a scream caught in his throat.

"Corey?" he whispered, his voice strangled. "Corey, what are you doing? What did you do to that dog?"

The counselor dragged himself out into the moonlight, crawling on his belly like a lizard, and rose up into a crouch, his smile stretching wider. Gabe inched back from him, glancing quickly down the alley between the two cabins. Then Corey was on him, pinning him to the dirt and kissing him, forcing his tongue into Gabe's screaming mouth, and beneath the horrible taste of the dead dog's blood was a sickly, cloying sweetness. Something sharp pricked the back of his throat.

The world turned into smoke and blew away.

Jo pushed the Glovers' screen door open, eased it in to rest against her back, and turned the knob of the front door. The living room was empty, the television turned to CBS at a low murmur. Rush Limbaugh's face danced distorted in the mirror under the stairs, his cheeks reddening as he shook his finger at the camera. Jo guided Brady past her and slipped in herself. Carefully, quietly, she closed first the screen door and then the inner, muting the sound of the sprinklers outside.

It was only a few steps to the study's door. Jo's heartbeat thundered in her ears as she crossed the Persian carpet and tried the handle. It opened. Relief washed over her in a pulverizing wave and then she and Brady were inside the little room, Brady shutting the door behind them. The sole window's curtains were drawn. They were heavy and red and looked almost like they were made of wool. In the sliver of moonlight that fell between them Jo could just make out a desk, a chair, the spines of books stacked neatly in their recessed shelves. And there, resting on a lace doily set on a side table, a powder-blue phone sitting in its cradle. The hair on the back of Jo's neck stood on end.

"Find a bill," she hissed in Brady's ear. "A letter. Something with an address."

In silence, as quickly as they dared, they began to search the office, rifling through drawers and sorting stacks of papers. Jo had to hold each one up to the moonlight to make out the words. *This is like something a detective would do in a movie,* she thought. *Except it wouldn't be grocery lists and coupons.* She held another sheet of paper up to the light. Something about toxicology. 3,4-Methyl enedioxymethamphetamine. Ketamine. A bunch of other shit she couldn't pronounce. She threw it aside. That was when she saw the little wicker wastepaper basket set between the desk and side table. She knelt and dug into it, wrinkling her nose as her hand touched a slimy black banana peel and the slick wrapper to some kind of yogurt cup. Under the thin layer of detritus, she found the letter.

A bank statement, thrust back into its torn and crumpled envelope. Her heart leapt into her throat when she saw the stamp, and beside it the chicken-scratch return address, ripped clean in half. Carefully, she folded the torn portion of the lip back over to match the partial return. In both it and the destination address, *Resolution, UT* stood out bold and dark. She put a hand over her mouth to stifle the delighted laugh that wanted to spring free of her.

"Brady," she whispered, reaching for the back of his shirt. He turned, eyes widening when he saw the envelope. He was about to take it when a voice came through the window, muffled by curtains.

"Come along now, darling."

It was Mrs. Glover. She was at the front of the house. Jo could hear her footsteps and the creaking of the porch. Hardly daring to breathe, she let go of Brady and moved with painstaking slowness back to the door and looked through the half-inch gap between it and its frame. The sticklike woman stood in the open front doorway, hand in hand with a shorter figure in a nightshirt, or maybe a too-big tee, who, as Jo squinted to bring the pair into focus, took a tottering step into the living room.

At first she thought it was Smith. It had the same flyaway hair, blond as a baby's first feathery tresses, the same frail frame and willowy limbs, but then it limped under one of the overhead lights, and where Smith's face should have been was a distended, eyeless snout, raw and pink and wrinkled as a foreskin, its mouth full of peglike yellow teeth, its nostrils oozing thick, yellowish mucus that gathered under its jaw to drip to the floor.

It's not real, thought Jo. *This is a nightmare. I'm having a nightmare.* She bit her tongue until she tasted blood, but reality refused to cooperate. The terrible thing remained. At her side Brady had his hands over his mouth. He was crying silently.

"We'll get you dressed and you can finish in the guest room," cooed Mrs. Glover, pulling the front door shut behind them. The starved and skull-faced woman's sunken cheeks were flushed. She looked emotional. "You're doing so well, honey. I know this time it's going to work."

This isn't real.

The pair passed by them, heading for the stairs. Jo listened as their halting steps began to fade. She tried to keep her breathing even as her headache pounded. It was getting worse. When she closed her right eye the point of white still burned in her left's vision. She took the phone from its cradle and hit the zero key, praying to no one in particular that she still remembered Oji's room extension. The crackling blare of the tone made her want to crawl out of her skin. *They'll hear. They'll hear and they'll bring that thing back down here, that thing with Smith's hair that can't be Smith, it can't be.*

Connection. A man's scratchy voice. "Operator. How may I direct your call?"

"I need a number; Akira Takahashi, North Caldwell, New Jersey. He's a resident at Green Grove retirement community."

"One moment."

Ringing.

The line connected. A scratchy recorded message played. "You've reached Green Grove retirement community. If you know your party's extension—"

A click. Ringing and ringing and more ringing as Jo's palms began to sweat. The phone was nearly stuck to her cheek by cold, stinking perspiration and her headache was jabbing at her over and over again as though a needle were being pushed through her pupil and into the front of her brain. She wanted to claw at her eye socket, to scratch until she couldn't feel anymore. A recorded voice answered. She dialed the extension.

Ringing.

Ringing.

"Hello?"

"Oji-chan, don't hang up," she started, her voice already quavering at just the sound of his. "It's Jo. I'm in Resolution, Utah. Mom and Dad sent me here, to a camp."

"Joanna?" He sounded far away, his voice scratchy and thin. "It's so late. Are you all right?"

She almost cried. "I . . . I need help. They're hurting us. Giving us drugs. They want to do something bad to us. There's a place in the city"—she read from the torn envelope—"Carter and Sons Feed, Fertilizer, and Farm Supply. We need you to meet us there as soon as you can. Do you still have your car?"

"Your mother sold it. Joanna—"

Running footsteps. The study door crashed open, knocking Brady back into the shadows as Enoch barged into the room. Jo's breath came in quick gasps. Enoch's eyes were on her. He took a step into the room. She thought how stupid he looked in his pinstripe pajamas, like an overgrown eight-year-old. "Resolution,

Utah," she repeated as clearly as she could through the sobs trying to force their way up out of her throat. "Please, Oji. It's—"

Enoch grabbed the side table and flung it across the room. The cord tore from the wall and the line disconnected as Oji shouted something Jo couldn't make out. She staggered back, ear ringing where the receiver had clipped her jaw. Enoch seized her by the arm. "You're in big trouble, egg roll."

A *ding* and then Enoch dropped to his knees. Brady stood behind him; he'd smashed the phone's carriage into the back of the bigger man's head. Enoch looked confused. Brady lifted it again and brought it down, harder this time. *Ding. Service to the front desk,* thought Jo as Enoch's hand slipped from her arm. She turned away before the third blow landed, but she heard the wet, brittle *crack* as something broke in the man's skull. Running footsteps overhead.

"She's fuckin' *Japanese,* you *moron,*" Brady hissed.

Jo grabbed his arm, and he dropped the phone as though it had burned him and wrapped her in a tight and desperate hug. Enoch lay very still, a dark stain spreading through the carpet from his dented temple. Everything felt like it was moving too fast. Footsteps coming closer. Brady crying. She was crying, too.

Oji has to come for us. He will. He'll find a way.

"We have to go," said Jo.

They ran.

XII

AND YOUR ASS WILL
FOLLOW

They were halfway to the crater's lip when they heard it: a high, horrible gobbling that rose up and up until it seemed to fill the air, to come from all directions at once. Jo could hardly think. She stumbled and staggered, her balance suddenly thrown off as an awful pressure built in her ears. Just when she thought her eardrums would explode, pain knifing hot and dirty deep into her skull, the shrieking ceased. She grabbed Brady's hand and dragged him onward. They crashed through a copse of magnolia saplings, knocking one of the slender trees askew from its braces in a shower of fleshy white petals. Her headache was getting worse, the white spot growing in size and a point of pitch-darkness now visible at its center, like the pupil of an eye.

Up to the next tier, panting for breath as the sounds of pursuit grew louder. The flat crack of a rifle shot. A clod of earth and grass leapt from the slope a little way ahead of them and then a woman's furious yelling, incomprehensible at a distance. No more shots came. They struggled onward in the dark. Behind them, the distant sounds of bodies breaking trail through vegetation. *This place is impossible,* thought Jo. *How did I ever fucking believe this could be real? All this water . . .*

"Where?" Brady gasped. His face was brick red, his legs trembling. They weren't dressed for the cold.

"Trees," Jo wheezed back. Her thighs were burning. She felt a ridiculous rush of gratitude toward Cheryl's brutal morning runs, which had, if nothing else, left her with legs that could stand toiling uphill with Brady hanging on her arm. She looked and saw his lips were moving. He was saying something, and with a galvanizing thrill of horror she realized that she could hear the same words his mouth formed.

I love to love ya, Joey baby.

She moaned in horror, despair bubbling in her guts as she thought again of breathing the world in, of inhaling reality so that it covered her insides and erased the barriers of skin and thought. *What's happening to me?*

You're digging up Roy, laughed the voice of her subconscious, Brady's lips flapping in time with its wet, throaty gurgle. *Let's see if old Roy still has his claws! Let's see if his teeth are still where we left 'em! You know a vulture'll ride a carcass miles and miles downriver till the pressure from gasses building up inside ruptures the animal? That'll be five seventy-eight, first window! Arentcha hungry, Joanna? Don't you want some of that* dee-licious *Szechuan spicy chicken, or are you running for office?*

Dead dog, guts spilling out of him, legs and neck twisted the wrong ways as he shivered in the driveway, piss and blood run down its slight slope. Eli. Roy. Names she didn't know. Her father stepping from the car. A man she'd never seen, big and broad and pale with thinning golden hair. No, dark. Choking her on the living room floor because of what she'd done to the dress. She ran uphill through soiled gore, clawing at the loose black soil, which was dog flesh furred in blood-soaked gold. Then it was over, the white spot in her vision popping like a pimple as she dragged Brady up over the final ridge and onto level ground. She sobbed, but only once. There wasn't time. Floodlights washed the crater in blinding light and stabbed at the dark above.

The white spot formed again, and this time she knew what it reminded her of, with its round form and its little glistening black head. A grub. A stupid little grub chewing at whatever was in front of it. *Oji heard me right,* she told herself, looking back down the tiered slope. Dark little figures coming toward them, but still far away. *He heard me right and he's going to figure out how to get here, and he's going to save us.*

She could just make out the brown smudge of the tree line at the nearest extent of the mountainous foothills, the dark outline of the peaks above just visible in the predawn sky. Pines dead and living, left withered by years of drought, marched over the rugged earth. "Come on," she panted, forcing herself to break into a jog. "Come on, come on. We can make it. We can do it."

Cuckoo! shrieked the voice in her head. *Cuckoo, cuckoo! Do you hear it, Joanna? You're not going home! Someone else got your seat on the bus, and she's just so excited to meet your parents, to meet that feeble old man rotting away where he's no good to anybody and wring a little something useful out of him. You wouldn't believe what you can do with just one tired old man, Joanna. With his skin and his fat and the soggy, failing neurons in his demented old head. You won't recognize him when I'm done, but he'll recognize you. He sure will. Cuckoo.*

Cuckoo.

Somewhere behind them in the crater, an engine roared to life. Another followed it. Jo ran faster toward the dark under the trees, Brady at her side.

Gabe woke as Corey pulled him out of the bed of the truck. His feet slipped off the tailgate and hit cold gravel. Corey had him under the arms and he couldn't seem to move, so he just hung there, heels dragging as the counselor hauled him onward. He was freezing and his thoughts felt like molasses. His breath came in puffs of mist. It was still dark out, but harsh floodlights bathed them. There was a house. A barn. A towering rock face. And around it all, impossibly, the garden the girls had told them about and which he realized he'd never quite believed existed.

Somewhere close by another truck peeled out, tires spitting grit and gravel, but Gabe couldn't see it. His head didn't want to turn when he told it to. He thought he might be drooling. *He gave me something,* he thought, and the grown-up phrase "slipped him a mickey" surfaced from somewhere in his subconscious like a shark's fin cutting water. A dog lying dead on the ground. A hand emerging from the dark. He was so cold.

Corey dragged him up the steps of a wraparound covered porch, past Garth and another ranch hand, who were looking out into the floodlit gardens, guns raised and eyes narrowed, and in through the front door, which was braced open with a chipped red brick. His ankles thumped against the edge of each stair, but he hardly felt it. The carpet in the entry hall was stained. Mrs. Glover sat in one of the high-backed armchairs by the staircase, a cigarette in her hand, a linen nightgown cinched around her tiny waist. Family photos marched along the steps at their backs, older and older as they rose toward the second floor. She looked like a toy beside her husband. He noticed a little girl in Mrs. Glover's arms in the first few, his mind snagging on the detail.

"Thank you, Corey," she said in her hard little voice. Her jaundiced skin was stretched so tightly over the bones of her face that Gabe thought she looked more like a skeleton than a person. "Take him down to the basement."

A door. A stair. A long, dark laundry room and at its end an open pantry. They passed by it all, Corey dumping Gabe against one of the dryers to free his hands for prying open a door concealed as part of the unfinished wall. A bloom of noxiously sweet air, fetid and hot, like a garbage can left out in the sun after a warm summer rain. He tried to move, but he could hardly curl his numb lips. He could feel drool soaking the collar of his T-shirt. He could feel cold cement under his backside.

Please, God, he prayed as he hadn't since the fourth grade when Father Dolan told the congregation there was "nothing gay about Hell." *Please, don't let them do to me what they did to Candace. Don't let them do it, God. Please. I'm sorry. I'm sorry for everything, I didn't mean it.*

Corey heaved him up over one shoulder so that all he could see was the back of the counselor's striped button-up and then they were going down again, each step a jolt through Gabe's stomach. The shock of level ground. Dirt floor glimpsed between Corey's boots and then the older man unlimbered him and dropped him without ceremony to the ground. Gabe sucked air, trying to fill his lungs as he stared up at the joists above, and then Corey set the toe of one boot against his cheek and tipped his face over to look to the right.

Once, when he was twelve, his class had taken a day trip to a local dairy farm. It was calving season and one of the cows was close to delivering, a sight some enthusiastic teacher had decided would do the school's coddled best and brightest some good. Get some dirt under their nails, or at least show them what it looked like to achieve proximity between one's fingernails and dirt. What that teacher hadn't counted on was a word Gabe hadn't known before that day. The word was "prolapse."

The thing lying there on the warm dirt floor looked much as the cow's uterus had oozing over the filthy straw, a great pool of bloody, hairy tissue inside which some fragile thing thrashed weakly, limbs like tent poles pushing at the near-translucent membrane. Except it was bigger. Much bigger. A shapeless, jiggling sac of flesh nearly six feet long and full of cloudy pinkish fluid, all covered by a dissolving layer of matted hair. It looked, he realized, like the strange owl pellets he'd found in the desert.

Gabe heard himself screaming, but it was as though he heard it from a great distance, an echo of the real thing that tore at his numbed and tingling throat. He didn't hear Corey walking away, or the door at the top of the staircase closing, or even—if indeed it made any sound at all—the sound of the dark humanoid shape in that prolapsed mass of flesh as it turned toward him, flailing through the soupy liquid in which it was suspended.

They reached the edge of the forest just as the truck's headlights came over the edge of the crater, swinging wildly through the dark and then stabbing out across the open ground. Jo chanced a look back and almost brained herself on the underside of a dead pine toppled against its nearest neighbor. She slid under it, twigs scraping her scalp, a huge swag of dusty cobweb clinging to her face and shoulder. The roar of the engines grew louder. She crashed through dry brush and dead branches, Brady flailing somewhere to her left.

They broke into a clearing. Headlights stabbed through the night around them. Jo clambered over fallen logs, dry-rotted wood giving way under her hands and knees. She cut her leg on something—she didn't see what—and warm blood slicked her shin and stuck her sock to her sweaty ankle. Car doors slammed somewhere behind them. Voices rose over the crash and crackle of deadfall underfoot. The slope pitched sharply up and Jo threw herself at it, kicking little landslides loose as she seized hold of roots and fallen brush, half slithering and half dragging herself up the grade. Halfway to the slope's crown she nearly tumbled into the darkness under the exposed roots of a gigantic pine. She made her decision without thinking, leaping up to catch one of the huge, stripped limbs. It creaked under her weight, dead wood cracking, and she scrambled up into a crotch set just above it, wedging herself into an awkward position to push with hands and feet as pine needles and loose scales of bark rained down on her. She was twenty feet up at her best guess before she thought to look for Brady.

He was sprawled in the dirt at the base of the slope. He must have twisted his ankle in a hole or under a root, because he couldn't get his feet under him. He clawed at the ground, sobbing in panicked frustration but still somehow with the presence of mind not to give her away by calling for help. *I have to help him,* thought Jo, but her hands refused to release their death grip on the old pine's trunk and the ground seemed so far away, so unrelated to her. When the first flashlight beam slashed through the dark off somewhere to the right she realized then she wasn't going to go back for him, that however brave Oji had told her she was, this was beyond the limit of that bravery. She was afraid down to the marrow of her bones.

Something came out of the dark just as Brady finally yanked his foot out of whatever root it had gotten stuck under. The thing had Cheryl's face, but her skin sagged, hanging in flabby folds from her arms and drooping under her eyes so that red, glistening tissue showed in little crescents under them. Raw sores gaped at her hairline and on her bare arms among constellations of boils and blisters. She tossed her flashlight aside, scuttled up to Brady on all fours, and planted a hand between his shoulder blades, flattening him against the ground. He screamed as she bent to sniff the back of his head, a low, despairing cry of horror that made Jo want to double over and vomit. *If I was brave,* she thought, *if I was really brave, I'd jump down now and help him fight her off. Maybe together we could take her, whatever she is. Maybe—*

The Cheryl-thing bent her head to Brady's neck. There was a wet, heavy slurping sound and Brady fell still, his cry cut off. When she drew back there was an oozing wound at the base of his skull, as though someone had slipped a scalpel in between his vertebrae. The thing threw back her head and let out a hideous shriek, that same high, frantic gobbling they'd run from in the crater. Jo nearly lost her balance.

They're going to kill him. They're going to kill him. Do something. Do it now. Now. NOW.

Pastor Eddie stepped into the moonlight at the clearing's edge, the beam of his flashlight playing over the ground and the Cheryl-thing where it crouched atop Brady's back. "Go and get the rest of his cabin. The girls from Four, too." He looked at someone Jo couldn't see. "It was that little nip with him, wasn't it?"

"Yes, sir," said a man. Garth, Jo thought.

Do it now. Do it.

"Cheryl, you'll have to wake it up." He bent and grabbed Brady around the middle, then straightened and slung the boy over his shoulder as though he weighed nothing at all. Brady's neck flopped horribly. His limbs swung limp. Pastor Eddie blew out a frustrated breath. "Tell it we've got another runaway."

Gabe stared at the wet, rippling surface of the birthing sac. Egg? Womb? Whatever it was. The thing inside thrashed pitifully, stub limbs churning murky fluid. Its lipless gash of a mouth stretched open wide. Wider. Jaw breaking apart, sticky strands of flesh stretching between the segments, pulling taut, and snapping as its forehead *wriggled*, furrowed, and split into three clawing digits. Within, dark eyes blinked furiously in no recognizable sequence as a loose wet slit contracted and fluttered its plump lips. A gap. A hole.

A single word slipped through the panicked morass of Gabe's thoughts, the snatches of grade-school kisses and the taste of lipstick on his tongue, his mother's hand, perfectly manicured, the news blaring from the old TV in the lake house living room as Tom Brokaw talked about the wall and the drone of a boat motor off in the distance like some ungodly huge fly, the scratch of nails on skin, and the word was: *Cuckoo.*

The thing spluttered out a cloud of silvery bubbles as its stump-ended limbs pressed at the surface of its sac. The translucent membrane bulged outward under pressure. Cilia like a jellyfish's tentacles bloomed from the face, and from the cunt-like gash within a curved black stinger slid to neatly cut a slit in its cocoon. Its egg. Warm, sticky fluid splashed over the floor, soaking the back of Gabe's shirt. The stinger withdrew. The tendrils flopped limp as the thing dragged itself out of the collapsing sac, dead tissue and sodden clots of hair clinging to its skin.

Don't cry, beautiful boy, a voice hissed inside Gabe's skull. **You're going home to mommy.**

The thing crawled toward him. The wooden bird emerging from the beautiful Swiss clock in his grandmother's living room, its little wings flapping stiffly, its neck thrusting out as it cried, and his headache roared back, piercing him through the skull between his eyes, and he saw:

A slab of meat and rough, dense bone plummeting through the atmosphere. Below, the jagged lines of mountain ranges crawling between lakes and deserts. Crosshatched farmland alternating brown and green. The glint of water. Closer. Great scar bisecting old, dead soil. Clumps of concrete growing tight and high like fungal stalks. The sea stretching away over the curve of the horizon. The lifeless plain rushing toward it, and then impact, body blown apart like a water balloon bowled through glass and nails, flesh strewn throughout the crater clawing back toward itself, brain waking by slow, sticky degrees as neurons knit and memories propagated through uncomprehending meat. Huddling in the shadow of a rock escarpment as the sun boiled its way across the sky, lung networks like bunches of grapes struggling to process the thin air as it fights to grow new alveoli better suited to its new conditions.

Minutes pass. Hours. The last straggling gobbets of its biomass join it in the thin band of shadow. Some it allows to fuse with its wheezing bulk. Others it crushes and discards, smelling cancer on their burnt and flaking skin. This place is killing it. Flesh sloughs from its bones in scabby, lifeless sheets. Not the paradise it seeks but an irradiated wasteland where poison rained down on its sensitive skin. It is dying. Every breath is hard-fought. It snorts thick yellow mucus from its half-formed mouths and oozing gills. Lesions bloom where its slack folds rub up against each other, auto-frottage lubricated with its watery, discolored blood. At last the sun sets. It shivers in the dark, temperature plummeting, and leaves a hunk of itself the size of a stray dog twitching and vomiting behind it as it presses closer to the stone outcropping, still warm from the sun's touch. Its thoughts race. Nothing living here. Nothing to take into itself and turn to its own purposes, to use as a fleshly lens through which to understand this barren place.

Nothing, until in the silence of the deepening night it hears a plaintive chorus rising from somewhere above. A bright, vulnerable cry. Its milky, watering eyes blink. It turns toward the rock face, struts of cartilage unfolding to support new tissue as its ears expand, and with palsied, trembling claws it finds a crevice in the stone and starts to climb. It secretes adhesives through the pads of its limbs, sprouts fat, muscular tentacles lined with suckers, and inch by torturous inch, even as its vision blurs and its blood—starved of the strange compounds of its native atmosphere—hammers through stiffening veins, it climbs toward that shrill, innocent sound. Little pink things hidden in a recess in the rock, beaks open in needy supplication, bodies so delicate it can see their frantic heartbeats through their skin. Blind and helpless, vestigial wings folded tight against their sides. It reaches out and they stretch up toward its twitching digits, begging, it thinks, to be fed.

Four of the five it eats, plucking them from the nest of brittle twigs and dusty, matted fibers and dropping them still crying out into a prehensile mouth. Bones as delicate as matchwood snap between its jaws and in the meat, the marvelous meat, so perfectly suited to this world of horrors, is the blueprint for the lungs it needs, a map of flesh, muscle, and organ tissue evolved to endure this world's leaden gravity, its caustic atmosphere and poison sun. Eyes that drink in the full spectrum of wild colors, nostrils lined with minute, sensitive hairs which capture particles of complex stink, and still the fifth thing cheeps at it, beak gaping. Waiting, it realizes, for its progenitors, the hosts from which its graft was cut. They will come and feed it. How perverse, to care for one's own leavings. Useful, though. It eats the last survivor.

It sheds a little lump of tissue in the nest, now empty as that gaping beak, and along the sympathetic link still binding them together it begins to whisper of another form. A feeble thing, its adult shape still months away, a hazy smear of genetic destiny extrapolated from the bulbous head, the blind eyes and tiny claws as delicate as glass. Even if it dies out here, even if its flesh fails and its long voyage is all for nothing, seeds of the meat will be sown, and as the crude little double begins to cry out to be fed and its true parent scurries down the sheer rock face, the harried egg-layer flutters back to light on the nest's rim and twitter in fear and confusion at her missing offspring before opening her beak to vomit in the upturned beak of her sole remaining nestling.

Her child, and its.

Jo stayed in the tree until dawn, dropping once or twice into gray dreams of pus and sores and clutching hands from which she woke in a cold sweat, ears perked for the sound of footsteps or the roar of engines. The chill seeped into her a little more each time she stirred. Her fingers ached. Her face itched where the wind had burned her. Once she dreamed she was lying on her back at the bottom of a tiled shower, cold water dripping on legs she couldn't move, a stomach she couldn't feel. She woke to find she'd peed herself. As the first needles of gray light pierced the thickening clouds she shinned down the pine's trunk and wiped her sap-smeared hands on the seat of her jeans. There was no sign of Brady. No blood. No claw marks in the dry, colorless earth. She pressed her fist to her mouth to stifle a sob.

Part of her wanted to lie down in the dirt and scream until somebody found her, scream and scream until whatever the fuck was happening out here at the ass-end of the world wrapped itself around her and dragged her under. Living meant making sense of what she'd seen last night. It meant making a place in her conception of reality for the thing Mrs. Glover had led into the basement, for the thing wearing Cheryl's face in the darkness under the trees.

They aren't just going to kill us, she realized. *They're going to take us. Our faces. Our lives. Oh, God, please don't let them get me. Please.*

That was when she heard the dogs.

XIII

BROOD PARASITES

Shelby heard the cabin's steps creak underfoot and knew the dream was over. No time to get out through the trapdoor. No time to hide under the bed or in the tiny bathroom. She didn't open her eyes. It would only make it worse, the moment they took her from Nadine's arms, from the peace of the other girl's sweat and sawdust smell and the thrill of being skin to skin with her, still tingling and tired. *This must be why they call it making love,* thought Shelby.

She was crying when Corey and Marianne came in and dragged her from the bed, crying when Nadine kicked free of the tangled sheets and threw herself on Corey's back, biting and clawing, raking his eyes with her nails.

When Corey's face broke open like a spider's legs unfolding, though, and the puckered mouth within snapped shut on Nadine's first two fingers, then Shelby began to scream.

The counselors zip-tied their arms behind their backs and marched them up a plywood ramp into the bed of one of the pickups, where Malcolm, John, and Felix were already sitting. They brought Shelby and Nadine up last, Shelby with duct tape over her mouth, Nadine bleeding freely where two of her fingers just . . . ended, as though someone had snipped them off with a pair of gardening shears. There was no sign of Gabe, or Jo, or Brady, just the five of them herded up over the tailgate.

"You think they're taking us to Disney World?" Malcolm asked, wishing he could scratch his nose. "It's peak season, so we're just gonna be waiting in lines all day."

"Malcolm," said John. "Could you please shut up?"

Malcolm swallowed past the lump in his throat. He couldn't stop looking at Nadine's hand. He'd thought she was so cool, so tough, so grown-up. How had he missed that she was just a fucking kid? They were all just fucking kids. "Copy that, chief."

The truck's engine turned over. It pulled away toward where two ranch hands stood by the open chain-link gate. Through the dirty glass of the cab's rear-facing window Malcolm watched Corey wipe blood from his chin with a handkerchief. The counselor's face was covered in angry red scratch marks.

Felix kicked the tailgate hard enough to rattle it. "Fuck," he snarled. He kicked it again. "Fuck." Again. "Fuck!"

"Take it easy," said John.

"FUCK!" Felix screamed, rolling onto his side as he doubled up his legs and kicked again, jolting the tailgate hard against its locks. He was crying. "FUCK! FUCK, FUCK!"

Malcolm wished he'd stop. He still felt so weird after whatever had happened the night before. As he met John's gaze across the bed of the truck, he remembered their mouths sealed together, their tongues thrashing, and the painful stiffness in his briefs. His thighs were still sticky from it. He'd thought it would be too much, John on top of him, but it had been . . . nice. Soft, like drowning in molten marshmallow. In the light of day he felt embarrassed by how eager he'd been. How much he'd liked it.

Something must have shown on his face, because John turned away from him and set his jaw as though determined not to cry. *You're the Tom Cruise of fucking up*, thought Malcolm. *You're the fuckin' Kyle MacLachlan of pulling a boner. Whatever. He's better off without you.*

"They're not human," said Nadine. Her face was ashen, her voice hardly audible over the rattling roar of the truck's progress.

Still, they all heard her. Malcolm watched her blood slosh back and forth in one of the truck bed's plastic channels.

"They're monsters, and they're going to kill us."

John rose awkwardly up onto his knees as the truck started its descent into a tiered depression in the shadow of a wind-smoothed wall of rock. He couldn't stop staring, could hardly hear Felix and Malcolm telling him to sit down before he fell out of the bed. Trees. *Grass,* which he knew from the summers his father had made him work at Shearwater Meadow, the golf course on the edge of town, drank water like a fish. And there was water to be had, entire pools and rivulets of it splashing down the tiers in miniature waterfalls through stands of bamboo and sumac, past overgrown flower and herb gardens. Scintillating blurs flitted here and there among the nodding blossoms. Hummingbirds, in the middle of the desert.

"Oh my God," he heard himself say. The look of ashamed anger Malcolm had given him earlier seemed all at once a tiny little thing, inconsequential against what he was seeing. Even if they were about to die, even if the camp's staff really *were* monsters, this was the most beautiful thing he'd ever seen in his life, an awe-inspiring waste of resources on a scale he couldn't begin to imagine. "This is impossible."

"Well it's doing an amazing impression of being possible then," Malcolm snapped. He was sulking. Probably embarrassed about how he'd begged John to climb on top of him and grind, how he'd come right away and broken down crying, mumbling nonsense as he fell deeper into whatever trip they'd been sent on. Doors and phlox and Mary's hand and *Mommy, Mommy, please don't do it.* John had felt so tender toward him then. He'd held the skinny boy, Malcolm's chin on his shoulder, and stroked his hair as he cried until it passed and they went back to kissing, to whispering sweet things and touching, still afraid but eager. Hungry. It was over now. It had crumbled at the first touch of sunlight.

John sank back down into the bed, trying to ease his legs out from under him. He nearly tipped over onto Felix, who'd been lying silent and unresponsive since his outburst when they were loaded aboard. "Sorry," he said. The truck hit a bump in the narrow dirt track and a flock of game birds exploded from the undergrowth to the side of the road, wings whirring loudly enough to drown out the noise of the motor for a fleeting moment. One came close enough for him to see the raw, sticky flesh of its underbelly, as though it had torn itself loose from something greater and gone winging off in terror on its own. Rags of skin trailed after it, and then the birds were gone into the bamboo, crashing through the pale green stalks.

In the yard outside the farmhouse they climbed down out of the truck with Garth's help while a few ranch hands kept watch at a distance, shotguns shouldered. Mrs. Glover stood smoking on the porch, a fringed shawl wrapped around her bony shoulders. She reminded John of his stepmother, all protruding ridges and hard angles, her skeleton resentful of the skin encumbering it. Her stare gave him the bizarre urge to wrap his arms around his belly, to hide it from her, to protect it from her fleshless fingers. She looked at him like he was something dirty.

"Where are you taking us?" shouted Felix. He was crying again, the most emotion John had ever seen from him. "Where's Gabe? Where are Jo and Brady? Fucking *answer me!*"

Garth slapped him hard across the face. Felix went over, unable to break his fall with his bound hands, and Garth kicked him in the stomach hard enough that he folded in on himself with a harsh, coughing sob. "Stop it," Shelby moaned through her duct-tape gag. "Stop it, stop it, stop it."

Garth seized Felix by the back of his shirt and dragged him the rest of the way to the porch as Corey and the other ranch hands closed in to force the rest of them toward the house. John brought up the rear. The guns were making him nervous. He'd never liked them, had turned white on the spot when his father gave him a rifle for his thirteenth birthday. It made his heart rabbit and his mouth turn dry when the sun glanced off those oiled barrels. *If we run, they'll shoot us.*

On some level, he thought as he climbed the porch steps, he'd really believed Nadine's plan would save them, that they'd swipe protein bars from the kitchen like Tom Sawyer packing his bindle and then traipse right out of camp and have a real adventure, that Jo's grandfather would pick them up in a big gold Cadillac and take them all for hamburgers and milkshakes. He'd never thought it would wind up here, kids held at gunpoint by grown-ups, a toe on the last line of the unspoken pact between their worlds: *If you obey me without question, I won't kill you.*

"It'll all be over soon, babies," said Mrs. Glover as they passed her by. Her bony fingers brushed John's face with something between lust and loathing, the expression etched deep enough into her skull-like mask of a face that he stumbled back a step and nearly bowled Shelby over. Corey shoved him back in line. They went into the house, and as John stepped over the threshold a white-hot needle of pain zapped between his right eye and the back of his head. He bumped against a side table. Something shattered on the floor. Porcelain.

If the moon is waxing gibbous and the limpid limpets shimmer, who is watching from its zenith as the bursar carves his dinner?

John remembered something as he fell to his knees and vomited, heaving bile and mucus up on the clean carpet. Something Gabe had said that night they'd all sat around drinking and talking about their dreams. About the holes they dug when they closed their eyes, and the things they found in them. His own face smirking up at him from beneath clods of runny, sucking mud. His own fingers curling around his wrist as he knelt to dig deeper. *Someone's beaming shit into our heads like Professor X? I mean, come on.*

The next thing he knew, he was sitting in a chair in a big, well-lit kitchen with one of Pastor Eddie's dinner-plate hands gripping his shoulder like a vise as the Cheryl-thing drew his blood. The syringe filled quickly, sucking at his forearm like a huge mosquito made of glass and metal. Someone had cut his zip tie. John let out an involuntary whimper and tried to jerk back, but the pastor's grip restrained him. The others stood all around and Dave and Corey barred the doors, incongruous in stocking feet. They must have left their boots by the doormat.

"Easy," the pastor rumbled. His voice made John think of a Morlock, hulking and filthy and secretive, toiling under the earth. His mother had read him *The Time Machine* when he was seven. He'd had nightmares about things coming up out of hatches in the ground for weeks. "It's just a little blood, sissy Mary."

Not since what happened at the lake.

The thought came from nowhere. He'd been noticing things like that more and more. He didn't have any memories about a lake. Nothing worth calling up, anyway. For an instant, as he looked away from the needle, he saw Gabe lying curled on the floor under the cabinets, but it was just his eyes playing tricks on him. Gabe was gone. Jo. Brady. Quiet little Smith, who he'd never really gotten to know. Everything was moving so fast. Stinging pain as Mrs. Glover drew the syringe from his arm. A little way off Nadine stood with her back to the oven, still pale but no longer bleeding. She wouldn't meet his eye.

"All right, big boy," said the pastor, heaving John to his feet. Blood trickled from the pinprick wound in his forearm. "Next."

The Cheryl-thing took an ampule from each one of them, working quickly and efficiently. When all five glass vials lay side by side in a little tin tray left out on the polished kitchen table, she took them all and left the kitchen. Pastor Eddie left a moment later, bending down to kiss his wife on his way to the back door. Their tongues flicked between their mouths. A wet sound. She looked so tiny next to him. John felt a momentary flash of embarrassment at the thought of what he and Malcolm must have looked like to the rest of the camp last night.

I am never going home again.

Mrs. Glover broke a match from a book left out by the salt and pepper shakers, struck it, and lit a cigarette. He'd never seen her smoke before that day. The others sat and stood around the kitchen. John joined Felix by the cabinets under the sink, lowering himself to the floor and letting out a long, slow breath. His whole body wanted to run, his heart pounding, his head still aching, but there was nowhere to go. Nothing to do. Men at the doors and Mrs. Glover sitting there and smoking, like nothing was wrong in the world.

"What are you going to do to us?" asked Felix.

Mrs. Glover took a long drag off her cigarette. Ash crumbled from the tip and she waved it away before it could settle on her skirt. "When my daughter was three," she said, blowing swirling trails of smoke from her nostrils, "she was diagnosed with leukemia." She took another drag from her cigarette, the cherry flaring orange and red. "Our church prayed. Our neighbors. Our families. We took her to tent revivals. Homeopaths. To Sloan Kettering and St. Jude's. Dieticians, hypnotists. I even took her to a shaman, near the end. He covered her in grease and gabbled over her, filled the tent with steam and smoke, poured cold water over hot stones."

She pursed her lips and exhaled a long plume. "I was so desperate. Janey was just skin and bones by then." One of her hands flew to her right collarbone, fingers stroking its prominent ridge without apparent thought. "You'd touch her arm, just while you were talking to her, and leave these big ugly bruises like you'd beaten her with a mixing spoon. I would have done anything. Believed anything. One night when I brought her home from a week of observation, when I carried her into the house in my arms like she was nothing and tucked her into bed, there was a message on my answering machine. Thelma Nielson, a woman I knew from church, telling me she'd heard from my mother-in-law's friend Sookie Carmichael that the week before she—Eddie's mother, Nora—had bailed him out of jail in Ranahoe County, and the word was he'd been caught blowing some seventeen-year-old boy whore with a purple mohawk, and did I need anything? Was I all right? Oh she hoped she hadn't upset me." A bitter smile. "Purple. I think she made the color up, to make it more delicious. To have a little extra texture to savor while she chewed on what was left of my life.

"He came home later that night. We didn't talk about it, but he knew that I knew. It was like that for months. He slept in his study. He hadn't touched me in years anyway. So we kept it up until Janey died, that May. It was nineteen eighty-one. After the funeral, the first moment Eddie and I were alone in the house, we had a fight. It was like everything we'd held inside ourselves came pouring out at once, more and more of it. Black bile. Ugly things. He begged me to stay, to stand by him in his struggle. He promised he'd get better, but all I could think was that he was going to use my daughter's ghost to guilt me into giving him a fig leaf while he carried on with his boys.

"In the end I walked right out of the house and into the desert. To die, I think. Eddie's problem. Losing Janey." Her face twitched. "That was part of it, of course. The way her little hand uncurled from mine. But to tell you the truth, what sent me out the door that night, what made me turn my back on Eddie while he pleaded with me, begged, sobbed, was imagining the way the congregation would look at me from then on, now that Janey was gone and there was nothing to keep them from digging their claws into us, the way they'd tilt their heads, speak softly, gently, like I was the one who was dying, like their feeling sorry for me . . ." She pursed her lips, expression sour. ". . . that it mattered. I couldn't face the thought of that much pity.

"So I walked. I walked until the sun came up. I was thirstier than I'd ever been before, and so weak I could hardly stand, but I did, and I kept going until it was dark again. I don't know how long I was out there. Two days? Three? But I remember the stars." Another exhale, smoke coiling around her skeletal wrist as she drew an arc in the air with the cigarette's burning tip. "The Milky Way . . . and I remember drinking water near the mountains. It made me sick. Shitting my guts out. Delirious. That was when it found me. It brought me here, to its crater, and showed me what it could do.

"A few days later I went home, and it came with me. It fixed Eddie. Now it's going to fix you, too."

Shelby was crying. Nadine had her arms around the shorter girl. John put his head in his hands. He felt sorry for her, for this starved and deranged woman holding their lives in the palm of her hand, for her long, lonely, frustrating marriage. And then he thought about what Gabe had said about Candace, about how she'd been replaced, which led him to the memory of Pastor Eddie's parting kiss just minutes before. *What kissed her?* The thought chased itself around his mind until it felt like he would never think of anything else. *What puts its mouth on her mouth? What did Jo hear her having sex with? What touches her at night? Does she want it? To let it touch her?*

"You're insane," said Felix.

Mrs. Glover smiled slightly. "Maybe," she said. "But soon you'll be dead, and I'll have my daughter back. It's been growing her for me. So what does the rest of it matter?"

Cheryl appeared in the doorway to the back hall, sliding easily past Dave. "They're clean," said the counselor. "It's ready."

"All right." Mrs. Glover stubbed her cigarette out in a porcelain ashtray. "Take them down."

In the laundry room a door stood open to the left of the machines. The air smelled of bleach and warm cotton and Nadine clung hard to Shelby's hand with her uninjured one, hoping no one in the kitchen had noticed her turning on the gas and palming the plastic knobs. They were in her pockets now. Probably someone would smell it and turn it off. Probably they'd all be dead long before anything happened with it at all. It still felt better, knowing she'd thrown one last punch.

Marianne took hold of a bar that must have been concealed behind shelving during laundry shifts and hauled back on it. A secret door, set flush with the wall, rolled smoothly out of the way. Behind it was another, plain wood with a tarnished knob. Smiling broadly,

Corey opened it. Thick, humid air stinking of corn syrup and cat shit rolled out over them. "Oh my God," breathed Malcolm, hands over his mouth and nose. "Oh Jesus fuck-me-running Christ."

Behind the door, a set of concrete steps led down twenty or thirty feet to a bare dirt floor, and a short way from the foot of the stair, Gabe lay curled on his side next to another boy with whom something was terribly, monstrously wrong. It was Gabe's size and shape, just about, but its face was split from chin to forehead just like Corey's had been, and from the slack-lipped gap spilled a thick mass of tendrils that stirred weakly in the muck surrounding the thing. Behind it lay some sort of hairy, membranous egg sac, now deflated. Nadine stared. Even after what had happened in the barn and then in the cabin, even with the stump of her missing fingers burning and throbbing through the handkerchief Shelby had knotted over and around it, the stench and the cavern and the thing lying down there next to Gabe in the fluorescent glare all made her feel like she was losing her mind. It couldn't be real. It couldn't be happening.

"Bye, princess," said Marianne, smiling broadly at Nadine.

"Suck my dick," Nadine snapped without thinking. Someone hit her from behind with the stock of a shotgun, knocking her forward a few steps. The doorframe caught her chin, reopening her split lip, and she spat blood as Shelby grabbed her arm and pulled her back from the stair. A few of the ranch hands laughed and it occurred to Nadine with a sick thrill of curiosity that some of them might still be human.

"It's okay," said Shelby. Her voice trembled, but it held. "I'm with you."

The ranch hands and counselors herded them through the door and onto the narrow steps. Nadine felt like a steer in a run, the air thick with panic, something ahead beyond her comprehension except that she was frightened of it. Those air-powered bolt guns punching their little metal rods through the beef's skulls. Two thousand pounds of meat coming down like a curtain. Marianne slammed the inner door behind them. The lock clicked. Below, the thing lying beside Gabe let out a low, sleepy burble like a baby talking in its sleep.

"I'm getting him away from that thing," said Nadine, and as the words left her lips the horror of the reeking chamber seemed a little more bearable, a little more real. She went down the steps and crossed the broad expanse of dirt. The subbasement was huge, poured concrete walls rising fifteen or twenty feet to an arched ceiling supported by graying, splintery timber joisted with rusted plates and struts. A tunnel yawned on the far side of the room and the smell was even stronger in its draft than at the top of the steps, flyblown garbage and orange soda drying into sticky chemical waste on car upholstery. Nadine put her face in the crook of her arm and made her way to where Gabe lay on his side, pale and motionless except for the flutter of his pulse in his slender throat.

She knelt, fighting the urge to gag at the sight of the thing lying next to Gabe. Its eyes were closed, the uneven halves of its face slack and dead-looking. It had four fingers on its right hand, its fifth no more than a tender half-inch nub of raw pink flesh emerging from what looked like a burst blister. It was a little more solid than Gabe, too, its shoulders broader, its muscles more de-fined except where they drooped like sleeping snakes from the curved bones of its malformed legs.

"Is this the thing?" Shelby whispered from a short way behind Nadine. The others stood gathered there, not daring to come closer. "You know, from our dreams? The thing that replaced Candace. Whatever you want to call it. Some kind of monster, or a—" She gestured with both hands as though grasping for some-thing.

"Cuckoo," John finished, and it sounded right. It sounded familiar. "No, I don't think so. Or, not all of it. That thing it came out of looks like an egg; something must have laid it."

Nadine turned her attention from that appalling thought to Gabe, slipping her arms under his and standing with some diffi-culty. He didn't weigh much, but he was tall and bony and awk-ward to move. The thing's tentacles slid from his face. It let out a piteous squeal, but didn't follow. She had him halfway to the steps by the time he started to stir, snorting and retching in her arms. "Easy," she said, trying to avoid his flailing hands. "It's me! It's Nadine. Just—"

That was when she heard it. People. It sounded like dozens of them at least, shuffling and wheezing and blowing, coughing and snorting and clearing their throats. It came from the mouth of the tunnel. A phlegmy, sputtering onslaught of respiration echoed and re-echoed from the tunnel walls, and the sound of something heavy dragging over rock and earth. A fresh wave of stench washed over her. As she backed gagging and coughing toward the steps, a dark mass appeared in the deeper gloom.

It squirmed through the archway, a tide of skin and greasy hair and raw, wet flesh pulled along by scrabbling limbs and bands of muscle cradled in buttery soft fat like the segmented body of some obscene grub. It was enormous, as big as an elephant. Bigger. Feathery limbs dripping with a cloudy, viscous fluid unfurled from its sides. The front of its rolling mass heaved and stretched, rings of doughy flesh forming and inverting as new limbs squirmed their way out of its bulk. It clawed at itself with soft, unformed fingernails, peeling away mats of sodden hair and flaking, scabby dermis. Dirty feathers covered its back like an eagle's ruff. Nadine couldn't seem to find her breath.

This isn't happening.

A particularly large crust of dead flesh tore loose and from the quivering vaginal wound beneath it came a face, wriggling its way slowly out into the open air. A girl of three or four, wisps of dark hair plastered to her scalp by that same nameless slime, eyes rolling from rheumy white sclera to huge black pupils. The pupils shrank. Muddy irises bloomed from them. The face began to age. Its skin grew tight, dried into brittle flakes, and tore, the pouty mouth cropping at loose scales of the dandruff-like refuse. Bones lengthening. Nose growing, baby fat melting away. Vestigial features formed and burst like boils in the sagging flesh of its neck. Another layer desiccated into eczema and ripped with a dry, satisfying tearing sound. It was almost to the other Gabe now as it picked away the dead mask, fresh clumps of black hair spilling from its scalp where its skin sloughed free. A woman, wrinkles at the corners of her eyes, brow furrowed in concentration. Its mouth worked, lips fluttering in separate segments before knitting together and pulling tight over crooked teeth.

"*Up*," it hissed, humping itself up on its own bulk, sluglike pseudopods of fat and muscle dewing from its belly to support it. "*Up*." It hit the sleeping figure with one of its knobby, sticklike fists. The thing opened its eyes. Gabe's eyes, round and baby blue but lifeless as the marbles in a doll's porcelain sockets. Whatever it was, however it saw the world around it, those eyes were just for show, no different from the way some bugs looked like leaves or bark, or predators. Camouflage.

Nadine stared, a picture beginning to form in her mind. A thing with her face getting on a bus back to Kansas, riding in silence until it came at last to her family's home, to the red front door and the old granite hitching post, and went into her mother's arms. What would it do with her face? Her life? She felt violated. She felt as though insects were crawling under her skin.

The creature looked at her and a smile split its face, a smile so wide its features began sliding back over the soft contours of its skull until all that remained was skin pulled so tight that it was shiny and translucent, and nightmarish rows of teeth nested in infected tissue. Then it spoke, and its voice left a white-hot hole in her mind like a cigarette burn on tender skin. She was on her knees. She was screaming as blood poured from her nostrils.

I will tell you what becomes of the flesh, Nadine. Lovely Nadine with your long, long legs and your hair like summer. Your father thinks of you as he touches himself. He dreams of your wet little holes, your long, graceful toes. You suspect these things. You understand them, but there is nothing you can do. This is the nature of separation. Pain. Loneliness. Deformations of desire, all to bridge a gap that cannot be bridged, save through union with us. With me. Aren't you tired of being afraid, Nadine? Of being lonely? Tess will never understand you. Nor will this sad little thing, trying so pitifully to reshape itself with neither art nor understanding.

She was vomiting. She couldn't see out of her left eye. Hands had her. Took Gabe, who was waking now, crying out and coughing up something thick and black and sticky. She was alone. She was alone and her brain was on fire and there was nothing, nothing but an endless darkness clawing at her stomach, eating away at her insides.

I can make it stop, Nadine. I can show you what the mushroom did, the dance of chemicals and electricity that will strip loneliness away from you forever. The final yielding up of meat to consciousness. The boundless freedom of the void. My servants have prepared you and the time has come, Nadine. Lovely Nadine. Let me in. I will show you true love.

A deep, tooth-rattling concussion shook the chamber. Dust and plaster sifted down from overhead and Nadine was halfway up the staircase, Felix and Shelby dragging her between them as below the chittering Gabe-thing skittered from the Cuckoo's path. It squirmed toward them, moving rapidly for its huge size. Up ahead Gabe staggered in John's wake, on his feet but covered in sweat and with vomit down the front of his shirt. John threw himself against the inner door.

Below, the Cuckoo reached the steps. Its bulk spilled into the narrow defile as with spindly fingers it seized hold of its lower jaw and wrenched it down, opening a bloody furrow in its mass. Teeth wriggled from the seeping flesh. Tongues spilled from the cleft. Over the top of its humped enormity she could see the rest of its bloated caterpillar form writhing in the chamber below, plaster and dust raining down on it along with the occasional chunk of concrete. Fat, hairy eggs slid from openings near its rear. Inside them, murky forms were thrashing. Thick snakes of muscle coiled around its flopping makeshift maw, giving it structure as the thing dragged itself toward them.

Another blast, this one followed by a thunderous, rippling series of crashes as something aboveground collapsed. More rock dust showered them. Nadine got her feet under her just as John kicked the inner door open, the lock splintering and tearing loose. They spilled out into the laundry room. Garth was on his hands and knees beside a workbench set along the far wall, a shotgun lying near him. He must have fallen in the tremors. John crashed into him and knocked him to the ground. The shotgun skittered away over the concrete as Gabe and Malcolm piled onto the fallen counselor, punching and kicking his prone form. As the man thrashed, John grabbed his head in both hands and slammed it hard against the floor. Garth's legs jerked. His back arched. He collapsed and didn't move again.

Nadine.

She staggered back. The Cuckoo had reached the top of the stairs, its swollen mass overflowing the frame as its toothy snout, draped in folds of quivering flesh, snapped at the air. Hooked claws and fumbling fingers pulled it slowly, inexorably into the laundry room, its neck extending as fresh lattices of muscle squirmed under its skin. In the depths of its gnashing maw, a pale eye blinked. Its pupil dilated.

Lovely Nadine.

The door frame buckled outward with a resounding *crunch*. Nadine staggered toward the steps up to the farmhouse, groping for Shelby's hand. She found it and squeezed hard, not caring that it sent a red-hot shock of pain up her mutilated fingers. Halfway up the stairs, Gabe just ahead of her and Shelby just behind, she caught a whiff of sulfur in the air. A rotten egg stink. *They didn't notice the gas, or whatever's going on outside distracted them.*

She looked back over her shoulder, only for a moment, and saw the thing drive one of its hooks through the back of Garth's skull as it squirmed past him. The counselor convulsed and let out a strangled sort of squawk. Above the limb that had dealt the killing blow, a mouth opened in the Cuckoo's sloping bulk and echoed Garth's gargling death wail.

Then they were pounding out into the hall that cut down the center of the farmhouse, framed pictures falling from their hooks as a third explosion—this one unmuffled by rock or concrete—shook the house around them. *What the fuck is happening out there?*

"Gas!" she shouted, pushing Shelby ahead of her toward the front door. She could hear the basement steps breaking like matchwood under the Cuckoo's weight. "Outside! Outside!"

Shelby looked back at her, eyes wide with terror, and Nadine wondered how anyone could ever have mistaken her for a boy. She had such beautiful eyelashes. Such a perfect mouth.

"Go," said Nadine. "I'm right behind you."

Halfway to the front door she ducked into the kitchen. Through the windows over the sink she could see the barn was burning, its roof mostly collapsed and a thick tower of black smoke pouring out of the wreckage. Flames caressed its sole standing wall. Cinders danced in the air.

There. The matchbook Mrs. Glover had used to light her cigarette. She started toward the table when it struck again. The white fire in her head.

Nadine, it whispered, its voice clawing at her forebrain, shredding her thoughts as she crawled to the table on hands and knees and fumbled for the matches, hardly able to see. *Lovely Nadine, aren't you tired of being so strong for everyone? Aren't you sick of how they cling to you, look to you, need you? Come and be my baby, sweet Nadine. Crawl into my arms and I will nurse you at my breast. Sweet girl. Baby girl.*

It made an obscene kissing sound just as her fingers found the pack. She grabbed it and lurched in the direction of the door, hoping she wouldn't smack full tilt into the wall. Everything was smears of black and white and red and she heard Shelby calling for her. She had to get to the front porch, to get out of the reeking gas before it got to her. Just a few more steps.

Just a little farther.

"We have to go back!" Shelby screamed, clinging to the door frame. John had a hold of her shirt and he was shouting about gas and the pastor and the other counselors. None of it mattered. Somehow, Nadine wasn't with them anymore. "She's still in there! *She's still in there!*"

And then she was back. Nadine lurched out of the kitchen a few yards back along the hall, washed in the blue static glow of the TV, and brandished something at them with a wide, bloody grin. A match torn from Mrs. Glover's matchbook, which she held in her other hand. She took a step toward them. Shelby felt an overwhelming crash of relief, as though a wave had broken over her and flattened her into nothingness, serene and empty. It was going to be okay. Nadine would know what to do.

The floor under the other girl's feet erupted, splintered planks and shreds of fiberglass insulation flying. The Cuckoo had Nadine. Its malformed jaws worried her legs and side, shredding fabric and flesh. Dog mouths. Little ratlike rodent heads and crooked human teeth tore at her flesh. Its claws and spines punched through her skin, which tented against the penetrating barbs, as it extruded a long, glistening stinger from its bloodied mass and rammed it through her stomach. Shelby stared. There was an awful roaring in her ears. Someone was pulling at her, dragging her through the door and out onto the porch. Voices shouting words she couldn't understand. Down the steps. Reaching out with helpless hands.

No, no, no.

Nadine still held the match in her uninjured hand, her thumbnail poised against its head. Her lips moved, forming words that cut themselves deep into Shelby's heart. Shelby screamed them back. "I love you," she wailed. "I love you!"

Nadine flicked her nail against the striker. There was a spark. A flame. A wave of blinding red and white and yellow, the house's windows flexing like sails catching the wind, and then everything was fire and flying glass.

XIV

VIRGINS

"No!" Shelby screamed, a sound so high and wild and desperate it put a lump in John's throat as he dragged her back from the inferno. It was nothing next to the scream coming from the burning house. It sounded like a cat in heat being fed backside-first into a blender, a high, thin, gobbling cry that jumbled his thoughts, making it impossible to focus on anything more complicated than staying upright and pulling Shelby along with him. Glass from the windows had cut them all to shit, but there was no time to stop and see if any of it was serious.

As they retreated, Pastor Eddie came around the corner of the burning house. His little glasses flashed white in the flickering glare. He was in his shirtsleeves. Behind him, under the pall of smoke rising up from the house and barn, John saw other figures staggering and crawling in the heat haze. Maybe they'd been trying to form a bucket brigade when it was only the barn on fire. Then Nadine had—he couldn't think it, couldn't touch the memory of her face framed in the open doorway. Shelby was just keening now, no words, only a long, terrible wail. John pulled her back another step, and then Malcolm was in front of them, grabbing Shelby by the front of her shirt.

"We have to go!" he shouted. He slapped Shelby, not hard, but hard enough. She blinked at him with those big soft eyes. "Shelby, baby," he said, softer. "We have to go."

That must have been when Pastor Eddie saw them, because he let out a bellow like a wounded animal and broke into a jog, and then a run, his long legs eating ground as he pounded toward them, so much bigger than Garth, who he'd—*don't think about that.* John took a step back, and another. Then he remembered the shotgun. Malcolm and Shelby were already running. Felix had gone on ahead, and he was so fast. John would never catch up. One moment of bravery in his whole chickenshit life and he'd wasted it breaking down a door and—*Garth's head in his hands, the older man wide-eyed and blowing spit through his teeth*—Felix darted past him, wielding a shovel like a baseball bat, and swung it in a brutal arc to bury the side of the spade in Pastor Eddie's face with a wet *thunk.* John fumbled with the gun, knowing there should be a safety, but not where to find it.

The pastor's arms flew up, flailing blindly as Felix steered him around John and down onto his knees. John stumbled back as Pastor Eddie's face came apart like a fist unclenching. Fronds and tendrils dripping with clear, viscous mucus uncurled as his features opened, skin unsticking from itself, features reduced to a random topography of bumps on the thick digits of its grasping orifice, a gaping, crotch-like fork where alien muscles met around a puckered anal maw lined with peglike yellow teeth that clicked together rapidly, shifting in their gums.

"Pull the hammers down!" Felix shouted, leaning hard on the shovel to trap the Eddie-thing's head against the ground. "At the back of the barrels!"

The whole of the verdant crater seemed to bow inward as John found the little metal catches and thumbed them down. The thing *gobbled* at him, a sound like a turkey drowning in mud, and wrenched its head off of the shovel's blade. It slapped Felix away, knocking him sprawling, and John brought the gun up, his hands trembling, and pulled both triggers at once. There was a titanic *boom* that left his ears ringing and the Eddie-thing's face and shoulder came apart in a cloud of flying blood and meat. It fell, convulsing, and then curled in on itself like a dead spider and went still. John stood there, staring.

Then Jo, covered in soot and dust, a heavy satchel at her side, was tugging at his elbow, shouting something at him that he couldn't hear. *Where had she come from?*

There was no time to make sense of it. They ran.

Betty kept wondering when the sound would stop. It was a high, insistent whine in her ears, an unpleasant sense of pressure as though someone had stuffed her head with cotton balls. There was something wrong with her leg and she was thirsty, terribly thirsty. She'd watched Dana die when the barn roof came down. They'd been mucking the stables. She dragged herself through the garden, clawing at the grass and pushing with her right leg, her left sliding uselessly after her and the heat of the burning house beating against her back. She was almost in its lap before she noticed the body.

It was Athena. There was blood all over her, and Betty could see bone poking through her jeans. "Princess," Athena breathed. Her bloody, lacerated hand reached for hers. She must have been caught close to the explosion. "My princess . . ."

Betty hadn't cried since her sixth birthday when her older sister Charlotte had pulled out a fistful of her hair in a fight over her Dolly Surprise. Not when her father died, not when she broke her leg during a soccer game in freshman year, or even when Edith van der Lee had a breakdown the year after and told wrinkled old Sister Mary what she and Betty had been doing in the girls' room between periods. She was crying now as she let Athena take her hand, as she crawled another agonizing foot and laid her head down in that warm, familiar lap, now wet with blood. Athena ran her fingers through her hair.

"What's happening to me?" Betty sobbed. Someone was screaming, but she didn't want to look. She didn't want to see anything else. "Am I sick? Am I dying? Athena—"

"Shhh, princess," Athena said, her voice cracking a little. "Shhhh, now."

Betty hadn't cried at her grandma June's funeral, even though

Grandma June had been her favorite, had always let her eat what she wanted and play in the mud or in the woods out back of the old house. She hadn't cried when her stepfather got drunk and broke her kitten's back by stepping on her. Not even when he'd found her alone that first time in the backyard, by the birch trees, or any of the times after. Maybe it was all coming out now, those unshed tears. She couldn't seem to stop, not until long after the hand stroking her fell still.

When the thing that had been Cheryl came for her, she didn't fight.

They met no one else on their way up and out of the crater, though both times Gabe paused to look back he saw silhouettes rushing through the dark, billowing clouds of smoke around the burning compound. He could still see snatches of the thing falling huge and awful from the sky, of the first tender bodies it had stolen to conceal itself. The white fire had burned deep into him, deeper than the drug trip, until it melted its way through the bedrock of his consciousness and dropped like a falling star into the mad pink void beneath, the place where skeletal women of pure light spun and danced in a tearing wind amid the sound of babies crying, where semen dripped from tubes of mashed and deformed lipstick and eyeliner ran down the cheeks of featureless faces veiled by rivers of dark hair and the plastic arms of Barbie dolls opened to receive him in a slender and jointless embrace.

And then they'd come for him. His friends had dragged him out of that terrible room where the slimy, mewling newborn thing had made itself his double, kissing and licking his body, leaving slicks of mucus that dried into greenish crusts that now flaked away as he scratched at them. None of it seemed real. He'd helped Malcolm and John beat Garth, maybe kill him. The thing, the *Cuckoo*, boiling up the steps. Nadine.

He blinked rapidly to hold back his tears. He was dehydrated enough already. They'd drained the single canteen Jo had brought with her on her one-woman mission to blow the farmhouse to hell before they even reached the forest's edge. Shelby had stopped screaming, at least. Now she trudged in silence beside John, eyes red and expression blank. Gabe tried again to think of something to say to her, but what could he say that would mean anything beside the awful fact that Nadine was dead, that the best and bravest and toughest of them was gone forever. If he closed his eyes he could still see the fire chewing at her thrashing outline. The blast had seared the image deep into his corneas, Nadine and the Cuckoo all one wild black tangle of convulsing meat.

It was getting toward afternoon, he thought. The sun was high and shadows were dwindling to murky little pools. His feet hurt. He'd had blisters his whole time at camp and it occurred to him that maybe he'd outgrown his sneakers, a thought that brought on a violent wave of disgust. Gabe imagined his feet stretching, growing, spreading wider as hair sprouted in wiry tufts from the knuckles of his toes. How long had it been since he'd shaved his legs? He could feel his leg hairs catching in the ventilated fabric of his shorts, but to look down would be to see his knobby knees, his ankles—ugly, undefined—and all the rest of it. So in silence he trooped after the others, scrambling up and down the banks of dry streambeds and crawling under fallen trees supported by their living fellows until at last, in the shade of a huge knotted pine somehow clinging to life, they collapsed by wordless mutual agreement to rest.

Gabe lay staring up through the pine's branches, the sky just slits and pinholes of bright blue between the canopy of needles. When he closed his eyes he saw Nadine's silhouette—the one he'd seen once through a gap in the fence around the shower, the one he'd coveted and felt so much inchoate rage toward—coming apart in the red tide of the explosion. Before the searing heat and light had forced his eyes tight shut, he'd seen part of her upper body strike the top of the door frame, the Cuckoo writhing in agony behind, withdrawing back into the basement as ton upon ton of wood and shingle plummeted down on its massive bulk.

Brady must have been down there, too. And Smith. It hurt to think of Candace, who had blushed so prettily when he'd smiled at her. He wondered when he'd be able to think of himself as a woman, when it would feel anything less than mortifying to think "she" instead of letting the leaden weight of "he" drop from his tongue. He thought of Courtney Love's messy red lipstick and unwashed platinum hair, of her mint-green dress and Kurt's hand on her pale, smooth shoulder.

After a while with only the sound of ragged breathing, John spoke. "How'd you do all that?" he asked hoarsely, looking at Jo. "The dynamite. Where did you even get any of it?"

"Malcolm's bunker," she said, leaning back against the tree's thick trunk. Her face clouded. "Things . . . these things were chasing me, after the counselors took Brady. Like dogs. I was running. I was so tired, I'd been up a tree all night and my whole body was so stiff. I ran until I puked, and then somehow it was like my feet knew where to go, like someone was telling me the way. I think . . . whatever it was that thing was doing to us, the stuff it was putting in our heads, it must have opened us up to each other, because I knew exactly where that bunker was and how to get there. I got in just ahead of them. They couldn't fit through the passage, the way in through the rocks.

"I found the dynamite and blew them up while they were trying to get through the tunnel. They were too big for it. I thought I was going to bring the whole thing down, or blow myself up too, but it worked. I think one of them got away, maybe. They were all tangled together; it was hard to tell. Anyway, my plan was just to blow the whole farm apart, and then while I was coming down into the crater I saw them pull in and take you into the house. I figured I had to get them to come running."

"I told you all I wasn't fuckin' lying," said Malcolm, sitting up and glaring indignantly at the rest of them. For a minute it seemed as though things would somehow snap back to normality, as though Nadine and Smith and Brady might come stumbling and giggling out from behind a nearby tree and they'd all cry together and feel somber about the kids who hadn't made it, but they didn't, of course. Gabe was starting to understand that nothing would ever feel normal again. He ran a fingertip along one of the scabbed-over cuts he'd gotten when the farmhouse's windows exploded, a thin, clean line just above his right collarbone.

"What now?" asked Felix. His voice broke. "What the fuck are we going to do now?"

Shelby kept losing time. She would walk for a while, following Jo between and over the dead pines, down gullies and up the far embankments, and the ground would change like a reel switching in an old-fashioned movie theater. She heard something about a phone call and an atlas and a feed store in a place called Resolution, but that was just noise. It came and went. In between, in the moments when the world dissolved into a kind of black and rushing static, there was Nadine.

I love you, she had said, but what was there worth loving? She'd let herself be drawn out through the door, had left Nadine behind and stood there helpless while she died. Who could love something so weak and slow and stupid? That smile, almost a smirk. The freckles across that crooked nose, broken and badly set. The raccoon bruises under her eyes. Sometimes, when her thoughts wandered, she heard Nadine speak in the voice of the thing under the farmhouse, the thing that had whispered to Shelby in her dreams and in the room under the earth.

Why don't you come and stay with me, Andrew? Why don't you come back to the house and crawl down through the charred and splintered beams, the loose wiring, the sheafs of scorched and smoking insulation? Most of her pelvis is still in one piece down here. You could fuck it, Andy. You could shove that fat little worm in your pants right up into it, to keep her close. Hair in a locket. Did you love her or were you just jealous of her cunt? I can make it go away. I can kiss it better, Andy.

Come and kiss me. I've almost got her lips right.

They went single file down a narrow canyon, the walls closing in until it became a tunnel and Shelby had to shuffle along
sideways. Loose earth rained down on her head. She heard John
cursing behind her and couldn't find it in her heart to look back
or to help him. The thought of seeing his fat body wedged between the rocks made her insides curdle with self-loathing rage.
If she'd been thin and strong, Nadine wouldn't have needed to
help her on the stairs, wouldn't have been held up waiting for her,
wouldn't have trailed behind while the rest of them ran out the
door.

There was blood on the canyon floor and walls and loose rock
everywhere at the juncture where Jo must have killed the dog-
things she'd told them about, but no sign of the bodies themselves. Maybe a surviving thing had dragged its packmates away
to mourn them in private. Maybe it was crying over them right
now, gnashing its mismatched teeth and shedding cloudy tears as
conjunctival buildup gummed the folds and wrinkles of its muzzle. Would the Cuckoo cry for its dead offshoots, for its procurers
and caretakers who had burned alive in the farmhouse? She knew
it wasn't dead. She didn't know why she felt so certain, but she
did. It had survived.

*I hope Nadine hurt you, you fuckin' wad of bubblegum and
pubes. I hope you're screaming right now, for yourself and all your
little jellyfish-face babies.*

Shelby came out into a little courtyard in front of the bunker's
open door. Roots crawled over the rock walls and the ceiling of
the cave above. A thin humus of dry soil, fraying plastic bags,
and fragrant pine needles lay underfoot. She followed Jo into
the darkness of the entry tunnel. The back of her neck prickled
at knowing she stood under who knew how many tons of earth
and rock, but it was a distant fear. Little white moths fluttered
through the air as fluorescent lights crackled to life in the great
room past the tunnel and the airlock entrance, both its pressure
doors long since rusted open. A strange sense of déjà vu as she
looked around the common area. *Pantry, bathroom, bedroom,*

she thought, marking each exit in turn. Like her certainty about the Cuckoo's fate, the knowledge came from nowhere, but after everything was it really so strange? Maybe they were telepathic now, their minds frozen open like the bunker's doors after weeks of that thing's dreams and the drugs and their bizarre conditioning in Ms. Armitage's lessons. She couldn't make herself care.

Jo came back from the pantry with an armful of black plastic packets as the others sank down to the floor. Shelby took hers without enthusiasm. The thought of spooning food into her mouth made her want to vomit, and the water Jo brought them in a little tin pail with a dipper tasted like rotten leaves and metal. It felt good on her cracked lips, but what was the point? What was the point of any of it? While the others pored over a flaking and yellowed survey map, she slipped away into the bedroom and lay down on the frayed and rotting sheets of the old double bed, not much more than a moth-eaten mattress on a slab of concrete jutting from the wall. There was no light in the bedroom, only a sliver of pale blue cast by the common room's fluorescents, and as she closed her aching eyes, the coarse texture of the sheets and the smell of dust and mold began to fade, crumbling away into sleep where something hot and soft and wet was waiting for her, strong hands on her shoulders, guiding her mouth down to taste the salt. The sea. The blood.

What's your name? Nadine's voice whispered in her ear. The close heat of a bathroom stall. Golden light pouring in through the high, narrow windows.

Shelby.

Jo dozed in Felix's arms. They lay together on a folded wool blanket he'd found in the linen closet, a few ragged sheets pulled over them. They'd kissed for a while after the lights went down, but exhaustion had been stronger than desire. She kept thinking about Pastor Eddie's face unfolding, about his huge frame thrashing in the grass after John had shot him. She'd felt nothing looking at the body. No, it was Celine who haunted her. Celine with her bulbous eyes and crooked buck teeth, who she'd watched hesitate, sick with guilt, before kicking Nadine, who'd stumbled across Jo while she was planting dynamite up on the crater's second tier behind some rhubarb leaves and trying to figure out how long to cut the fuse. It had all happened so fast. Rolling through the rhubarb, the stalks crunching wetly under them, her hand clamped over Celine's mouth as they wrestled over the clippers the other girl was carrying.

It had ended so quickly. She wasn't quite sure how. The long scissor blades buried in the other girl's throat and Jo kneeling astride her, hands over her mouth, until the jerking stopped. Had she cried then, as Celine's last breath husked against her spit-slicked palms? She couldn't remember. She'd almost forgotten to light the fuse before creeping away, low to the ground and moving fast but part of her wanting to run back and throw herself onto the dynamite where she'd left it half-buried in the rich black earth. The shock of detonation—not the sticks in the rhubarb patch, but two she'd left at the northeast corner of the barn—had slapped her to the ground like a giant's hand and for a moment, rolling over to her back, she'd seen the plume of brown and red expanding to fill the whole sky, burning fragments of the barn borne up spinning with it, and thought that she was staring into Hell. Scraps of wood raining to the ground around her, trailing arcs of smoke across the sky.

Celine's dead, flat eyes among the rustling leaves.

Shelby woke all at once. For a moment, before the day came rushing back, she had no idea where she was or why it was so dark, the air so dry and close. Her throat was parched. It hurt to breathe. Slowly, feeling her way through the blackness, she slipped out of bed and found the doorway to the common room. A cold wind slithered low around her ankles, blowing in through the open airlock. A line of moonlight lay aslant the room. Someone's leg.

A hand. By the door, stars swimming on its surface, the water pail. She picked her way with painstaking care across the forest of sleepers and knelt down to drink, savoring the stagnant water even though it numbed her teeth. Her clothes felt grimy, the tender skin under her belly rashy and inflamed. She drank another cupful and then turned, mouth aching with cold, to find John sitting up in the moonlight.

"What's going on?" he asked, voice bleary. He looked beautiful half-lit in silver, his pale skin smooth, his soft, round shoulder and the spill of his belly somehow delicate. His stretch marks shone like rivers and she wondered how it was that she could hate her own so much when they were so tender and so otherworldly on him. She went to him slowly, on her hands and knees, and laid her palm against that quivering slope as he stared at her, not speaking. His big, dark eyes. She could feel things where she touched his skin, feel them the same way she'd heard the Cuckoo's voice or seen the dreams the others stumbled through alongside her own, as though through a fluttering tear in the world. Nights spent starving in bed. Calories and supplements and the guilty hum of the refrigerator after midnight, the whole house dark and poised to pounce at the first creak of a floorboard, the first sticky hiss of an ice cream carton's lid pulled up.

How many hours spent pulling the skin of his face taut over the bones beneath, imagining his features hard and definite, the cream and butter of him all sliced bloodlessly away in one ecstatic pass of the knife—the same knife she'd imagined kissing her own flesh so many nights as she lay staring at her ceiling, begging the universe that tomorrow she might wake up right, that it had all been just one long, sick joke and now she could leap free of the body in which they'd caged her, surplus flesh abandoned in a shapeless steaming heap—and they were kissing, his hands recreating the generous curve of her hip, the crease at her waist, the velvety heft of her tit.

If I'd never gotten fat, she thought, kissing his throat, *I wouldn't even have them.*

Someone touched her leg and she was watching Aimee Mann sing "Stupid Thing" on *Late Night,* her hand down the front of her striped pajamas, while her friends dozed all around her in the living room. A voice murmured not far from her ear and she was listening to the slap of flesh on flesh as her parents made love in the next room over, her mother crying, "Oh, Stan, put a baby in me. Please, Stan. God. God!"

Someone peeled off her underwear, working them over her thighs and out from under her weight. She was on her back now, shredding tulle and taffeta with hands and scissors, the sink and the tile floor all covered in locks of her long, dark hair. Their memories flowed through her like tributaries into a river, the rush of smells and fractured images growing louder with each passing moment. A dog lying broken on hot pavement. Wind turning the green and silver leaves of a great willow. Something dark and spicy simmering in a pot on the stove, the smell of it blooming out in a translucent cloud as her mother helped her lift the lid. A little hand gripping the edge of a doorframe and phlox nodding in the sunlight and the feeling of dark mud, fine sand, red clay between her toes and here and there the visions overlapping, spliced together awkwardly so that the images formed ghosts of one another twisting in the particolored daydream haze. Exhaling weed smoke as the world dilated around her. Stealing into a laundry room to paw through leggings, skirts, and panties, to let another boy dress her as though the pilfered scraps were finery and she was Marie Antoinette. She was Nadine, stepping from the fire into her open arms.

Tawny hair spilling soft over Shelby's shoulders. It felt like Nadine was with them, or she was, or would be again someday. Shelby kissed her. She pulled the other girl's grinning face up to her own and made a seal between their mouths, sucking and licking hungrily as hot tears ran down her cheeks to salt her lips. There was a finger in her, spit-slick and tentative, and someone was licking her hip where it met the curve of her belly, and someone was kissing her, someone's mouth was at her little breast, someone's hand held her jaw gently cupped. There were hands that feared her, hands that held desire and disgust in equal measure, hands that wanted her with a deep, burning heat, and all of the hands were Nadine's and none of them ever would be again. She had never come with someone else before, but she came then, not once but twice, first in an emptying rush that left her gasping at the center of their human knot, fireworks in her ears, and then in a long, slow shudder which seemed to cover all the world's sounds in a thick drapery of silk.

Shelby fell asleep still tangled with the others, still seeing what they saw, and dreamed of swimming somewhere warm and blue and trackless. In the morning they lay for a while in the pale light of dawn. It felt strangely grown-up, that hour in that empty place, chatting in hushed voices as one by one they rose and drank and started to prepare to leave. It felt to Shelby as though she were peering into her own future, into a world of bills and paperwork and answering phones with a big fake smile in her voice in which nonetheless there would be moments like this, moments of clarity and love when everyone around her would understand the things she'd been through in her life, when they could be together in the arms of something greater than themselves. In the bathroom, the dead man's skeleton curled in the shower, she cried for Nadine until no more tears would come.

They left the bunker not long after.

XV

THE DESERT

Jo led the way down through the foothills, following the path of a dry stream. The others walked strung out behind her, no one talking about what had happened last night in the bunker's soft, enfolding dark, that pale stripe of moonlight falling across their backs and limbs and open mouths. Her legs and pelvis still thrummed with the power of it, like static building in her veins, but it no longer felt completely real. Shame and exhaustion crept back in the farther they walked and the more the world became about wet socks and blisters and the crackle of dry air in thirsty throats. Felix's best guess was that they had a two-day walk ahead of them, maybe more.

They had just passed beyond the forest's edge and out into the flat country when the noises began. Jo turned at the first distant blast of wood exploding under pressure. The treetops swayed far back along the slope. *That's close to the bunker,* she thought, her heart hammering. She still had the shotgun, for all the good it would do. Wood splintered. Groaned. Cracked with gunshot reports as forty-foot ancients toppled to the forest floor some miles behind them, the thunderous boom of impact presaged by the rippling crackle and snap of branches breaking. They stood in silence as the giants fell.

The squeal and clatter of stone against stone soon joined the cacophony. Dust rose up from among the trees and plumed from rockslides which grew and spread, gouging vee-shaped wounds in the dead forest. A scream came from the midst of all of it, not the strangled choral wail that had risen from the burning house but a sound like dogs at hunt in an old movie, a layered baying interspersed with a shrill screech of rage. It echoed in the hot, dead air until another cry, smaller and more distant, came up from the fading sound to meet it.

"We need to go," said Jo, finding her tongue.

They walked, quickly at first and then slower as the heat pressed down on them in earnest. For the most part the ground was flat and barren, the soil dry, what little vegetation clung to the earth brown and dead and desiccated. Here and there it dipped where rain had rutted it, plates of dried mud peeled up separately from one another.

The next time she looked back, it was waiting at the forest's edge. They must have been almost a mile away then, but the size of it made distance hard to judge. A landslide of flesh, white and pink and brown and scabby red, banners of wet hair hanging like moss from limbs that coiled around dead tree trunks. Delicate fronds waved among the branches as the thing heaped itself higher, cresting like a wave but never quite breaking for all that it strained toward them.

It doesn't want to be out in the sun, Jo realized. She thought of her Oba-chan's melanomas near the end, those dark, raised moles where the skin had died and replicated over and over and over until whatever engine drove it came apart in a rush of flames and screaming metal. Was that thing, that alien or monster or demon or whatever the fuck it was, afraid of getting skin cancer? The others looked back, following her stare.

"Oh God," Shelby sobbed, burying her face in John's chest as he wrapped his arms around her. "No, no."

A voice cut through Jo's thoughts. Her mouth hung open, drying out. Drool dripped from her chin. *Come back, Jo! Please, come back! It has us! It won't let us go! Please help us.* Flesh parting like a sigh. A green eye opening in the raw meat beneath, gazing at her through its thick eyelashes. *Help me, Jo.*

She staggered back, retching. Hair the color of wheat and honey wriggled out of the ground and caught at her legs, caressing her, wrapping itself in wet, clinging coils around her shins and ankles. Loose earth shook from the tresses as she struggled. Someone had her under the arms. They were pulling her, yanking her back. The earth from which the hair had sprung began to part, solid wedges of dirt rising as something beneath pushed its way to the surface, plump lips puckering, milky slime dripping from a cat's rough tongue.

Only you can give me what I need.

And then, like a soap bubble popping, the voice was gone. No hair. No silky wet caress. Just the distant bulk of the Cuckoo at the edge of the wood, a vast serpentine thing coiled tight around a huge dead pine, fronds and feelers blooming from its fat segmented sides and shapeless head. It loosed another scream, raking empty air with scythe-like forelimbs. Shelby was still crying. Malcolm's face was ashen, his hands trembling. Jo stared at the bloated thing, John still holding her up, until at last it uncoiled itself slowly from its perch and squirmed away into the wood, trees swaying and crackling as it brushed against them or used their trunks to anchor its progress.

None of them spoke until the sound of its retreat had faded into the distance, replaced by the hiss of the wind scouring the open flats. "It has her," Shelby said, and Jo knew it had spoken to the others, had uncoiled the dirty tendrils of its mind and offered them its luscious, dripping gift. They had felt their own version of it last night, she realized, the dying embers of whatever telepathic fire it had worked so hard to bank in their minds giving them a single moment outside of aloneness, a little chemical byblow of its attempt to digest them into its protozoan bulk. Union, pure and true and beautiful.

"We have to go," said John, his voice cracking.

Slowly, one by one, they turned and walked away from the memory of that sandy hair, those green eyes, the bruises and split lips and bloody teeth. Each of them, in their own way, left the ghost of Nadine and all the others behind.

* * *

They were out of water by the end of the first day. Jo thought maybe they should walk at night, avoid the sunlight that had left them all red and peeling, lips cracked, hair stiff, but the cold was worse, the ground riddled with gopher holes and squat dwarf cacti bristling with two-inch spines. A short while after sunset they stopped in their tracks, the sound of ragged breathing suddenly unbearably loud in the absence of their footsteps, and sank down to the dirt to bolt their MREs—a brownish paste masquerading as veal cutlets in tomato sauce—and collapse into exhausted, dreamless sleep.

In the morning Jo woke so sore she almost cried just getting to her feet. Her shoulder where Celine had clawed her throbbed and burned and the joints of her knees were swollen. She'd started her period sometime in the night and her underwear and the crotch of her jeans were soaked through and drying to an itchy, iron-stinking crust. At least her head had finally stopped aching, even if her stomach was in knots. She shuffled over to where Felix and John were poring over the atlas, spread out on the dirt and anchored at the corners by stones.

"We just need to keep heading for that rise," croaked Felix, pointing toward a brown smear on the horizon where the flat, endless hardpan rose slightly into a small hill. He cleared his throat, tapping a finger against a faded illustration on the map. "My uncle's a surveyor; these lines mean elevation. The town should be a little way past it."

"I'm so glad we're following the map of a guy who built a fallout shelter in the middle of nowhere and then slipped in the shower and died," said Malcolm. He squatted not far off, picking at the wrapper of an MRE. "I can't wait to fall into some fucking sinkhole he forgot to chart."

"Shut up," snapped Jo. She took a step toward him, suddenly unable to stand the sound of his whining for another second. "If you don't have anything useful to say, just shut up. Shut up. Can you even do it? Can you do anything but fucking run your mouth?" She pushed him. He fell back on his ass and it felt *good* to see his eyes go wide. He scuttled back from her on his rear, heels kicking dust. "Shut up!" she shouted, catching his shin with a glancing kick. "*Do* something or *shut up!*"

He whipped something at her, a rock the size of a walnut. A bright, infuriating pain like being flicked by a giant just above her eyebrow. She staggered back. She felt raw flesh when she probed the wounded spot, and her fingers came away sticky with blood. She squeezed her eyes shut, fighting down an urge to scream and throw herself on Malcolm, to claw his face and gouge his eyes. It wasn't his fault he was a stupid fucking clown. When her pulse finally stopped hammering, she looked down at him.

"I'm sorry," he said. His voice was small.

The others stood around them, tense and tired, John with tears in his eyes. Jo swallowed. "Me too," she forced out. It was still so cold. For a moment they all stood there, saying nothing, as though they were trying to find the thread that would take them forward out of this huge, flat void of broken earth and empty sky. Those who could eat did so.

Gabe was almost done pissing by the time Jo thought to shout at him to stop, to finish in one of the canteens.

In case they needed it.

Every step found a new way to hurt John. A grinding, burrlike pain in his heel. A molten sting as torn blisters shifted between shoe and foot. A dry, feverish stiffness as his calves cramped, and the gummy chafing of the skin under his belly, which shifted each time he swung one leg ahead of the other. His head ached. His mouth was dry and cottony. He kept thinking about a hot summer day when his mother had taken him out for homemade strawberry rhubarb ice cream from the little place a few miles from his grandfather's cabin on Lake Superior. He could still taste the tart, sweet ice flavor on his tongue. He could still see the tears in his mother's big blue eyes—his father had been sleeping on the couch for months by then, and had for years until her diagnosis—and the soft weight of her belly in her lap. He knew even at nine that she didn't think of herself as beautiful, but to him the sun rose and set with her smile. *Mama's boy,* his father had called him more than once, lip curling in disgust.

Phillip Bates said it again the day he found John's magazines, all those muscular, sweat-slicked bodies so unlike John's own— *I've been patient with you, learned to live with the laziness, the lying, the mama's-boy theatrics, but I'll be damned if I raised a queer*—and now his son realized that he'd just been guilty. He hadn't been able to love her, his soft round wife with her wavy golden hair and ruddy cheeks, the product falsely advertised by the thin, hollow-cheeked woman in their wedding photo, and he hated that John hadn't minded at all, that his fat wife and his fat son had adored each other, had even sometimes been happy in spite of the cold, looming presence of his martyred disapproval.

It felt strange, to realize something like that out here where it didn't matter at all, where it couldn't shield him from the dust and grit the hot wind drove across their path or prevent the sun from crisping his face, his arms, the back of his neck. His skin was hot and tight. What a joke, a fat boy thinking about ice cream as his body started shutting down. How'd that old chestnut go? *I love you like a fat kid loves cake.* He'd heard that one a lot at the fat camp his father and Sheila had sent him to a few years back. Sometimes it had snuck into his thoughts as he lay in his bunk at the end of the day, heartsick and crying for his mother, who'd been buried just a few months earlier. *I love you like a fat kid loves cake. I love you like a fat kid loves cake.*

It was so dumb on its face, so bluntly simple in its cruelty, that he hadn't figured out until the humiliation of his final weigh-in the deeper, more insidious barb it had hooked deep inside him, tangled up in bone, impossible to remove: that he could never again hear the words "I love you" without finishing the sentence in his head.

Like a fat kid loves cake.

* * *

They had to drink it, of course. By noon they were all practically delirious, so dehydrated they could barely cry, and so when the canteen came around Gabe tipped it back without hesitation and swallowed a mouthful of acrid piss. It wasn't as bad as he'd feared, really. He'd tasted it before while sucking cock, a little trace of bitterness in the gamey bouquet of an unwashed groin. At least the hunger was easier to bear. It made him feel good. Special, almost. Like he was sacrificing something for the greater good by leaving his unfinished MREs scattered across the desert. Maybe he'd never get a chance to be a girl, not really, but at least when they found his body out here his collarbones would be standing out like the prows of battleships.

I'd have to pick a whole new name, he thought. *Buy new clothes. Hormones, somehow. And then what, spend my life saving up for someone to cut my thing apart and shove it up inside me?*

He tried to make it a hateful thought, a lash of punishment thrown back over his shoulder, but just the idea of it brought such a wave of relief that he almost stopped in his tracks. That was exactly what he wanted. His whole life he'd been creeping along with the weight of his manhood crushing him as flat as a cockroach, dirty and untouchable even when a lover was inside him, when someone blushed and smiled just at the sight of him. It was like the minute he'd slipped out of his mother the doctors caught him in a trash bag full of putrid sludge and tied it off, trapping him inside for the rest of his life.

Shelby was a few paces ahead of him. He wondered if she'd felt this way, if she still felt this way. How long did it take to slip out from under their burden and start life as something new? He watched her hips move, her ass swaying from side to side. She looked like a girl. A real one. A sudden spasm of misery cramped his stomach; he would never look like that, those curves, that hourglass shape. Shoulders too broad, hips too narrow, chest too wide. He would be a cheap knockoff of a woman, a slouching scarecrow in garish lipstick and blue eyeshadow.

He found himself wishing he was home in Idaho again, walking somewhere in a shaded wood. It was so much easier there to feel safe, to feel unseen and anonymous. Here there was no escape, nowhere to hide or shelter or rest, just the unrelenting emptiness stretching away on all sides, heat haze shimmering at the horizon, and the sun staring down at them like the eye of God. A formless little nothing in a plastic bag full of filth, writhing as it drowned. He wanted to lie down in the dirt and curl into a ball. He wanted Shelby to hold his head against her chest and whisper that he was a good girl, he was pretty, he was good and sweet and perfect. He wanted his mother, though the thought of her touching him as she hadn't since the lake made him sick to his stomach. He wanted her to tell him it would be all right.

She sent me here to die, he thought. *They both did. They're home now with Mackenzie and they're not thinking about me at all. They don't care that it's been three weeks. They don't care that I haven't called. They want me to go away so they can go back to being perfect, so she can forget the lake and try again with a fresh kid. She'd never do it to Mackenzie. She'd never do it to her little girl.*

Her only daughter.

They stopped to eat as their shadows lengthened, spilling dark over the rocks and soil. Gabe's legs felt like overcooked spaghetti. His spine ached and his head felt curiously empty, as though his thoughts were draining out his ears to dribble on the sand. Ham and scalloped potatoes. It tasted like ashes. A swig of piss to wash it down. This time he swilled it through his teeth to ease the rasping dryness in his throat.

"Are you going to finish that?" John croaked.

Gabe felt a surge of selfless euphoria as he handed the plastic packet to the other boy. Now it wasn't his decision. He *had* to go hungry, because someone else needed his share. In a perverse way it comforted him to watch John eat, to see those soft, round shoulders move as the other boy scooped grayish paste into his mouth. His bulk was reassuring, every calorie poured into it one more that separated them, that assured Gabe he would never look that way, never have to drown in a body like that, wrists creased like a baby's, heavy rolls spilling over the waistband of his shorts.

You're being cruel.

They started walking again not long after. For a while they went in silence, Jo leading them and Shelby at the rear, their shadows slithering huge and dark and spindly beside them. It seemed impossible that just a day ago they'd all been in each other's arms. Maybe it had been a dream. Maybe all of it had been one long and terrible nightmare, and any minute now he'd trip or pinch himself and wake up back in his bunk at a good old regular American torture camp for troubled teens. In another few weeks they'd drive him home and his father would say gruffly that he liked the short hair and his mother would make a comment about his color, and then at some point he'd climb into the bath and slit his wrists with a broken Coke bottle and they'd find him there, face slathered in clownish makeup, staring at nothing while flies cleaned their forelimbs on his glassy, open eyes.

There's no place like home, he thought bitterly. The rise in the distance didn't seem any closer. His feet hurt. His head had started to swim, and his sunburns were peeling. By sunset he knew he'd look like one of Francis's lizards midmolt. He wondered if he'd still have pee in his stomach when the coroner cut him open, assuming anyone found their bodies out here. The desert was probably full of half-grown bones. He was still mulling that unsavory thought when Malcolm, his voice hoarse and ragged, started singing.

> *Great big globs of greasy, grimy gopher guts*
> *Mutilated monkey meat*
> *Hairy pickled piggy feet*

Jo groaned. Felix looked back with a grin. Behind Gabe, Shelby took up the uneven chant, yelling in something like harmony with Malcolm.

All comes rolling down the dusty, dirty street
And I forgot my spoon!

And then they were all singing it, belting it out loud enough that their voices pushed back the endless emptiness, loud enough to take the worst of the sting out of every step, to wash away the morning's stupid arguments and scuffles and make them feel, if only for a little while, that the thing they'd left behind was nothing but a slimy lump, an overgrown Jabba the Hutt, and someday its voice would stop echoing in their heads and its memory would leak away, and they would feel clean again.

Great big globs of greasy, grimy gopher guts
Mutilated monkey meat
Hairy pickled piggy feet

As if to say, you're nothing special, you Spencer's Gifts–looking bitch. You dillhole. You're just a sack of roadkill and old wigs. You're a pound of hamburger somebody dropped on the carpet. They sang until their throats were raw, their shadows starting to dissolve into a deeper darkness, and even after the words trailed away Gabe felt lighter, more free. He was still smiling when his knees buckled, firecrackers of incoherent sensation going off in his head, and he dropped face-first into the dirt. Grit on his lips. Taste of blood. Then nothing.

Malcolm held Gabe's head in his lap as the others clustered close around them. Gabe was breathing, but his pulse felt fluttery and weak when Malcolm pressed two fingers to his throat and his bruised eyelids twitched as though he was caught in some awful dream. He hadn't stirred, not even when slapped and pinched. The sun was getting low.

"We'll sleep here," said Jo. Her whole face was peeling, right up to the hairline, and her dark hair was stiff with salt and dirt.

She looked like shit. They all looked like shit, and now stupid anorexic Gabe—could boys even get anorexia?—was down and the rest of them wouldn't be far behind.

Malcolm stroked Gabe's hair for lack of a better idea. "It's okay," he murmured to the other boy. "You're okay, baby."

They ate in silence. The thought of drinking from the canteen made Malcolm want to hurl, even though his mouth felt like it had been packed with sawdust, so he waved it on. John broke out a gas lantern he'd found in the bunker and in silence they tried to find the most comfortable patches of dirt. Malcolm could just see the first stars coming out over the mountains, pinpricks of white in the bruise-purple sky.

The coyotes appeared not long after the sun had set. Three of them, waiting on their haunches outside the pale circle of lantern light. They were gangly things, no bigger than collies but with long, slim legs and pointed snouts. Their tongues hung from their grinning jaws and in the dark their eyes glowed flat and cold as coins. *They're waiting for us to die,* thought Malcolm. He was tired enough that there was no drama to it, just an exhausted sense of resignation.

John sat down beside him. For a while they said nothing, Malcolm still stroking Gabe's hair, the coyotes fading in the gathering dark until only the glow of their eyes and the gleam of light on spit-slicked teeth remained. A tight knot of anxiety formed in Malcolm's chest as the silence stretched on and on. It was getting cold again, the icy chill of night in the open desert creeping back into his bones. Finally, John spoke.

"I like you," said the other boy. Malcolm could practically hear him blushing. "Do you like me? I honestly can't tell. If it was just the drugs, whatever they gave us, that's fine. That's okay. It's just that I'd like to know."

"You know there are literally scavengers waiting to, like, pick our carcasses clean right now," said Malcolm. He didn't like how snippy his voice sounded, how panicked and defensive. He sounded like his mother when someone pointed out she wasn't making sense, or caught her in one of her lies.

"I know," said John.

Malcolm thought of the other boy's weight on top of him, of the feverish intensity with which his body had given itself up to John in the midst of whatever drug trip they'd been sent on. Part of him wanted to lunge back into those soft, strong arms, to spend however long he had left rubbing himself off against John's thigh, but another part, one he didn't fully understand, that spoke not in words but in the silent language of sidelong looks, knew that to be with John was to give up something precious, some indefinable cachet that everyone knew by sight without ever having heard its name spoken aloud. That same sense had driven him to mock the fat boy on their first day digging postholes for the fences, and it kept him silent now.

Something screamed in the distance, breaking the unpleasant stillness between them. Not the Cuckoo, but something like it. Some nasty little tumor, he thought, that must have wriggled loose from its vast bulk and slunk out after them across the plain. One of Jo's dog-things. The coyotes fled at once, the glow of their eyes vanishing into the gathering dusk. He wondered if they knew to fear it from experience, if it had crept out here in the years before it found Mrs. Glover and snatched their pups, if it had given them sweet little replacements, balls of fluff with too-big paws, mischievous, panting grins, and cold, dead eyes like little chips of glass. Malcolm felt like his guts were full of ice water.

Jo bent and lifted the lantern. She had the shotgun in her other hand, its stock across the crook of her arm. "Can you move him?" Her voice trembled. Her pupils looked huge in the hissing white light. "John, can you carry him?"

John scrambled over and after a false start got his arms under the skinny boy and heaved him up into a fireman's carry, then straightened with some effort. Malcolm tried to help, standing with him and supporting Gabe's head where it lolled against the other boy's back. The others were on their feet, too, pain and exhaustion forgotten. Something yelped out in the dark, whining and whimpering before it fell suddenly and totally silent. It sounded like one of the coyotes. Malcolm realized as he backed away from the sound that he'd pissed himself, urine soaking the crotch and leg of his jeans, and before shame he felt despair at wasting water.

A voice came from the darkness, high and desperate.

"Wait! Please, wait!"

They froze. Malcolm's own breathing seemed suddenly thunderous. He knew that voice. It was Nadine's.

"It's a trick," Felix whispered.

"Malcolm, take the light." Jo shoved the hissing Coleman lantern at him. "I need both hands. Quick. *Now.*"

He took it, fumbling with the handle, his fingers half-numb in the cold, and Jo broke the shotgun, checked the barrels, and then closed and cocked it. *Click, click.* She brought it up to her shoulder. He wondered if he could get it from her, if he could shove both barrels in his mouth and still stretch to reach the trigger. That or run. *Run.* His whole body ached for it, but he was so tired, and the dark was so complete out here, even with the whole sky bathed in a bright sea of stars. He'd never seen anything like that in Connecticut.

"Okay," said Jo. "Everyone, walk. Follow Felix."

"Help me. Please, you guys. I'm hurt. My leg . . . there's something wrong with my leg." The voice trailed off into a thready sob. *"Why won't you wait for me?"*

"Move," Jo snapped. She started backing away from the voice and Malcolm stumbled forward just to keep ahead of her, the lantern's light swinging wildly.

"Keep it steady," said Jo, her voice terse and taut. "I think it's the thing, the one I didn't kill back at the bunker."

"What if it's her?" Shelby sobbed. "What if she's alive?"

"Pleeeeeeeeeease."

It sounded closer now.

"You saw the house," said Felix. He had her by the arm and he was dragging her after him as John shuffled forward, bent under Gabe's weight. "She's dead. She was dead before it even blew. That thing ripped her apart. The roof caved in."

"It hurts. Please, it hurts so bad. My leg . . ."

Close enough now that Malcolm thought he could hear the scratch of claws on rock and dirt, the soft weight of padded footfalls. He caught a whiff of something rancid, a septic reek mingled with something like the bright, bitter tang of grapefruit juice. He kept moving backward, trying not to think about whether anyone else knew he'd peed his pants. How long had it been since he'd wet the bed? Four years? Five? He'd lived in terror of sleepovers in middle school, when people had still invited him to sleepovers. He'd lain awake at night staring at the ceiling and willing himself not to pee, or sit hunched and miserable on the toilet, horribly certain that somehow there were just a few more treacherous drops to squeeze out.

"Help me. Shelby, is that you? Shelby? I love you. I love you. It's the last thing I said before you left. Why did you leave me?"

Shelby was screaming now. No words, just animal shrieking, raw and awful. It reminded Malcolm of the time his uncle Marlon had shot a rabbit. The thing had been eating Marlon's cabbages and the bullet had severed its spine, leaving it to drag itself through the rows of tilled earth as it squealed and squealed in high-pitched agony. The worst sound he'd heard in his life before the last few days.

"Just keep walking," said Jo. "It must not want to get too close. Keep walking. Don't listen."

"I'm so cold," the thing whimpered. Malcolm caught a glimpse of something at the edge of the lamp light's circle. A glimmer of white fire reflected in huge eyes. The shine of spit on teeth as long as a woman's manicured fingernails. *"Please don't leave me. I can't keep up, you guys. Shelby . . . John . . . Please . . ."*

They kept moving. Malcolm felt sick to his stomach. His arms burned with the strain of holding the lantern up, but he didn't dare lower it. He could almost feel the thing's jaws closing like a vise around his throat. He could feel its claws unzipping his belly. The Cuckoo couldn't chase them, but it had sent a little part of itself after them, a guided missile of flesh and fat and bone streaking out across the flatlands, keeping out of the sun because the thing it was made of hated the sunlight, feared the cancerous blaze that baked the desert by day.

After a while the pain no longer seemed so urgent. The thing's pitiful whispers and entreaties became just white noise like his grandmother's *The Healing Sound of Rain* CD. *Greasy grimy gopher guts,* he thought, and almost giggled. At the light's edge the thing still lurked, pacing them effortlessly. John was red-faced and sweating bullets. Shelby had gone silent and let Felix lead her by the hand. Malcolm wondered how long they'd been walking. It might have been an hour. It might have been five minutes. He was so tired. The night seemed to swim around him. The starlight gleamed in the oiled barrels of Jo's shotgun.

This can't be happening, he thought, remembering the thing that had sniffed at the door of his cabin, the thing that had scratched at the planks. Had it been the dog? He missed her horribly. Gabe said she'd died, that Corey—or whatever the thing that called itself Corey was—had killed and eaten her. Had she belonged to someone? A stray lost in the trackless waste, or maybe abandoned by the side of the road. Or maybe there were other dogs out there, hunting gophers and hares and sleeping in big matted piles to stave off the cold, and they were mourning her right now, howling at the moon together.

I'm sorry I couldn't protect you.

Mary's hand in the door. Later he'd snuck her some of his Halloween candy, had told her jokes until she laughed and threw her arms around his neck and forgot the throbbing pain in her little fingers, which still didn't close quite right. Hairline fractures. Reese's peanut butter cups. Her little face against his shoulder. *You got your boogers all over me! Thanks. Now I'll have a snack for later.*

Ewwwww.

She'd called him Mallum when she was little. She couldn't make the hard *C* sound, not until she was almost six. He wondered as he took what felt like his millionth step of the night if he'd ever see her again. The lantern swayed at the end of his shaking arm.

The thing slunk along with them, smiling, drooling freely. Sometimes its claws caught at the edges of the light. Brown and cracked and curved, like the raptors in *Jurassic Park*. *Click click, click click*. He could see its humped back and the line of thick, bristly hair running along its spine.

"Shoot it," he begged. It felt like days had passed, slipping by in drips and dollops. His arm was on fire. He switched the lantern to his other hand, the light shuddering over clawed fingers too much like a person's. Snout a nightmare combination of weasel and girl, blond tresses dragging in the dirt. Lips wrinkling back from pretty little teeth. Rows and rows of them, all moving slowly, rasping at the air. "Shoot it. Please, Jo."

"Quiet," said Jo. She kept backing up, each step slow, steady, and deliberate.

"Mommy's hurting me, Malcolm."

Mary's voice.

"Kill it," Malcolm begged. He felt like he was going to lose his mind. "Kill it. Shoot it. *Shoot it.*"

"She shut the door on my hand again. She caught me touching myself and she held my hand there and she slammed the door like Grandma Ella did to her. You remember when she told us that story? You remember her eyes?"

"Stop, stop," Malcolm sobbed. His hand shook. The lantern's light danced wildly over that smug grin, those glistening eyes and under them the slow, meticulous shifting of something like a spider's mouthparts, palps rubbing against each other, mandibles clicking excitedly. Long ropes of drool shone bright.

"Mommy," it simpered in Malcolm's voice, pursing fleshy buds that came together into something like a pair of lips. *"Mommy, why'd you do it? She's just a little girl, Mommy. She doesn't know anything."*

"Easy," said Jo. "It wants you to freak out."

We're all going to die.

"Don't know how much longer I can . . . go," puffed John. His face was red, his back bent. Gabe showed no sign of stirring.

How far have we come? How long has it been?

The sky seemed a little lighter, the stars a little fainter. Would it stay with them once the sun was up? Malcolm kept moving. The thing had fallen silent. Only its smile showed in the deep dark, a ruthless Cheshire Cat grin. Then, suddenly, the lantern flickered with a sucking hiss. The pilot light guttered, dark and light stuttering over the ground and the others around him. Shelby let out a long, terrified moan.

The voice came again. So small. So vulnerable. Malcolm wanted to scream. He wanted to die.

"I'm scared of the dark."

"Off, then on," Jo hissed.

He stared, uncomprehending. The flame flickered again. Outside its shrinking circle, the thing smiled and stole a little closer, sinking lower to the ground.

"Off, then on again!" Jo screamed.

Malcolm twisted the lantern's key. The flame went out. He fumbled for the igniter, found it, punched it twice, three times, dry coughs from the pilot light, a shriek from the dark as claws scrabbled over stone and soil, the fitful hiss of gas, and then light, light like a star, and an earsplitting boom as Jo fired both barrels into the huge shape plummeting down on them like a pouncing cougar from above. It struck the ground near John, thrashing and squealing in agony, claws slashing at the air, the huge hairy duster of its tail sweeping clouds of grit into the air as it slobbered and vomited. It must have been ten feet from its pointed muzzle to the tip of its tail, its coat long and matted and patchy with something like mange. The others stumbled away from it. John fell, Gabe sliding from his shoulders to sprawl in the dirt, and Shelby was screaming again. Blood covered the ground, black in the dwindling light, and Jo was loading one last shell into the shotgun's breach. She shoved both barrels right down the thing's throat, ignoring the little fleshy digits and bony claws that scratched at the polished metal. She fired. Malcolm dropped the lantern to instinctively clap his hands over his ears.

Glass shattered. The flame roared, licking at the breach, and then went out.

The echoes of the last shot faded. The thing fell still except for a slight spastic twitching in its eight gnarled and bandy limbs. As Malcolm's eyes adjusted to the starlight and his pulse slowed to a dull, distant roar he could make out the human eyes set far back on its skull, and see the little traces of freckled skin, the hints of thin-lipped mouth pulled taut over alien bones. Had it been Corey? He didn't know. He didn't want to know.

He took a few unsteady steps back from the carcass and heaved up his guts. More wasted water. When he straightened, wiping his mouth on the sleeve of his filthy flannel, the others were helping Gabe to his feet. The skinny boy was pale and shaken, tears shining on his cheeks, and as Malcolm watched he threw his arms around John and the two held each other tight, crying, and he realized for a fleeting instant of embittered clarity that he'd let something slip through his fingers, and that he might never touch it again.

They went together down a slope of scree and loose red earth into the town of Resolution. A single main road cut through ten or fifteen side streets, a dull little grid of boxy stucco houses with flat roofs. Jo had never really thought about it, but with no snow to worry about you could pretty much build whatever kind of shoddy little box you wanted out here. No need for an incline or tight shingles. Just ugly shoebox rectangles of varying sizes, bigger the closer they got to the main drag, smaller the farther away from it you went.

At the base of the slope Jo paused to look back up the way they'd come, watching the eddies of sand and rock fragments. In a few moments it had all ceased, their tracks already starting to fill in as the wind wailed across the incline. She could still see the *thing* thrashing madly out there in the dark, its voice Nadine's one moment, her mother's the next. *Bad girl! Bad girl!* The way her mother spoke to her when Jo had really pissed her off, as though she were a dog that had piddled on the carpet.

If it heard me calling Oji, this is all for nothing.

They crossed a stretch of empty ground and passed into a cul-de-sac framed by three houses. Heavy red curtains hung in every window. Lawns were overgrown, fleshy stalks of sumac swaying over salt-eaten fencing and pushing up through the sidewalks. Hummingbirds danced in the morning chill. No one was out. It all felt half-real, the way things did after staying up all night; like seeing the world through one of those mounted binoculars they had on the boardwalk in Atlantic City. The big blocky kind you had to pay a quarter to use.

They'll be waiting at the feed store. They'll take us back.

Fremont Street to Thornton Avenue to Rumfitt Parkway. More red curtains. More greenery. More silence. There were no cars. Dawn was breaking now, pale pink and rosy red and a thin blush of gold, and Jo wondered half numbly when the things inside the houses would wake up. The houses on Rumfitt were nicer than the others they'd passed, big two-story sprawls with terra-cotta tile roofs.

Even if it hasn't been able to get word out here, they'll smell us. They'll see us. Even if they don't, even if we make it another day, or two, or a week, what if Oji isn't coming? What if he couldn't get out of that place? What if he couldn't get a car?

They turned onto Ransom Court Road, passing a shuttered pizza parlor and a corner store with a CLOSED sign hanging in the window. Inside were metal shelves of chips and candy, engine oil and shaving cream. A revolving rack of videotapes in black plastic cases, the names of the movies written in magic marker on strips of masking tape. She could just make out the names. *The Last of the Mohicans. Single White Female* right below it, and then something obscured by the edge of the front counter and the big plastic cases of scratch tickets atop it.

At least it will be over. At least I'll get to sit down and close my eyes. Maybe we can hide out in the sewers. Maybe—it occurred to her suddenly that it was probably down there already, wallowing in filth and runoff, feeding on the town's rancid sewage and waiting for some idiot to pop up one of the grates and wriggle right into its grasping claws. Eaten alive with her mouth and nostrils coated in the stench of shit. She put one blistered, aching foot in front of the other. There was blood leaking through the side of her left shoe, she realized, but the thought of bending down to see what was wrong made her want to collapse and roll into the street. Let it bleed. It didn't matter.

Savage Street. An auto repair place named Bud's, piles of tires beside a whitewashed cinder block garage. A tow truck and a few older station wagons parked in the oil-stained lot. Jo's heart leapt before she realized that chances were the engines were all dead, some crucial wire or cable cut. This place was like a duck blind painted to blend in among the waving reeds. Not nature, not really, but a lifeless imitation of it meant to lull the idiot prey into a false sense of security. People probably drove through every day, never noticing anything out of the ordinary.

They came to Main Street. A Chinese restaurant. A post office. Diners and shoe stores and cars parked in front of steel and plastic meters and a record shop with BLACKTOP VINYL stenciled on its storefront window. They stood on the corner for a little while, the sun in their eyes, and then Jo set off following the building numbers downward from 361. It was the longest moment of her life, going down that sidewalk, all those still, dark buildings pregnant with the threat of the things that would wake up and crawl out of whatever brackish pools they slept in to open up and make this place seem ordinary, just another no-name dump in the middle of nowhere, too small and sleepy to spare a second thought about.

She saw her mother's gray Lincoln before she realized they'd reached the feed store. It was parked out front, Oji asleep behind the wheel. He'd changed its Jersey plates out for dirty Ohio ones that read BIRTHPLACE OF AVIATION in little red letters under the serial number.

"Is that him?" croaked Gabe. He looked like a skeleton, skin stretched tight over his cheekbones, lips peeling and flaking. He gripped her arm. His hand was feverish. "Jo, is he really there? Is this real?"

"It would really be something if it was just some other old Japanese guy," said Malcolm, but Jo wasn't listening. Oji must have heard them talking, because suddenly his eyes were open and with a cry he levered himself up out of the driver's seat and hobbled toward her, arms outstretched. She ran to him and flung herself into his embrace, the last four days crashing down on her all at once like an avalanche until she was sobbing so hard into her grandfather's shoulder she could hardly stand. "My girl, my girl," he said, his frail voice cracking as he stroked her hair. "What did they do to you?"

It wasn't until the town was far behind them that she told him everything.

Part II

ABBY

"I keep seeing these people, all recognizing each other. Something is passing between them all. Some secret."

Invasion of the Body Snatchers,
Directed by Philip Kaufman, screenplay by W. D. Richter
1978

XVI

IT'S NOT YOU

Cook Canyon, Nevada
May 29, 2011

Canned food didn't keep as well in the car as Felix had figured it would. The heat was too much for it, which he'd discovered when he opened the trunk one day and found burst tins of beans and chickpeas soaking into the dark upholstery. Dry cereal. Granola. Nuts and raisins. It had to be fine sitting in the glove compartment for six days, or else it wasn't worth buying. It had been a little easier when he was in North Dakota scoping out the New Day Youth Wilderness Retreat. Dry, there. Cool at night. Kids shivering in tents while counselors smoked and gossiped around dying fires or fucked each other or, sometimes, slipped into silent tents by moonlight and fucked the kids.

He'd left a sheaf of glossies in the office of the Bismarck DA after a month of skulking after hiking parties, sleeping outside, and picking ticks off himself in truck stop bathrooms. A month later, with nothing in the newspapers and trucks still coming and going from the ranch where New Day had its headquarters, he'd sent copies of everything to lawyers and reporters all over the state, along with xeroxes of his notes—his handwriting carefully neutral, smoothed into typeface by years of practice. New Day were monsters, but only the human kind.

So, New Mexico. Six months trying to track down the full extent of the Integrity Pledge, a "personal mastery program" for delinquent boys he'd heard about on one of the parenting forums where he lurked, only for it to fold while he was in the middle of mapping out its leadership and investors. A boy in the program had died of appendicitis after his counselors ignored his screams and pleading for three days. The parents, being rich idiots, sued immediately, and the whole thing fell apart inside a month. He'd tailed staff and administration long enough to write them off as anything worse than callous grifters.

So, Nevada, eating macadamia nuts and sipping lukewarm water from a Nalgene in the boiling interior of his 2006 Civic as he watched traffic rocket past his hiding place in the shadow of a sun-bleached billboard reading JESUS KNOWS in huge, faded red letters. Every few minutes he checked the short list of license plate numbers he'd scribbled on the back of a takeout menu from a Chinese place in Carson City.

The trick to finding these people was: first you found an IP address for a mother looking to forum support groups to assure her she was doing the right thing by sending her twelve-year-old across the country into the care of unlicensed strangers. Then you staked out the house—a split-level an hour outside Louisville, husky always barking in the fenced backyard—and when a van came (and it was always a van) you noted the license plate. You couldn't follow them. Not really. Even an idiot gets suspicious with the same car in his rearview for a day at a time. So you run the plate—get scammed a few times on the dark web, then find someone halfway legit who tells you Cook Canyon, Nevada, and a last name, Glover, that makes you shrivel up inside, as though someone has sucked all the fluids out of your body with a straw.

All of that for the moment a white contracting van roared by doing eighty-five on the flat, shimmering stretch of road. Felix looked from paper to plate and back again. A match. He made himself wait, heart in his mouth, as the van dwindled into the distance before he turned the key in the Civic's ignition and eased out onto the road, the engine's hungry growl reverberating through his aching body. How long had he been sitting? Six hours? Seven? *Lactic acid builds up in your muscles when you sit,* his ex Tucker had told him once. *If you don't warm up before a set it can fuck with your joints.*

Why think about Tucker now? He hadn't seen the other man in years. No calamitous breakup, no big fight, just a slow, numb fading out, like it always was for him. A few tears. A few awkward phone calls.

Feels like you don't wanna see me, man.

I'm busy. It's not you.

No, I got that. Feels pretty much like it's you.

Okay.

That it?

I guess.

Okay, Felix. I love you.

Goodbye.

He kept the van just in sight for close to half an hour, squinting into the sunset. It was easy to get hypnotized out in flat country like this, nothing to look at for miles in any direction and the distant shadows of the Rockies lost in the glare. Easy to lose focus and drift too close to a mark, flip the switch in their head that made them go from treating you like landscape to following your every move. Felix was careful. He didn't even slow when they pulled off onto an unmarked service road, just blew past and waited until they were out of sight to pull a U-turn and mark the turnoff on his roadmap. He'd used GPS a few times, but he'd never quite been able to shake the feeling that if he were a parasitic hive mind slowly and stealthily spreading itself across the continent, the first place he'd want to be was wherever they monitored those satellites. He had a lot of thoughts like that.

He's paranoid, he'd heard Mal tell John when he'd stayed with them briefly back in the winter of 2004, before the two of them split up. *He's fucking insane.*

You remember that thing, John said. *You remember it just the same as I do.*

We don't really know what happened. We were kids. They were feeding us drugs.

Nadine died in front of us. I remember that.

Felix had left the next morning, slipping out while his hosts had tearful makeup sex in the next room, and that was the last time he'd seen any of them since. Their little band of rejects had fallen apart, the memory of the summer that had brought them together finally eating its way through their bonds until all they wanted was to be as far from one another as they could get. It was why, in spite of everything he'd seen on the forums he trawled, he almost hadn't gone to that house just outside Louisville, the split-level with the dog chained up and barking in the backyard, where Mark and Nancy Donovan had moved after their daughter died in a terrible accident at Camp Resolution in the summer of 1995, and where a few years later Nancy had given birth to a boy, the couple's first, a little late-in-life trauma baby to get them through the loss of Nadine.

In 2008, Nancy had begun soliciting advice from forum dwellers on what to do with her *sensitive* boy, who was getting a little too old for playing dolls with his big sisters and crying when he saw dead animals in the road. In 2009 she'd caught him playing "dress-up" in her oldest daughter's clothes, and by 2010, after his expulsion from Saint John Francis Academy for what the priests characterized as "lewd behavior" she began asking in desperate earnest for suggestions.

im at the end of my rope. i feel like i failed as a mother & now the whole nightmare is happening again. god gave me a second chance but what if i am the problem . . . ???

A flood of support. Praise for her courage, for her steadfast love, for her willingness to *sacrifice* for her son. Suggestions poured in, and buried among the military schools and wilderness retreats was a place called Integrity with a website full of misspelled testimonials and pictures of smiling teenagers, and that was the program Nancy Donovan chose. Of course it was. Felix didn't know how it had forced the issue, that disgusting thing that had haunted his nightmares for more than a decade. Maybe it lurked around families it had already fed off once. Maybe it wanted to get even.

Maybe it was just taking so many kids now that it snapped this one up by chance. Somewhere off the highway Tommy Donovan, age thirteen, whose most heinous crime seemed to have been asking that her parents call her Abby, was probably getting her head shaved right now.

Felix put it out of his mind. He had it. Sixteen years of robbing vending machines and shoplifting energy drinks as he crept inland from California, sniffing after rumors and clipping newspaper articles about dead kids and tough love, and it had finally slipped up. It had gone back to the scene of one of its crimes. He had the fucking thing in his sights.

XVII

CAPGRAS DELUSION

Boston, Massachusetts

Lara lit another cigarette from the glowing butt of her last, then sucked in a final drag and flicked the nub under the tires of the cars whooshing through the rain past the departures gate at Logan. The overhang kept the worst of it off but the air was still damp and cold, clinging clammily to her skin. She hunched deeper into her coat, shivering as she exhaled and drew the coils of heavy blue smoke up into her nostrils, savoring the earthy burn before blowing it out again. The coat was Michael Kors, a gift from a longtime client, and it was absolute shit for Boston in late fall. The wind cut right through the marled sheepskin and its dark silk lining. She took another deep drag.

Lung cancer, here we come, she thought as she watched rainwater hiss through a sewer grate a few feet from where she stood. The butt, caught in the gutter's current, swirled through the corroded iron and was lost to sight, borne down into the dark and out to—where? Boston Harbor? The Charles? Some scenic reservoir or wetland? Or maybe, some hateful corner of her brain suggested, it was Boston's version of the farmhouse basement. Maybe it lurked just out of sight, sifting the rainwater that fell through the grate, searching for anything edible, for anything it could hollow out and imitate.

New England always made her think like this. It was the cold, the rain, the ceaseless fucking humidity. Akira dying didn't help. He'd been kind to her, put up with her shit without so much as a raised voice, cooked for her night after night even knowing she'd just puke it up afterward. She closed her eyes and tapped her silver cigarette case against her hip. A gift from a client, a silver-haired old man named Rudy with a tan like a Ritz cracker and a dazzling white smile. He was waiting for her in Palm Springs, would be there to pick her up from the airport in his big silver Corvette, the top down and the light flashing in his sunglasses and from the band of his Rolex. They'd kiss, his cologne enveloping her in a cloud of heady musk, and she'd blow him while they did ninety on the highway, the Stones or Jefferson Airplane blasting from the Corvette's speaker system loud enough that she could feel it in her bones. She'd straighten up after, fixing her lipstick as the wind blew through her hair, and he'd say something like "You're a hell of a girl, Bunny," before dropping her off at her hotel with an envelope and a promise to call her sometime that week.

It would be warm there. She'd have a room overlooking the lagoon. She'd lay out by the hotel pool, feeling like a movie star, watching men and women check her out in passing, feeling the outer edges of their lust the way she had since the summer of her fifteenth year. A trace of the wild power that had danced in her that summer, that had woken her screaming so many nights with fragments of the others' dreams replaying on an endless loop lodged in her mind and made the psych ward such a deafening hell of overlapping want and misery and hatred. She always knew when someone wanted her.

"Think I could get one of those?" asked a man in a Red Sox sweatshirt and blue jeans. He'd sidled up on her left while she was lost in thought. He looked like money in spite of his getup. His nails were manicured, his haircut the kind of effortlessly rumpled waves only a three-hundred-dollar trip to the barber could produce. Finance bro, she decided. Probably dressed down for a long flight. She dug out a cigarette for him and handed him her lighter, which he flipped open and shut with expert precision before exhaling a stream of smoke.

"Thanks," he said, smiling. He had a hungry look in his eyes. She could feel it pouring off him, that familiar impatient yearning.

It always reminded her of a little dog yapping to be let out. Men like him didn't really understand their money yet. They didn't have Rudy's comfortable largesse, or the cold, sharklike affect of a real executive who knew exactly what he wanted and how to take it. They were nervous, resentful, impulsive. Stupid.

Lara pocketed her lighter. "No problem."

They smoked side by side for a while in silence, his scrutiny uncomfortable but bearable, but when she flicked her butt away in a shower of sparks and ashes, he raised a hand and touched two fingers to her forearm, like she was a waiter who'd ignored his signal.

"You're Bunny Vixen."

God, not again.

"No, sorry, you have me confused with someone else."

"Come on, you don't have to do that." He flashed her a wide, bright grin that didn't reach his eyes. "I'm a fan."

She stepped smoothly away, shrugging off his hand. "I'm not working right now." She turned to leave.

"Five thousand."

He was smirking when she looked back at him. It made her want to kick a heel off and put the spike through his eye socket. "Excuse me?"

"Come back to my hotel room for half an hour. Have a little party with me. Five thousand dollars."

"How about we go back to your car instead?" She stepped back toward him, resting a hand on his chest. She could feel the heat of his erection even in the chill. The musky funk of how badly he wanted her to do something little and mean and boring to him, something he thought was the apex of perversion. "I can jerk you off, wipe your cum on the upholstery, and then next week I'll find you out at brunch, and I'll come up to you and your wife and your kids while you're eating eggs Benedict and say, 'Fancy running into you here, Bill. What are the odds? Remember me, the tranny who gave you that handy in an airport parking garage?'"

He stared at her, his mouth hanging open, then seemed to find himself. His face went hard and tight. "Fuck you, cunt."

"Yeah," she sneered. "Fuck me."

It felt good to leave him standing there, though her stomach roiled at turning her back on him. Men had hit her for less. Her only defense now was an affect she'd spent years cultivating from one of breathy vulnerability to a sort of steel-clad cuntiness with a spine of fuck-you money. She'd probably made more than the little shit last fiscal year anyway. Let him hit her; she'd take his beach house and slice off his balls in court.

Her phone started vibrating as she stepped through the sliding glass doors and into the echoing clamor of check-in. She took her sleek little iPhone out of her coat pocket, pushing her fogged-over glasses up onto her forehead to read the caller ID. She answered, but somehow her voice had dried up in her throat.

"Lara? Are you there?"

Her palms felt damp and clammy. She licked her lips. "Yes," she said, her voice a strangled croak.

"I found it," Felix said, and she knew what he meant, had never been able to bury the knowing of it even when it had eaten through her twenties like a cancer, had put her in a psych ward in Rhode Island and then, a few years later, another in upstate New York. The line crackled. "I'm just outside Reno. The Star Motel."

She thought of Palm Springs, of lying poolside like a lizard in the sun, a mimosa close at hand and clients cuing up to smell her dirty panties, to suck her toes and drink her piss and beg her to step on their faces and put her cigarettes out on their nipples. Clamps and spankings and ball gags. It was the best job she'd ever had. The only thing she'd ever been good at.

"I'll be there tomorrow."

Clearlake, California

That first night, all of them crammed into a motel room in a Podunk town just across the Idaho border, Jo had told Oji what happened at Camp Resolution, switching back and forth between English and her broken Japanese until she was pretty sure she'd gotten it all out, had vomited the entire nightmare onto the dirty carpet. He took her hands and said, "I believe you." She saw how it hurt him to mean it, how badly he wanted to tell her she must have hallucinated, must have misunderstood something while out of her mind on whatever the administrators had given them— probably mushrooms—but he hadn't. He'd believed her, believed the whole insane mess of it.

For seven years he'd worked his fingers to the bone however and wherever he could to keep a roof over their heads. Technical drafting, night shifts at convenience stores, stocking shelves at Walmart, telemarketing for a company that sold steel wool and industrial solvents in bulk to factories. He'd done it all without complaint, just like he'd worked through the tantrums, the depressive episodes, the fights and breakups and suicide attempts, the anorexia and petty theft until one by one the others went off on their own. Until it was just the two of them.

For eight years after that he'd lived with her in her little third-floor apartment on Gate Street. It was during that time he'd told her about his marriage to her grandmother, about the matchmaker in Hokkaido who'd known the signs and led them to an understanding. He told her about the men he'd loved, showing her letters full of poetry by someone named Yoshi who he said had been the most beautiful man he ever saw, long black hair and a little mustache. Like Clark Gable. A few weeks after that, Oji had gotten his diagnosis. Cancer, hospice, and pneumonia, bam, bam, bam. Three months start to finish, and now, in the back of a cab, all that was left of him was the little copper urn in her lap, no bigger than a potted plant.

"... *another tragic entry in what psychiatrists have termed an unprecedented case of mass hysteria. A Ventura County mother murders her teenage daughter in cold blood before turning her gun on herself. Friends and family say the deceased, forty-one, struggled with a rare disorder known as Capgras delusion, the persistent belief that a loved one has been replaced by an identical or near-identical copy. Police have thus far been unable to locate—*"

The driver changed the station. "That's all there is on the news these days," he groused. "Mamas killing babies. They oughta do something about it."

"They should," Jo agreed. She always agreed with cab drivers, just like she always looked down when she passed by a cop. There was no way to know how far the Cuckoo's work had spread. There was no way to know who was safe and who was just a glove of skin around a knot of alien muscle. Mostly she managed not to think about it. Mostly. The cabbie pulled up to the curb outside her building. "Thanks," said Jo. She dug in her coat pocket for cash and handed it over without counting. Oji had always said it was bad character to count money in front of someone you were paying. She slipped out of the cab and shut the door, the urn cradled like a baby against her breast.

When she turned, the car pulling away, she found Shelby sitting on the steps of her walkup. For a moment the old fear seized her, the hair on the back of her neck standing on end, but if Shelby had been a copy she would surely have called ahead. She would have taken pains to make sure Jo felt comfortable. The fear passed. Shelby's round face was flushed in the unseasonable chill. She flashed a sad smile. "Lara told me," she said. "I tried to get here for the funeral, but you know what LAX is like. I'm so sorry, Jo."

A cold gust blew down Gate Street, past the little pizza parlor— which was terrible, but the best you could reasonably hope to find this far from Jersey—and the head shop where Jo's ex, Fiona, worked most days. It had been years since she'd seen Shelby. Christmas of 2009, she thought, when Lara had come out from Boston with that awful boyfriend, Max or Mack or something, who wouldn't shut up about how Facebook was going to change the world. She took Shelby's hand and pulled the other woman up and into a tight hug, and before she knew what was happening she was crying at her kitchen table while Shelby made coffee and rifled through the cupboards, making an unholy mess that would, Jo knew from experience, result in the best chocolate chip cookies she'd ever tasted.

"He was such an awful cook," said Shelby, cracking an egg on the lip of one of Jo's metal mixing bowls. "You remember his pancakes?"

Jo made a sound, half laughter and half sob, and rested her head in her hands. "Raw in the middle, burnt around the edges."

It was strange, being together again. All through the end of high school they'd been caught in each other's hair, trapped in a succession of tiny apartments and unable to stop seeing what had happened to them that one summer every time they caught sight of each other. She still felt it, even fifteen years later. Just a glimpse of the old scars on Shelby's forearms and she was back in their blood-spattered bathroom keeping pressure on the wound and wishing she was anywhere else, even back home in the airless tomb of her parents' house. It wasn't that they hadn't been close, it was that they'd never been able *not* to be. They were her family, and seeing them made her feel like she was drowning.

Time passed. Shelby ordered Chinese food and they ate it in the living room, trying and failing to watch one of the old Japanese movies Oji had always put on at holidays. They were all three hours long and called shit like *The Tale of the Dreaming Chrysanthemum*. Jo hated them with every fiber of her being. Her aunts had always called her a banana, yellow on the surface and white inside. Maybe they were right. Maybe if she didn't love watching handmaidens throw themselves into wells and samurai nobly sacrificing their lives for the shogun, she was betraying the memory of the man who'd raised her, who'd loved her even while she had the spins and puke in her hair, or when she'd crashed his car drunk the week before her nineteenth birthday, or flunked out of her GED program. Maybe she'd lose his memory, like she lost everything else. She was already on thin ice at her barista job at Bean Counter, and Rosalie at the print shop had taken her aside to let her know if she missed another shift they'd have to find someone else. More shitty jobs down the drain.

Three beers later she started crying again, sobbing into her lo mein as Shelby rubbed her back. "I'm a banana," she wailed. "I'm a fucking banana."

"What?"

Another beer and they were tearing at each other's clothes, kissing so that snot and tears ran together. She pulled one of Shelby's big, heavy breasts from her bra and took the other woman's puffy nipple into her mouth, rolling it on her tongue, letting it slide through her teeth until Shelby moaned and squirmed beneath her. Not their first time together, but the way Shelby filled her mouth always surprised her. Her jaw ached, a blissfully all-encompassing sensation. Shelby's fingers in her hair, pulling her closer while on the television Doug Bradley rasped, *"Your suffering will be legendary, even in Hell."* Shelby and her scary movies. Lara and John couldn't stand them, but Jo liked the thrill, the black cavern of a screaming mouth, the oozing drip of dyed red corn syrup. It made her feel naked. Vulnerable.

In bed, Shelby softening, easing Jo's hand away from her dick. Lube, delightfully cold, and a husky sigh of satisfaction as she slid a finger up inside the other woman. Tattooed arms around her, thick and soft, Krazy Kat lighting his cigarette on the fuse of a bomb, a spray of hibiscus blossoms, mushrooms in a riot of strange colors. She wrapped her legs around one of Shelby's thighs, grinding frantically as she built a rhythm, easing a second finger up the other woman's asshole. The room was spinning, but just a little. Just in a soft, pleasant way.

Afterward they lay together, trading memories and sipping water, talking about the times Lara ran away and when Mal had gotten drunk and done stand-up at open mic night at the White Horse in Seattle. *You guys remember when Bush got really mad at France for a while and it was all freedom toast and freedom fries? Imagine being the guy who had to explain that to the French parliament. Respected ladies and gentlemen of the assembly, the president of the United States has changed the name of that wet bread thing they have over there.*

Shelby blinked, a tear falling from the corner of her eye to trace the curve of her cheek and then soak silently into the sheets.

"It's okay," said Jo. She kissed the other woman, tasting duck sauce and Pabst Blue Ribbon, and let Shelby's plump lower lip slip from between her teeth. "It's okay, baby."

They slept. Jo dreamed of an ex-girlfriend, faceless and brooding, shaggy blue mullet and snakebites, and of hummingbirds swarming like iridescent wasps around a gigantic hanging nest of woven grass. She woke to her ringtone drilling at a pounding hangover. Ke$ha singing nasally about brushing her teeth with Jack Daniel's, which didn't sound like such a bad idea. She leaned across Shelby's sleeping warmth to grope for the sound, layered with the irritating shudder of vibrating plastic against the fake wood of the bedside table. Gray morning light bathed her pigsty of a room, the floor drifted in takeout wrappers and dirty laundry, the bookshelf full of waxed paper coffee cups and used acrylics scabbed with glue.

She found her little Motorola brick under a stack of coffee-stained *X-Men* comics one of her hookups had loaned her and never taken back. The caller ID blinked: Felix. She rolled onto her back and held the phone up to her ear, wondering what he was going to ask her for, if he needed money or had gotten his car impounded or himself arrested again. *Fuck you,* she thought as the call connected with a hiss. *I have my own problems.*

"Hey, Felix."

His voice was husky, the connection fragile and crackling with static, but she knew at once he was afraid. The same fear stirred inside her. It had spent the last fifteen years nestled in her guts.

"I found it."

Brooklyn, New York

John had always thought he might get thinner as he got older, that as he stretched and grew his body would find what his younger self had conceived of vaguely as a kind of equilibrium. He'd felt then like he woke up only to make his notch in the wall of his cell, his prison of rolls and folds, waiting for the day when it would all, somehow, be over. *There's a very handsome boy in there,* his stepmother, Sheila, had told him more than once as he stood on the precipice of some diet or another. *Once he's out, you'll be beating the girls off with a stick. Just you wait.*

Once he's out. It always made him think of *Alien,* of John Hurt screaming in agony as that penis-looking snake thing burst out of his chest and splattered everyone around the table with its gory afterbirth. Shelby had probably borrowed that movie from the library a dozen times. His body was just an incubator for a form of life that owed it nothing, that would hollow it out from within and then slit it up the front with a sharp black claw and step out slim and muscular and perfect, glistening with the last of his vital fluids, to begin a *real* life, whatever that was.

It had never come, that joyous moment of liberation. Not with Mal, who had alternated tweeting body-positive word salad about their beautiful fat boyfriend and treating John like a sex toy they didn't want anyone to know they owned; not with any of the chubby chasers or curious twinks who'd come after. Not even with Louise, who'd been with him since she swept into the bar where he'd been working odd nights at the time, a mountain of creamy, freckled curves poured into a white dress dusted with sequins, flushed and sweaty from her act at Whispers, wet with rain, and dropped herself onto a stool, chin resting on her tented fingers.

Who's a girl have to do to get a drink around here?

More people flooded in out of the unseasonable rain. Regulars. Friends. He'd hardly noticed them. They'd gone home together. She broke two acrylics clawing his back before he even got inside her. She kissed his belly. Left dark hickeys printed on his breasts. Under the golden curls of her wig, her hair was fiery red and damp with sweat. Loose tresses tickled his thighs as she went down on him. She didn't like to be touched down there, but they did other things, so many other things, and then it was rides to the airport, nights in instead of nights out, and the slow sliding together of their circles. He'd met her parents a year ago at Christmas, out in Sacramento. Kind people. Sweet and gentle.

Matching coffee mugs and eight-hundred-piece Where's Waldo puzzles spread out on the coffee table.

No release, no sense of finally shedding the weight he'd carried with him all his life, but he'd found a species of uneasy peace in his love for the expanse of her, for the warmth between her perfumed rolls and the sparse copper curls on the pad of milky fat beneath her belly and above her cock. The things he had loathed in himself since he could remember had become beautiful, had lost their power to curdle and suffocate him. How could he despise himself when he lay next to her, his arm around the swell of her belly, his face buried in the silky soft skin between her shoulders?

And now she was gone. He'd fallen apart after Felix called, and after the panic attack, after vomiting in the sink and shaking in her arms for half an hour, he told her everything, all of it, and she looked at him as though he were a broken-down old tramp raving on the bus about wiretaps and second shooters on the grassy knoll. She left a few minutes later, not saying goodbye. He wondered where she was now, which of their friends she was crying to, whether or not there were paramedics coming to perform some kind of wellness check on him. He had a ticketing site up on his wheezy little secondhand laptop, a red-eye flight to Reno ready to book. He could afford it, just about, with what he'd saved from temping in Punta Gorda and working at the Waldenbooks in the Cross Trails mall until it shuttered in late July. He'd be fucked for December rent, but he was already fucked.

He'd been fucked since the summer he turned sixteen. That first fall and winter together they'd talked about it constantly, gathering whenever they could between the collage of part-time jobs, all under the table, that had carried them through high school. The Cuckoo and its babies were the one inexhaustible subject they could always turn to, no matter how little they'd had to eat or what run-down shitbox they were living in. Where did it come from? Outer space? A government lab? The Earth's core? Why had it singled *them* out as its prey, the queers and fags and transes, and what was it doing now?

There had been no manhunt. That had always surprised him, until he realized the thing would have had no problem producing bodies, and that it was probably tracking them itself. It had made them all paranoid, especially in those first few years and after Shelby's first attempt. Any cop, any truant officer, any nosy neighbor could be one of those things. Their summer in Reseda had ended with all of them bolting in the night after Lara got herself arrested for solicitation and some fancy lawyer called the station to say he was representing her. Maybe it had really been a high-stepping pro bono type, but John could still remember the fear that had filled the station's reception area when the officer on duty had relayed the call. Eighteen hours later they were sleeping in a warehouse in North Coast with six hundred dollars between them and no prospects whatsoever.

They'd talked about it less as time wore on. First Mal wanted to put it behind them, especially after they came out, and even more so after the two of them got together. Then Lara left. Then Felix. By 2000 it had all felt like a bad dream. There were other things to worry about, rent and work and Y2K and the Ebola virus. The president smirking and sweating at his podium and the towers coming down as though someone had killed the pumps in the world's biggest fountain, concrete collapsing in on itself like water. The sky all full of dust and smoke. Wildfires and the ozone layer. Baghdad burning in the alien green glow of night vision while Fox News played "America the Beautiful."

Except it hadn't been a dream. He couldn't pretend anymore, not with the girl's name stuck in the back of his throat like a chicken bone. Abigail. Abby. Whatever its reasons, wherever it came from, it was back, and it had already started to wrap its tentacles around his throat. Louise was gone. She might never come back. He sipped his beer, long since gone warm and flat, and thought of the first time he'd climbed on top of her, the way she'd stroked his face with her plump little hand, pale and soft as fresh dough.

Don't be afraid. You're not going to hurt me.

We're the same.
He bought the ticket.

Chico, California

Mal stared at the half-finished painting. It was their latest, the white arc of the nun's wimple still blurry where they'd fudged around with the still-drying acrylics, rubbing their thumb over the canvas. The blunt iron hooks holding her mouth open were wrong somehow, the quality of the light on the burnished metal distracting from the dark glow of her skin, the empty pools of her eyes. *I am never going to finish this,* they thought. *Which is fine, because nobody's going to buy it anyway.*

Their little canvas travel bag lay packed on their air mattress. They'd been sleeping on it since the guy in the apartment downstairs dragged that bedbug-infested couch into the building and they'd had to throw their mattress out. The thought of the hard-bodied little insects still filled them with revolted panic. The bites on their lower back weren't fully healed yet. *The bugs are gone,* they told themself for the hundredth time. *They tented and sprayed. They're gone.*

They'd have to hitch to make sure they could afford the train and the two bus tickets to get them to Reno, but at least they wouldn't bring bedbugs with them. At least the others wouldn't know how things were with Charlie, who they loved, they really loved, they loved so much it hurt sometimes, which was good because everyone says love hurts. The hurting's how you know it means something. Not that they were hiding anything. People didn't understand how sensitive Charlie was, how hard his childhood had been. Sometimes they thought Shelby knew. Not that there was anything to know, but still.

I'm here if you ever need to talk.
I know how hard things can get.
Been thinking about you lately.
They zipped up their bag. Fuck anything they'd forgotten to

pack. Fuck the painting and the other six in the series under their little canvas shrouds against the wall, and fuck Felix for calling and telling them the one thing they couldn't ignore—that for fifteen years it had been out there doing to other kids what it had done to them, that it was stealing lives and faces, insinuating itself into the fabric of the country, and they'd decided to look away and live their lives while it did. Years of therapy to convince themself they'd imagined it, then denial, then drinking, and somewhere in that sparkling haze they became Mal, clawing their way in a disgusted frenzy out of what was left of grinning, joking Malcolm, and Charlie came into their life.

They kept thinking of the smell that had washed over them in the basement under the Glover house. Cat shit and warm root beer, a rancid sweetness that had made their mouth water and their gorge rise at the same time. The summer Shelby showed them *The Thing,* all they'd been able to think about was what it smelled like, that tame little stop-motion monstrosity wreaking havoc against all those grown men. Had Childs and MacReady caught a whiff of boiling aspartame and diarrhea as they slunk through the claustrophobic halls of their research station? Had they smelled it on the thawing tangle of cooked meat dragged back from the Norwegian base?

In their dreams sometimes they saw the Gabe-thing sit up and open its baby-blue eyes. They had painted it once, though they'd later burned the canvas behind the Big Lots where they'd been working at the time. *What if she saw it?* John had asked them. They were in love with John, then, but already angry with him, suspicious of his kindness and embarrassed of his body. Fat and getting fatter. Overflowing. Not like Charlie, skin and bones and sunken cheeks, the knobs of his spine like the heads of pushpins. Mal couldn't stay hard for him, not even before getting on spiro, but that was just part of being together as long as they had. Charlie's body was like a model's body, sharp and clean. It was perfect, and sex would only demean it.

"What the fuck are you doing? Are you *leaving*?"

He stood in the doorway in his sweats, dark circles under his eyes, his mop of curly hair disheveled. He'd been going shirtless ever since top surgery. Mal had once made xylophone sounds while tapping their fingers on his stark, protruding ribs. They could almost hear his giggle now. He'd loved that bit. They wished with a sickening intensity to be back in that moment, to be pleasing to him and not the thing making his face shake like that, his lips press together tight and bloodless. What could fix it? What could they say to make it right before it all spun out?

The best they could come up with was: "What?"

"You're obviously going somewhere." Charlie's pale eyes bulged in a way that suddenly reminded Mal of Mrs. Glover. "You didn't think about *telling me*? We just had that entire discussion about abandonment triggers and you weren't even listening."

"I was going to tell you—"

"Why the *fuck* should I trust you? You lied about your date with Lillith, you lie about money, you lie about food—"

Mal grasped for words. "I got a call," they said, and their voice sounded as though it were coming from behind a thick stone wall. They watched themself speaking and thought how strange, how artificial their body language looked. Hadn't they been loose, once? A clown. Now their arms were folded tightly, their shoulders hunched. "From an old friend, Felix Vargas. We grew up together. Someone . . . someone we knew back then is in trouble."

"You're a liar."

"Please don't say that."

"Right, fine, because I'm not allowed to say anything. I should just shut up and let you do whatever you want, let you forget I exist. You use me to get better, use me to sleep around, but I can't have anything because I'm so terrible."

He had moved closer, his spit on their cheeks. They stood, slinging their bag over their shoulder. "I didn't say that."

"Because it's my fault," he shrieked. He stepped back to block the door, blotches of color in his sunken cheeks. He had such beautiful cheekbones, sharp as cut glass. "Everything is my fault. You've never done anything wrong."

"I'll only be gone for three or four days," they said quietly, hoping and dreading that soon the crying would start, the pleading for forgiveness and the perverse feeling of power that came with it. Like looking down from a crucifix on their weeping executioner. "They need me. I promised I'd go."

"Why? Why do they need *you*?"

They thought of Abby, of a kid with Nadine's crooked smile and wheat-blond hair curled crying in a narrow bunk bed. They thought of the pallid monstrosity unfolding itself in the dark under the farmhouse, of how they'd stood frozen, doing nothing. Of Nadine swallowed by a wall of rippling light.

"I can't tell you about it," they said. Their voice shook, and with every fiber of their being they wanted to shrink back small into the corner, to apologize and cry and say they wouldn't go, it didn't matter, they'd been selfish and thoughtless and awful. "It's something we went through together, when we were younger. I—when I get back, I can try to explain."

"You're gonna get raped," he spat at them. He stepped aside to let them through the door, then fell in close behind them. They blundered through the kitchen, banging their knee on the edge of the rusted gas stove with the faulty pilot light as he ranted at their back. "Do you even care how I feel? Do you care how much I worry about you when you're out there? What are you going to do for money? What are you—*Look at me when I'm talking to you!*"

He hit them on the shoulder. It wasn't hard, more of a faggy little slap than any kind of punch. They yelped in surprise, wheeling to face him and retreating at the same time until the backs of their legs hit the threadbare sofa under the front windows. "You hit me," they said. Their voice trembled. The darkness outside their apartment seemed suddenly incalculable, huge and yawning and unsafe. At least in here they knew what came next. At least it was safe.

Charlie's expression curdled in an instant from shock and

guilt into one of pure contempt. "Oh please, I didn't hurt you. Are you gonna start crying now? Boo-hoo, boo-hoo-hoo, poor baby."

They broke for the door, Charlie stomping after them. Down the stairs past the reggaeton blasting on the second floor and the furious screams from the first and out into the cool, dark night with Charlie still ranting at them from the window above, screaming that they'd never loved him, that they wanted him dead, that they owed him four thousand dollars for rent from when they'd first moved in together. Silence, then the sound of canvas filling with air and the painting arcing out over the street to bounce off the curb. Mal started walking, their thoughts blazing with static. They headed up the street toward the lights of Sacred Conception, trying to ignore the eyes that followed them.

"Dykes are fightin'," laughed one of the men on the steps of the building across the street. There were two of them they knew by sight and one they didn't. "Trouble in pussy paradise." He raised his voice. "You all right, girl?"

Charlie was still screaming. Mal, not slowing, looked at the man. "Nothing your sister can't fix!" they shouted, and burst out laughing at his shocked expression. They picked up their pace. The night seemed to open itself up around them, the smells of rain and garbage and late-blooming snapdragons in the overgrown yards of foreclosed houses twining together, the light mist brushing their bare skin—they'd left the apartment in a tank top and loose drawstring pants.

"Use your eyes, stupid," said the hard-faced white woman sitting on the steps with the men, ashing her cigarette onto the sidewalk. "Those bitches are transgendered."

XVIII

THE BIGGEST LITTLE CITY
IN THE WORLD

Someone was jiggling Shelby's ass, gripping a handful of soft flesh and shaking it gently so that waves rippled across her cheeks. It was getting her hard, a breathless heat poised on the edge of dysphoria. She reached under herself to stroke it, the morning sunlight warm on her bare back as the sheet slid down, her breathing coming faster. Cool silicone between her legs. Leather and skin against the backs of her thighs.

God, breathed a voice Shelby knew, husky and raw. The hand kneading her ass tightened its grip until she gasped, stroking herself faster, the heat rising until her face burned. *Your ass got so big.*

A playful slap. Her breath caught in her throat as she arched her back to meet the next. Harder this time. Hard enough to sting. She could see the red palm print forming in her mind's eye. Another, the lubed head of the strap pressing hard against her asshole, Nadine's lips on the edge of her ear and that voice, grown up now but unmistakable.

You want to know what it feels like? the other woman whispered. *You want to know what you're trying to take from us?*

A white-hot flare of pain as something sharp and cold cut her across the taint. She opened her mouth and someone forced a wet cloth into it, the rough fabric soaked with iron-stinking menstrual blood. Hands gripped her right arm and leg, dragging her off of the bed, the sheets sliding off her body. Enoch and Dave pulling her down the front hallway away from Nadine, who sat burning alive at the kitchen table, hair a torch, skin blackening and cracking, peeling back from muscle and bone beneath, lips splitting over shining teeth.

Help me.

Shelby woke, her T-shirt soaked with sweat. The alarm clock on the motel room's bedside table read 6:13 a.m. Pale light filtered through the dusty Venetian blinds and in the other bed Jo was mumbling to herself, her calves sticking out from under the tangled sheets and ribbed green blanket. Had their blankets at Camp Resolution looked like that? Shelby thought they might have. She rubbed her own between thumb and forefinger. The texture was wrong; the blankets at camp had been broken in, soft to the touch. These were new and coarse. She sat up and peeled the wet shirt off, tossing it in the general direction of her suitcase. She ran her thumb idly along the faded ridges of the scars from her breast augmentation, first under the right, and then the left. Her Jessica Rabbit job, as her girlfriend at the time had called it. That had stung.

Never been an hourglass, never will be.

She got up and made coffee in the tiny electric pot on the room's dresser, her reflection staring blearily back at her from the water-spotted mirror on the wall. Nose piercing infected again. Two days of personal time left before the studio canned her and she went back to doing key frames for Cheerios commercials. She'd burn through her savings in a month. Things were already rocky with Christa and now she'd fucked it up worse by sleeping with Jo. Maybe Felix had finally gone off the deep end and none of this was real anyway. Maybe the Cuckoo had died of the world's biggest melanoma back in the Utah desert and there was no little sister of Nadine's getting force-fed mushrooms and trained to recite gibberish from a textbook with a lighthouse on the cover. Maybe it was all a bad dream, and tomorrow they'd all go their separate ways and everything would be like it was: two or three of them getting together every couple years, less now without Akira to mortar the cracks between them. A few texts, a few emails. Just six kids who'd been at camp together, once upon a time.

She slipped into ratty sweats and took her coffee outside in a

Styrofoam cup. It was dry and cool in the shade of the motel's overhang. Concrete walkway, then a strip of dead brown grass and then the crumbling pavement of the parking lot and the front fender of her rented Honda. She'd texted Felix their room number after they checked in last night. He replied *see u soon,* but there'd been no trace of him since. She plopped herself into one of the sagging, sun-bleached deck chairs and checked the charge on her vape pen before taking a long hit. Fuck it. As long as she was throwing her life's work away chasing ghosts in Reno, she was gonna get baked and take the edge off her stupid carpal tunnel.

No one else at the motel was up. Cars whizzed past on the main road and by the concrete divider she could just see what looked like a jackrabbit dead and mangled and crawling with flies. She blew out a long plume of smoke. *What if he just doesn't show? I guess this turns into the world's shittiest, most expensive vacation and then we go home. Back to drawing Princess Sadako's moon-steel katana until I start having sex dreams about her. And Jo. That apartment. Bills piling up. Empty bottles. Living like a freshman, except we never went to college.*

The motel coffee tasted like bitter wallpaper paste, but it was hot and between it and the weed she was starting to mellow out, the nightmare fading into a collage of vague, unpleasant shapes and half-remembered scents. Maybe she could loan Jo a little money, just enough to get her through losing Oji. She could make it work if she paid her electric bill with her Discover card, maybe. Maybe. Her friends had told her more than once to cut Jo off, but hadn't the other woman been there for her more than anyone else, except maybe Oji, when she'd tried to kill herself for the first time? She could still remember the look of pure, vacant horror in Jo's eyes looking down at her, the bathroom ceiling receding down a long black tunnel and Oji slapping her face, saying her name, slapping her face.

She had her own apartment. She had friends, lovers, a job that didn't pay under the table or in free drinks. So what if Jo was a mess? She'd gotten them out, after the house went up. She'd saved them all, led them into the forest and across the desert, killed that thing when it came after them in the flickering lantern light. Sometimes Shelby still dreamed about those long, slavering jaws, those scaly talons and the soiled fringe of its shaggy coat. She realized she was crying and wiped her eyes, sniffing. She shot Felix another text—*where the fuck are you?*—and finished her shitty coffee. Before she could go in, Jo came out. The other woman looked tired, her hair flattened on one side, dark circles under her eyes. In her baggy pajama pants and ratty T-shirt she looked, just for a moment, like a teenager again, and Shelby thought her heart might break.

"How'd you sleep?" Shelby asked, coughing.

Jo took the pen and sucked on it, cheeks hollowing. At the far end of the lot a hunched old woman shuffled from her room to her car, the aluminum storm door clattering behind her in a sudden gust of warm, dry wind. Shelby hated the heat. It was why she'd moved to Rhode Island in the first place, to get as far away as she could from all those beige flyover wastelands with their endless howling wind and the shadows of their circling buzzards and the dead white smiles of their Mormons.

"I'm afraid," said Jo, smoke pouring from her nostrils and uncoiling from between her lips. She blew a ring and stared past it with unseeing, glassy eyes as it came apart in the fading breeze. "I don't want to see it again." Her voice was far away, a little higher pitched than usual. A child's voice. "I don't want it to be real."

"I know," said Shelby.

Jo sank down onto the ground beside the chair and leaned her head against Shelby's hip. They stayed like that for a while as the little old lady got into her car, started it after a few clunking coughs from the engine, and pulled out of the lot, joining the light traffic on the main road. Everything was the same out here. Chain gas stations. Office parks. Flat-roofed buildings and beyond the few bland streets of the city's edge, the desert stretching dead and vast and featureless to the distant purple blush of mountains. Little brown birds perched in rows on the telephone lines. It could take a place like this so easily.

They ate lukewarm scrambled eggs and flavorless wheat toast at a diner a few blocks down the road, and when they came back John was pulling into the motel lot in a rented hatchback. He heaved himself up out of the driver's seat, waving at them. He was huge, big and solid in jeans and a bomber jacket, his brown hair grown out in waves. When he folded Shelby into a crushing embrace she could feel the thick cables of muscle shifting under his soft exterior. The three of them chatted for a while about his shitty adjunct job, about Jo's girl trouble and Shelby's latest grueling animation gig, which consisted mostly of drawing a single sword fight over and over until she wanted to rip the stupid katana out of the ninja-maiden's hand and behead whoever'd done the storyboards. Light things. Small. They weren't ready to touch it yet.

Lara was next, arriving by cab and stepping out neatly onto the sidewalk, her long salmon dress swishing around her slender ankles, her big, round sunglasses reflecting the motel's unlit neon sign and the chain-link fence around the pool. She looked like a movie star with her little peach-colored rolling suitcase and broad-brimmed sun hat. Some of her smiles were fake and some of them were real and on the first finger of her right hand she wore a platinum band set with what looked like real diamonds. It was funny that out of all of them she was the only one who had money. Shelby assumed it was from escorting, because if it had been movies or singing or any of the other careers she'd tried on and discarded with such restless impatience in California, she'd never shut up about it.

Mal came just before dark, meeting the rest of them in the same sleepy diner where Shelby and Jo had eaten breakfast. Lara had told her a while back that Mal and John had broken up badly, and the look on John's face as the door swung shut behind them agreed. It had been longer than that since Shelby had seen either of them. Mal looked good, but tired. Estrogen agreed with them and they'd finally put on a little weight. Their hips were padded, the shadow of a double chin under their pointy jaw. They wore tight black jeans and a graying hoodie over a thin, ragged tank top. They smiled and Shelby felt them lie about how good things were with their partner Charlie, a leaden, heavy lie straight from the gut, and then they were all ordering from a hard-faced waitress in an apron and a faded peach-colored uniform, the table filling up with wilted salads and burnt hamburgers. They had already started eating, Lara only picking listlessly at her greens, when the bell over the front door tinkled and Felix walked into the diner.

He looked so different from the last time Shelby had seen him, six or seven years ago at Lara's going-away party, right before she moved out to the East Coast. His hair was thinning. His shoulders were a little hunched, and he had the beginnings of a potbelly. In his Wranglers and leather jacket, scuffed work boots with broken laces on his feet, he looked like someone's contractor uncle who made book on the side. For a heart-twisting moment she almost thought Nadine might walk in after him, not the girl she'd known but a woman, tall and strong and beautiful with a throaty voice and waves of sandy hair that stank of cigarettes and grease.

It came to Shelby then just how insane this was, just how little sense it made for five broke queers straggling one by one out of their twenties—and one rich bitch, same—to drop everything and race to Reno fucking Nevada on the say-so of their disturbed foster sibling who lived in his car. Only Lara could really afford to travel like this. The rest of them were blowing rent money, or had blown it already. And for what? A story that had been true, once, until a thousand, thousand tellings and retellings rendered it a soup of resentment and grief and hormones. A thing that had seemed like the end of the world until life in its wake kept unfolding with its relentless, monotonous procession of bills and work and dates and oil changes, until years of dodging truant officers and landlords and the dead-eyed drones from California's child and family services department left it lumped alongside the wars in Iraq and Afghanistan and the subprime mortgage crisis and the opioid epidemic and penal slavery and every other miserable thing you had to ram into the back of your mind to get out of bed in the morning and push yourself through another day emptying grease traps. Who were they to think they could take this thing on, much less beat it?

Felix pulled out the last chair at the little round table. It was dark outside and their reflections swam in the water-spotted glass of the diner's storefront, haloed in light. They were silent. It stretched on until Mal leaned toward Felix, cleared their throat, and said gravely: "Freddie Mercury's corpse called. It wants its mustache back."

John looked at the pictures Felix had given him, a folder full of four-by-six glossies, a few blown-up printouts of digital photographs—all of a compound not too different from the one he remembered, except that the cabins all had shitty vinyl siding and the main house—if that's what it was—stood much closer to the camp, just outside the chain-link fence on a rocky ridge maybe fifteen or twenty feet high. Even in the grainy image John could see greenery pushing its way through lifeless soil and between piled stones. It had bothered him ever since that summer. What made it grow like that in the middle of a desert? Whenever he thought about it he would always come back to a single awful thought: it must be bodies. All those little corpses, their copies already cleaned and pressed and sent marching off into the world, mulched and buried, nutrients seeping into the earth.

There were people in some of the pictures. Mostly kids, but he recognized Dave, new lines at the corners of his mouth and eyes, hair a little thinner, maybe, leading a line of boys across open ground into the desert. A few other counselors looked familiar. He'd had dreams about Garth for years after Camp Resolution, sometimes that the older man was chasing him through the burning maze of the farmhouse, sometimes that they were twined together, sweating and grunting, Garth whispering something in his ear in a language he couldn't understand, but there was no sign of him in Felix's pictures. It had happened. John and the others had killed him. There was Marianne, the woman Nadine had bitten, looking older and a little heavier.

Mal's phone kept buzzing. John had been trying not to look at them, not to notice when they looked at him in turn. It had been so bad between them, at the end. He recognized the way they were looking at that glowing screen, the desperate, twitching hunger etched into their face as their thumbs danced over the keypad. Someone back at home was tugging on the umbilical cord they'd never quite managed to shed, even without their mother hanging on its other end.

That's not your problem anymore. They can be fucked up with whoever they want.

He wondered, as he thumbed through a second sheaf of pictures, noting sticky, hairy pellets and stands of something like bamboo pushing their way up through the rocky soil, what Louise was doing now. She hadn't called. She hadn't texted. He'd left her half a dozen messages but by now she was probably with her parents telling them he'd had a breakdown, that he'd fled the apartment after babbling about his alien abduction. He'd gotten Steph—a friend of theirs—to agree to feed the cats for a few days until he and Louise could figure something out.

It's over.

It had been a kind of joke, really. One of those long, pointless, rambling jokes Mal used to love to tell, fifteen minutes of setup for the corniest punchline imaginable. Some pun that made them all groan and throw things at him. *A fat little faggot, some transsexuals, and a couple of other gays get sent to a conversion camp— stop me if you've heard this one.* Fifteen years of borrowed time spinning their wheels in dead-end jobs, flaming out one by one, over and over, and now it was pulling them back in. They'd never left that basement. Nadine was still burning.

Felix was talking, answering a question Lara had asked. "You remember how they drew our blood right after they brought us to the house?" he said. "How they kept us waiting before bringing us down to it? I think they were worried we might get it sick, or that one of us might be on something that could fuck it up if it got into its system. They drugged us, then gave us a drug test. It doesn't make a lot of sense, right?"

Pictures of red curtains in the windows of another sleepy desert town. Armed guards in scuffed denim on the wraparound porch of a half-built farmhouse. Men on horseback leading kids through the wasteland. He could almost feel his blisters reopening. Mal's phone buzzed again. They looked so tired in the screen's blue light.

"They're testing for club drugs. Ecstasy, ketamine, molly." He smoothed a sheaf of stained and crumpled papers that looked to have been shredded and then taped together out among the plates and coffee mugs, flattening the crinkling mess with his palm. "I found these in their garbage. Whatever it is, I don't think it likes getting high, at least not in a very particular way."

Lara looked skeptical. "Then why *did* they drug us? That night, with the mushrooms or whatever they were."

"I only have guesses," said Felix, "but I think it was to get us ready to be copied. To soften us up, open our minds."

Jo broke the silence. "So your plan is what, we lure it onto Willie Nelson's tour bus and hotbox it?"

"No. My plan is we hook up with a dealer I know in Vegas and we buy him out of all the ketamine he's got, then we find that fucking thing and send it on the trip of a lifetime."

John cleared his throat. "How are we gonna buy this guy of yours out, exactly? I teach fiction writing at a community college; I'm going to be paying off my plane ticket for like four months as it is. I probably have about a hundred and seventy dollars in my checking account."

"Lara has money," said Felix.

"Oh, help yourself," Lara snapped.

We could tell the governor, thought John. *We could tell the police. We could tell child services.* They weren't real thoughts. They'd had each one of those conversations a thousand times in their youth. No one cared about a little reform farm for faggots. No one gave a shit what good, honest ranchers did to the sissies and dykes and the rest of the freaks. Fix them or fuck them, kill them or cure them—as long as it was quiet, who cared? And beneath that, a darker thought: that it might already be entrenched in those same institutions. They had no way of knowing how many it had infected, how far its influence spread.

"You're the only one of us who can afford it."

"So? Who says I'm going to bankroll you? Why the fuck is this *my* responsibility?"

"Lower your voice. The waitress is looking at us."

"Oh, I'm so sorry, snake. Think you can salvage the op?"

"None of this matters," said Shelby. The rest of them shut up. They'd always liked her best, back when they'd lived together. She had a kind of indefinable mommy-ness to her, a sense that if you cried in front of her she'd rest your head on her breasts and stroke your hair. Maybe it was just that she was pretty and fat and patient and had big, sad eyes, or that after Nadine they'd all made a point of loving her a little more than they loved one another. Whatever the reason, they listened.

"How are we going to get close to that thing?"

The first time Lara had been sectioned it was for telling her therapist about waking up beside her half-formed twin in the basement of that farmhouse, and the things she dreamed as she slept beside it. The meteor of flesh and bone. The false bird chirping in its nest. The Cuckoo, stealer of faces and skin.

Reciting that little stream-of-consciousness epic to one Dr. Bethany Weaver had earned her a night on a locked ward which became, after she spat on a nurse for refusing to use her real name, two weeks of isolated observation. The funny thing was that she'd seen it coming, had felt the tide of Dr. Weaver's confidence in her recede like the ocean did before a tsunami. She'd kept talking anyway. That had been her first time hooked on Klonopin, skin crawling, fried and anxious, desperate to drag that soothing benzo blanket over her thoughts, to deaden things enough that she could make it through another night. Looking into the trunk of Felix's Impala, she felt the old itch again for the first time in years.

The upholstered floor of the trunk was covered with guns, all secured with strips of Velcro. A hunting rifle, three holstered revolvers and a pair of plain black automatics, a shotgun with its stock and barrels filed short like in a mob movie, and a long, mean-looking thing with a wooden stock Jo thought might be a Kalashnikov or AK-47 or whatever they were called. There was ammunition, too. Boxes of it, and metal cases fastened with heavy clasps. Walkie-talkies and a first aid kit. Road flares. Grenades. It reminded Lara of that sad, lonely bunker in the desert, and the man lying dead in its shower.

"Jesus, Felix," said John. He sounded faint.

Felix shut the trunk and locked it.

"And what if the drugs don't work?" asked Mal. They sounded a little hysterical, their voice tight and frantic. "What if it just gets sick or wigged out and then shakes it off?"

"We're going to need to test it," said Felix, scratching his chin. The parking lot lights buzzed dully overhead, moths and other insects circling around their glow. "I thought we could use one of the replacements. The doubles."

Lara spoke without thinking, her voice coming as though from a long way away as she thought of a house on the edge of the woods and a hide-a-key under a rotten old porch and a little boy who had played there in the years when his dog was his only friend.

"I know where to find one."

XIX

LAYLA

So much had gone wrong for Betty Cleaver since the summer of her sixteenth year. Sometimes it felt like *wrong* was the only thing that happened to her anymore. First the accident. Her parents hovering over her in a hospital room somewhere in Utah. Concussion. Malnutrition. Something bacterial in her urinary tract that just wouldn't give up. The gray fog of the nine months that had followed, all neurologists' offices and therapists asking her what happened, what was she repressing, who had touched her, until she broke placid old Dr. Kuzik's nose and was barred from the only practice in the city that took their insurance. Then the infection in her leg, the moles and skin tags sprouting faster than dermatologists could cut them away, the fever, and the end of her boxing scholarship, and now here she was, pushing a mop at a quarter to midnight on New Year's Eve in the glittering, colorless tomb of the Lansing township's only Target superstore.

Stiff-legged and slow in her orthopedic brace, Eric Clapton wailing *"You've got me on my knees, Layla!"* through her headphones, Betty worked her way back and forth over the off-white linoleum of the cosmetics section near the checkout lanes and the front of the store. Fifteen minutes until 2012. Outside the wind was blowing snow over the parking lot where Diego and Miguel were probably still racking shopping carts, unless the spics had fucked off to smoke a joint behind the loading dock. The post-Christmas sales were always brutal. Immigrants rushing the racks for half-price dinner sets and discount linens, filling the aisles with the smell of rotten cabbage and the sinus-stripping spices she'd heard they used to cover up the taste of putrid meat. Ragheads and wetbacks and everyone else Obama had opened his arms to. It was enough to make her miss Clinton, who'd at least known where *they* belonged.

"Three strikes and you're out," she muttered to herself, not realizing her stepfather had often said the same thing four or five beers into the evening. "He was right about that one."

The little clutch of moles on her hip stung with a sudden, painful intensity. She winced, reaching under the elastic waistband of her scrubs to scratch the insistent itch, then yanked her hand back with a grunt as wetness and a jolt of sickening agony met her touch. She stumbled, her bad leg sliding under her, and hip-checked a Revlon display, spilling compacts and lip gloss to the floor in a waterfall of brushed black plastic. "Shit, shit, shit!" she hissed, clawing for purchase on the shelving. A dark stain seeped through the hip of her blue scrubs, and she'd dislodged an earphone somehow, so now Clapton's hollering had taken on a ghostly, doubled quality.

"Cleaver."

The bottom dropped out of Betty's stomach. At the end of the aisle, shelves of plastic storage tubs and toiletry organizers at his back, stood all five-foot-five of Richie Messeder, who had just turned twenty-two and might have weighed in at a hundred and twenty pounds if you dipped him in shit first. He was what Coach Parcell would have called a *welterweight,* she thought. He was also what Coach Parcell would have called a faggot, or at least Betty thought he looked like one, the way it puffed him up to order around decent people.

"Tripped, Richie," she croaked, trying on a smile. It felt ghastly. She was sweating bullets. "I'll clean it up. No problem." She pushed herself off the shelves and a lone tube of liquid eyeliner clattered to the floor and spun a few times before falling still. Betty fumbled for the scuffed old Discman's pause button, but it was stuck and the CD must have been scratched because Clapton kept belting out a mocking loop of *got me on my knees got me on my knees* and for some reason she was thinking of Athena, of kneeling in the darkness of their cabin—*what cabin?*—and taking that plump, downy pussy into her mouth, sixteen and insane with lust, practically clawing at herself in her need.

That's just how I like you, baby. On your knees.

Richie was coming toward her now. His eyes were practically popping out of his narrow head. "Are you drunk, Cleaver? Are you *actually drunk* right now?"

Something was wrong. Terribly wrong. Her whole thigh felt hot and sticky, like gum left out on the dashboard on a sunny day. She clamped her hand over the spreading stain in her scrubs and nearly blacked out from the pain. She vomited, doubling over as a searing cramp ripped through her belly and pelvis, like a dozen periods hitting all at once. Blackness shuddered at the edges of her vision.

Am I dying?

"Cleaver?" Richie crouched a few feet off, a look of anxious disgust on his pimply little rat face. "Jesus, do you need a doctor?"

got me on my knees got me on my knees got me on my knees

There was something squirming in her vomit. Something black and fragile, thin as living strands of angel hair pasta.

And then the pain was gone. All of it, and not just in her thigh but the constant ache of her bad knee, the knots in her back, the wire-taut sting of tension in her shoulders and the nagging, sickly hot throb of the molar her ex-girlfriend Jenna had kept telling her to show a dentist. Gone. In its place was a velvety, enfolding warmth, a sense of contentment she couldn't remember ever having felt before except, in some neglected corner of her mind, in a formless, hazy memory of sucking at her mother's breast. It took her a few moments to realize through the fog of her new bliss that she had Richie pinned against the floor.

You will need his meat.

He fought her, thrashing with all his pitiful might. She rolled him easily onto his belly, locking her arm over his throat. No muscle fatigue tonight. No ringing in her ears. *Tinnitus,* the doctors had called it. No. Her thoughts were clear and her body sang with strength, and in her thigh she could feel something moving slow and syrupy beneath her skin, closer and more tenderly than any lover had ever touched her. She twisted, shoulders straining, and Richie's neck snapped with a dry, brittle crunch. He jerked once, then went limp in her arms, but his right eye still moved, still stared back at her in mute, unthinking terror. She bent to grab the little man by the ankle and set off for the empty registers, dragging his unprotesting weight after her as her right shoe slowly filled up with something warm and safe and wonderful. It squished wetly with each step she took, and when she looked back there was a trail of gray-blue droplets, some smeared by Richie's body, leading all the way back to cosmetics.

"Gee, Rich," she said dryly. "I sure hope you can find someone to cover for me."

The automatic doors slid open for her like the Red Sea parting for Moses and she hauled the unresisting sack of flesh that had been Richie Messeder out into the squall. Her beat-up Baja was parked close, and she'd filled it up that afternoon. That was good. The warmth inside her told her that she had a long, long way to drive, but she didn't mind. She had Richie for company, and her good buddy Eric was still singing in her ears, the loop cutting shorter and shorter each time it ran through.

on my knees on my knees on my knees

It would be so *good*, seeing everyone again.

The first day on the road went by without incident. Betty made good time, cutting through flat, endless Indiana with its cookie-cutter cities and its half-dry canals and crossing most of Illinois before the warm little voice in the back of her mind directed her to get off Route 80 in the suburbs north of Peoria. Streets lined with identical split-levels. A labyrinth of cul-de-sacs and dead-ends, boring people living out their boring lives, the glare from their televisions flickering on the snow outside, to a house with red curtains hanging in the windows where a man her age was waiting in the driveway, tall and clean-cut in a black wool winter coat and dark sweater.

"Must have had a long drive," he said, smiling as she stepped out of the truck and slammed the driver's-side door behind her. Glare from the floodlights on the front of his garage lit nothing but his mouth and throat, leaving the rest of his face in shadow. The air was cold and clean after six hours in the truck with the stench of Richie's voided bowels. He lay under a blanket in the back, motionless but still, last time she'd checked, alive.

Betty coughed. Something about him looked so familiar, so comforting. He smelled like cloves and cooking oil. "Not bad."

It was smotheringly hot inside the stranger's house, the air close and humid and full of the sound of running water. It smelled of warm root beer and diarrhea. He took her jacket and led her from the mudroom with its coats and scarves hanging from wooden pegs over ranks of winter boots and out into the kitchen, where his family was waiting. An older man and woman—they must have been the original's parents—and two younger women, early twenties maybe, all blond, all blue-eyed. They knelt naked on peeling linoleum where a kitchen table should have been, leaning together to form a sort of shelter. Where their skin touched it was scabbed and warty, growing together so that heads and shoulders all formed part of the same flaking, oozing clot. Fingers twitched at the ends of their limp arms. Piss stains marred the floor and the exposed particle board where the synthetic tile had separated. A few of their eyes followed Betty as she passed, but mostly they stared dead and milky into space.

"They'll be ready very soon now," said the stranger. "Have you seen a chrysalis before?"

"No," said Betty. She felt calm staring at the family, the stench of their putrefying flesh and accumulated waste so thick in the air she could almost chew it. She felt good and right and satisfied. "What does it do?"

"It will protect me, when it's time for my change." He smiled.

Even inside under the even yellow lights it was hard to get a sense of what he looked like. A smile. A smile between flesh and shadow. "Come."

Through the silent living room and up the carpeted stairs. A hall. Bathroom, tub full of black fluid. Mushrooms growing from the sodden carpet outside the open bedroom door, the bed itself a collapsed, moth-eaten mess. Dusty wings beat silently as their footsteps disturbed the feast. A guest room at the hall's end. Narrow twin bed. On the side table, a plate covered in raw ground beef and a glass full of cloudy liquid.

"You must be tired," the stranger said. "Eat. Drink. Sleep. In the morning you continue west."

Betty sank down gratefully onto the bed, which creaked beneath her. She took the plate into her lap and scooped up a handful of raw meat. It tasted sweet. She thought of the family downstairs. She thought of Richie, lying boneless in the truck, and Athena smiling cruelly down at her so many years ago. She had died in the garden. Died in her arms.

"Will I change, too?" she asked, her voice soft.

His smile widened. She thought of the Grinch, Boris Karloff narrating as that lipless green slit curled into spiral dimples. "Only a little."

In her dream Athena came to her like a breeze through the open window. It was warm, not winter, and they were girls again, curled together in Betty's bunk and whispering about their firsts. Winnie Prince, blond and mean and two years ahead of Betty, making her kneel down in front of the sinks in the little bathroom on the third floor—the one by the music department, that nobody used—and guiding her mouth between those strong thighs. Pink nails like talons digging into her scalp. Cigarette smoke coiling around fingers stained red from the tampon Winnie had pulled out and dropped into the sink.

Do you suck your daddy off like this?

But Daddy never touched her. Not like that. He would only say *Jesus Christ, you just ate, fucking mower blade's bent, is this your fucking glass here with the milk all dried inside,* and then he would hit her, sharp and quick like you hit the big steel bell on the carnival game. Test your strength. How high would she whizz up that thin metal rod? The *clank* when the weight struck home. It was her stepfather who'd done the rest. The dark, wet things she'd known even then were wrong. Athena's first, a teacher at her school who'd later killed herself. The light from the refrigerator. Picking the crust off a quiche and savoring the buttery pastry as she listened for footsteps on the stairs.

You want to look like a pig, you can eat like one. Get down on the floor. The smell of her mother's menthols. Was that why she hated smoking? Dirty habit. She'd gotten drunk and hit Tricia once after finding that mint-and-silver pack crumpled up in the bathroom wastebasket. Closed fist. Cheekbone broken. Bruise like an apple dropped on the floor, but hadn't she wanted to be back on her knees? Winnie blowing smoke from her nostrils, like a dragon.

Here, piggy, piggy.

It was why, she understood on some dim, guilty level, the thing under the farmhouse hadn't wanted her the way it had the other children. She and a few others it had saved for the camp, the next generation of Garths and Enochs and Mariannes. It preferred to keep such people close so they could do its fighting for it. It hated fighting. Hated work. It had a great task, something it had come to Earth to do, but it left the little things to humans. Insects it paid in replicas of loved ones, in diseases cured, in deformities rectified. It had come to her, she now remembered, as she lay burned and half-conscious with her head in the lap of Athena's corpse. It had spoken in a voice like ten thousand buzzing flies.

You will want for nothing.

The smell of cigarettes and urine and that tang of menstrual iron. Why did people always talk about how clean girls' restrooms were? Strands of mucus glittering between her lips and Winnie's, caught in the flickering light.

There will be no loneliness.

It had set its many lips against her skin. It had placed its hands over her torn and bleeding leg.

And it had smiled.

Betty woke to find what was left of Richie lying beside her in the bed. For some reason it didn't bother her, though he smelled worse than he had in the car. He must have shit himself again. He was painfully thin, his skin gray and wrinkled, his hair gone colorless and brittle as dead grass. He looked like a Capri Sun pouch someone had sucked until their cheeks hollowed out and the reflective plastic collapsed in on itself.

She reached out to touch his shoulder and found his flesh spongy and yielding. It held the imprint of her fingers even after she withdrew her hand. Her hand? It was a third again as large as she remembered it, though in the warm peace that had descended on her this felt right and good and reassuring, like the name of a close friend she'd forgotten and just now recalled. Her fingers were long and thick, wormlike blue veins crawling along the back of her hand. She sat up, the blanket sliding from her body, and saw herself. A snippet of some stupid shit she'd read in high school rattling through her brain like a beetle's dead husk.

One morning, when Gregor Samsa woke from troubled dreams, he found himself transformed.

Except she wasn't vermin. She was beautiful. Perfect. She pushed Richie off the bed onto the carpet. A little sack of foamlike skin and broken bones, he hardly made a sound. She rose up and stepped over him, and in the doorway the handsome man stood, and he was small now, a head and a half shorter than she was, and smiling, smiling wide, and she thought as she ducked through the doorway of what he'd said about the things that had been the family of someone who had once looked much like him: *They will protect me while I change.*

"I need something for the road," she said, her voice hoarse and deep. Her head brushed the ceiling as she made her way toward the stairs. "Meat."

Meat, whispered the voice of peace.

"It's in your car," said the handsome man. "You know, we needn't talk like this. Not any longer."

She turned back toward him and found that his face was open, that its fleshy petals had parted and the mandibles and fronds within uncoiled. Her body answered. From her left leg came a questing tendril of pink, dripping flesh that wriggled through a tear in her straining scrubs. Another followed it. Another. Pseudopods grappled and entwined. Slippery flesh deformed. Communion. He gripped her. She him. Thoughts and images melted together like tin under a welder's torch. Smoke and cunt and the doctors probing at her knee, freezing warts and slicing skin tags, and the Cuckoo dragging itself toward her from the wreckage of the burning house. The eyes. The kiss. Bags of muscle, meat, and suet dragged out of a freezer in the garage and loaded into the truck's bed. A boy, something like a boy, thrashing frightened in the dark. Malcolm curled around her leg as she stood over him, hands braced against the cabin wall, spittle dangling from her mouth as she drew her foot back for another kick.

The man and Betty broke apart. They smiled.

Cuckoo, said the voice of peace. *Cuckoo.*

It had seen something. The closer Betty got to its nest, the more she comprehended the finer nuances of the call that had woken her up and drawn her south and west across the map. The sentinel flesh it had placed in telecom and in Silicon Valley had found it quite by accident in their sweeps of email logs and traffic cams and motor vehicle records: a beat-up old Impala, different plates each time but always the same dings and scratches, in twenty-minute proximity to three different youth wilderness programs. A tall, blank-faced Mexican man glimpsed through the dirty windshield. *Felix,* the voice told her, conjuring a lanky brown girl-child from the haze of memory. *Inez.*

So, an excess of caution. Betty and a select few others plucked from the thing's precious reservoir of servants—not its hatchlings, growing year by year in number but occupied in their entirety with grand designs beyond the scope of single minds—and called home for communion with the mother cyst, that huge impacted womb that had reached out to them and found their thoughts young, eager, and aching to be molded. They would defend it with their lives and afterward, the voice of peace had told her, there would be a sweet reward. A kiss. Well done. Good girl.

It was a thought that warmed her as she slept in the truck's unheated cab at a rest stop a few hours west of Omaha, the limitless void outside the windows blanketed in a thin crust of frozen snow. Barren cornfields. Pig runs full of squealing meat with steam rising from their flanks. It made her wistful, not for places she knew, but for places her flesh remembered. Nautilus spirals of something smooth and shiny, decorative bodies merging and splitting in the pulsating light, wet strands of skin and mucus stretched between them. The chilly existential thrill of communion with rare strains of isolated flesh, alien ideas denuding her neural net. So much excitement in allowing separation to curdle and ferment, to bloom with the fungal growths of differentiation, to allow it—in more senses than one—to *culture.* Reabsorb and feel it break against the final hegemony that was its own endlessness. Exaltation. Like a crown lowered again and again and again onto your brow.

You are the only way. The only thing.

There were others everywhere. She could feel them. See them in a crowd, as though they emitted some form of secret radiation. Three skinheads at a biker bar in Cascade where she stopped to eat. They fed with her in the alley after closing time, holding down the little dyke she'd pulled. A plain-faced housewife in Lamoine. Her six-year-old son in the back of her car, though not the older girl beside him. Not yet, anyway. A state trooper sitting silent in his car beside Route 5 in Northern California, eyes hidden by mirrored aviators, who watched her blow past going a hundred and five without moving a muscle. It had spread so far in the years since it had come to her. Its children were everywhere, on school boards and on naval bases, in churches and in hospitals. What it loved best, though, was the home.

In a home it could draw the blinds, lock the doors, and do its work in private. It could spread from flesh to flesh, not in the careful way with which it made its cuttings in the desert, but through crude assimilation and replication. A boy went to sleep one night, and the next day a thing wore his face to school. It was the miracle of modern life, the insular nature of the home. Work, church, education could all be satisfied with only the most trivial investment of energy. It let relationships wither. It fell away from extended family, allowed its cuttings' memberships in clubs and in societies to taper off to nothing, and slowly, meticulously, it created streets, then neighborhoods, then entire counties ruled by a dark and watchful silence.

Chico's outskirts weren't yet part of that hidden country dug deep into the sclerotic corpse of America, but its day was coming. There were houses with red curtains. Strange plants growing in neglected lots. The sewers swarmed with things that were no longer rats. On a hill overlooking a vacant lot where locals dumped used batteries and broken electronics among the rusted hulks of vintage cars, a line of stucco row houses kept a lonely vigil. In one of these lived a man named Charles Sutter, and in Charles Sutter's phone, the voice had determined, was a way to find the people who might mean it harm.

For decades it had ignored all attempts to expose it, hiding in plain sight in an ocean of incoherent conspiracy theories. There were YouTube videos—not many, but no longer very few, either—in which people spoke with terror and heartbreak of loved ones going blank and empty, of mothers disappearing from their lives, of children going through life's motions with no sign of their former spirit. Whole families irreparably ruptured by sudden changes in a loved one. They were dismissed as cranks. Laughed at. Scorned. It could fool most doctors ably enough, and in America it was not so unusual to avoid a physician's office for years or even decades.

These people were different. They had injured it. They had escaped it. They had eluded it ever since, vanishing for a decade and a half, until Vargas gave himself away by surveilling the Cuckoo's lair. From there a complex web of facial recognition software and digital necromancy led its cuttings to old emails, now inactive but preserved in the bloated wasteware of corporate code at Google and in the shell of America Online, and in the contacts of those accounts were a few precious phone numbers, long since abandoned but which led in turn to other numbers. Current numbers. Charles Sutter's was one of them, and his social media overflowed with pictures of a tall, gangly Black lover whose whimpers Betty could still call to mind. Malcolm, now Mal.

She parked across the street from Sutter's building and waited for night to fall.

XX

GABRIEL

It felt strange to Felix to be around the rest of them again, even just Lara and Shelby, after so many years apart. They drove and slept in shifts as desert gave way to farmland, farmland to flat prairie, and prairie to deep forests and clear rivers. Traces of snow became frozen lakes and icebound marshes became strip malls with four-foot drifts plowed up against the raised beds sectioning their parking lots. They didn't talk much. Lara's iPod had a little adapter that connected to the Impala's tape deck and sometimes they'd listen to her music: Goldfrapp and Bauhaus and other art-goth white-person stuff. Other times she'd spend minutes on end paging through his nylon binder of CDs, briefly unselfconscious as she read the little tracklist stickers Tucker, his ex, had used to label all his mixes. She smiled a little when she saw the one he'd made, FOR TUCKER on the torn sticker, and he fought the urge to look away from her, to hunch and shield himself instead of watching the road.

The meeting with Rashad in Vegas had gone smoothly. He didn't bat an eye at Lara's seventy-three thousand in cash—bundled up in newspaper and grocery bags and spirited nervously from the local Bank of America branch to the sun-drenched apartment on West Bonita where Felix had stood feeling awkward while the beautiful man he'd once fucked weighed a brick of special k for them and made small talk with Shelby. He gave them a tote, like they'd just donated to a PBS pledge drive, and threw in a few am-pules of Narcan. Lara looked just the way a tasteful buyer should, immaculate in her peach slacks and blazer, button-down open at the top to show her collarbones. It made Felix feel dirty next to her, a grubby nobody in unwashed work clothes that felt suddenly constricting, itchy and coarse against his skin.

It's not me. It's you.

Was this really what a decade and a half's obsession had led him to? Speeding through Idaho in a car full of ketamine and unregistered guns with people he hardly knew anymore. It felt so inadequate. It should have been a bomber wing and twelve platoons of the National Guard. It should have been tanks and artillery and all the clean-cut men in uniform the movies said would save you, but nobody cared, and no one was coming. He'd tried so many different ways to make them see.

It had started snowing. The wind picked up as they drove through Boise in the gathering dark, old redbrick mill buildings slowly vanishing into the blowing white across the river, the lights in their windows sharp and fragile. Vaporous wisps of powder blew across the surface of the highway. It glittered in the headlights of the other cars—compacts creeping along through the slush and trucks with shoulder-high grilles thundering past—and swirled pale and ghostly in their wakes as they vanished into the gray void ahead. Lara slept in the back seat, her dark hair falling across her face, her cheek pancaked against the window. She always looked so inelegant asleep; it made him smile.

"We can switch at the next exit," said Shelby. "You've been driving for, like, eight hours."

"I'm fine."

She smiled. Felix had never really been interested in women, and the two of them hadn't gotten along particularly well when they were younger, but she looked beautiful in the dark, all soft and smooth with that deep, shadowed dimple in her left cheek. Her voice was a little smokier than he remembered, her dark hair falling in waves over her rounded shoulders. "You really haven't changed that much, have you?"

He shrugged, vaguely irritated. "Been busy."

"I didn't mean it like that. Just . . . it's good to see you again. I'm grateful for everything you've done."

Everything he'd done. What a small way to talk about ten years spent glued to screens reading posts by people who wanted him dead and breaking into locked dumpsters to rifle through stained and dissolving paperwork, ten years of cruising through the middles of a dozen nowheres and watching kids go through what they had, bullied and fucked with and raped by the adults to whom their irritated parents had thrown them. All his years of stealing to eat, of siphoning gas with a cheap rubber hose until just the sight of a filler cap put the taste of it in his mouth.

"You have no idea what you're talking about."

He felt embarrassed as soon as the words were out of his mouth, his resentment curdling at the back of his throat. Who'd asked him to throw his life away chasing their shared bogeyman across the country? They'd come, at least, when he called them. They'd stopped acting like it had never happened.

"You're right," Shelby said after a while. "I don't."

Waves of ghostly white slithered across the highway. The headlights of other cars cut tunnels through the squall. It had been a long time since he'd come this far north.

"Honestly, Felix, I don't want to do this," Shelby stammered, her voice cracking. There were tears pouring down her cheeks and she was speaking quickly, words spilling out of her so fast that he felt like they were flooding the car, like he would drown in all those frantic words. "I didn't want to come," she sobbed, "and I still don't want to be here. I don't want to see it again. I don't want to know if . . . if it copied her. If it gave her face to one of those things. I've probably already lost my job. My girlfriend keeps calling and I don't know what to tell her. How did you do it? How did you do this alone for so long? I'm so sorry. I'm sorry, Felix. I'm sorry, I'm sorry."

He took her hand, not knowing what else to do, and for a few nerve-wracking moments drove on one-handed through the storm until, with a gentle press of her lips to his knuckles, she released her grip and let him focus on the road.

"I don't want to do it either," he said after a while, laughing a little past the sudden knot of grief in his chest. The Impala's engine growled as they started up a hill. "I never wanted to do any of it."

Lara hadn't been home in sixteen years, not since the summer *Needful Things* had come out and she and Jason Proulx had gone to see it half a dozen times, making out discreetly in the air-conditioned gloom of the dilapidated Boise Regal. No one from Saint Michael's ever went there; they liked the big AMC a few miles down the drag with its high, soaring ceilings and its arcade where you could play *WaveRunner* on a lacquered model Jet Ski that moved with you when you shifted your weight in the seat. The summer her parents had sent her to Camp Resolution.

The house hadn't changed much. Same off-white trim—the plastic kind, machined to look like wood grain—same above-ground pool covered with the same frayed blue-and-silver tarp weighted down by bricks. The place where she'd grown up was a sprawling cape with a two-car garage attached and a pair of dormers on the street-facing side, like a chameleon's bulbous eyes peering out at the infrequent traffic and the cyclists and dog walkers. Lara couldn't see the road from where she stood up at the tree line with the others, but if she closed her eyes she could recall the way the glare from passing headlights had washed over her bedroom in the night. She could imagine the two maple trees in the front yard and the snow-covered field, wild wheat pushing through the frozen crust, stretching out and up the rocky hillside toward the belt of pines between her parents' property and the Wingardt farm.

They were forty minutes from the nearest grocery store out here. Not quite in the sticks, but sticks-adjacent. Miles of woods behind them. Miles more across the street where the ground fell away into wetlands and rose up again under thick carpets of rust-colored pine needles and clearings where in the spring lady slippers bloomed from beds of soft green moss and fiddleheads swayed, curled and dreaming. It was out there that she'd sucked off Max Shannon on a hot, sticky summer day. Out there that she and her dog, a border collie mutt named Eli, had found the doe laid out on the logging road, hit by a truck and left blowing blood and mucus in the dirt and struggling hard to get her legs under her. It was land where you could hide things, sink them into murky water or leave them lying far out in the woods, past the sound of cars, for the black bears and the buzzards.

"There," whispered John, pointing. His nose and lips were red and chapped with the cold and raspberry brambles had left his thick forearm ribboned with scratches. They'd been in the woods to the west of the property for most of the morning, waiting for the things that had once been Lara's parents to leave for work. "The window. See?"

Lara followed the line from his finger to the shadow gliding black across the kitchen curtains. A man in silhouette, tall and slender against the red fabric. They weren't her mother's curtains, which had been white linen with a simple fringe of lace, but heavy doubled panels of red wool. The same kind hung in every window, all drawn flush and heavily backlit by some unseen light source.

It must be sweltering in there, thought Lara as the shadow vanished, gliding on toward the breezeway. *Hot and wet and thick. Like morning in August.*

"We should just burn it down," hissed Shelby. Her pale, round face was flushed from hiking through the woods, her black hair plastered by sweat to her throat and forehead even in the biting chill. "I don't want to go in." She swallowed. "I can't. We should burn it. We should burn it and watch the doors. So it doesn't get out."

"We have a plan," said Lara, wiping spit and perspiration from her upper lip with the sleeve of her worn, greasy flannel shirt. With her free hand she tested her backpack's frayed left strap. Her shoulders were raw where the straps had rubbed against them during their hike through the snow in from the woodlot off the nameless logging road at the town limit. "No fire."

We can't get what we need from a corpse.

They began their advance across the snowy lawn not long after, John looking up from his watch and giving Lara the nod. It was just past eight in the morning. The sun shone pale on the backs of their necks and the wind blew loose powder over the frozen crust that cracked and gave under their boots. She couldn't remember the last time she'd been outside like this in winter.

Near the western corner of the house, a red door stood out against the oyster-colored siding. In front of it sat a decaying wooden stoop, a single step built flush against the few inches of concrete foundation exposed under the trim. Lara knelt down beside it, squinting into the dark between the short, stout wooden legs she'd watched her father measure and cut in his workshop on a muggy afternoon seventeen or eighteen years ago. His big, callused hands, his sweaty blue-gray T-shirt with the Horn & Carter Building and Remodeling logo on the chest, the text stylized to fit within the outline of a two-story house.

You wanna hand me the level? Can't have your mom tripping on her way out to the pool.

Lara groped along the underside of the rotting stoop, fighting to breathe past the lump in her throat as her fingers encountered nothing but spongy wood and empty spiderwebs. *It's gone*, said a small voice in the back of her mind. *They found it, took it. You'll have to break a window and he'll hear you, and he'll get you, and*—Her forefinger found blessed plastic, pebbly and cool to the touch. She slid the hide-a-key's tongue out, pressing down to pop the plastic teeth loose from their tracks, and the key fell into her palm. Still there, the same one she'd copied at the Home Depot in the Heights the fall before her parents had sent her to Camp Resolution. She straightened up, brushing her sweat-damp hair out of her face, and tried the back door. The lock hadn't been changed. She nearly sobbed with relief when the key turned without sound or resistance and the flaking red door drifted open.

They took off their boots and went single file into the bathroom, slinking past their own reflections in the water-stained mirror over the robin's-egg-blue sink and peeling Formica countertop, opposite the washer and dryer. The stifling humidity settled over them like a film, smothering all memory of the chill outside. The yellowed linoleum was cool under Lara's bare feet. Felix eased the outer door shut as Lara wrapped her hand around the inner's handle, pressing down on the thumb plate. A low growl of metal on metal, burrs or rust scraping away, and a wave of humid air broke over them, bringing with it a sugary-sweet stench. Orange soda drying to a sticky chemical mess in the heat. Aspartame dissolved in sour milk. Lara gagged, hand flying to cover her mouth and nose as her eyes began to water.

The heat was on full blast in the living room, boxy humidifiers gurgling in three of its four corners, condensation sliding down their sleek white plastic casings. Pale greenish light leaked from a single bulb in the uncovered overhead. Mold grew in feathery gray-white swathes over the upholstery of the couch against the east wall and the love seat against the south under the big bay windows, now curtained. The television burbled, a sitcom wavering on a magnet-spoiled screen behind a partial skin of mold and lichen. Jim Belushi gesticulating in dead silence. The closet door and beside it the door to the westernmost part of the house, the old part from before the fire, looked sealed by how much they'd swollen, bulging in their frames so that wood deformed against wood in rolls that seemed to Lara almost fleshlike. Only the bathroom door's heavy coats of varnish had preserved it from the same fate.

East to the kitchen, clammy sweat beading on her forehead and running into her eyes. The air was thick and wet enough to chew. Something black leaking out from under the refrigerator. Fungus forcing its way up between the narrow floorboards in spongy clamshell ridges of brown and orange and something— spores or seed pods—drifting gauzy in the air. Her father had slapped her there for the first time, between the cabinets and the breakfast island. Clang of pots and pans from under the butcher-block countertop and then the window seat where her mother's little dogs had stood, forepaws on the windowsill, to bark at the cars that pulled in and out of the long driveway. Across the room, the door to the breezeway stood open and shadows moved over the wood-paneled stretch of wall beyond it. The sound of running water drifted through the doorway, a steady gurgle underscored by sonorous plops and plunks. Felix stepped into the lead, pistol drawn.

She looked to the others. Bloodless faces. Watering eyes. They looked sick, and the sticky-sweet smell was getting stronger. John had a crowbar they'd bought in town. Shelby gripped a can of mace. Mal hung back a little, face ashen. Lara chewed the inside of her cheek and fingered her backpack's shoulder strap, the feathery-soft fibers of its fraying edge gliding over each other beneath her touch. The music of the falling water seemed like the only sound in the world. She wanted more than anything to run from this place, to forget it existed, to forget all these people she loved and the things they'd been forced to know and to carry, alone.

Felix was first through the door. John and Mal followed, Jo behind them, and then Lara was stepping down from the cracked wooden threshold, the inside of her mouth coated in that cum-and-melted-Skittles smell, gluey and saccharine, her skin washed in fierce blue-white light from the banks of rack-mounted grow lights overhead.

Somewhere, she knew, were the front door and another, leading into the garage and the barn above it where her father's business had been headquartered, but all that she could see were rows of hydroponic towers, and all that she could hear was the low snarl of the tower motors circulating water out of the cisterns at their bases where dark shapes like tadpoles wriggled and squirted among vascular traceries of vines. Sticky green-white fronds caressed her bare arms and slid over her cheeks, leaving behind snail trails of slime. Other things, fleshy and half-formed, twitched among the vegetation. The air was almost unbreathable now. She heard the dull thunk of metal striking flesh.

They had it pinned by the time she reached them. It lay on its back, Jo holding its legs, Shelby kneeling on its right arm, Felix on its left, John behind it with its head pressed against his belly and his crowbar against its throat. Its eyes were squeezed shut, swollen and red, and blood matted its short, light hair, but she knew its face. Knew and loved and hated it. Had filled in its thin, colorless eyebrows and plucked the fine wisps of its mustache from its upper lip a thousand times. Had traced its jutting cheekbones with a contouring brush and tugged turtlenecks up over its protruding Adam's apple. It had stared back at her from the mirror every morning of her life.

It wasn't a dream.

She approached and knelt at its left shoulder between Shelby and John, swinging her backpack off her shoulders as she did. Overhead a ceiling fan turned slowly, its blades dragging skeins of ghostly moss. She fished through the bag, pushing past power bars and bottles of Gatorade, and found what she was looking for. She flicked the safety toggle on the butt of the cordless drill. It was heavy in her hands, a satisfying weight.

"Hurry," John puffed, pulling back on both ends of the crowbar as the thing squirmed, nails scratching at the flagstones.

Lara set the bit against the thing's high forehead, forcing herself not to look into its puffy, Mace-burned eyes as it forced them open, forcing herself to ignore the things that it was saying, the sound of her own voice pleading for its life, offering them money, and with a squeeze the drill came whirring to life, the molded black rubber of the grip deforming under her fingers. The bit churned skin with a rough, chugging squelch. The drill bucked in Lara's hands. The whine of the electric motor deepened as it caught and began to grind through bone. A fine thread of white smoke rose from the bloody wound.

"Jesus Christ," said Jo, and for a sickening moment, as the thing screamed itself hoarse with the drill's bit between its eyes, Lara was convinced they'd made a horrible mistake, that this was just some weird, reclusive botanist and they were about to murder him, that they'd had some kind of trauma when they were teenagers and it had broken them and the story they thought they remembered was nothing more than fragments of science fiction and Stephen King paperbacks glued together over the years.

Bone broke. The bit plunged in.

The thing's skull opened up like a time-lapse clip of the world's most disgusting crocus blooming. Wet flaps of meat lined with mismatched and broken teeth snapped at Lara as John hauled back on the crowbar across its throat.

"Now," said Felix. He looked so calm, even with the Gabe-thing clawing at his forearm with its free hand. Mal had its other arm pinned tight. Shelby stepped forward and tipped the little plastic dime bag into the red gape of the thing's writhing face. Blue-white dust coated raw flesh. Malformed tongues lashed in drooling panic, only succeeding in licking up more of the crushed pale blue crystal. A yellowish eye rolled in the soup behind its opened face. It sneezed, spraying blood through its teeth, and its back arched like a bow as it began to scream. Lara lost her grip on the drill. She fell back, her mind blank.

The thing boiled. There was no other word for it. Its flesh heaved and bubbled. Its bloodied and distorted features swelled, splitting down the middle. Its scream de-synced like a corrupted video file, the right half of the face gibbering unintelligibly as the left gaped in a raw wail of anguish, strings of muscle and sinew struggling to form some kind of throat. There was a little half face taking shape halfway down its right forearm, a whimpering mouth sliding like a fried egg on a greased skillet toward the back of its hand. Bones unstuck themselves from joints and sockets, dragging sails of skin behind them as they fragmented and re-formed, serpentine vertebrae squirming away from the shrinking knot of matter. Fingers wriggled like maggots away from wag-gling metacarpals. Belly splitting, intestines slithering between withered thighs from which skin hung in gummy tatters.

The others backed away from it as something in its chest col-lapsed, flesh tearing, slick lumps of meat worming their way out through the holes. Lara couldn't move. She sat pinned to the spot, watching. A lung. The heart. Raw, stubby limbs propelled them over a morass of sagging skin. Wattles of excess dermis. For an instant, amid all that writhing ugliness, its face, *Gabe's* face, came back together, the halves of its discordant scream united in an ear-splitting shriek, and then its jaw popped from its hinge and folded back over itself, inverting to show only slimy membrane and the bizarre architecture of a mouth reversed, teeth raining down onto the floor like a fistful of dropped M&M's, and the sound became a wet and stifled moan, and ceased.

A toddler-sized chunk of its torso, which fell free and dragged itself on rejointed rib bones a few inches across the mold-furred tiles, was the last thing to stop moving, folding over on itself again and sagging from its bones. The smell of it burned Lara's nostrils. "Come on," said Felix, taking her arm. "Come on, Lara. Let's go."

It was only as Felix pulled her to her feet that she saw the sad little forms lying curled among the overgrowth. Withered lips peeled back from blackened gums. Eyelids sagging into empty sockets. Felix caught her as she threw herself against him, sobbing.

"Mom," she moaned past the lump in her throat, a knot of love and hate and loss swelling huge in her chest. "Oh God, Mom."

They filed out of the house the same way they'd come in. Lara tried not to think about the grasping hands she'd seen among the leaves, the kneeling figures clinging to each other in a grotesque human archway, bodies scaled with fungal growths and flaking skin. She tried not to think of her mother's hand—the same hand—twitching there on the warm, dirty stone tiles, of the shell of her father staring vacantly at nothing, pale vomit dribbling down his chin, and behind him something that might have been her sister. She tried not to think of her own face unzipping itself like a plastic bag full of spoiled soup.

"Okay," said Lara, not looking at the others. Her breath smoked in the air. She started back toward where they'd left the gas cans in the shadows under the trees, snow crunching underfoot. The cold stung her face as she looked back over her shoulder at the house. "Now we can burn it."

XXI

CLUSTER B

It was past three in the morning when John pulled off the highway on the outskirts of Boise and navigated a maze of empty streets to the parking lot of the Motel 8 Shelby had mentioned in her text. He took the space next to Felix's Impala and killed the rental's engine. Jo had ripped the GPS out of the dash for him and changed his plates not far outside of Reno; the agency had called repeatedly for days until they'd all tossed their phones and bought burners at a strip mall. He wondered, as he hauled himself out of the driver's seat and stamped his aching feet on the cracked pavement to force some feeling back into them, if he'd ever be able to rent another apartment after all of this.

Jo and Mal piled out of the back, Jo rolling her shoulder and blinking sleepily as Mal interlaced their fingers and lifted their arms high above their head, stretching until their knuckles popped. John watched as they rose up onto their toes and arched their back, their sinuous frame like a line of calligraphy against the parking lot's dim lights. Their nose ring and the studs in their ears caught the muted glow and for a moment John could remember nothing but the way their ass felt cupped in his hands and their breath—smelling of cinnamon chewing gum—washing over his cheek and ear and the corner of his mouth. It was easy to forget the silent treatments, the sneering remarks in the grocery store and at the table, the fake concern concealing a desire to wound he'd never fully understood. They were beautiful and brilliant and sometimes when you touched them you pulled your hand back and found it cut to ribbons.

They went in. The others were waiting in the hotel room with

Chinese takeout cartons spread over the side tables and on the quilted nylon comforters. Three beds and a cot set up blocking the closet, Lara already curled asleep on it with her mouth hanging open and her hair across her face. She snored softly while Felix pored over a dog-eared road atlas annotated in black Sharpie. "Day after tomorrow," he said, not looking up as they dumped their backpacks by the door.

John stifled a yawn with the back of his hand. "What?"

"We'll be there."

John sank down onto the unoccupied bed and ran a hand over his jaw. He needed to shave. He needed to shower. He needed to find some way to stop seeing that thing with Lara's face whenever he closed his eyes, to stop seeing the things that had been her family drooling and twitching among the overgrowth spilling from the hydroponic towers. They were ashes now. The house had gone up like a pile of greasy rags.

"Drive okay?" Shelby asked around a mouthful of eggroll. She had her headphones in and John could just hear the tinny beat of some hyperpop earworm. She'd always been his favorite. They went together easily, the only two fat kids in the bunch, but her taste in music made him want to follow his own grandfather's example and go deaf. Oji had hated it, too, though he'd been too kind to say it to her face.

What's wrong with Bob Dylan? Akira had asked once over coffee, some morning when it was just the two of them awake. *At least with him, the words make sense!*

"Not bad," said Jo, snatching up a carton of beef and broccoli and shoveling it into her mouth. "Some idiot hit a deer on the highway. I-70's all backed up for about twenty miles." She swallowed. "Other than that, fine."

"This is scintillating, but I'm getting cigarettes," said Mal, turning back toward the door. "Anyone want anything?"

"Remember, no credit cards," Felix answered automatically. He was busy making a note on one of his printouts. "We can't leave a trail."

They did their best Vanna White strut and gesture, presenting a sheaf of ones and fives to an imaginary audience with a wave of their free hand and flashing a dazzling fake grin. "I'm not a fucking idiot," they said, still smiling. "Thanks."

The door slammed, a blast of cold air washing over the rest of them, and John wondered how often he'd sat in other rooms with the same feeling of leaden failure in his chest, the sense that there had been some test, inscrutable and swift, and he had failed it.

Mal's cracked phone screen glowed in the dark under the stairs at the end of the motel's first-floor gallery as they thumbed back through days of Charlie's texts, the words flowing through the spidered and flaking section of the faceplate like water rushing under the surface of a frozen river. Distorted. Deformed. They'd thrown away an old protein bar when the others tossed their phones. Nice to be able to afford to do that. They couldn't throw Charlie away. They couldn't.

i canr lbelieve ur doing this to me
ur so fckikng selfish
i should have linstend tos ara and fucking left u

For the first time it felt less like an imperative and more like a glimpse through a window into a room they didn't live in but where they knew something terrible was happening. How many times had they ranted like this at John and Dorian and all their other boys? How many times had their own therapy sessions, when they'd been on state insurance and could afford them, devolved into embittered recitations of every petty slight—real and imagined—they'd endured in their week? *Jo texted me on my birthday, just a fucking text, and last year I bought her that face cream and pitched in for her septum piercing. Lane hates me. Lane, at work. I heard him talking about me, saying it's "weird" that I'm vegan. It doesn't matter. It's the same everywhere; I try so fucking hard and nobody wants me, nobody gives a shit what I go through.*

And then, inevitably, the stiff-lipped smile, the *I can't help you* and the referrals to other offices, half of which had already brushed them aside like bird shit off a porch. Borderline. Narcissism. Their body eaten through with the invisible leprosy of a cluster B personality disorder and none of these hard-faced white women with their pin-straight hair and their Buddha statues willing to cut into the necrosis creeping up the limbs of the grinning, joking Black transsexual who went on and off their estrogen every few months and sometimes dissolved into screaming fits over unwashed dishes or partners forgetting to text after traveling.

They'd had Dr. Paris for a while, before his heart attack. The first Black therapist they'd seen. He'd been better. Gentle but firm, pushing back against their explosions of venomous temper until little by little they began to emerge from the cocoon of their own aggrieved self-victimization, to set aside the defense of presuming themself loathed and persecuted at every turn. It was like picking glass out of bathwater, even two years in.

As they played their messages and lifted the phone to their ear, though, it felt clearer than it ever had before. Charlie's voice crackled and hissed.

"You used me, and now you don't need me anymore and you're throwing me away like *garbage,* because you never loved—hate me—fucking *bitch* fucking *cunt* shit cunt I *hate you, I'm going to kill myself*—" and then it was just an unintelligible wail, a whining, sobbing shriek that poured out of the phone like sewage from a burst pipe, garbled words lost in the dark rush of it and Mal could feel a tugging in the pit of their stomach, a single filthy, dripping thread pulling them tight against the phone's sweat-damp screen. They wanted to climb through it and into Charlie's shaking arms, to let their partner close the circle they had ruptured by leaving the house, by running away when they should have stayed and let the door slam shut on their hand like it had on Mary's, like it must have again and again on those delicate little fingers when Malcolm never came home, when there was no one to stand between those big, frightened dark eyes and the thing that had wormed its way beneath their mother's skin long before they'd seen the horror under the Glover house, the thing they could feel stirring under their own skin even now, a desperate, directionless need grasping at everything and finding purchase nowhere. Nails sliding over cold and sweating glass.

No one loves me, because I am unlovable. Because I've failed them. Because they hate me and wanted me dead from the beginning and every kind word they ever spoke was just the flashlight held to hypnotize the stupid fucking loudmouth frog.

This is why you've sabotaged your life every time you've had the chance.

"Mal?" John's voice, soft and gentle. He stood a little ways off, his leather jacket thrown over his pajamas. Striped, like their father had used to wear. *Float like a butterfly.* "Are you okay?"

For an instant they imagined throwing themself at him and falling into his strong arms. Then they remembered the cell phone, and in the same second realized he'd already seen it. "I really fucked up," they said, the words half a sob. "John, I fucked up." They wanted to scream at him, to push it onto him somehow, make it *his* fault for not asking them politely enough to toss their electronics, or not explaining himself adequately. Glass in the bathwater. They took a steadying breath and said: "Help me."

John came close and took their phone without a word, worked one of its rubber guards open, and teased out the SIM card between his thumb and forefinger. He snapped the card, then went to the hooded trash can sitting on the curb and tossed the pieces and the phone into the bin together. His shoulders slumped. He looked much older than thirty-two, and for the first time they noticed that his hair was thinning, that there were lines at the corners of his warm blue eyes. For a moment as he turned back toward them his stare wasn't warm at all, but cold and black in the long shadows of the parking lot's lamp posts, and Mal thought fleetingly of all the nights they'd lain awake in the little room they shared with Felix, wondering if one of them had carried something out of Camp Resolution, if it was waiting for its moment hidden behind the face of someone they loved.

It's John, they told themself, wishing they'd had time to fill their Klonopin script, wishing they had weed or Benadryl or anything to declaw the thoughts racing back and forth through their head. *It's really him, or he'd have killed you already.*

John took their hand and a wave of revulsion washed over them, not at John but at their own stupidity and worthlessness. He pulled them into his arms and they thought they might scream, but it passed. They cried for a while and thought of all the times they'd been cruel to him. "I'm sorry," they sniffled. "I'm sorry for everything. All of it."

He kept stroking their back. "I know."

"Do you think we have a chance?"

He was quiet for a long time before answering. "I think more than anything, it wants to stay hidden. That's why it uses us. Queers. No one comes after us. No one believes us if we get away from it." He stepped back and let go of them, though he kept holding their hand. They wanted him with every fiber of their being then, wanted his big, soft hands and the huge muscles buried under the warm and giving curve of his ass.

His fingers slipped from theirs. "I don't know if we have a chance," he said, "but I know it doesn't want us coming after it. I know it depends on nobody caring about the kids it preys on. Nadine died getting us out of that place; we owe it to her."

That long, beautiful body pierced by hooks and spines and claws. The fire. The shock wave, carrying broken glass. Mal still had a little scar on their left cheek, and another just above their collarbones. They all dreamed of Nadine, sometimes.

"Come on," said John, not unkindly. "We should get everyone else. We need to go."

He was halfway to the door before they called after him. "Do you think we could—would you ever—would you try again, with me?" They knew it was a mistake as soon as they opened their mouth, but the words wouldn't stop coming, slipping out of them like entrails through a wound. "I've done a lot of work, I know last time it was bad, I fucked up, I hurt you a lot, but I keep thinking of you, John." Their voice broke. "I'm always thinking of you."

He stood there, not moving, and they thought their heart would burst until finally John said, his eyes welling with tears: "We have to go."

"Right," they said. "Of course."

Lara had one of her headaches. She got them three or four times a year, and even through the gauzy film of her dream—she was trying to clean her parents' house as slick, hairy flesh spilled from the cabinets and pushed its way up through the floorboards—she could feel the sick pulse of low-grade pain and nausea washing over her in waves. When John shook her awake it was all she could do to scramble to the toilet before she started heaving up half-digested sesame chicken while he tried to explain something about cell phones and Mal and GPS. Five minutes later they were piling back into the cars and she was leaning out—Felix holding on to the back of her top as she vomited again out the rear driver's-side door. A man's voice echoed through the silent parking lot from one of the second-floor rooms, loose and drunk and cruel.

Cunt bitch, he shouted, but he wanted her. He wanted her so badly, not like a man wants a woman but like a baby wants its mother or a dying dog a cool, dry place to crawl into and curl up. *Faggot.* Something breaking. Lamp. TV. *Not mine. He's not mine.*

That was when she saw the woman walking toward them from across the parking lot. She looked like any other older white woman, maybe sixty, careworn and a little weathered, with long, wavy gray hair. She had a pistol in her hand.

"Go," Lara choked out. "GO!"

Felix pulled her upright and reached across her to slam the door as Shelby backed out of their space. The other car was already pulling into traffic. The woman's gun came up. There were other people in the lot now. A red-faced man, short and fat. A teenage girl in a heavy coat and winter hat. Lara couldn't talk, couldn't reach up to brush aside the hairs caught in the sick around her mouth. She could feel the thing that had stolen her life writhing under her. She could see it standing at her parents' bedside, watching the slow rise and fall of their chests, watching the part of the mattress where Lara had once tucked her small and frightened self between their sleeping bodies as lightning scribbled outside the north-facing windows, flashing again and again over the field. She saw it slip into bed beside her mother, soft and gentle as a whisper, and open up its face to give her a secret even her cold, hard-fingered hands had never found.

The gray-haired woman fired, cracking the Impala's right rear window and drawing a hot line of pain across the bridge of Lara's nose. She screamed, jerking back and falling into Felix's lap. Shelby spun the wheel and peeled out, tires squealing, fishtailing into the sparse traffic—mostly truckers. One stood on his horn, his trailer drifting ominously as he braked. She was drenched in the hot torrent of his desperation. He was driving high on Adderall to make his schedule; the smallest accident and his license would be gone, his living evaporated out from under him.

She felt the driver of the SUV behind him die as a stray bullet caught him in the temple. He was—*call Mary in the morning, tell her you're sorry, tell her you want to do better. God, if anything happened to her*—and then he was nothing. A line jumping. A line holding still. A scream of metal. Sirens whooping. *Oh God,* she thought. *Oh God, it has cops. Of course it does.* She felt the ripples of shock and terror in surrounding drivers as the dead man slumped against the wheel and veered into the other lane, side-swiping a cab. The cab driver praying *please, please* as he spun out. The guardrail. Tangled metal. Fire.

Felix was talking to her, saying something soothing as he smoothed her hair back and cleaned her face with a baby wipe that smelled strongly of aloe and disinfectant. He was saying, *It's okay, Lara,* only it wasn't okay. The pain was getting worse. Her eyeballs felt as though they were being forced out of their sockets. Her sinuses burned like white-hot wires pushed through her face, and she could taste Felix's fear, too, and feel in him an echo of the white fire burning in her mind's eye, the fire kindled in the summer of 1995 that had never gone out, not really, and she could feel the children sleeping in the Mercury that sped past them on the left, the panic and relief of the parents looking back at the pileup. They pulled up at a red light. Lara didn't know if she was breathing anymore. There was a weight on her chest. The dark bulk of the overpass loomed ahead of them, the on-ramp poorly lit by a light post with one bulb out.

The light turned green. Shelby followed a semitrailer onto the ramp, and suddenly Felix wasn't cleaning Lara's face anymore. "Oh," he said quietly.

As Shelby accelerated up the on-ramp toward the light and thunder of I-70, Lara turned, her head feeling as though it weighed a thousand pounds, and looked over the rail and across the intersection. The motel was burning. Gouts of red and orange boiled in the wind, which teased the blaze into strange shapes and fanned up a great rampart of smoke behind it. There were people running in the parking lot and flashes that looked like gunfire. Little figures fell and did not get up. She felt it like withdrawal from her meds, brief zaps of thought-annihilating static as want and fear and rage dissolved into nothing, blown away like dandelion seeds.

Felix was on his burner, talking to John and pushing down the center armrest to grope in the backseat as Shelby merged into traffic and cut around the rubberneckers slowing down to gawk over the guardrail at the towering sheets of flame licking up at the sky. Felix drew out a pistol and a pair of what she supposed must be clips and slammed one into its magazine, still talking. The connection must have been bad, because it kept crackling, but as she laid back against the seat and closed her eyes, Lara could still hear Mal screaming in the background.

XXII

HALF WINDSOR

"What were you thinking?" Felix shouted at Mal as they climbed out of the passenger side of John's rental. In the dim light filtering down through the trees that overhung the access road down which they'd pulled the cars, they looked as bad as he felt, deep shadows under their eyes and their hair flattened on one side where they must have slept against the window. From what he could see of their arms—they were wearing one of their shapeless, cowled black cardigans—they'd broken out in some kind of hives, too.

Good.

It felt good to see their pupils shrink in miserable terror as he strode toward them. It felt like doing something about the people he'd seen killed in that parking lot, the little body he'd watched flopping on the pavement as Lara shivered and dry-heaved against his shoulder. It felt like going back in time and wrenching that phone from their hands to smash it on the sidewalk. "What the fuck were you thinking?"

"I fucked up," they whined, their voice hoarse and raw. They shrank back against the side of the car. "Felix, I'm so sorry."

"Take it easy!" Jo yelled, scrambling out the driver's side.

"Those people are dead." His voice cracked, pitching up into a girlish shriek that made him want to crawl into a hole somewhere and staple his mouth shut. "They're all dead because you're fucking codependent, because you're a nightmare and you've always been a nightmare you selfish, awful bitch."

He slapped them. Felix knew as soon as he'd done it that he'd gone too far, that he'd let fifteen years of frustration and rage and unprocessed loneliness tear its way out of him and go straight for the most vulnerable target it could find, but before those thoughts could form belief he had slapped them again.

He never saw John coming, but suddenly he was on the ground and the huge man was straddling his chest and had his wrists pinned. "Felix," he said, panting a little, and his voice was soft but firm. "I understand, but it's done."

Mal was crying softly, not the hysterical screaming he'd heard over the phone but a congested, snotty whimper that made Felix want to hit them again. They were so *weak,* so wishy-washy. It woke something ugly buried deep under his subdued affect. Manny Vargas, a red-faced ghoul with broken glass and scraps of tulle embedded in his skin, clawing his way out of the son he hadn't wanted. Felix looked away from John, hot tears of shame burning his eyes. He watched a line of ants march over the rutted ground. They were carrying things. Other insects. Little bits of leaves. The things they needed to live.

"They're dead," he sobbed, and he meant not just the people in the parking lot but his mother, who in 2008 had fallen down in the kitchen of his childhood home, her mind wiped clean by an aneurysm, and his tío Lalo, her brother, who had stood up for him once during one of Manny's rages, putting his body between the two of them until the storm was over. Lalo hadn't been allowed back in their house for most of a year after that, and a few months after his sister died he was diagnosed with liver cancer and spent eight agonizing weeks sliding helplessly out of the world. Felix had spoken to Leo only a few times in the years since Camp Resolution, never daring to go further than that, always insisting he tell their mother nothing but that he was alive, and he'd missed his chance. He'd missed everything. Now Oji was gone, too, and he hadn't even flown home for the funeral. Akira had taught him how to knot a tie.

Like this. Over the finger. The half Windsor.

"They're all dead."

They slept at the end of the access road that night, Felix tossing and turning in the back seat of his car, the others out on blankets under the thin canopy. They were maybe two hours from St. Louis, a city he'd never seen before. He wondered if he'd ever see it now. It had some kind of arch. A bridge. He couldn't remember. How many nights had he slept in his car? Thousands. Whole years eaten up staring at the Impala's roof, breathing the chemical stink of its upholstery and the warm, cheesy musk of his own body odor. How many shots had he missed, too far away from any of his hookups, or too broke, or too exhausted?

John and Mal were talking outside, their voices low. Felix remembered sweating between them in the cool, musty darkness of that nameless bunker in the desert. His first time. Their thoughts running together, their bodies entwined among the others. He'd held John's nipple in his mouth as someone pushed inside him, as Mal's slender fingers found his cock and teased it from its hood, as his world took its first desperate breath of free air. He slipped out the other side of the car, easing the door shut behind him, and detoured back toward the main road to squat in the undergrowth. Headlights whisked through the trees as he peed. A deer stood revealed a few yards away, its eyes reflecting the bright glare, light sliding over their dark, liquid depths and passing on, and vanishing. He wiped himself on a leaf and tugged his jeans up, goose bumps crawling up his thighs and ass as the cool night breeze picked up.

Another car passed. The deer was gone. On his way back to the cars he paused to listen to the others, their hushed voices carrying in the stillness. The thought of slithering back into his car, back into that close, cloying smell they hadn't been able to steam clean out after what had happened in Idaho, felt like contemplating nailing himself into a coffin.

. . . *anyone like you. Baby, oh, baby. I miss you. I miss you. Yes, there, yes, there, God . . .*

. . . *only wanted to watch rom-coms and Disney movies . . .*

. . . forgot how good you felt . . .

. . . can't tell you, sweetheart, I know, I'm sorry, but I'll be home soon. I love you . . .

The wind picked up again, the leaves whispering, and Felix felt a terrible emptiness boil up from somewhere deep inside him. *I have no one,* he thought, trying to swallow past the lump in his throat. He saw Mal's eyes widen again, saw them shrink back against the car. Their weakness made him so *angry,* but it wasn't their fault. Not really.

If I die, he thought, *no one will miss me.*

Jo sat with her back against John's stolen rental, watching the stars through the branches. She and Shelby had tried fucking for a while, but exhaustion, stress, and the lumpy ground under their scratchy wool blanket had won in the end. Shelby cried for a few minutes and then fell asleep while Jo, feeling frustrated and overwhelmed, stroked her hair. It was cold out, even with the sleeping bags Felix had given them. She was pretty sure it was past New Year's, but she hadn't seen a calendar in days.

It felt strange to know that her stuff was out on the curb by now, or in a liquidator's warehouse. Her job was gone. Her clothes. Her music. The yukata Oji had given her for her seventeenth birthday, the summer after camp. The threadbare stuffed rabbit she'd slept with. Little pricks of guilt and loss. The things that had made up her life were falling away, like the last fifteen years had been a parlor trick, cards fanned out and shaken to entice and now snapped flush and made to disappear with a flick of the wrist to reveal that they were right back where they'd started. Scared, broke, alone, and running from something they didn't really understand.

A shooting star flitted across the sky. Jo thought awhile about how fucked up it was that she felt better on a suicide mission than she did in her own life, about how she hadn't had a drink in three days without noticing it, about how she hadn't had a nightmare since the motel in Reno. She loved these fucked-up people. It had killed her when they left, when one by one they fled the nest until it was just her and Oji. On the far side of Felix's car someone was having sex, mingled voices and the wet, desperate sounds of inelegant kissing. John and Mal. That was good. They brought out the best in each other, when they weren't ruining each other's lives.

Felix got out of his car, an indistinct black shape against the dappled moonlight. Shelby stirred at the gentle thump of the door shutting, squirming closer and burrowing deeper into the sleeping bag. "Love you," she murmured.

Jo tugged up her jacket's zipper with her free hand, wriggling down into the soft collar. With Shelby against her, the night seemed almost warm. "I love you, too."

Lara wiggled the SIM card out of her burner, snapped it in half, and slotted in a fresh one. Without Andrea's voice for company the woods felt suddenly threatening, full of mysterious sounds and moving shadows. She probed gently with two fingers at the bandage over the bridge of her grazed nose and wiped the blood that had seeped through on the sleeve of her coat, too exhausted even to be horrified at using a Michael Kors piece as a tissue, and started back toward the access road, picking her way carefully among the weedy birch saplings and clinging raspberries. Her thoughts kept racing ahead of her. Andrea had been upset with her, probably afraid she was having another breakdown.

You need to tell me where you are, Lo. This isn't like you. Please, I'm so fucking scared, I'm not even angry anymore.

It was easier with clients. You could just tell them "I'm out of town" and they'd make little sounds of disappointment, maybe try to bribe her into changing plans with spa treatments and Jimmy Choos, but in the end they always let her go. They knew she wasn't really theirs. Loving someone was what made it hard. Andrea and Adrien and Kevin and all the other hookups and friends and exes who revolved around and through her life in Boston. She missed them so much it was like a lead weight in her stomach, missed them with the terrible pain of knowing that when she went back they were all going to think she'd lost her mind. She thought of the psych ward at Albany Medical, of its bare, water-damaged rooms with their bolted-down beds and of Dr. Weaver's thick white hair and cool, icy gaze. Those words scratched out in thin, looping handwriting on a legal pad.

Gender confusion . . . part of systematized delusions?

Something moved out in the dark beneath the trees, dead brush rustling and crunching, and she quickened her pace, her heartbeat hammering, until she caught sight of the moonlight gleaming on the cars. It was like that feeling you got as a child after reading something scary after dark, when even the thought of turning off the lights put your whole body into fight or flight and only bed— feet off the ground, covers over the head—could possibly provide the slightest safety. She would have liked to feel that again, the thrill of being terrified by something that couldn't hurt her, the ecstatic, shivering relief of escaping its imaginary clutches. The real monsters didn't care about the rules.

Lara stepped out onto the access road. The forest was only a forest. The only things in it were deer and rabbits, mice and foxes. Things that knew to fear people. The others were asleep against the side of John's car, their breath smoking in the cold, their bodies curled together, and for a moment she remembered how it had felt to give herself to them, how beside the grave of their childhoods they'd become, in some confused and frightened way, adults. It would have been nice to feel that again, too. Carefully, trying her best not to wake them, she knelt and wriggled between John and Felix. John shifted, draping his arm over her, and she burrowed into his reassuring warmth. Mal lay dreaming fitfully on his other side.

At least it was almost over.

The next day Felix had them take the Impala farther in along the logging road to where the forest gave way to a scar of clear-cut land, crumbling earth and gray, dead stumps. Mal hadn't wanted to wake up, hadn't been quite ready to leave the warmth and safety of John's arms, but Felix insisted they get in a day of target practice before crossing over into Nevada. John, who had taught himself to shoot years ago, had gone into Boise to talk to a liquidator they'd found in the phonebook. Felix wanted him to check out stock at some local folded department stores. There were things they'd need for their trip to Cook Canyon.

Waiting for their turn with the rifle, which Jo was currently firing at cans of Sprite Felix had set up on a stump fifty yards away, Mal sat slumped in the Impala's driver's seat and listened with mounting dread to a spotty, crackling radio broadcast.

"Sixteen dead in what Boise chief of police Franklin Gerhardt called the worst mass shooting in Idaho history at a press conference this morning. Between three and five unknown gunmen converged on a local motel, where they opened fire without warning on guests and motorists. A fire claimed the lives of a further—"

They turned it off. It was their fault. Someone had been waiting for them to make a mistake, and they'd walked right into it and gotten every one of those people killed. The boom of the assault rifle firing sounded like a church bell tolling, calling in the townsfolk to see the traitor hanged. Mal deserved to die. They'd thought about it while the others were setting up, and while Felix explained basic gun safety. It was funny to watch Lara choke up on a shotgun, her acrylics catching on the trigger guard, but nothing could pull them away from the pit that had formed in their stomach as they drove away from that burning motel.

People are dead because of me.

They should never have answered Felix's call. They should have stayed with Charlie, let him keep grinding them down into a squeaking little nub afraid of its own shadow. It was what they deserved. Oblivion. Emptiness. And beneath that, deep down, a little voice—their mother's, though they were no longer conscious of this—said guiltily that it would be a relief, too. Not just for their friends and loved ones, who had to live with their disgusting burden, but for themself. A relief to let the engine of their mind, grinding white-hot metal on metal for years now, finally flame out.

The passenger door opened. Felix slid into the seat. Outside, Lara blasted a can of Sprite into flying metal shreds. Jo and Shelby cheered. Mal tried their best not to act like a wounded animal. They didn't deserve to be pathetic. They weren't going to let that be their family's last memory of them.

"I'm sorry," said Felix.

"You don't owe me an apology," Mal said woodenly. "I did it. I killed them."

Felix didn't contradict them, but after a few moments he reached over the console and took their hand. His grip was strong and warm. "What are you going to do now?"

Mal started to cry. The tears came softly, their shoulders shaking just a little. "We're all going to die, aren't we?"

Felix squeezed their hand. "Maybe," he said. "But we'll take it with us, if we can."

"And Nadine's sister?"

"If some of us live, we'll do our best for her. Like Akira did for us."

"I miss him," said Mal, their voice wavering.

"Me too." Felix pulled him into a one-armed hug, then got out of the car and walked over to help Shelby load the rifle. Mal wiped their eyes on the sleeve of their cardigan. They inhaled sharply, closing their eyes.

I'm sorry.

XXIII

JABBERWOCKY

The three of them made the trek from the rest stop off of I-80 in just under two days, picking their way over broken stone and bare earth and down canyons choked with shale and drifted sand until they emerged in the shadow of the rock wall to the north of Cook Canyon. It had been weeks since Felix had done laundry and his shirt was grimy and soaked under the armpits, the bridge of his ill-fitting gas station sunglasses digging into his sunburned and peeling nose. A quarter mile or so down the gritty slope, set back from the winding hillside road at the end of a long dirt drive, a two-story hacienda squatted like a tortoise under its shell of red clay tiles. Two well-used Ford pickups and a mid-century Cadillac in the shade of gold only old people seemed to buy were parked out front, and things that looked like men loitered on the porch, some smoking, others face-to-face as though embracing lovers, their skin knitted together and roiling with alien muscles.

"What if it got them?" Shelby whispered. She was crouched beside him behind the fallen petrified tree he'd chosen as their blind, her sweaty hair tied back in a loose knot, Lara beside her with her eyes closed and her back to the trunk. "What if they didn't make it in?"

"Then we'll try our best," said Felix.

"This is so fucking insane," Shelby continued, faster now. "What are we doing here? That thing in Lara's parents' house, I can't see that again, I can't do this—"

"Shut up," said Lara, and, mercifully, Shelby did. "They're all right. I can feel it."

Felix took off his sunglasses and dropped them in the dirt,

then unzipped his rifle case. He fitted the telescopic sight and checked the magazine and chamber. Shelby was right, of course. At any moment the thing under the house might think to check its own backyard, might question the likelihood that its prey and nemeses had decided to drive straight down its gullet without any apparent plan. John and the others might fuck it up. One of the cars might break down. Their phones were bricks out here—it had probably killed the nearest tower—and they'd all agreed walkie-talkies were too big a risk. He squinted down the sights, watching the things on the porch as they milled and smoked and knew each other, faces opening and closing, features swimming in seas of formless skin.

"I can feel it," Lara said again. Her voice sounded oddly far-away. "They're close now."

"How do you know?" Shelby asked.

"I just know."

Felix let out a long, steady breath and flipped the rifle's safety off. "Knock wood," he said, and rapped his knuckles on the dead tree's trunk.

They were maybe half a mile outside downtown when they saw the roadblock. A pair of beige cruisers with COOK CANYON SHER-IFF'S DEPARTMENT and a big gold star stenciled on their driver's-side doors sat parked headlights to headlights across the two-lane in front of an empty lot and a shuttered OneWest branch. The dull glint of spike strips shut off the lots to their either side. John could hardly breathe. He couldn't feel his own hands gripping the steering wheel.

"Now?" Jo whispered from the back seat. She sat beside one of the mannequins they'd picked up at a clearance sale in Fort Marsden and dressed in some of Mal's dirty clothes, one of Felix's submachine guns in her lap. John shook his head, slowing.

The cruiser on the left flashed its lights, its siren *whoop-whoop*-ing, and John nearly wept with relief. It wanted them alive, just like Felix had said. He pulled over ten or fifteen yards from the blockade so that the rental's passenger side was parallel with the two cars. An officer came toward them, his face expressionless, his mirrored sunglasses shining in the afternoon sunlight as he put his hand on the butt of his gun.

"Now."

Jo opened fire, her submachine gun jumping and shuddering in her hands, the rental's rear passenger window exploding outward. The thing walking toward them shrieked in agony, its face and upper body erupting in a writhing mass of feelers and tendrils as the Uzi shredded its uniform and ripped open its throat. The other cop-things ducked behind their cruisers, and by the time they began to straighten, John had Felix's Kalashnikov braced against his shoulder. The assault rifle thundered, kicking like a mule, and the first cop went down screaming and writhing, dragging its bloody, mangled body across the pavement with a sudden blooming multitude of shapeless limbs. The next ran jerkily in circles like a decapitated chicken, leaping every so often and convulsing in midair until finally he stumbled and collapsed. Rounds punched through steel and plexiglass and one of the cruisers exploded with a sound like a giant bringing its hand down on the world's biggest blown-up paper bag. Flames engulfed the road. John couldn't hear. His ears were full of a low, dull roaring as he swept the gun back and forth across the roadblock.

It only cares about staying hidden, Felix had said. *It's not a hunter. It's not a soldier. I don't think it has any real firepower, nothing that would draw attention, and most of what it knows about us it learned from the children it's taken. It might know we're coming, but it has no idea the kind of shit an American can buy at a gun show.*

He stopped firing. His ears were ringing so bad he could hardly hear himself breathe, and the only thing moving was one of the cop-things pulling itself piteously over the blacktop, its own entrails slithering after it. Jo was laughing in the back. She had little cuts on her hands and face where glass from the broken window had caught her, and little pieces of it glittered in her hair, but she was laughing.

"Okay," said John. "Let's start some fires."

The Glover house's driveway seethed like a kicked anthill. Smoke rose in thick black clouds from the town below, the tile roofs and church steeple of which were just visible from the hillside. Sweating, Shelby watched as counselors and ranch hands thundered down the porch steps and piled into the idling trucks, checking guns and shouting at each other and shivering through grotesque transformations. Claws like skinning knives tore open soft fingers. Mouths split and distended, tongues squirming in vertical slits lined with teeth like fishhooks. They scrambled roachlike over one another into the trucks' beds and the men at the wheels sped off down the drive, jouncing over every bump and rut. A minute later they were gone into the canyon below, their dust clouds lingering in the air.

Felix fired. The last man left on the porch shot to his feet as though he'd been jabbed with a cattle prod, staggered a few steps, and then collapsed against the railing, his shotgun slipping between the slats to fall to the driveway below. *Human,* thought Shelby. She didn't let herself dwell on it. Another man burst out through the front door and Felix fired again. Gore slapped the faded siding. The man's skull parted, a vertical mouth tearing open from the crown of his head to somewhere below the neckline of his T-shirt, needlelike teeth gnashing mindlessly, and Felix let out a slow, patient breath and shot him again. The third round put him down as he scrambled back toward the door.

"Okay," he said, stepping out from behind the petrified tree trunk. "Let's go."

Shelby rose and followed him, holding Lara's hand as tightly as she could.

*   *   *

They hit the thing going fifty and he went up over the hood, cracking the windshield on his way. Jo twisted in her seat just in time to see him spin through the air and smack into the ground a tangled, bleeding mess. With numb, fumbling fingers she stuffed the booze-soaked rag into the next bottle's neck and touched the lighter to its edge. It smoldered. Caught. She flung it by the neck as John slowed and watched breathlessly as it arced over the house's front lawn and smashed through the window. The red drapes caught at once, and by the time they reached the street corner the whole facade was blazing, black smoke pouring out like a thunderhead that had lost its way and wound up trapped in a suburban living room.

She'd missed a few at first, but even then most of the grass in Cook Canyon was dry and dead, and it caught readily. There were fires all over town, and they were spreading. The streets behind them were flooding with panicked things. Some of them were burning. Others had lacked time to compose their faces so that loose flesh hung in veils from their skulls, obscuring their features. She caught a glimpse of Felix's car at the next intersection, Mal behind the wheel, and bent to snatch another fifth of vodka from the car floor. She unscrewed the cap and forced a rag into place, unable to stop herself from looking back over her shoulder to where the crowd was thickening, its leading edge racing after them on all fours like a pack of dogs with the faces of middle-aged homeowners and teachers and teenagers and weather-burnt gas station attendants. It was like one of the dreams she'd had during high school, where she was shuffling along the sidewalk in the city when suddenly she noticed everyone was looking at her, their eyes following her labored steps. Then they stopped walking. Then they started to give chase, and no matter how she strained she moved as though through syrup until finally—

There were trucks full of men parked at the next intersection. The barrels of shotguns and rifles tracked them. Jo stared, her lighter flickering in her hand, the bottle's contents forming a shimmering slope as John took the corner hard. She thought of Oji showing her his faded old photographs of Yoshi, the most beautiful man he'd ever seen, of how tenderly his gnarled and shaking fingers had brushed the photo's torn and curling edge.

The men in the trucks opened fire.

Up the porch and into the house. Lara could feel it below them, frightened and angry. She stepped over the bodies and past the threshold of the swinging front door with its blood spatter and its splintered bullet hole. The front room was bare. Plastic tarps hung between raw pine framing. A kitchen—an old Coleman refrigerator and a stainless steel sink piled high with dirty dishes. An overflowing plastic trash can. There were things on the gouged and splintered butcher's block countertops, little scraps and ends of raw pink meat tinged grayish green around the edges. Lara could smell it from the doorway. She could feel something in it. Tears. Snot. Hard hands and crushing pressure. *Mommy, mommy.*

They searched. An office full of steel filing cabinets and loose paperwork. Scorched and smoke-damaged photo albums stuffed with pictures of children standing in front of the admin trailer at Camp Resolution and digging postholes in the Utah desert. A wet room, the floorboards spongy with rot, fungus blooming up between them. Bathroom unfinished. A hole in the floor. And then, finally, her room. Mrs. Glover lay wheezing on the soiled sheets, her oxygen mask fogged by her erratic breathing. What Lara could see of her withered body was hideously burned, her skin waxy and livid, her left eye little more than a swollen slit. At her bedside sat a woman in her early twenties, slim and fair-haired, dressed modestly in a pale pink button-up and cream cardigan. Without hesitation she came over the bed at a four-legged run, her face opening, sawtooth jawbones trailing spittle and slime.

Felix drew his handgun and shot the thing. He kept firing as it crashed to the floor with an otherworldly shriek, limbs lashing out at random. Mrs. Glover tried to move, but she lacked the strength to leave her bed and fell back on the sweat-damp pillow after a single convulsive attempt to push herself up onto her elbows. Her breath fogged her oxygen mask. Felix ejected the little automatic's magazine and slapped another into place. He shot the thrashing thing again and it curled in on itself and was still.

Lara went to the bedside and plucked the mask gently from Mrs. Glover's face. She slid the band over the older woman's peeling scalp with its wisps of brittle hair. Mrs. Glover pawed at her arm with a fleshless hand, her touch like the caress of dried flower petals. "N . . . no," she moaned. Her lips were already colorless. Her good eye was wide with panic. A tear leaked from its corner and made its way down her sunken cheek, silvery and clean as she reached with a burn-scarred hand toward the dead thing bleeding on the floor. "Fuh . . . fuh . . ."

Lara bent down until her lips were almost touching the old woman's ear. "This is for Eddie," she whispered, not quite knowing why, knowing that the man had been a coward and a weakling and a hypocrite, but knowing he'd been one of *theirs,* and he'd died for it. "The real one. He's waiting for you in Hell."

"Is she dead?" asked Shelby.

"She will be soon," said Lara, and she ran her fingers through the shriveled woman's hair. Mrs. Glover stared at her, mouth open, eye still leaking. Lara straightened up and turned away. "Let's go."

Gunfire blew in the rest of the rear windshield, glass cascading over the back seat as they fishtailed through the intersection past a movie theater—*The Sound of Music* up on the marquee, but all the ticket booths papered over and the front doors locked with a length of rusty chain—and what looked like some kind of town hall, and the men in the trucks shooting guns at them. "Hold on!" John screamed. Something grazed his cheek and left a line of white-hot pain sketched smooth and clean across it before punching a spiderwebbed hole in the windshield.

He looked back as they straightened out. Jo lay slumped against her window, blood dribbling from a hole in her throat.

The expression of surprise she wore slowly went slack. Her hand slipped from the wound and fell into her lap, bloody fingers twitching. John couldn't seem to breathe. There was blood in his mouth. He looked away from the scene and took the next turn fast, still floating in the airless moment, still trying to make his thoughts connect to some kind of world that made sense, because he was seventeen and Jo and Shelby were showing him *Prince of Darkness* after a bad breakup and he was nineteen and Jo was vomiting in the sink while he held her hair and he was twenty-five and so angry with her and loaning her money again and this couldn't be happening, it couldn't be real, he would turn back again and she'd be crouched in the broken glass and firing at the things still chasing them, because it couldn't—

He never saw the third truck, which barreled into his stolen rental doing what must have been sixty. The world caved in. It screamed. Glass in his arms. In his legs. Huge shards standing out and Louise sinking onto the stool in the little dive where he tended bar like a big beautiful scoop of ice cream just starting to melt. Her sequins flashing. Glitter. Sharp little red fingernails. He flew through the air. Pavement. Sky. A burning building. White-hot pain as his shoulder hit the street. A swath of skin torn off like an old Band-Aid.

Who's a girl have to do to get a drink around here?

Crawling. Car on fire. Jo's Molotov cocktails. Flames pouring from the doors. Dripping to the pavement. Fire like the night Nadine died. He crawled toward it, fumbled the AK from the well of the driver's seat, tearing its bandolier where it caught on something. He stood and his head did a kind of wriggling belly flop, the world swaying and spinning all around him. There was blood. He thought of Mal, of their first night together. *Please, I want you on top of me.* Their fights. Limping around the burning wreck to where something was hauling itself from the truck, its bony scythes digging furrows in the softened pavement, torn clothes hanging from its muscular, amorphous bulk. Human arms hanging like useless sleeves of meat from what looked like a chest. Breasts weeping black discharge. Its matted, greasy ginger hair made a sort of ruff along its spine and its skin was peeling and sunburned, dusted with constellations of freckles. Weirdly beautiful. He brought the rifle up, though it hurt to raise his arms. He had at least one broken rib, and probably more, and his bloody finger slipped from the trigger twice before he managed to fire.

The thing screamed, rocked back against the truck, and rose up like a grizzly bear half-covered in chitinous armor plates. When it turned toward him, its repulsively human face twisting into a deranged snarl of pain and hatred, its lower jaw splitting in half to reveal a gnashing hell of slick black mouthparts, John saw that it was Betty Cleaver.

Lara led the others down the basement steps. No false partition this time, just a hole in the foundation wall leading into a braced dirt tunnel that sloped down and into darkness, out of sight. Wherever they worked their campers half to death now, it wasn't here. She drew her gun with shaking fingers and with her free hand felt for the baggies of ketamine she'd sewn into her old army surplus jacket. More in her pockets. Thousands of dollars' worth, which was funny now that she thought of it.

They had to crouch to get into the tunnel. Felix pushed past her, but gently, and took the lead. She followed the beam of his flashlight as he crept along. He was so handsome, she thought. His olive skin and little mustache. His dark hair, always so effortlessly rumpled in the morning. She'd had a crush on him for a long time when they were young.

The smell wafting up to them was terrible. She remembered it, and smelled it in her nightmares still. They came out into a larger chamber, cut and blasted stone and packed earth making up the walls, and dark, glistening things hung above them, mucoid sacs like the chrysalises of huge caterpillars turning slowly into chemical soup that dreamed of flying. Lara didn't want to know what was in them, but she knew. She started to cry.

There were other chambers branching off the first. Chambers overgrown with fungus and chambers opening onto brackish aquifers and chambers full of the hairy, womblike membranes in which it gestated its cuttings, some with dark forms curled within, others deflated and dried. Everywhere were psoriatic drifts of pale, dead skin and clumps of wet black hair. There were bones, too. The bones of cows, and of burrowing things, and of children. Lara followed Felix in a daze, Shelby close by her side. Little voices whispered in her ear. Little fingers plucked at her sleeves. They came at last into a massive stone cavern split by a shallow stream flowing swift and clear on into the darkness. Across it, picked out faintly by Felix's flashlight, an archway of stone slabs yawned like a mouth, and—like a tide of vomit—it was already coming through.

The Cuckoo dragged its raw, slimy bulk through the arch, sprouting new limbs to brace itself against the stone. It slobbered and shrieked as it came, its unintelligible cries overlapping wetly as mouths formed, bubbled, and burst on pseudopods and nodding skin-draped skulls like sped-up footage of necrosis in action. Features Lara still recognized, even fifteen years later. Dana's nose, an unmistakable point. The plump, pouty lips of a girl whose name she had never been able to remember. Celine's big, bulging eyes. Pruny, soft-nailed fingers groping blindly from the side of its wattled throat as vaginal slits discharged thick streams of yellowish slime. At the center of its thrusting foremost segment, a black oval of chitin like a caterpillar's head gazed eyelessly out at them, mouthparts moving like inscrutable machinery.

More little limbs formed and collapsed as it pulled itself toward them. It reared up, a bloated serpentine arch dotted with grasping cilia and filmy eyes, rolls of slack flesh bunching where its bulk overlapped, dirty feathers bristling from its bedraggled, stunted wings. A bloom of fronds and tendrils erupted from its back all at once, bioluminescence flashing among rags of filmy skin torn by its transformation. The air seemed to flex and throb. It fixed its empty stare on Lara.

A migraine split her head like an ax, a flash of dirty white and then a world, a marble of mottled browns and blues and greens hanging fat and webbed with constellations of electric light upon the depthless black. World in blacklight, skull coming apart in her hands. Closer. Lightning splitting fat pink trees and clouds of oily feathered seeds erupting to be swept up by the sulfur-smelling wind and borne down from the foothills of a great peak honeycombed with pits and quarries and fans of broken scree to the valley below where they met the sluggish flows of streams and rivulets and then were vomited into the broad green sewer of a river flowing down over tiers of broken stone where fat, ulcerated silos with mouths lined with spirals of baleen stood in the waterfalls, their broad backs and stumpy legs aswarm with biting parasites, and on until the flow broadened, slackened, drooled into endless marshland separated into grids by lines of glowing buoys where the low meat—the subjugated flesh—toiled endlessly with hands bent into scoops and huge, pale eyes to peer through murky water for the mollusks—or something like mollusks, fat and pale and fleshy in broken toroidal shells—which they heaved over their shoulders into sacks of woven grass.

From time to time a part of the laboring flesh would fail, over-worked or sun-stricken or poisoned by polluted silt or bitten by one of the flat, rubbery creatures that lurked in the mud of the paddies, and its fellows would bear it on their shoulders to a temple of the flesh to be drained and strained and reprocessed into something new, a little turd of barely sentient biomass pinched off a great and greedy whole and set again to toiling, or some-times discarded, too overworked and riddled with the tumorous scourge of the remaking sickness to be of use. *It is of the body,* Lara thought nonsensically, *but it is not the body.*

The things they harvest are loaded up in vats of bog water and pushed through the great gills of something else, another dull automaton of meat which on a thousand sturdy legs conveys its sinuous bulk along a trampled earthen track, guts bulging heavy with the harvests of a dozen terroirs. It thunders on through swamps and valleys and passes blasted through great berms of rock to a city where a thousand, thousand other paths converge, a city like a great emphysemic lung, heaving, straining, never satisfied no matter how it pants and wheezes, and more meat unloads the meat the meat has harvested and it is pickled, sauteed, seared, and fried and fed into the billion, billion mouths of the high flesh, of the one that is many, the changing seed from which all thinking life on this world now grows. It splits and changes and experiences reunion, calving and melding, sloughing off outré manifestations and mashing itselves together like the Play-Doh figures of some monstrous cosmic toddler, thoughts and lives spun off to dance and mug a little before reabsorption, the thing entertaining itself as it dines on the fruits of a world it has devoured and excreted a hundred times over, a world of acid soil and vast, dead oceans where the sky—*Oh, God, the sky*—is a roiling hellscape of thunderstorms caught in atmospheric gyres where the planet's gravity well dips and deforms, storms within storms, lightning stitching clouds together and through the occasional gap a sickly green sun poisoning the skin it touches, blistering, sewing tumors like seeds in the changeable dermis.

Once there were herds and flocks and shoals and schools and the thing that changes was a few thousand clots of thinking flesh propagating itself over tidal forests and through boreal chasm-mazes, leaving its youngest grafts to mature in the lairs and nests of creatures that it learned to imitate, learned to charm and tame to parenthood until the flesh was ready to rejoin the whole, sire and dam sucked dry and discarded. Then the clots began to meet. Some fought. Others fucked. There was little difference, and neuron by neuron it began to recognize itself, began to dew from the collective thinking muscle of the flesh that changes, began to realize its hungers and the things which it despised. Suffering. Tedium. Need. Now everywhere it turns it finds only itself, a starving animal the size of a planet curled in a panicked ball and shitting into its own open mouth to quell its hunger pangs. *What happens?* it thinks, synapses leaping from body to body, twining tight in glistening braids so that thoughts echo, sync, and join together seamlessly, so that it is never alone, never and always alone with the thoughts that chase it through the labyrinth of its own consciousness, the single thought, *What happens when the meat runs out?*

And so in a spiral hall dug deep into the earth—the *Nythith*—the flesh brings itself together in great coral ridges of brain matter, turning its leviathan mind to matters alchemical and scientific, arcane and epistemological. For long and torturous years it plans and frets and does what it most detests—labor—until its self is fractious with rogue impulses, frustration climbing between dendritic webs like a parasite, whispering ghostly in the great machine that this is work for the *feet,* for the *digits,* not for the body, until on the verge of cataclysmic egomorphic rupture, the greatest psychotic break the galaxy might have ever seen, it unlocks the object of its search. A door. A wet slit between dimensions which may be wriggled through, which may be traversed by just enough of its noble and cunning matter that on the far side it might feed and grow and reach back to the *Nyth* across the dark ocean of space to join hands with itself, to become a bridge of braided fat and muscle spanning hundreds of thousands of light-years to secure the only thing that matters.

Fresh meat.

Another sizzling flash of white and the seeing was done, the headache it left behind the filthy, stabbing pain of an infected tooth. Lara doubled over and vomited on the cavern floor. The Cuckoo was all around her. She could hear gunfire, but she couldn't see the others. The skin of its flank split, reversed, and squirmed over her shoulder to cling to her neck like a thawed chicken cutlet, wet and cold and rubbery. Fingers grew to stroke her chin and cheek, to fumble at the corner of her mouth. Soft nails. Wrinkled knuckles. Its skin tasted of neroli and civet, sugar and cardamom, a nauseating, gluey flavor smeared across her face. Fingers knit together, a hand bubbling up behind them. It pried her mouth open, forcing thumb and forefinger inside. A pinkish membrane slipped over her eyes, veins pulsing in the expanse of fragile skin. Against her ear formed tender lips, a pointed tongue which brushed the fine hairs of her cochlea.

You will never be alone again.

Mal ran sobbing through the streets. The things were chasing them. They'd shot a few, though the submachine gun frightened and disoriented them, but they still came snorting and snuffling on like a pack of bloodhounds, faces trailing flaps of loose skin and delicate tendrils tipped with suction cups and airy fronds and fine, dark hairs. More spilled out of burning buildings. The fire was catching. Mal turned and tore down the narrow gap between two houses, vaulting a low chain-link fence and eating shit on the far side. They scrambled to their feet, spitting dirt, and kept running. Bodies packed the slice of lawn behind them. Runners leapt the fence in graceful arcs. Mal turned and fired into the crowd. The submachine gun kicked and roared. A nearby window exploded outward in a blast of flame.

Onward, sprinting across a stretch of lawn where sparks were already beginning to catch, the grass so dry it crunched under their sneakers. They'd been lucky not to break anything when they crashed Felix's Impala. Stupid. So fucking stupid. Too fast. Skidding out into a telephone pole. It was nothing like Riverside out here, but they felt like they were running through their hometown, like it was finally rising up all around them to show them what it thought of that loudmouth crazy bitch and her brats. They could see it in the eyes of every faceless thing that boiled out after them into the street.

We were trapped in there with her, and she was trapped in there with us.

The boom of John's AK tore through the sounds of the spreading fire and the mob on Mal's heels. They dug deeper, legs pumping, chest on fire and black dots at the edges of their vision as they ran toward the intersection at the street's end, and suddenly the mob was silent at their back. They looked over their shoulder and saw them halted in among the blazing buildings, filling the street on all fours and in bestial crouches. The things weren't chasing them.

What?

Another shot. They headed left at the intersection, away from the fires, ducking under the hanging boughs of thorn trees the roots of which had begun to buckle the sidewalk's concrete slabs. They ran faster. Strength came into them, not as ease but like fuel burning, as though the marrow in their bones was catching fire, and down at the end of the street, beside the wreck of his car and the truck that had T-boned it, John lay in the street with something huge crouched over him. It had his head in one scaled claw, and the great scythe-tipped limbs that rose up from its shoulders were dark and dripping with blood.

"Get the fuck away from him!" they screamed, their voice cracking. Mal staggered to a halt and fumbled with the Uzi's shoulder strap and safety, trying to eject the mostly empty magazine. Where was the button? Groping in their pocket for another clip. *Please. Please. Kill me, not him. Kill me. Kill me.* "Look at me, you piece of shit!"

It looked up and a smile split its face, a bloody nightmare grin of teeth and chitin and shredded meat, and it was Betty. Betty kicking them behind the bathrooms. Nadine bruised and limping after Betty and the others beat her senseless. Betty crawling dazed and blinded as the farmhouse burned. It was impossible, but she was there, and she was smiling at them.

She charged.

Mal got the clip in. They brought the gun up with both hands, the way Felix had shown them. *He isn't dead,* they told themself, not daring to look at where John lay not moving in the street. *He's not dead. He's not. He's NOT.*

They fired.

Shelby scrambled after Felix over loose earth and tumbling shale, clawing her way along the tunnel. She'd lost track of where she was, or where they'd come in. Whatever had happened between the Cuckoo and Lara had left her reeling and disoriented. It was hard to string two thoughts together. She kept seeing things. Pearlescent rooms and corridors full of laughing monsters. A bird's nest hidden in a crevice in a cliff face. When Felix turned and pushed her down to fire back over her prone body, she went limp with relief. Why run? They'd made a mistake. They'd fought back against the way the world worked, tried to snatch a queer kid from the jaws of its cruel indifference, and they were going to die for it.

Then she looked back under her own arm and saw it coming up the tunnel after them, unfazed by the bullet wounds in its soft bulk. Slowly, like a newborn crowning, Nadine's face emerged from the loose, flabby folds of foreskin at the end of a serpentine neck it had grown. The folds pulled gradually taut over the dead girl's skull. Tufts of slimy hair erupted from its flesh to fall over one flashing eye, swinging wet and heavy near the dirt. Sharp canines flashed in a vicious smile. *"I miss you, baby,"* it whispered in her throaty voice as plump little insect limbs dragged it along. Its left eye's swollen pupils shrank, met, and collapsed into one inky pinprick. Thick black tongues like condoms full of garbage juice slid slow over its teeth. *"My little dumpling."*

"Look at me, Shelby," shouted Felix, and even as he kept firing he grabbed her hand and squeezed it so tight she thought he might break her fingers, squeezed it hard enough to break the spell of those eyes the thing had stolen, of that smile it was wearing wrong, because Nadine had never smiled at her like that, like she was looking at food. It was just a trick. That's all the thing was. Tricks and lies, all of them cheap, all of them ugly. They only worked because nobody cared about the truth.

"Don't look at it," Felix said, and she curled into him and wept, sobs shaking her so hard that even the boom of the gunshots in the enclosed space barely registered. "I've got you."

Lara had been ready for it since she was a teenager, her mind rewired by Armitage's nonsense lessons, by the slow breaking down of her young body, by psychedelics and sex and a riot of hormones, and she was ready still. The difference was that now *it* wasn't ready for her. As it engulfed her and their bodies flowed together in a molten crucible of fat and flesh and bone, it slowed. One of its mouths began to emit a thin, plaintive keening sound. The eyes dotting the inner surface of its digestive chamber rolled and spun, looking at its own formless mass, staring at each other, at Lara's dissolving body with the stumps of its legs and her beautiful hair all burned away, and in them she saw a flat, uncomprehending terror, a lack of recognition as its million parts began to dissolve into their own tiny and fractious wholes. She spat blood, smiling. It had eaten about half a pound of ketamine along with her.

Goodbye, you ugly fucking thing, she thought. *I hope it hurts.*

Flesh boiled over her in a screaming wave. Her skin burned. Coils of muscle seized her throat as keratin pushed messily through pulpy fingertips and clawed hands dug into her scalp. A dreadful weight bore down on her and she felt things give beneath it, felt them pierce her organs in a thought-bleaching rush of chemical anxiety. She could feel Felix and Shelby somewhere close, and Mal and John beyond them, fainter, and fainter still the echo of Jo, who had saved them all as much as Nadine had. Dead now.

It got Felix's gun hand while he was reloading. Nadine's jaws crushed his fingers. Tore them loose. In the confines of the dead-end tunnel there was nowhere to retreat, nothing to do but scream and beat at it as its limbs grasped at his clothes, his crotch, his hand where it gripped Shelby's tightly. It had her, too. It was dragging her back down the shallow slope toward a huge, drooling maw that gaped beneath the neck it had grown. He stumbled after her, jerked along as it bit his thumb in half and lunged to sink its teeth into his forearm. There was so much blood. He felt little teeth gnawing at his right ear. Snip. The lobe gone, more blood sheeting down his neck. It was pushing inside him now, and he beat his head against its pliable softness, trying to hurt it, trying to make his hatred for it mean something.

"I'll kill you!" he shouted, and he bit it back, its taste unspeakably foul on his tongue, like spoiled meat and lukewarm vomit blended together and seasoned with just a touch of fecal decay. He didn't care. He bit at the limb coiled around his throat. He bit and tore and spat as its bulk surged over him, bearing him down to the dirt, as its eyes split like doubled yolks and its mouths grinned with indecent delight. Slowly, with great deliberation, the rough shape of his father's face emerged from its putrid mass just above Felix's. Bull neck, hooded eyes, the dark mustache and jutting chin. It smiled at him. It bent.

Don't worry.

It kissed him on the mouth.

I'm here with you.

Bullets tore at Betty's side, but each impact felt like a gentle caress. She sprinted toward the thing that had been Malcolm. The world shook with her every footstep. All around them the people of Cook Canyon, who were not really people at all, watched in delighted silence, smiles on the masks of their faces. It was watching through them, she knew, and it made her heart burn with pride.

She bore down on Malcolm and swiped at him, her arm bubbling like boiling water, bones parting as muscle and sinew stretched. The limb smashed through the pavement where he'd stood a moment before and tore a furrow clean across the road before bringing down the facade of a burning split-level. Dust rose. Masonry and wood spilled out with a thundering roar.

Betty whirled, her arm humping back up against her shoulder, and shrieked at the sight of Malcolm vanishing behind John's burning car. She lashed out again, upending the wreck of the car and sending the fat man, dead or unconscious, rolling over the broken street. The car flipped twice in the air and crashed into the storefront of a pharmacy. Malcolm scrambled backward away from her on his ass. He looked ridiculous, little breasts pushing at his T-shirt, inner thighs crosshatched with neat, precise little scars, like hating himself was a job he'd clocked into and out of on a schedule.

She padded toward him and crouched down, pushing him effortlessly to the pavement, grinding his face into the dirt and loose granules of road. "I told you what I'd do if I found you sneaking around again," she snarled, and with hundreds of mouths the Cuckoo laughed and clapped appreciatively, a sitcom audience plucked out of a rancid wet nightmare.

"Kill him!" it shrieked with one mouth. "Make him eat his cock!" it screamed with another.

Betty thought of Athena stroking her hair as she died. She brushed her own thumb over Malcolm's braids. Something felt wrong. Something in the air had shifted.

"Kill him!" the crowd chanted. "Kill him! Kill him!"

Betty bent low. She felt tired. Sick, somehow.

"I'll make it quick," she whispered.

"Fuck yourself," Malcolm snarled back.

Lara fell into herself, and as her consciousness began to come apart she thought of her half sister, Celia, who had been so beautiful at seventeen as she read "Jabberwocky" out loud from where she lay draped on the window seat in their kitchen. Ashen hair and pale, pale freckles and those long, thin hands and delicate wrists which then had made Lara feel a burning, needy jealousy, a species of devotion that had only faded when Celia left for college and stopped talking to their father.

> 'Twas brillig, and the slithy toves
>   Did gyre and gimble in the wabe:
> All mimsy were the borogoves,
>   And the mome raths outgrabe.

She reached out with the fire that it had woken in her by pure accident, and she thrust herself as deep into the Cuckoo's roiling mind as she could go, tearing and clawing and smashing everything she found, ripping at the alien wiring of its dirty baby-snatching mind, kicking and spitting and crushing even as its oneness, its unity began to calve chunks of random traits and memory like a glacier melting in nuclear fire. It ran wailing from her and she chased it, squeezing its frightened giblets to death in her soul's grip, or her mind's, or whatever it was that had made her crazy and alone and a fantastic fucking dominatrix.

> He took his vorpal sword in hand;
>   Long time the manxome foe he sought—
> So rested he by the Tumtum tree
>   And stood awhile in thought.

> And, as in uffish thought he stood,
>   The Jabberwock, with eyes of flame,
> Came whiffling through the tulgey wood,
>   And burbled as it came!

It was afraid. It was so terribly, terribly afraid, alone in a way it had never been before, on fire with the ecstatic terror of it. Their minds were burning in the same molten light and she could feel its shrieking misery as it came apart into the things that it had eaten, stolen, raped and digested and shat out. It was trying to hide. It was trying to find something to imitate. Its huge body boiled with deformed likenesses. Campers and counselors and somewhere in among the gnashing jaws and empty eye sockets were what was left of Nadine, and Pastor Eddie. In there somewhere were the coyote cubs that it had stolen from their packs' dens and the birds whose nests it had raided and the grinning masks of Smith and Brady and fat, lovely Candace who had smiled at her and blushed.

> *One, two! One, two! And through and through*
> *The vorpal blade went snicker-snack!*
> *He left it dead, and with its head*
> *He went galumphing back.*

> *"And hast thou slain the Jabberwock?*
> *Come to my arms, my beamish boy!*
> *O frabjous day! Callooh! Callay!"*
> *He chortled in his joy.*

Lara let go. She began to drift, lines of red and purple light flaring wild in the void. She felt what was left of her crushed beneath a massive thrashing weight, and the fire of her mind flared bright, and things were falling away, layer after layer of skin peeling back as she rose up like a plucked note hanging in the air, shedding everything, and thought, *I love you, I love you, I love you.*

Be good.

The Cuckoo let out a low moan of pain and confusion and suddenly the head of Manny Vargas was just flopping meat, expressionless and dead. Its limbs slid from Felix's body, the tongue that had coiled around Shelby's leg falling slack to the ground as it undulated backward down the tunnel, heaving its huge mass along faster and faster, throwing itself against the tunnel walls until earth showered down on them and Felix felt sure it would collapse and bury both of them, and then they were *out*, they were staggering after it into the great chamber with its stream where something that looked horribly like Lara lay dead half in the water and half on the stony bank, her cheek pillowed on grit and rock, its flank—where she must have spilled from it—split open and puckered like the world's biggest mouth had just sucked on a lemon.

"Felix," Shelby sobbed.

Felix limped after her, tearing out the hasty stitching where he'd sewn part of the ketamine stash into his jacket. He slit it partway open with his knife, fumbling a little with his missing fingers, and flung the packet at the Cuckoo. Its wings flapped out of sync as it listed and stumbled. Pale bluish powder sparkled in midair. The packet hit its side, spilling more of the drug onto gnashing mouths and heaving gills. He helped Shelby cut her own share free of her sweatshirt and tossed it after his before sinking down to sit beside her, watching the thing tear itself apart.

The great bulk reared up, splitting like a lightning-struck tree, and two serpentine heads took form, teeth pushing out through bloody gums as jawbones slid into place to give structure to flop-ping, sleevelike mouths. Tentacles unfurled from its heaving flanks, leaving furrows in the flesh into which molten fat poured like hot lead into a mold. The left head struck at the right, viper-quick. Tentacles coiled around one another, tugging and squeez-ing, sprouting spiral rows of serrated yellow teeth, and in the space of a few seconds the entirety of it was at war with itself in a dissociative fugue, unable to recognize its own amorphous horror. The drugs had worked. Arms still slick with thick white discharge grappled within collapsing tents of skin and cartilage. Effluvium spouted from puckered blowholes as bear-trap jaws crushed bone, tore flesh. Felix led Shelby around it as it ripped itself apart. They lifted Lara between them. Even with his maimed hand it wasn't hard; she was so light. Her legs were gone. Much of her skin had dissolved.

They were most of the way back to the exit when its convul-sions brought the cave roof crashing down on it. The sound was

astronomical, a physical presence pushing them along in a hail
of dust and grit as they toiled up that last dark stretch and up the
basement steps and left the house by the bloody, bullet-scarred
front door, carrying Lara with them.

The Betty-thing drew back from Mal so suddenly that they assumed
it meant those anvil fists would come rushing down to crush their
head. Instead, the thing that had once been Betty Cleaver started
screaming. She lurched back and forth across the street, smashing through a telephone pole and upending a station wagon with
a convulsive heave. Live wires showered the pavement in sparks.

"It hurts!" she shrieked, and her voice was horribly normal, a
worn-out woman's hoarse, strained cry of pain.

All around them other screams rose from the mouths of the
townsfolk as they reeled through the streets. Mal scrambled to
their feet and ran. John lay on his face at the corner, covered in
blood, glass protruding from his arms and side. They dropped to
their knees at his side, struggling to roll him over.

"John," they begged. "John, honey. Please answer me. Wake up.
Please, I can't—I can't."

Behind them, Betty clawed at her own face and bone and flesh
gave way under her gnarled fingers, her bottom jaw swinging
loose by a flap of discolored skin, blood pouring out onto her
throat and chest. She drew back a massive fist and punched herself, hard, in the face. Her nose caved in. Her cheekbones were
distorted, snapped like matchsticks. She seized one of the townsfolk crawling near her on hands and knees and tore him in half,
lifting his thrashing legs to what remained of her mouth and biting ineffectually at it. Strings of flesh stretched between it and
her teeth. It put out tendrils, flailing limbs, and brushed her face
with awful gentleness in the moment before she fell to one knee
and vomited up a tide of half-digested meat. There was a girl in
it. Parts of a girl. Mal threw up with her, then, leaning away from
John to do it.

Betty toppled with a crash that shook glass from the traffic lights and nearby windows. She was mouthing something to herself, her eyes glassy, her huge frame shuddering. Blood pumped from her bullet wounds and the gashes and scrapes she'd given herself at an alarming rate, until it slowed to a trickle, and then a seep. And then it stopped. The townsfolk started falling, too. They were keeling in the streets and running into their burning houses. They were screaming until their eyes popped like rotten grapes and blood poured from their mouths.

After a long time had passed, it was quiet except for the sound of fire. Mal sobbed as they bandaged the long gash that ran from John's shoulder to the top of his belly with strips torn from his bloodied shirt. Betty had clawed and cut him in a dozen places, or he'd been hurt in the crash. It was impossible to tell. They cleaned his wounds with water from their canteen and touched his face and looked at him, and tried not to look at Jo's body where it sat in the still-burning wreck.

After a while, John's eyes flickered open. He cleared his throat and looked at them. "Am I dead?" he whispered hoarsely.

"No," Mal sobbed, and then they bent and kissed him, still crying, and he took them in his good arm and kissed them back, and that was how Felix and Shelby found them.

At a fenced-in camp in the desert a half hour's drive outside the town, Shelby stepped out of the minivan Felix had hotwired and found twenty-odd confused and angry teenagers staring at her through the chain-link fence. She felt suddenly absurd and monstrous, every bit the playground predator TERFs shrieked about in their think pieces and blog posts. Here she was rescuing a teenager who didn't know who she was or that she existed at all.

She cleared her throat. "Abby Donovan?"

The little crowd milled, kids exchanging sideways glances, until at last a short, chubby girl—how could any mother have looked at this child and not seen her for a girl?—stepped forward. "Where are the counselors?" Abby asked, her voice small and frightened. Her head had been shaved recently, and tawny peach fuzz the same color as Nadine's grew from her scalp. "What's happening? What are you going to do to us?"

"It's okay," said Shelby. She fished the keys she'd taken from Mrs. Glover's room out of her pocket and unlocked the fence. "It's over. I'm getting you out of here. All of you."

The girl was crying now. Some of the other kids drew back as Shelby opened the gate, but Abby stayed where she was. "Who are you? *What's happening?*"

"I knew Nadine—knew your sister," Shelby said, a lump in her throat as she remembered that long-ago bathroom and the dry heat of the stall where they'd first kissed. "A long time ago."

PRIDE

San Francisco, California
2018

Sometimes Abby couldn't believe Margo wanted her. The other girl was so beautiful, so tall and graceful and stylish in her shimmering silver tank top and her glittery eyeliner, bleached hair falling pin-straight to her shoulders. At first it had made her afraid that one day Margo would wake up and realize she was dating a chubby little nobody, plain and shy and boring, a weirdo raised by broke oddballs in a succession of awful apartments, who at twenty-one was still finishing her GED. Then, slowly, as day after day began with that sleepy smile, those painted nails tracing the curve of her cheek, it began to make her feel beautiful.

The real story had never come out. A cult. A mass suicide. Some-one had cleaned up in Cook Canyon, or someone had been high up enough to make the nightmare wreckage disappear, but the things she'd seen at Integrity still haunted Abby's dreams. Those first months with John in the hospital, the rest of them sleeping in cars and stealing to eat, the other kids and their parents giv-ing fringe radio interviews about torture and brainwashing and Satanic rituals until one by one they gradually went dark. "We'll take you home, if that's what you want," Felix had told her a hun-dred times. "All you have to do is ask."

What would have happened if she had? Her mother's love and desperation had been equally cloying, her father's disinterest painful and his white-hot rage at her transition terrifying. Maybe they would have learned their lesson the second time. Maybe she would have wound up in another camp. The four of them, Felix and John and Shelby and Mal, had done their best for her. They had wanted her the way she was. Lara and Jo, who she'd never known, had died trying to get her out of that place.

She would never have met Margo, who one sweaty, sun-drenched afternoon two years ago in Punta Gorda had seen Abby coming off her shift at the Daily Scoop ice cream shop and screamed from across the street, "I'd like a scoop of *that*!" Her drunken apology had become a half-sober invitation to dinner, had become electric sex at her cramped and cluttered apartment, full of books on Python and C++ and particle physics, had become coffee mugs of Cap'n Crunch for breakfast and a long, rambling discussion about Kurt Russell and trans drama and their favorite smells. Little things.

She would never have found herself here, walking down the street shoulder to shoulder with half a million gays for Pride. It was easy to feel hot at the march, even if the organizers *had* allowed corporations to join in again. At least they'd kept cops out this year. An older cis dyke had checked Abby out near the water station at the corner of Main and Desmond, her eyes sliding over Abby's ass and down her bare legs. It felt good to be wanted like that. She'd kissed a few friends, giddy with the sunlight and the glitter and the last slow, soothing waves of last night's edible. Now she was hand in hand with Margo in the thick of the parade, the late afternoon sun bathing them in its warm red-orange glow, the group of big, hairy men ahead of them marching with a sign that read THE B STANDS FOR BEARS, glistening beautifully with sweat in their vests and chaps. Before they'd left, Margo had put on phosphate-red lipstick and planted a kiss on Abby's cheek in front of the hall mirror.

So everyone will know you're mine.

It had made her want to suck the other girl's dick right there, even knowing Margo's roommates were asleep a wall away. She felt wrapped up in that moment as they rounded the corner onto Washington Avenue, the sun hitting their faces, people cheering and waving and holding up their phones to film the parade from

behind the barricades at the curbs. Shelby was out there some-
where, probably being gross and corny with her new girlfriend,
Sid, and John and Mal were supposed to meet them all later, after
John's physical therapy appointment. His scars had been bother-
ing him lately. Felix hadn't called in a few weeks. He was out in
Colorado again, hanging around a wilderness discipline camp.
He said he couldn't sleep in the city.

That was when Abby saw him. A boy stood at the parade's edge,
staring at her. He was a little younger than them, maybe sixteen
or seventeen, and dressed in tight black jeans and a ragged Mitski
T-shirt. His hair was a vibrant green and in the shade of the aw-
ning beside him his face, except for the slight smile curling his
lips, was difficult to see.

"You okay, babe?" Margo asked her. "Did you take your meds
this morning?"

Abby watched the boy as he stepped down off the sidewalk and
came toward them, and she thought as her heart came up into her
throat that this was worse than cops or soldiers marching, worse
than the Citibank float up near the front of the parade or some
corporate PR mutant tweeting that the Keebler Elves were demi-
sexual. None of it, no matter how it gnawed at everything they'd
fought and bled and died for, was as bad as this. She tightened her
grip on Margo's hand, anxiety closing her throat as the boy drew
nearer, sliding between marchers, his face hidden by wigs and
signs and baseball caps. Was he coming for her, or had he only
seen a friend somewhere nearby?

"Babe?" Margo asked.

Nothing was worse than this: to look at her people, her family, and not know if they were real or if their smiles would split,
their skulls bloom red and stinking like corpse flowers as they bent
to wrap the tendrils of their faces tight around her own. To never
know, even in a lover's arms, who was *us* and who was *them*.

ACKNOWLEDGMENTS

Thanks to my parents and grandparents, who kept trying to understand until it finally clicked, my brave and brilliant sibling Elliot and my kind and giving brother-in-law Huey, my writing partner and dear friend Sara, my beautiful Dana and Julian and Darcy and Ezra, my loving partners Sam and Carolyn and Quinn and Carta, my dear friends Josh and Lydia and Arielle, Vince and Alice and Jacey and Hazel, Millie and Sean.

My fantastic agent, Connor Goldsmith; my dynamite editor, Kelly Lonesome; the whole Nightfire team—Kristin, Jordan, Laura, Valeria, Dakota, Janine, Sara, Jaime, Rafal, Steven, Greg; cover designer Esther S. Kim and cover artist Sarah Sitkin.

Special thanks to Philip Kaufman, W. D. Richter, Clea DuVall, and Jamie Babbit.

ABOUT THE AUTHOR

GRETCHEN FELKER-MARTIN is a Massachusetts-based horror author and film critic. Her debut novel, *Manhunt*, was named the #1 best book of 2022 by *Vulture* and one of the best horror novels of 2022 by *Esquire*, *Library Journal*, and *Paste*. You can follow her work on Twitter @scumbelievable and read her fiction and film criticism on Patreon and in *Time*, *The Outline*, *Nylon*, and more.